The Unfinished Storm

The Unfinished Storm

A NOVEL

JACKIE AHN

Cover and book design by Christian Storm.

This is a work of fiction. Names, characters, places, and incidents are the product of the author's imagination or used fictitiously, and any resemblance to actual persons, living or dead, businesses, companies, events, or locales is entirely coincidental.

ISBN (paperback): 978-1-7364303-1-6
ISBN (ebook): 978-1-7364303-2-3
ISBN (hardcover): 978-1-7364303-3-0

VIGGO BLU PRESS

*To my beautiful mother,
Linda.*

The brain is a fascinating machine, designed to protect the user from moments too unbearable to withstand. It hides memories deep inside the hidden vortex of the unconscious, a function of survival that keeps us moving in the present. Such a memory can stay locked away for years —

    sometimes forever —

        although the body always remembers.

The Unfinished Storm

CHAPTER 1

It's Time

Four weeks into her new school, Mia Storm had the same two nagging thoughts. *Don't slip down the marble stairs again*, and *don't forget, after fifteen years of being told he was dead, your father is alive.*

Taking her seat while a pleasant chorus of bells rang, Mia logged into her device while catching a glimpse of her teacher propped in his usual pose — meditating or napping, she wasn't sure. At the last chime, Dr. Fern stood and adjusted his rimless glasses while welcoming the students with promises of another stimulating class.

"It is time for our biogenetic group midterm . . ." The rosy-faced teacher removed a sleeping student's arm from a beeping keypad. "This report will count for half your grade. I ask, in utmost sincerity, that you choose your group with *careful* consideration. I will not tolerate requests from parents to fire group members."

"Jade!" an icy-blonde called. "Over here!" The class had begun to separate into groups, while Mia scanned the room, deciding her best option was to wait for everyone to pair up before looking for a comfortable place to join. She hadn't made friends yet, although her attempt at *trying* was a forced smile in the hallways. So, it surprised her when a girl came over and stood in front of her.

"Hi." She smiled broadly, her bottom teeth covered in braces. "Would you like to be in my group? I promised my cousin he could pair up with me, and we need a third." She pointed to a boy who thought he was in the clear to dislodge something deep within his nose.

". . . anywayzz, I'm Yu-Ting."

"I'm Mia. Okay." Mia said cautiously.

"Yay. So, we can come over to you since our spot is crowded. Call me *Ting*, by the way, only my parents call me *Yu-Ting*." She signaled for her cousin to join them while she slid into the seat across.

"Your stuff," Ting's cousin plopped down, his gaze drifting to the group of girls in the corner.

"Terry . . . Terry!" Ting nagged. "This is Mia, our new group member. Say hello —"

"*Ni hao*," Terry said, and Ting flicked his ear.

"Stop! I told you I gelled!"

"Go get the passcodes from Dr. Fern, as that would be *super* helpful since you *need* to do well on this project, RIGHT?"

"Right." Terry stood. Walking in the opposite direction of the teacher, he reached the classroom doorway and turned around. "But first . . . nature calls."

"Terry!" Ting yelled across the classroom, but he was gone. Blushing slightly, she turned back. "I swear, he wakes up plotting how to complicate my life. But on the bright side — he reminds me of the perks of being an only child and . . . right about now my auntie is losing it," Ting said, pleased by the sudden pinging of her phone. "His parents are tracking his every move since his last detention."

Mia laughed. "Really? They're tracking his bathroom usage?"

Ting snorted. "No, no, trying to crack down on his casual approach to life — my auntie's greatest fear is Terry never moving out . . . or getting married —you know, Asian parents. What are yours like? Nice and normal?"

Mia hesitated. How *was* she meant to share about her new version of family she barely accepted for herself?

"It's probably not considered normal — I live with my mom," Mia said, mulling over the rest. "So, my dad lives in LA, and we moved to be closer to him." She paused, thankful for the student rushing in.

"Miss Romeno, please join a group of less than four. Allow them to update you on the midterm expectations." Dr. Fern glanced up from scraping wax off his apple with a metal ruler.

Two girls waved over the latecomer, their group now complete alongside a boy named Jackson, whose dislike of shoes had been threatened by Dr. Fern with antifungal spray.

Shelby Romeno slammed her handbag down. "My dad — he's dead to me."

"What happened with Pops?" Jackson leaned back his chair, tossing his lacrosse ball against the side wall with repeated thumps.

"I thought he was joking when he said I had to wait for my license, but nooo! He rigged my car and *I* got escorted to school today by the COPS!"

"Mr. Skinner, Miss Romeno, I am old, not deaf. Please keep to an acceptable noise level." Dr. Fern eyed the athlete from above his glasses, relieved his shoes were still on.

Vivian looked mortified. "Shelb, did anyone see?"

"Who gives a — "

"Miss. Romeno!"

"That car is mine in ten days!" Shelby balked, only this time a little quieter. "I can't believe he would be so . . . I swear it's this new ho he's dating, putting dumbass ideas like boundaries into his head." Shelby ran her hands through her sun-streaked hair and looked up to see a few students listening in. "Can I help you!" she snapped, and the girls quickly tucked their heads back together.

"Well," Ting said, shaking off her distraction from Shelby's entrance, "I'm excluded from the normal camp since I live with my grandma — my parents too, but they're divorce lawyers and work a lot. Gram's good, though — she doesn't like little kids, which means it was rough a few years back. Where did you move from?"

Mia and Ting spent the rest of class chatting and working out details for the midterm. Ting was fascinated with all the places Mia had lived, questioning her life in Texas, while Mia found herself wondering about this new LA life. How much was going to change now with *her father* in the picture, not that she was ready to call him family.

"Class," Dr. Fern said forty-five minutes later. "I assume this is obvious; however, I must express the use of caution and need for confidentiality with the algorithms. I suggest you show a bit more seriousness than one of you who decided to icon their photo tag with the buttock of an animal . . . Mr. Skinner?"

After exchanging numbers and expressing concern over where Terry had disappeared to, Mia waved goodbye to Ting and joined the staggered thread of sophomores waiting to board buses for the school field trip. Something in Mia felt different, and it dawned on her that she may have just made her first friend.

The thought of an outing in downtown Los Angeles (with minimal supervision) seemed to be sending the already rambunctious students into a mild form of hypermania. Even Mia found herself smiling as she anticipated getting off of the school grounds for the day.

Boarding the motor coach, she plopped herself in the plush reclining chair and noted how her new surroundings were a far cry from past school buses, where duct tape held together ripped pieces of vinyl and foam that carried the lingering smell of body odor. Crowing under his breath, the driver muttered at the students ignoring his request to keep their feet off the seats. Sitting at the wheel, the man looked to be in his late sixties, a worn hat on his bald head and many years of life etched around his eyes.

Noticing Mia's smile, his face softened. "Ah . . . to be young again . . . really, I was worse."

"Hey, Pops, how about some beats?" said a boy whose spidery legs spilled into the aisle, a gold chain around his stretched neck.

"Phillip!" the bus driver howled as the kid retorted.

"Sorry . . . Mr. Henness — please may we have the pleasure of stokin' some beats?"

The old man shook his head. "Doesn't make good sense . . ." and seeing Mia watching, he added, "Been doing this since I retired, and I still don't understand half the things you kids say. What's your name?"

"Mia — Mia Storm," she said, only to have to repeat it two more times over the purring of the bus.

"That's a different name. Do you bring the storms, Mia? See, I grew up in Oklahoma. Not many can say they chased a tornado, but we did, always the big ones."

"That's interesting . . . *I* was born in Oklahoma." Mia said, startled by the coincidence, though she was too young to remember.

"Well, you're practically storm-born then." The old man winked.

As the bus pulled out of the parking lot and through the tall iron gates, Mia's stomach lurched. Her insides churned and she felt something bubble up inside her like an unwanted trespasser.

A feeling. A sense.

Mia had never told anyone about whatever "it" was, but when it came, it seemed to foreshadow something *troublesome*. Like the arrival of her father's letter. Or the time her mother overdosed. Or whenever they had to pick up and move.

Pulling her hair into a ponytail and resting her head, Mia tried to shake the feeling off. She looked at the picturesque ocean view they were leaving behind and told herself she was reacting to all the changes happening to her. There were too many.

Naturally, with life feeling so unpredictable, she couldn't trust herself. Feelings weren't reliable, at least not in this case. Not this time. Looking at the bright aqua sky, Mia sighed. Everything looked promising. Cloudless and serene. There was no indication of a storm brewing.

She hurried off the bus, waving to the driver and heading toward the glass dome building that carried the name Contemporary Art Museum of Los Angeles across the top in mirrored lettering. Once inside, she was grouped together with a few self-proclaimed jocks and the class president Will, and together they toured the museum's special exhibit on angels and demons.

Mia studied the paintings as Alfonso, their tour guide, droned on (in his thick Italian accent) about the various artists' inspirations and painting techniques. Pausing at the biggest Alfonso said, "dis painting says to me: di'vorld will bloop by di-dieath of a 'voman," while Mia caught her classmates smirks.

"Really? I see more of an evil-killing-good concept," Will argued, sparking an animated lecture (from Alfonso) for the next fifteen minutes.

Stepping closer to the painting, Mia studied the angelic woman cast in hues of gold and yellow and thought for a second, she could almost see her own mother's reflection staring back.

Her mother was the most beautiful women Mia had ever seen, so it wasn't far off to say the goddess like painting resembled the woman who raised her. Not just in her own opinion, but most people whose paths they crossed admitted her mother's beauty was undeniable. Only somehow, her beauty was one of the many traits Mia *hadn't* inherited.

When the tour finished, she made her way to the first-floor lobby ready to board the bus. Breathing in the smoke-filled city air, Mia turned her thoughts to what she would do once she got home, as most weekdays she was on her own for dinner, though, she always had Chip. She couldn't forget her stubborn little Shibu, who kept her company on the many nights her mom was working. She had her homework, chores and Chip duties, but any extra time tonight, she was determined to crack open her driving manual so she could keep studying for the written test.

"Okay everyone, the bus is leaving in ten!" Will yelled again, his look of confusion from the limited number of students boarding the bus. "So ninety percent of the school got a ride home?"

"Why, hello again, Miss Storm — how is the other side?" Mr. Henness was finishing a banana when a small plastic tube rolled down the bus stairs as Mia boarded. Reaching down to grab it, she held up what looked like lost lip balm.

"Sorry, kid, that's beyond my expertise. Maybe whatever it is, belongs to one of those gals?"

"Sure, I'll go check." Since the bus was fairly empty, Mia only had to ask a dozen students, all of whom claimed the small cosmetic didn't belong to them. Two girls sitting together insisted Mia throw it out before diseases spread.

"I'll just check it isn't hers." Mia said shuffling over to the girl named Shelby from Dr. Fern's class. Shaking her head, Shelby continued complaining on the phone to a Louie, while Mia headed back to ask if the driver had a lost and found.

"Just put it there with the extinguisher . . . and hey . . ." He made Will wait on the stairs. "I hope you have a great year. You know, this crowd looks a little tough, but there's some good ones." He glanced at Will, who smiled curiously back at Mia.

Mr. Henness was pulling the bus out of the parking lot when Will jumped up yelling for them to stop. Craning her neck, Mia caught a glimpse of a bobbing head running alongside the moving vehicle. Moments later, Ting sat across the aisle, huffing from losing track of time in the bookshop. "That's a lot of books," Mia said watching her stop the top book from sliding off the stacked pile that broke her shopping bag in the rush.

Leaning toward Mia, Ting whispered, "My grams loves the Renaissance nudes."

"Well, she needs to come down here for a visit." Mia laughed as they drove by a long-haired singer busking in nothing but his guitar strap.

"Mia, LA is crazy. Believe it or not, I'm probably the most sane —" But Ting never finished her sentence.

A blast erupted, silencing everything around Mia as she watched the entire front of the bus explode into hot acrid flames.

Mia felt her body lift into the air, floating unhinged for a moment before it slammed against hot, sharp metal. Tiny shards of glass pierced her flesh. She was sure her back was on fire. A faraway cry of agony hit her ears; clouds of black smoke enveloped Mia's senses. Her heartbeat paused, her mind stopped, her body . . . everything drifted into a world of complete darkness.

CHAPTER 2

Survivor

When Mia awoke Sunday afternoon, her body knew something terrible had happened.

"How can this be?" asked a muted voice from outside the hospital room. Stirring from a heavy, dreamless sleep, Mia caught fragments of her mother's panicked voice.

"A survivor . . . is that what she is?"

"We're waiting on ballistics to confirm our suspicions," spoke a man. "In the meantime, call us when she wakes."

"Did you see the latest about the former governor . . . ?" a pleasant voice asked hours later as Mia succumbed to consciousness. Gentle hands wrapped her arm. "Sure did. All this time he had a son."

A raspy moan escaped Mia's lips as the blood pressure cuff tightened on her bruised limb. She felt sore everywhere. Even her eyes hurt. As she fought to open her eyelids against the brightly lit room, Mia discovered two nurses watching her. "Welcome back to the world," the taller nurse said, replacing an empty bag of clear fluids next to Mia's bedside. "Mom?" she whimpered, hardly recognizing her own shaky voice.

"Sure thing, your mama's been here round the clock; should be back any minute. Think she said she needed to make a call . . . Of course, you wake when she steps out; see it all the time. The fighters like to come at no one's mercy but their own."

As if manifested by the mention of her, Mia's mother appeared in the doorway. "MIA!"

"MOM!"

Dropping her soda can and spraying brown fizz all over the sterile floor, her mother ran to her. "You're AWAKE! You're awake!" she sobbed, grabbing Mia's bruised hands. Ignoring the sharp jabs of pain from her mother's grip upon her IV, Mia caught the familiar scent of sandalwood and vanilla and burst into tears. Smiling, her mother sniffed, "I can't believe you're awake. They told me you might not wake up until . . . they had to give you extra meds, you were fighting so hard."

"Mom? Wha — happened?"

"Please don't strain, honey, I've been so worried. The nurses kept saying what a fighter you are. That you came through the accident with — well . . . minor injuries comparatively — I've been hoping —" Her mother wiped her tears on her gray oversized sweater.

"Yes, we don't always see such a quick turnaround," the nurse added, smiling at her mother. "You have some strong blood in you," and she went back to wiping up the soda mess.

"But what happened?" Mia persisted, her rusty voice improving.

Her mother hesitated. "You — you don't remember . . . *anything*?

"Maybe . . ." Mia closed her eyes. "I . . . I remember the field trip . . . getting on the bus .

. . the driver . . . ." Mia searched her mind for remnants of the *accident*.

"Oh, Mia — I'm so sorry — it was terrible."

Mia stared at her mom. "And . . . ?"

"I can't tell you any more yet." She stroked Mia's damp hair off her smooth forehead.

"What do you mean you can't tell me *yet?*"

"Let's get you checked by the doctor, and the good news is you're awake — you're safe."

"What. Do. You. Mean. You. *Can't.* Tell. Me. Yet?"

Looking at the nurses — or to avoid Mia's glare — her mother hesitated. When she spoke, her words were calculated. "Mia, we have to wait until you can speak with the police. A few detectives have been visiting and —"

"Detectives?" Mia gasped, her movement causing immediate pain. "What would a detective want with *me?*"

"They just want to speak with you about what you can remember. Please, I don't want you upset."

But Mia's mind buzzed.

"Let me get this straight . . . something happened to *me* — *you* have some knowledge of but won't tell me. I'm waking up after God knows what — bandages all over — feeling like I got hit by a *bus,* and I'm expected to lie here and just *wait for some crusty old detective to talk to me?*"

As Mia's anger intensified, so did a fresh wave of her mother's tears, the nurse's despondent stare only agitating her more.

"WHAT!?"

"Mia!" Her mother wiped her cheek across her damp sleeve.

"Oh, it's okay," the shorter nurse said tenderly. "It's common for patients to experience mood swings after such a —"

"THIS IS NOT A MOOD SWING!" Mia yelled, but as quickly as the anger surfaced, her feelings of fierce resolve began to wane; her back seared in pain.

"Whose revving up my patient?" a robust voice teased, and in strolled a man who looked to have stuck his head in a tub of liquified coconut cream. "Miss Storm, Dr. Millard. I'm glad to see you've perked up." He extended his hand to shake Mia's. As if fresh from a shower, Mia picked up the scent of Irish soap and rubbing alcohol while he checked her vitals. "How is the pain?"

With everyone watching, Mia hoarsely blurted, "Fine," and tried to avoid staring at the curly wisps of hair poking out of his tightly buttoned silk shirt. "Doctor, what happened to me?"

"Dr. Millard," her mother interjected, "we can't tell Mia until she speaks with the police and —"

Holding up his hands, the doctor shook his head. "Say no more Divana, as we previously discussed." His grin at her mother revealed an orderly row of pearlescent whites. Turning to Mia, he sighed. "I'll tell you what, when we can let you know what you need to know, then we'll let you know." He winked, mostly for her mother.

Mia groaned internally at his obvious gaze of infatuation for her mother. Suddenly, an image of a golden-haired angel flashed across her mind. *The painting . . . the painting in the museum!* She remembered!

"Dr. Millard, I'm sorry to interrupt," said a young curvy nurse who'd accompanied him into the room. "You're being paged by Dr. Kirchum about Monday's surgery."

"I'll call back." Dr. Millard shifted his focus back to Mia. "You are incredible. Nine-hundred-and-ninety-five — no, 996 stitches, here and here . . . ." He swept his hand in quick arching movements to illustrate where the stitches lay across her back. "Would have been nice to make it an even thousand."

Mia tried to imagine what a back with 996 stitches looked like.
What *her* back looked like.

"Nurse Rose, tell me what you saw a moment ago when you checked our patient."

Rushing to Mia's side, the shorter nurse padded her shoulder. "Remarkably, the skin has already begun to seal," she explained while the doctor leaned Mia forward. Grabbing the sides of the bed rails, she steeled herself while he pulled and tugged, strips of bloody gauze falling into a sterile pan. Blood that had come from her back and, from what Mia could see, carried bits of burnt flesh with them. She was seconds away from throwing up.

"Correct." He continued to examine Mia. "Ladies, right here is the power of youth. Our patient's epidermis is working triple time — so speedily that we need to remove some stitches early. Lucky me!"

Dr. Millard dug to dislodge the threads. "We can all see where this girl gets her incredible genetics from." He passed her mother another wink. "Oh, this one is deep . . . Nurse, how's she holding up?"

"Honey?" Divana leaned in at Mia's paling color.

"Done and done." The doctor snapped off his gloves and moved away so Nurse Rose could clean up the blood oozing from Mia's examination.

"You are in good hands." Dr. Millard looked at his own. "Keep up the great work, and I'll see you in a few days when it's time to send you home." Mia listened with her eyes closed as the doctor lingered on to speak with her mother. "I'll have the nurses give you my personal contact number, should you have any questions . . . ."

"Thank you." Divana followed him into the hallway for what Mia presumed was a more private discussion.

Left alone with Nurse Rose, the caregiver eyed Mia. "How's the pain?"

"Could be better," she whispered, wishing someone would either knock her out or muzzle her. She'd never been inside a hospital before, and she hated it.

"Sure. We'll get you comfortable. Good that your body is tolerating everything so well." She injected something into the IV while Mia longed for a silent room that wasn't spinning. "The doc was impressed with your healing, good signs! Just you and your mom?"

The drugs brought the nauseating throbs down to a dull ache.

"Yeah, just us." Mia opened one eye at the sound of her growling stomach. "Actually, no." She paused. ". . . I have a father."

"Not on good terms?" The nurse handed Mia the hospital dinner menu and a paper cup. Mia sipped the cool sweet water.

"I wouldn't know; I've never met him . . ."

"Well, that wouldn't be the first time I've heard that kinda somethin' around here. Sometimes I think this city is cursed . . ."

And while Mia chose between chicken alfredo and tofu curry, her mother poked her head in the doorway.

"Honey, how comfortable are you with me stepping out for a few minutes to make some calls?"

"Sure." The pain medication had vastly improved her mood.

"But if you need anything, there are half a dozen nurses outside your door, and I'll only be fifteen minutes."

"Fine here." Mia gave her best attempt at a smile and turned on the TV with the remote Nurse Rose had slipped into her hand. After flipping through the channels, she turned it off and stared at the abstract piece of art sitting above the couch when she heard a knock.

Another knock. Mia ignored it.

Another knock.

"Geesh . . . come in," she called, hoping it was her alfredo.

In walked a foodless man. "Miss Storm, I'm Detective Tommy Batair." And while he spoke, he unclipped a police badge from the side of his belt, flashing it to Mia before rehooking it. "It's good to see you awake."

"Thank you." She'd imagined someone much . . . older.

"How are you?" He studied her while taking a few steps away from the door.

"I'm . . ." She paused ". . . good. The doctor says I'm going to be fine." She reasoned it was technically true.

"That's good news. I've been hoping to speak with you, Mia." She watched him pull out a small leather notebook, dark and brown like his smooth skin. *What decade was he from?* "I'd like to ask what you remember from the day of your school field trip." The detective began, and Mia became aware of how papery thin her hospital gown felt.

Delicately working herself into a comfortable sitting position, she pulled her blanket up to her neck and listened to him ask if there was anything *unusual* about the day.

"Unusual . . ." she repeated, letting the question linger in the air while she touched her hair to confirm it *was* a giant mass of frizz. She didn't even know when she'd last showered although she assumed hospitals did nice things like bathe unconscious patients.

"How about the art museum?"

"I really can't . . ." She felt like whole pieces of her memory had been stolen. Mia watched the detective observe her and was sure she saw his eyes flash from warm brown to a golden amber.

Like a gust of warm air evaporating layers of fog — Mia's body started to remember. The flash of an angelic woman — it was a painting Mia had seen at the museum. Lunch with Ting in the cafe, the venerable smile of the bus driver — blurred face of the students . . . . Either Mia's mind was spinning or the room had begun to revolve again because now she could only see the faces of the people on the bus — the last images she had access to before everything went dark. The detective studied the look plastered on Mia's face, and although she opened her mouth to speak, nothing came out.

"Miss Storm?"

What happened to Ting? What happened to the others?

"Miss Storm — are you okay?"

Does alive . . . mean okay? Mia opened her mouth but again closed it without making an audible sound.

Detective Batair checked his watch. "I need to know if you remember anyone paying attention to you during your visit to the museum. Possibly following you? Could someone have gained access to your belongings, specifically your bag while you visited?"

Her foot twitched. She shook her head and thought how insane he sounded. No one had followed her . . . Why would someone follow her?

Clearing her throat, she winced. "You — have to be mistaken. There's no way —"

But maybe . . . long skirt, heels — some type of accent . . . .

Mia had never seen a face, but someone had bumped into her after she'd collected her bag from the coat check. It was a woman. Mia remembered her ramming into Mia's side outside the bathroom without even uttering an apology. How was she only just remembering this?

Something must have happened to the temperature in the room because Mia felt a deep chill. She pulled the thin hospital blanket up to her neck again, wondering if the detective could feel the cold too — like someone had opened the freezer door.

After a minute or so of waiting for Mia to continue, Detective Batair spoke. "Mia, we believe a self-detonating micro bomb was planted in your backpack at the museum last Friday between the hours of 12:00 and 3:00 p.m."

Mia gasped.

"A bomb designed to destroy anything within a ten-foot radius," the detective explained and for the briefest moment, flitted his eyes away from Mia's.

"Oh . . ."

"We got lucky. The bomb was at the bus front. After exploding, the tail end of the bus was blown away from the fire, sparing you and the other survivors."

Time paused as Mia tried to absorb his words.

A bomb. Spared. Other survivors.

"You and your classmates Yu-Ting Chen, William Turlington, and Shelby Romeno survived. Sarah Petterson, Tiffany Remmington, and the driver, Carl Henness —" And he went on, listing name after name of all the ones who hadn't survived although Mia couldn't bring herself to use the honest word. *Dead.*

Relief and terror hit Mia, as if she had been slapped in the back of the skull. For a second, she felt a heavy weight upon her chest, like someone had dropped a thick library book right over her heart.

Clutching the blanket, she remembered something else. Something she'd never told a living soul.

Sure, Detective, I have this thing that happens . . . a feeling that, when it comes, something awful follows. So, that being said — maybe I manifest bad news, considering you're telling me someone was hunting me down, looking to use me to aid explosives that would . . . . But she couldn't bring herself to finish the thought.

"There was a woman," she said, and as she named her, she knew the woman had something to do with all of this. "We bumped into each other outside the bathroom . . . She could have put something in my backpack then — I dropped it. She picked it up and handed it to me . . . ."

The hospital door opened to Nurse Rose's backside as she pulled a dinner cart inside. Turning around, she was startled, "Oh — it's not visiting hours." But even before anyone could answer, Divana appeared.

Snapping shut his notepad, Detective Batair nodded. "Good to see you under better circumstances, Divana. Just finished collecting your daughter's statement. Thank you, Miss Storm. I'll be in touch." And he walked out before anyone could utter a goodbye.

"If I was twenty years younger . . . ." Nurse Rose mumbled and maneuvered the rolling cart over to the bedside.

Mia felt jolted. Left behind with too many thoughts. He hadn't even asked what the woman looked like — although she wouldn't be much help on that. Running the conversation in her mind while Nurse Rose unwrapped plates of steaming food and the taller nurse returned with fresh bed linens, she caught the scent of garlic and butter and remembered her hunger.

"Thanks."

"You're so welcome, sweetie. Most of my patients complain it's not takeout." Nurse Rose busied herself unwrapping Mia's salad dressing and silverware, all marked with orderly green stickers indicating only the use of eco-friendly, organic materials.

Mia rolled the creamy pasta around her fork and took a bite. She chewed and tried to swallow, but despite her hunger pangs, the food stuck in her throat. After a few smaller bites, she put her fork down and massaged her neck. Turning to her mother, she watched the woman, who sat cross-legged in the chair, easily contorting her long legs to fit between the narrow armrests.

"Mom, the detective told me about the bomb," Mia said while the nurses slipped out of the room but not before Mia caught them exchanging glances.

Looking to Mia with sadness, Divana murmured, "I assumed," and tears flooded her eyes. Her mother cried a lot. "I don't know why someone would do this, honey." Divana sobbed. "I've been communicating with your father about everything, and he doesn't either," but Mia saw something in her mother's face that looked like it had on the day the letter had arrived.

One of the worst feelings in the world is catching someone breaking your trust. Again.

Divana shook her head. "I know you are reluctant to trust him, but I do. I trust him. When you meet him, I want you to trust him too. Relationships that don't begin with trust can't grow." Divana looked off and out the window.

"But *does* he have *anything* to do with this?"

"No. He is as upset as I am. He cannot wait to meet you." She looked at her daughter with her deep-set emerald eyes.

"But *who* would do this? Why? Nothing makes sense. Someone *must* have made a mistake!" Small sharp jabs ran through Mia's back as if someone had turned the pain switch back on.

"Mia — there's something you should know about your father . . . and his family . . ." Divana began, and Mia's stomach dropped. Looking at Mia as if she was one of the most fragile things in the world, she began. "I — well, when I found out I was pregnant with you, everything I thought I knew — changed." Clasping her hands as if searching for something to hold, she smiled. "This tiny blessing within me, I knew you were going to be my life, my new life. And your father . . . he had such a sensitive spirit . . . always trying to hide his real self from the world, but I saw his sensitivity. I loved it. I guess being with me brought it out more . . . perhaps." Divana sighed. "Your father had a brother, a twin. Never a mom, only a dad and brother. They were close. When I came into the picture, Charles started to change, and his family . . . they hated me for it. They blamed me for his change. It's hard to understand that level of hatred, but your father became — afraid. Some people just don't know how to be brave. They settle for less because they can't imagine something different, something better."

Divana took a sip of Mia's juice from the tray.

"Is that why he left us?" Mia couldn't understand that level of selfishness. Maybe he was born with it — the man she was now linked to.

"Mia — he didn't leave us. Your father's brother — he was elected mayor and things got complicated. We had to go."

"What! But why? Why couldn't —"

"Because his brother attacked us! His father ordered it!" Divana's tears stopped at the mention of Mia's grandfather, something in her steeling itself. Mia stared at her mother. She was so confused. She had once believed her father had died of an attack from a stranger, but now her mother was telling her there was no stranger, but a brother and a father, trying to kill her mother, to kill her.

Mia was repulsed that the blood of these people also ran through her. What did this mean? How was she meant to think of herself now that she knew where — or who she came from? Was it all the truth? Why was it so hard to get the DAMN TRUTH?

"I thought everything would be okay —" Divana continued, her expression pained, her voice soft. "With Charles's father and brother gone, I believed it was safe to come back. I never foresaw *this*, but then again, that's not my gift."

"You mean that someone still wants to kill me?" Mia wanted to laugh. This was ludicrous, all of it. She was an ordinary fifteen-year-old, needing to fit in at school and go through the phases of teenage life like driving and graduation — maybe going to a dance with a date at some point. Looking to the blank ceiling, she attempted to sift through the added layers of debris that now made up her life's narrative. Her head pounded. All this was happening, and she hadn't even met him. After this, she wasn't sure she'd ever know what to say to him. Because of him, she and her mother had nearly been killed. The man she pitied wasn't the one in harm's way; he was a coward. Sending them away because it wasn't safe. Well, the joke was on him because apparently it still wasn't safe.

"Mia, I'm sick with the thought that someone would try to hurt you. Maybe they are after me? I don't know —" Divana stared at the floor, shaking her head. As if coming to life again, her mother stood. "I've protected you all my life, and whatever it takes, I'll keep you safe." She leaned down and hugged Mia tightly.

Mia stiffened in her mother's embrace and then, unable to help herself, softened into the warm comfort of the one person she'd always loved. The one person who'd been there. The one person who loved her fiercely. It didn't even matter that her back was bleeding again from the pressure on her stitches. For the moment, locked in her mother's comforting embrace, Mia decided she *was* going to believe her.

CHAPTER 3

A Detour to Friendship

Mia breathed out a sigh of relief at the *tick-tick* of the car blinker. She'd won the argument. After two wrong turns, Divana pulled the clunky Honda up to a large brick fence crawling with ribbons of persistent ivy that concealed the Mediterranean-style home.

"This should be it . . . ." Mia said, approaching the iron gate and slowing to read the handwritten note. Taped to the intercom box, it read, *Postal persons — please leave packages at the front door so I don't have to walk. Gate code #3980.*

Shrugging, she entered the code and opened the gate while her mother followed down the stone driveway. Two brass dragon heads adorned the front doors, Divana lifting one of the dragon's jaw with a loud *clack* to announce their arrival. After a moment, Mia knocked again while her mother admired the verdant landscaping. A pair of wide eyes stared at them through the tempered window while someone cracked the door open enough for Mia to hear a high-pitched dog barking inside.

"What you want?" the woman asked, and Mia could just make out cat-eye glasses and shades of purple hair.

"Hello, I'm Mia Storm — a friend of Yu-Ting — "

"Ohhhhh!!!" The woman snapped the door shut as the dog, who had quieted for a moment, began barking again.

Mia and her mom exchanged looks and waited a few minutes when the door flew open wide. Ting jumped out, onto the porch and threw her arms around Mia in a fierce hug. Standing still with her arms trapped in her friend's embrace, Mia held her breath as she was squeezed in a painful bear hug.

Releasing Mia, Ting clasped her hand. "Mia! You're okay — how do you feel?"

"Good, I'm good, really —"

Her mom gently put her hand on Mia's back, soothing the prickling pain. "We were headed home from the hospital, and I wanted to come see you — Ting, this is my mom, Divana."

Ting and her grandma drew their attention to Mia's mother, who seemed to brighten in their gaze.

"You *her* mother? I thought you her nanny." Ting's grandmother said.

"Why, thank you." Divana laughed.

"When I open door and saw you standing," Ting's grandmother continued, looking at Divana but talking about Mia, "I knew my Ting so happy her friend not dead."

"Grams!" Ting blurted. Looking serious, she explained, "I was really worried when I didn't hear from you . . . ."

"I know, my phone —" But Mia stopped short of finishing the sentence that would have involved saying anything about getting blown up in the bombing. She was adamant about not triggering her mother; it was already a delicate risk trying to speak with Ting alone.

Thanks to Ting's grandma, she didn't have to work too hard for a distraction, as the bemused woman proceeded to fixate on Divana while welcoming them inside. "How you recover so well from having baby? My daughter not so good . . . She lawyer and work too much. I tell her, she need yoga . . . but what can you do? Do you need divorce lawyer? She and my son-in-law, they the best, if you need any help at all."

With her own wide eyes, which mirrored her grandma's, Ting mumbled, "I don't think Mia's mom is looking for a lawyer, Grams . . . This is my grandmother Nori, by the way . . . ."

"But *you* call me Gigi. I *only* allow Ting to call me *Grams*."

"Will do." Mia followed the hosts inside the foyer of the modern ranch-styled home.

"Would you like anything to drink?" Ting asked.

"Yes . . . some tea?" Gigi added. "We have hot and iced . . ." Gigi stared Divana down.

"That's so kind of you, but we won't be staying long," Divana explained to a disappointed look from Ting. Mia was distracted by a bubbling fountain in the middle of the spacious entrance; it seemed to be spurting violet-colored water into the large copper basin.

Ting's grandmother took Divana's hand as she, too, admired the fountain. "Place your hand here, make wish, and touch water. Whatever you wish will come true . . . so you think of good one . . . ."

"Well, I can use the help." Divana glanced at Mia, allowing Gigi to plunge her hand into the water as droplets splashed on her clothes.

Ting's grandmother examined her hand. "Maybe you wish for husband." She smiled at Divana while Mia laughed.

"Umm Grams . . ." Ting chided.

"Or wife? Whichever you like, you choose." She smiled at her granddaughter, who seemed to be giving up on civility.

Divana closed her eyes and ran her hand against the falling water. For a moment, she was quiet. When she opened her eyes, the three women were staring at her.

"Good . . . now you wait and see," Gigi said, as Ting asked her grandma in Chinese to not make Mia do the ritual.

"Ting . . . do you think I could ask you a few questions about the midterm while I'm here?"

"Sure — but we have plenty of time left in school . . . and actually, I kind of mostly finished it — I knew Terry was going to be helpless . . . Are you okay?" Ting watched Mia widen her eyes and lean her head toward her mom.

"Yeah . . . just worried about the project. Such a big part of our grade . . ." Mia sighed.

Ting narrowed her eyes at Mia and asked her grandma if she wanted to show Divana the garden. "After you get some tea, of course. Gram's a wonderful gardener if you want to meet all her plants . . . ."

"Meet them?" Divana asked, but Gigi was already grabbing Divana's hand.

"Come on . . . I have to feed Chloe anyway . . . but no shoes outside," Gigi chided as she led Divana away from the girls and toward the kitchen. Waving to her mother and wondering if Chloe was a tree or the still yelping dog, Mia followed Ting down a hallway.

"I wasn't expecting company . . . Sorry, it's a little messy." Ting hurried over to pull up the duvet on her king-sized bed. The room was decorated with a brown leather couch, oversized white dresser, and corner office desk holding three screens and an assortment of empty chip bags. The wall-length pinboard was packed with magazine pictures, ice-pop sticks, colored sticky notes, and candy wrappers.

"So . . ." Ting threw the last decorative pillow onto her bed ". . . you wanna work on the project?"

Looking at Ting, Mia shook her head. "I've been hoping to talk about the accident."

"Me too, Mia." Ting hesitated. "Are you okay? I mean really okay? You were in the hospital for over a week . . . and I can't make sense of how you were the only one who was injured when the rest of us didn't . . . I mean besides the others who . . ." Ting stopped and stared at the floor.

"Did you know the girls who . . . ?"

"No . . ." Ting admitted. "I never met them . . . Terry did — said he borrowed a pen once from the girl Tiffany . . . she rode horses. The bus driver was the grandfather of a kid named Phil — he was a volunteer . . . Most people would rather go to court than spend time with teenagers . . . ." Ting sighed.

"Ting?" Mia bit her lower lip. "I have to tell you something." Taking a breath and holding on to her nerves, she blurted out. "The bomb — the bomb was meant for me . . . ."

"What???"

"That's what a detective told me . . . I never meant for any of this to happen; it's all been so . . . shocking and . . ."

"Wow, that's crazy, Mia." Ting shifted uncomfortably next to her desk.

"I understand if you think I'm — well . . . dangerous."

Picking up a pile of sticky notes that ribboned as she pulled them apart, Ting mumbled a distracted, "Yeah . . ."

"Oh." Looking at the floor in disappointment, Mia pictured herself carrying out the remainder of her three years at North Elite High as an outcast. "Right . . . well, I guess maybe we can just get through the midterm and . . ."

"Huh?" Ting came out of her daze.

"I mean, I don't want it to be awkward doing our group work, I get not wanting to be friends . . . ."

"Mia! What? I don't care about that! I mean, I care . . . but not about the midterm . . . Well actually, I do care a lot about that class in particular but — not that you're dangerous . . ." She saw Mia's confusion. "No, you're not dangerous — I mean I don't think you are . . . ah, Yu-Ting, come on! Okay, see . . . I kinda already know the bomb was meant for you." She flopped on her desk chair, flustered.

"But . . . what? How?"

"Oh," Ting said, "well . . ." and without warning she flung herself into her messy desktop, stale popcorn kernels blowing onto the floor. "Mia, I'm sorry . . . You think I'm this good girl, but no one knows . . ."

"Okay . . ." Mia waited for Ting to go on.

"No one knows . . . not even Grams . . ."

"Knows what, Ting?"

"Knows the truth." Ting kept her head on the desk but tilted it slightly to wipe off the cracker crumbs that had stuck to her cheek.

Mia stared into the right side of her friend's face . "And . . . ?"

"And . . . AND — Mia!" Ting shouted sitting up with a face that looked as if she'd smelled something rotten. "Mia — I'm a grey hat hacker! A federal offender . . . peruser of the dark web. Hacktivist, Cyber thief, flower puller — " Staring at Mia with a self-loathing scowl, she continued, "My parents are *always* going on about how people *casually* break the law, and here I am, their own daughter, breaking into and decrypting police and medical systems!" She shook her head in disgust.

Mia walked over and kneeled on the floor next to Ting's desk. "I'm sorry, but . . . I'm a little confused . . . Why is this worse than being the cause of almost getting us killed?"

"What! Why? Because Mia — I'm a bad influence! I've tried to stop, but I can't. I'm so damn good too. Did you know recently . . ." she whispered, looking around the room, "people have contacted me . . . asking me to help them . . . you know . . . hack?"

Mia couldn't help but form an idea as she listened to her friend. "So, does this mean . . . you could — help me find out more about the bombing?"

"Yeah. Whaat?"

"I only know what the detective told me, and that's not much . . ." Mia wondered how much Ting had been able to find out already. "I mean, do you know much more about what happened to us . . . ?"

"But why don't you think I'm a terrible person? And I didn't find out much, as I was mostly trying to figure out if you were, you know, okay. When I didn't hear from you, I checked the active hospital records, and . . . I thought it unusual that you were in the isolation wing. Usually, that's the place for high-security patients . . . I tried asking the detective about it, but he gave me nada to go on, so . . . I kinda looked at what was on file in the police database. You came up as the suspected target for the bombing . . . but the woman who set the bomb is believed to have fled the country," Ting added. "Although they believe she's connected to someone, maybe even working for them like a hitman — in this case a hit-woman . . . ."

". . . working for someone," Mia repeated, letting it settle in.

"Oh, and Detective Batair is bringing someone in from San Francisco to help with the case . . ." Ting continued. Seeing Mia's distress, she added, "Mia, I'm sorry, I can get so logical about things . . . This must be so scary for you to hear —"

"No . . ." Mia began. "I mean — yes, it's scary but . . ." Mia leaned her head back against the wooden side board of Ting's desk. The cold, steady wood felt good against her prickly back. "When I was in the hospital, my mom told me some things . . ." and as she began, a flood of uncomfortable feelings fell out. Before she could stop herself, she began telling Ting everything she had learned about her past. Even if she wanted to filter her thoughts, she couldn't. The words and all that she had discovered and felt about her family trickled out into shards of a life story, while Mia cried and wiped her snotty nose with Ting's Hello Kitty tissues.

Her friend listened while Mia shared, gasping in shock at some parts and thoughtful during others. When she finished, Mia felt tired as she sat on Ting's floor, drawing circles with her finger on the tan carpeting. Her tears had dried up for now.

"Feels good to share with you . . ." Mia wiped her nose.

Ting's eyes were kind. "I'm glad you did . . . and thanks for, ya know, not judging about the hacking stuff . . ." Ting gave an awkward laugh. "It feels good to talk to a friend . . . I mean, Grams is great, but . . ."

"Yeah, I know what you mean."

"Maybe we're lucky we almost got blown up together," Ting said, thinking the timeline for inappropriate jokes about death was probably limited to this conversation. "Mia," Ting continued, seeming cheerful, "do you remember what I said to you right before the explosion?"

"I think . . . that your grandma liked naked paintings?" Mia tried to remember.

"No . . . well, yes . . . but not that. I said, 'nothing interesting ever happens to me.' I . . . I haven't exactly had the best of friends. I mean, my actual best friend is in her seventies, but meeting you . . . it's like destiny brought us together maybe —" Ting stared at the ceiling.

"But what if something happens again?"

"My dad always says life doesn't discriminate when it comes to hardships," she said in a fatherly voice. "And he's seen a lot of divorces."

Looking at the lines in the carpeting and wiping them clean with the sweep of her hand, Mia decided something. "I don't want to not live because I'm afraid . . . you know?"

"Yeah, I do . . ." Ting agreed, electrified by a thought. "Mia — hey, maybe we can keep looking into things . . . investigate . . . use my . . . ah, um — skills for a good reason . . . ." Ting blushed on her smooth cheeks.

"Yeah . . . would you be willing to help me with something specific?" Mia asked knowing Ting would be the right person to ask. "My mom told me all this stuff about my family's past but . . . not specifics, and I have this feeling that somehow my uncle is involved."

"You mean the dead guy?"

"Yeah, it's not a very solid theory, but . . . it's just this gut feeling."

"Okay, but why won't she tell you?"

". . . she says it's up to my dad to explain the rest . . . but considering we've not yet met . . . I won't be in the dark anymore. " Mia resolved. "It makes me so . . . weak."

"Sure, Mia, what's your uncle's name? I'll start there . . ." Ting grabbed a piece of paper. "I'm assuming his last name is different from yours considering you were unwillingly on the run and everything . . ."

"Gosh, this is so lame, . . . I don't even know his name —" Mia realized she needed to start changing a few things about her life, the first being figuring out who the heck she was related to. "He died a few months ago, so just look him up through my dad, twin brother of Charles Marazza . . . ."

"The ACTOR???" Ting yelled. "Your uncle is Charles Marazza's brother? Wait, I mean YOUR DAD is Charles Marazza!!!" Ting stared at Mia in shock. Studying Mia's face as if trying to see the resemblance, Ting shook her head. "Mia, he's like — Charles is pretty famous — I mean, there's a lot of actors around here, but he's kind of that different level. My mom loves him; she's always wanted to do his divorce, but apparently, he never married . . . ." Ting stopped herself mid-sentence. Mia was stoic, hard, her expression cold.

Willing herself to not show any emotion about Charles, she quipped, "Yeah, he's fantastic. Abandoned his family, never met his teenage daughter but . . . has a great career." Mia's words dripped with sarcasm, but she hoped Ting didn't take them as directed at her. Talking to Ting about everything had opened the vault.

"Mia, no success is worth missing out on you."

Clearing her throat, Mia smiled. "Hey, whatever you can find out, regardless, would be amazing, and — no, I didn't know he was famous."

"Oh, Mia, I'm sorry."

"Thanks, but it's — whatever. If I'd met him before, I'd probably have figured this out, but I wanted some time and then the accident, so — here we are. Anyway, I'm going to school Monday, no matter what my mom says. I'm happy I could see you today . . . that you were home and we could talk." Mia tried not to appear sappy.

"Mia . . ." Ting whispered, upon hearing footsteps and the voice of her grandmother down the hall, "you're not alone."

"Thanks."

"Seriously, I was on that bus too. Whoever messes with you — messes with me." Ting looked protectively at her friend, and something in Mia softened. The feeling of having someone on her side expanded her heart. She felt somewhere, deep in there, somehow there was a bit more space for what she felt was the budding feeling of . . . hope.

To avoid another painful hug on her sore back, Mia took Ting's hand and the two grasped fists in a silent gesture of friendship.

"People died that day, and we got to live. I think that means something," Ting said, and Mia agreed.

The drive home from Ting and Gigi's was a pleasant one with lots of impromptu singing and laughter as Mia and her mom sang the wrong words to their favorite songs. "Mia, you should sing more. I sometimes forget how beautiful your voice is." The truth was Mia's mother was the singer of the two.

"That's because I like singing in the car and shower, and that's about the extent of who will hear it and that's you, chip and neighbors, when the windows are open." Mia laughed.

Pulling into their apartment parking lot, Mia thought about something. "Mom . . . don't you think it is strange Ting doesn't have any injuries from the accident, not even a scratch?" Mia gently took off her seatbelt while her mother turned off the car engine.

That fact had been bugging Mia since she'd left Ting's house. She hadn't realized how odd it was until Ting had said it.

Mia's mom opened the car door and began collecting their things from the back seat. "I think they are very lucky to be okay, as are you. Now please let me get excited about this surprise I've been hiding from you. By the way, how is pizza for tonight? Ting's grandma wouldn't stop asking me if I wanted dumplings, and I'm starved."

Following her mom as she carried in most of their things, Mia handled the fragrant bag of lemons Gigi had insisted on sending them home with; Mia trudged behind, reaching the top of the stairs to hear Chip's wild barks upon seeing Divana's face. As the door opened, he beelined it to Mia, bombarding her with kisses and yelps. Trying to scratch him while he rolled around and sniffed her, Mia bent down and laughed at her Shiba. She loved him, even if he did steal her underwear.

"Tada!" Her mom stood in the middle of the living room that no longer resembled the room she'd left.

Taken aback, Mia realized her bedroom had been redecorated, from the color of the walls to the rug placed over the hard tile, both a light shade of blue gray. The once worn couch was replaced with a pull-out futon, dressed by a soft lavender duvet dotted with black polka dots and cozy fur pillows. A small pile of packages sat on her new desk. A few of Mia's favorite books, drawings, and keepsakes decorated the bare shelves.

"I wanted to leave the little details for you to do, but what do you think?" Divana clapped and smiled ear to ear.

"Mom! This is amazing! How did you do all this?" Her mom must have sneaked out of the hospital at night while she was sleeping.

"Your dad and I did it! He was wonderful, and look, he sent these!" Acting like an excited schoolgirl, she handed Mia three elegantly wrapped packages. "Open!"

"Wait —" Mia paused, feeling her excitement stifle "— he was here? In our apartment?"

"Oh gosh, no, he's too busy to do it himself. He has an assistant and hired people, but I picked everything out. Can you believe it? I feel a little envious thinking of all the things I could get done with an assistant and endless budget. He wanted to get you something special, so I gave him a few hints, knowing you're kind of a practical girl." Divana handed Mia the beautiful boxes. "Open!"

Mia sat on the silver swivel desk chair and carefully opened the smallest box. Untying the silky ribbon, she unlidded the flowered box to see a brand-new smartphone inside.

"Your father said this isn't in stores yet. Fun, huh? He wanted to have it all set up and running, but I told him it would be better to let you do it yourself."

Divana's smile was so genuine, Mia didn't have the heart to tell her what she was feeling. Honestly, she wasn't sure.

"Wow, this is . . . helpful."

"Now, this . . ." Her mom bounced on Mia's bed as she pointed to the second larger package.

Mia opened the larger box, to reveal another electronic device, this time a small, sleek laptop. It was a light purple color, and she knew it was one of the special editions that some of her classmates had at school. On the front was her name, engraved in large sweeping cursive letters.

"Woah, Mom . . . this is too much." Mia started to feel uncomfortable at such extravagant gifts. If there was one thing Mia and her mother never had much of, it was extra funds to spend on new things.

"I know, I told him you would feel that way, but Mia . . . he was so worried about you, and he begged me to do something to make things easier for you as you adjust to life here in LA. Technically you need these for school, so I consider it part of your schooling materials that he's replacing. Now . . . the last present *is* a little much . . . so if you don't want to use it, I understand, it may be hard to explain it, though . . . but he insisted . . . so here!" Divana gave Mia a large black box tied with a black satin bow.

Pursing her lips, Mia undid the ribbon and looked into a mass of tissue paper that covered a leather backpack. "Oh . . . wow." Mia breathed in the warm scent.

"Phew. He literally had the saleslady try every bag in the store. This was the one I thought you would like best." Divana jumped up and kissed Mia's forehead. "Okay, that was fun, but I'm starving and need a shower. My feet are covered in dirt from Ting's backyard," her mom said, heading toward her bedroom.

Mia looked around the unrecognizable room, sighing once her mom closed her door. Chip perked up at the sound of her voice, and she scratched his little head. "I mean, I admit, it's nice things he's trying to do, right, bud?" The dog pawed his ear. "But what about the past fifteen years?" Chip continued scratching and stared into her wondering eyes. He always did this when she was having a heart-to-heart; sometimes she almost believed he possessed the ability to understand her. "Well, at least I'm prepared to back to school."

And she pulled the tag off the backpack to throw into her new rose-scented waste bin when she noticed the price tag.

"WHAT???" She stood up and dropped the bag on the bed; the leather backpack cost more than her mother's car.

"Mia?" her mom yelled as she threw open her bedroom door, holding her phone and staring at her daughter.

"Ahhh, sorry — I was talking to Chip," she said as her mom gave her a *don't-scare-me* look, sighed, and went back to her pizza order. Grabbing the backpack, Mia went to the hall closet and smushed the present inside the already crowded space. Changing into her favorite nightshirt, she crawled into the silky bamboo sheets and breathed in the delicate scent of lavender. She was happy to be home, even if the room didn't feel at all like her own. Intending to close her eyes to rest only until the pizza arrived, Mia quickly drifted off to sleep. Maybe it was the new comforter or the buttery sheets, but Mia began to dream she was a young cherub, flying among the clouds with golden wings and wisps of linen covering her from the cool night air. She flew for hours only low enough to see the earth and high enough to see the heavens and belonging to neither. When she did awake, early the next morning, Mia felt tired. Her sleep had been restless. She had no idea that someone had been parked outside her apartment all night, watching her and waiting.

CHAPTER 4

The Memorial

The arched wooden front doors opened promptly at 8:00 a.m., but a flash of her lanyard ID to the burly security guards and Mia was able to enter her school at half past seven. It was Monday morning and North Elite Preparatory was quiet as she walked to her locker.

Everyone at school had a key code programmed into their lockers, only Mia was having trouble remembering hers after two failed attempts.

"Hey!"

Mia turned to watch a young man jogging toward her (hair still wet from the shower) his smile widened as he caught up with her. "It's Mia, right?" He tossed back a few unruly pieces of his wavy chestnut hair, while Mia studied his scratchless face.

"Yeah."

"Hi, officially — I'm Will, Will Turlington. It's good to see you back at school. How are you?" He looked intently with his light gray eyes at the greenish-blue bruise on the left side of Mia's forehead.

"I'm good . . . you?" She shifted under his stare. Something about the way his nose crinkled when he smiled.

"I'm fine. Still having a hard time absorbing how everything went down. With some of us completely fine and others . . ." He paused.

"I'm helping with the memorial today." He glanced at Mia's outfit, and she fought the urge to check for a cereal remnant on her uniform shirt.

For a moment it crossed Mia's mind that she should have stayed home like her mom had suggested; she'd had no idea the school memorial was today. "Ohh, that's — good."

Will leaned against the lockers. "Yeah, we want everyone to be able to pay their respects — this hits us all in different ways," he said quietly. "It's weird, Mia Storm, I don't know you at all, but after Friday, I think we should be friends. I mean," he went on, "I do know you came from Texas, but you weren't born there. You've played enough sports to be athletic, moved a lot — which might be why you have this 'I don't need you to like me' vibe . . ." He paused. "You seem to like school enough, and oh yeah, you're considering studying psychology in college." Her mouth went ajar, and Will smirked. "I have class president access to student files. Probably not the best way to get to know you, but I was curious. You don't have social media, you're a bit of a mystery."

You have no idea. Reminding herself not to fixate on his dimples or the way his pose looked like a back-to-school ad, Mia was about to joke about stalking when someone, again, called from down the hall. This time, Mia turned to see Ting land face-first on the cold, squeaky floor.

With a look at Will warning him not to laugh, Mia hurried over. "Ahh, Ting, are you okay?"

"Eww, shoes . . ." she murmured and pushed herself up into a sitting position. "New shoes," she explained, twisting her wrist and picking at the fresh hole in her tights. "This is why people like me *don't* wear heels."

"People like you?" Will asked.

"I'm convinced they do something to these floors." Mia offered her hand for Ting to grab. As Mia pulled her up, Ting grabbed her bag and took out a pair of purple striped sneakers.

A quiet *ahh* escaped her mouth as she eased her feet into the high-tops. "Thankfully, I brought backup."

Amused by the interaction, Will smiled. "Did you both give your statements to the police?"

"Yep." Ting stuffed the heels into her bag.

"Did you?" Mia wondered.

"Yeah, had to go downtown to work with a sketch artist," he explained, to the surprised looks of both girls.

"You saw her?" they both asked.

"Yeah, I mean, I think so. I'm pretty sure it was her, although obviously, I didn't know at the time . . . ." Will frowned.

"What did she look like?" Ting and Mia exchanged looks. All week Mia had been imagining a terrible behemoth disguised as the woman who had tried to kill her; her latest creation convinced her she was searching for a hideous wart-faced witch.

"Well, she was a brunette — thin eyebrows, high cheekbones — um, no freckles, but a small mole below her left eye . . . good nose, ya know, not the artificial kind, and . . . she was wearing this long dress, split at the top," Will explained to the girls' stare. "And — I think she had a small gold chain around her neck too . . . couldn't see what was on it but I keep thinking it was a letter or a third eye," he said as if disappointed.

"Too bad you can't tell us what kind of underwear she had on," Ting said as Mia stifled a laugh.

Will looked taken aback. "Why would I see that?"

"I think she is just noting how observant you are," Mia said.

Shrugging, he mumbled, "Yeah, a curse sometimes . . . ."

Click, click went heeled shoes against the floor as a spindly woman rounded the corner.

"Mr. Turlington, thank you for coming early," said the school's principal as she neared the group.

From afar, Mia had always thought Principal Florence resembled a flight attendant.

"Miss Storm!" She extended both hands to Mia. "I am so glad to see you! We have been thinking about you since the accident, sending you all our positive energies for your full recovery. What a relief, to see you standing here, all of you — looking ever so healthy," and the principal released Mia's hands and stared bittersweetly at the others. "Never could one ever anticipate such an unexpected tragedy at our school. How devastating a time this has been. I keep reminding my staff, it's the hard times that can shape us into greatness."

The students nodded.

"Mr. Turlington, I am so sorry to take you away, but can you accompany me to the gymnasium — I need help arranging some chairs."

"Yes, of course." Will looked reluctant to leave but bid goodbye to the girls. "See ya later."

Principal Florence turned to Mia. "Miss Storm, I would love to speak with you personally. Let's meet sometime — Ms. Courtney, my assistant, can help you find a time that works."

"Ah, okay?"

"Good, now we must be off!" Principal Florence motioned for Will to follow her as she clicked back down the hall rather fast for a woman in a tight wool skirt.

"Mia, how did *that* happen?"

"I just saw him while going to my locker, which reminds me, I've gotta grab a book. Ting . . . do you think Principal Florence knows much about . . . ?"

"Hmm — I don't know . . ."

Mia finally remembered her code and clicked open her locker. "What the . . . ?" Mia ripped off a yellow sticky note stuck to the inside of the silver door. Showing it to Ting, together they read the sentence silently: *Wish you'd blown up instead.*

"Oh my God!" Ting said. "This is — who would do this?" Ting stared down the two students walking by as the morning rush began. Not wanting to show how shaken she felt, Mia crumpled the note and stuffed it in her bag. She'd never had someone say something so cruel. "Mia, you should show the principal," Ting suggested, noticing Mia's expression.

"No way. It's just some kid being vile . . . anyway." Mia grabbed her book and closed the door in hopes of changing the subject.

"But someone got into your locker!"

"Look, it's probably someone close to . . . Well, I suspect it's someone venting on me. I can't worry about it right now. There's too much else — I'd rather know what you found out about you-know-what."

Ting bit the side of her lip as the hallway swelled with students visiting their lockers and talking to friends before the morning bell. Speaking quietly, she said, "Okay. Well, I've been looking into you-know-who —" The noise of lockers opening helped cloud Ting's words, but Mia began to notice a few students whispering and pointing their way.

"And — I didn't find a lot."

"Oh."

"Well, the thing is — your dad is actually listed as adopted and not as having any siblings."

Mia stopped her slow walk down the hall. "But my mom said —" Her stomach dropped.

"I know, right?" Ting leaned in. "But don't worry, I have an idea. There's this DNA test you can mail out for, to find distant relatives or your heritage and stuff. If you wanted, you could get a kit and send it in to see who comes back as a close relative. If your dad was a twin, even fraternal, the test would show."

"Ting, that's genius! But why would he be listed as adopted?"

But Ting was concerned about a sizable group of students gathering around a locker, throwing dirty looks the girls' way. "Um — wanna go to the gym early?"

"Yes, please," Mia said, as the two hurried off in the opposite direction of the gawkers. "Hey, Ting," Mia asked, when they made it to the first floor, and her thoughts turned to the school day, "why aren't you in your uniform?"

"Ahh, Mia! That's why I came looking for you! We were asked to wear black for the memorial. I tried calling your mom to let you know."

"Great. Wonderful." This was *not* the day she wanted to stick out in her wrinkled school uniform. Severely annoyed at Chip for playing weekend hide-and-seek with her mother's phone, she promised herself she would stay as unobtrusive as possible.

"It's not so bad, but here —" Ting took off her black cardigan and handed it to Mia. "Oh geez, it's got pit marks already —"

"Oh, I don't care." Mia put on the sweater and buttoned it up to disguise her stark white shirt. "Your sweater smells good — what is that?" Mia asked as they made their way toward the gymnasium.

"Gram's homemade perfume. But I can't have the recipe until she's dead."

When the girls got to the gymnasium, a teacher ushered them to their allotted bleacher sections, Mia to the sophomore class, and

Ting across the gym where the freshmen sat. Waving goodbye, Mia headed straight to the top tier of the bleachers, plopping herself on the hard metal seat and opening her leather backpack to grab her phone. She lost the morning argument with her mom that a grocery store plastic bag was better for schoolbooks than the silk-lined leather bag from her father. She frowned, remembering how much it cost.

When her phone screen flashed that its setup was complete, Mia hurried to look up the website for the DNA test Ting had mentioned. The screen checked the total cost of the kit and mailing at $275. "Shoot." She did not have that kind of extra cash lying around.

Looking out at the gymnasium, now packed with a mass of students in various collections of black attire, Mia wondered how she could come up with some cash. She was surrounded by a sea of rich students, all sitting soberly and talking without their usual ebullience. With a perfect view of the temporarily constructed stage set in the middle of the gymnasium floor, Mia stared at the empty rows of cushioned chairs, all probably set up by Will and the partial chamber orchestra seated off to the side stage. When the musicians played, Principal Florence led a procession of people down the runner-lined aisle, signaling the memorial had begun.

Family members, teachers, and a few students ambled their way down the center aisle, all holding a handful of roses which they placed atop a row of empty chairs. Mia recognized her classmate Phil from the bus, looking sullen in his charcoal suit and tie. Shoulders slumped, he placed his flower on a chair and followed a tall woman to a seat. "Ahh," Mia said quietly, making the connection between Phillip and Mr. Henness.

Standing at the lectern, Principal Florence watched as the last flower was placed on the overflowing piles cascading to the floor. The music stopped, and she spoke.

"Today we remember and honor the lives of our beloved students — Miss Tiffany Remmington Scott, Miss Sarah Veronica Petterson . . . and beloved friend Mr. Carl Henry Henness." Stifled cries came from around the gymnasium, while a woman seated in the first row sobbed. The principal continued her speech rather stoically, talking of each student's school accomplishments and contributions to the student body throughout their freshman year. Formal pictures were flashed across projector screens that surrounded the stage, highlighting happy and joyous moments of their lives, so full of potential, so alive. Mr. Henness looked strong and young in uniform and then with his wife, Esther. Phillip broke down in tears as images of him and his grandfather from his elementary years rolled across the screen.

Concluding her speech, Principal Florence welcomed a singer to the stage who crooned a wispy song about walking along the clouds. It was beautiful and eerie; Mia couldn't help but feel responsible. Thinking back to the vile note that had been eating into her mind all morning, she wondered if it was true — *should she have died instead*?

The rest of the memorial was filled with words from loved ones, some too distraught to speak, some unable to express their feelings, and others just sharing versions of the love they shared for the lost. Mr. Fallabee, Mia's English literature teacher, concluded the ceremony by inviting staff members to the stage while the orchestra played a final selection of songs. The staff gathered every rose and began weaving the individual flowers, one by one, around and into a circular wire frame, creating what the teacher named *wreaths of love*. "Let our hands send them out into the great unknown. Let their eyes see unveiled, let them run, unbridled, and soar beyond the limits of this limited life, into the next," the teacher read, wiping a tear from his youthful face. He concluded the memorial by inviting family and close friends to join the staff in a private ceremony down in the escarpment, where they would launch the wreaths into the sea and share moments of silence.

Following the crowd outside, Mia walked into the courtyard to see it had been transformed into a space for a reception. Hired waiters and waitresses served students drinks, as they walked along white-linen-dressed tables. Candles sat in crystal holders, centerpieces of red roses set among shoots of ferns. Students were filling the buffet line. Respectful conversations about the memorial turned to unrelated topics like bombs and gratitude for personal driving services.

Mia took one look at the tables full of fellow students and frowned remembering the freshmen class was eating elsewhere. Considering she had no hopes of sitting with Ting, she turned around and headed the opposite direction of the reception. Despite feeling hungry, she found herself walking along the school garden, admiring the leathery-leaved trees in abundant hues of green and pendulous autumn-colored flowers. The beauty of things that grew from the earth captivated Mia, somehow making her feel centered. She needed that today. Things that grew always made her feel alive, a welcome change after spending the morning thinking about death (and dwelling on someone wishing for hers).

The garden was set to the side of the courtyard and ran along the length of the colonnade archway, touched with ivy-climbed pillars and marble benches, although she preferred the large stone pathway that ran inside, feeling the preference to be closer to nature. Running her hand along a sharp blade of grass, Mia bent down on a steppingstone to smell the fragrant salvia and picked a tiny flower from the lion's tail growing next to her foot.

"There you are!" a girl snapped, her voice too close for Mia *not* to eavesdrop.

"Has anyone been watching the news coverage of all this?" asked a muffled male voice.

Mia smelled the scent of cigarette smoke wafting toward her and covered her nose before she could cough. Thankfully, from her spot in the garden, she couldn't be seen or see who was on the other side of the brush.

"Put that out, man."

"Mell out — there's no teachers around," said a smooth male voice.

"Yeah, but the teachers will be up here soon, along with a ton of parents," said the male voice that, to Mia, sounded somehow familiar.

"Not my parents."

"Will," said a female voice, "we miss hanging out with you . . ."

"I think she misses your tongue," said a second girl, and Mia realized why the voice was familiar.

"God, Liberty . . ."

"Oh, that's right, Gretchen, Mark's tongue has been working just fine," Liberty retorted.

"Have some class." Gretchen sounded highly annoyed.

"You and Mark, huh?" Will asked.

"My God, no . . ." Gretchen laughed. A new crowd could be heard exiting the building as it dawned on Mia that her chances of getting out of the garden unobtrusively were lessening by the minute.

"Hey!" A new set of male and female voices joined the group, while Mia debated busting through the topiaries and just dealing with the backlash.

"Hey, Mark, Natasia." Liberty said coolly, "Speak of the devil."

"We're looking for someone to take a table with," Mark explained.

"I can't, gotta go," Will explained. "President stuff."

"Wait, Will —" Gretchen said, "Mark is having a party this weekend and everyone's going. You gotta come."

"We're celebrating the well-lived lives of Tiffany and Sarah . . . and the old man," the smoker guy added.

"Thoughtful," Will said. "But I'll have to see. It's my little sister's birthday, so I'm doubtful my parents will let me out of that one."

"But I thought your sister just had a birthday." Gretchen sounded disappointed.

"See, Gretch," Liberty started, "some people have siblings — even more than one, believe it or not. Will here, he has a whole boatload of what they call sisters. Maybe, like, two of his sisters were born close together. Imagine that!"

"You're lame. Will, I'll come help you. I'm not staying here while she acts like such a —"

"Okay," Will said, cutting her off, "if you really want to help — I have to hand out some gift bags, for the families."

"Oh, shoot," Gretchen interjected, "I can't do that. I mean, I'd be too uncomfortable to speak to the families. What would I say?"

Sounding earnest, Natasia spoke up, "I'd not say much. People usually prefer less verbiage during such times."

"Yeah, thanks, Gretchen, but I'll just do it myself."

"Okay, but if there's anything *else* I can help with, let me know. Like if you need anything, I know the accident was so awful."

"Yeah, Will," added Liberty, "we're here, if you need anything. Can't be easy going through what you did."

"Thanks," Will said, "I appreciate that."

"You were sooo lucky — can you imagine if you got hurt?"

"Gretchen, some people *did* get really hurt," Will said to the instant silence.

"Right — I just meant like that one girl, wasn't she in the hospital?" Without moving a muscle, Mia began to sweat. "And you would think she would be appropriate today, with the memorial and all."

"What are you talking about?"

"Didn't you see her?" Gretchen said. "She's wearing her uniform, and Principal Florence asked everyone to dress in black — for respect, obviously."

"Yeah, show some respect man," said the guy who had been quietly sending a constant stream of cigarette smoke toward Mia through the mini evergreens.

"I haven't met her, but I think her name's Mia. Have you ever spoken to her?" Natasia asked.

"No," murmured a few voices.

"What about you, Will? You were both in the accident — I wonder how she's doing," Natasia said, while Mia made a mental note to like her in the future.

"Nah," Will said, and Mia's heart began to thump. What? Hadn't he just said something about wanting to be friends?

"I heard she's adopted," Mark added.

"Look," Liberty interjected. "This is fascinating and all, but I'm famished . . . anyone wanna go get something to eat before they haul it all away and I'm stuck living on a protein bar?"

"I really do need to go," Will said. "I'll come with you, Liberty . . . ."

"I'm not hungry. Too much coffee this morning," Gretchen said.

"Fine . . . adios, peeps," Liberty called, and Mia could hear someone walking away.

"How *does* a girl like that get in? I mean the application process is so thorough," Gretchen said.

"How did we all get in?" the smoker boy asked. "Is it our destiny? Potential? Parents like mine willing to buy their way?"

"Adean, stop —" Gretchen said flirtatiously. "You're sooo talented . . . and that reminds me, where did you end up putting your latest tattoo?"

"I'll show you this weekend."

Mia heard someone suggest getting something to drink, and like that, the group dispersed to go find a waiter. Getting to her feet, Mia was about to ease her way out of the covered garden path when someone spoke from behind.

"Looking at something interesting?"

Mia jumped, yelled, and whacked her arm on a spiky bush. It wouldn't have mattered if her sleeves hadn't been rolled up, but they were, and she scratched up her forearm, drawing blood and causing her head to pound.

Annoyed, she turned around to see Shelby Romeno standing behind her.

"Whatcha doing in the dirt?"

Mia sighed. It was bad enough overhearing people talk about you, but now she had to explain why she was listening in. Pulling herself out of the shrubbery, Mia stood and dusted herself off. Clenching her jaw, she shrugged. "I guess . . . eavesdropping."

"Hmm," Shelby said, assessing Mia. "That's odd . . . Did you at least hear anything good?"

Unable to hide her annoyance, Mia replied no, not wanting to say more; she was certain this Shelby girl was friends with Will.

Shelby's scrutinous gaze made Mia feel squeamish, which only added to the awkwardness when Mia's stomach gave a loud growl.

"Hungry? Or dieting?"

"I just missed breakfast," Mia admitted.

"Okay, then — let's grab some food." Shelby turned around and followed the stone steps out of the garden. Watching Shelby, Mia imagined she'd just come from the beach in her black cutoffs and a ribbed tank, sunglasses holding back her silky hair, and wondered why she *was* following after her.

Mia walked behind, watching Shelby grab a clean plate off an empty seat and walking straight to the meat cutting station. The server nodded as Shelby told him to "pile it on," while Mia had to cross three tables until she found someone willing to part with a clean plate. Walking back to the food, she headed to the charcuterie board, where she grabbed some crudites, and bite-sized desserts.

When she looked up, Shelby had sat herself at a table a waiter had begun to clear and waved Mia over. "I ordered you a lemonade."

Mia took a seat. "Ah——thanks." Mia picked at the fruit.

"Must be thirsty, hiding in the bushes and all." Shelby stuffed her mouth with a buttered roll.

"Long story." Mia felt the deepening sting of Will's denial — not that she cared. He was nobody to her.

"Well, I can't imagine anyone in this school has much to say that would be interesting to you." Shelby took another roll. "Oh, thank you, dear heifer, for making me so happy." She made Mia choke-laugh on a strawberry. The girls at the next table took offense, while Shelby leaned in. "I bet you a thousand, they are only meat-less for show. So, storm watcher, what's been going on since the big blowup?"

Mia spurted out her lemonade.

"Whoa — you okay? Did they spike it?" Shelby looked around.

"No, I just, umm, you want to talk about the bombing?"

"Well, yeah. Who else can I talk about it with?"

"But we've never — we're not friends."

"You're a funny one . . . Most new girls would just be happy I'm talking to them."

"Well, I'm not most girls." Mia stood. "Do leave me in the bushes next time if that's what you think."

Staring at Mia, Shelby held up her hands to stop her. "Whoa, listen, I'm not trying to rev you up. I like you. You're not as soft as I thought, storm girl."

Mia looked around to see a few tables staring at them.

"Sit, please." Shelby smiled and waved to the tables whispering about them. "Really, it will only fuel them." Mia hated the people staring at her because of what today meant. Wanting to disappear, she sat back down and grabbed a cracker, spreading the soft cheese onto it and shoving it in her mouth to stifle the hunger. "Storm girl, it's strange how you show up and some of us almost get blown up." Shelby leaned back and patted her taut stomach. "What kind of trouble are you in?" *How the hell did she know Mia was in trouble?* "Your mom didn't work for the mob? Bad exes . . . not paying your taxes?"

"I —" But Mia didn't want to lie. Something about Shelby told Mia she'd know if she did. Not that she cared — or did she? "Truthfully, I don't know. I don't know but I'm going to find out."

Shelby nodded. "Of course, so how?"

"Ting's helping me," Mia said, careful of students milling nearby. "But *why* do you care?"

Shelby laughed as if Mia had cracked a joke. "Well, I guess because almost dying kinda bonds people."

"Not for everyone." Mia caught Will in view from the far end of the tables.

Shelby followed her gaze and, landing on the class president, narrowed her eyes. "Yeah, well, some people don't know who they want to be yet." A bell chimed over the loudspeaker, followed by an announcement: "North Elite Students, please follow your traditional class schedule commencing at 1:00 p.m."

"Well," Mia said, regretful that she hadn't eaten more, "I need to go."

"What, you're ditching me?"

Mia shrugged. "I have class and — I'm pretty certain you do too."

"Nah, too nice a day to be stuffed inside." Shelby grinned.

"Well —" Mia grabbed a slice of meat and headed toward school.

"Hey!" Shelby called, jogging after her. "Wait!"

"Why . . . ?" Mia stopped and turned around. "Look, I don't understand what you want from me."

"What? I don't want anything." Shelby stared back hard at Mia's glare.

"You sure?" Maybe it was the memorial, the annoying students pointing at them, or the cruel note . . . but Mia wasn't in the mood to be toyed with anymore. Not today.

"Look, ever since the bombing, *bombing*," Shelby said, lowering her voice, "I've not been able to, to be around certain people. They all drive me crazy, more than usual. No one gets it. My dad thinks I'm depressed, and my friends are so dull I would rather do homework." Mia was taken aback by Shelby's admission. She hadn't expected her to be . . . sincere. "I'm not trying to screw with you; I just kinda wanted to talk. You like bubble tea?"

"I've never tried it," Mia said to Shelby's dramatic gasp.

"Wow, I mean *wow*. That's just . . . wow. Let's get some." Shelby gestured away from the school building.

"Wait, now?"

"No better time than the present. Like I said, too pretty to stay inside . . ." Shelby added, "and I hate brainless questions . . . *hey, what's it like to almost fry to death . . . morons*."

"No, I can't. I missed too much last week."

"Sure," Shelby said, her expression unreadable. "Then how about Saturday night? You seem like the charitable type. My dad hosts this huge fundraiser for the children's hospital, and it happens to be this weekend . . . It's nearly impossible to get a ticket, but I can bring any-one I like . . . ."

"I don't have extra money right now."

"Huh? Oh, don't worry about that. His friends will donate plenty.

I'm celebrating my birthday — for dinner, him and his girlfriend . . . he wants me to bring a friend . . . so how 'bout you come?"

"Wait." Mia paused and looked around to see if anyone else had surfaced into their conversation. "Let me get this straight . . . you want *me* to come to *your* birthday dinner?"

"Yep."

"Because . . ."

"Because . . . I can't stand anyone else."

"That's a terrible invite."

"Well . . . it's true. Come on, don't you feel it? Things just feel different since the —" and with her mouth and hands, she made a gesture and sound like an explosion.

"I guess."

"Okay, so you'll come, save me from going back to the creepy therapist my dad is threatening me with?"

Mia thought about it. This girl was on a whole other level, and yet, something about her interested Mia. Despite her rough edges, she seemed — honest. Speaking before she could change her mind, she agreed. "Okay, I'll come . . . *if* Ting can come too . . . and if my mom agrees . . . ." Mia said, unsure the latter would be possible.

"The clumsy girl? Yes. Definitely bring her. She's one of us, bonded by bombs," Shelby said, while Mia watched the crowd disperse inside the school.

"Look, I really need to get going." Mia hoped hard that Ting didn't have any plans for Saturday.

"Okay, what's your number? I'll text you all the details." Shelby whipped out her phone from her back pocket.

"I don't actually know — it's a new phone . . . ."

"Nice bag." Shelby eyed the expensive backpack where Mia's phone was stashed.

"It was a gift."

"Fancy friends," Shelby said, but Mia shook her head.

"Not really." And she wished she still had her plastic grocery bag.

"You don't trust people, do you?"

"Not the weird ones."

"Ha!" Shelby laughed, adding her number to Mia's empty contact list. "Direct and clear, I like. Oh, and I'm not trying to screw with you."

"Sure."

"Well, I better peace out." Shelby threw her keys up and caught them, while Mia looked to see that most students had gone inside.

"Shoot, me too." Mia hurried toward the school. "Oh . . ." Turning back around, Mia smiled and called, "Hey, happy birthday."

Looking out at the ocean view, Shelby shrugged. Their school was set on a cliff, nothing but sea and sky from the north view. With the wind blowing Shelby's hair and an unguarded look of memory, Mia caught a brief glimpse of a very young girl who seemed almost sad.

A second later Shelby yelled, "Saturday, make sure to dress up!"

CHAPTER 5

Divine Meeting

Staring at her mother's bed, Mia pointed to the emerald knee-length dress. "I'll wear this one, though I don't love the sparkles." She referred to the faint shimmer that reflected off the textured material. The two other black dresses were more in her comfort zone, plain and unassuming, but she needed to go with the only option that didn't showcase her scarred and healing back.

"It's going to look lovely on you," her mother said. "You should wear green more, it looks so pretty with your skin." Divana held the dress up to Mia, while they both surveyed her look in the mirror. "Now . . . about your hair. Would you like me to curl it . . . or at least smooth it out?"

Admitting the look of total neglect was not her goal, Mia agreed to let her mom try to work at her hair. An hour later, she was transformed into a silky-haired beauty as she stood waiting for her ride, the babydoll dress showing Mia's budding figure. Having only played with makeup as a kid, Mia fought the urge to wipe off the tacky lip goo her mom had used to color her pout.

Chip barked when an unfamiliar Cadillac pulled up outside their apartment. "He's here, Mom," Mia said, while Divana slipped on her sandals and leashed the dog so together they could walk Mia to the car.

"And you're *sure* you can drive Mia home no later than eleven?" Divana asked, tapping her foot.

Louie the driver had proved successful in handling Divana's interrogation. His calm nature sealed her reassurance that Mia was in safe hands, especially when he explained he'd been Mr. Romeno's personal driver longer than Mia had been alive.

Hugging Mia and kissing her forehead, Divana whispered, "Be smart — okay? No dumb stuff . . . be safe."

Mia nodded. "I'll be fine, Mom. I'll be a perfect little angel," she joked as her mom pulled back. "What?" Mia asked, seeing a peculiar look on her mother's face.

Divana's eyes, a mix of green with flecks of gold, seemed to glow as she gazed at her daughter. "Just some fuzz on your cheek," she answered, brushing Mia's pink-hued cheekbone with her thumb. "You *are* perfect."

It took an hour, with traffic, to pick up Ting and arrive at the casino. Just as they were pulling away from the street the Chens lived on, a woman ran out of the gate, pleading for Louie to take her with them. Mia would have considered it, if Gigi wasn't only in her bathrobe. On the way to meet Shelby, the girls indulged in an assortment of sour candies and chocolate-flavored caramels. "Now that she has her own car, I don't need to keep them stocked for Miss Shelby but old habit."

Finishing an extra-gooey caramel, Ting looked at Mia disapprovingly. "Oh, great. You're in green and I'm wearing red — we look like a Christmas card."

Mia laughed. "Then we'll make Shelby stand in between us."

Louie turned the car onto Lucky Lane as they hit a wall of traffic, cars so close they were almost kissing as everyone inched their way down the congested road waiting for their turn to drop off the important guests. Lights pointed to the red carpet spilling out of the casino's main entrance, a crowd of onlookers and journalists begging for pictures. "Whoa," Ting said, watching the organized chaos along the street, while a man in an earpiece approached Louie's vehicle, asking him to roll down the window.

"Personal driver for Mr. Romeno, just delivering some VIPs." Louie flashed his ID. "We need to get to the back entrance," Louie explained while the man slapped a magnetic sticker on the front and relayed the message through his mic.

"This, ladies, is the biggest poker charity event of the year. I hope Miss Shelby told you all about it, makes millions for the children's hospital. Mr. Romeno launched it the year Shelby was born," Louie said. Exchanging surprised looks, the girls watched him weave the sedan in and out of the long line of SUVs, while waiters brought cocktails to car windows.

"Ohhhh nooo!" Ting cried, smashing her face against the darkened window. "I think . . . I see . . . Terrance X-Code!!!" She tried to find the window button while refusing to remove her suctioned face from the fogged glass. Panic-stricken, Ting cried, "Excuse me! Mr. Louie! Could you PLEASE roll down the window?"

"Of course."

As he did, she popped her head out in awe at a man sporting a pink tracksuit with thick black braids running down his back.

"He . . . he's there." She pulled herself back into the car. "I can't believe he's here." And she slumped herself down in the seat to catch her breath.

"Ladies —" Louie announced as he pulled up to the side of the building, "Miss Shelby will meet you inside."

"You're sure she wanted me to come?" Ting whispered to Mia while waiting for someone to open the back door. "I was just thinking, what if — it really wasn't Shelby who texted me? What if someone stole her phone, duping me to come . . . ?"

"And for what reason would someone do that?" Mia rolled her eyes.

"Fatal embarrassment. It's a thing." But Ting forgot her concern when, minutes later, their senses slammed with the sounds and sights of spinning wheels pinging wins from hundreds of gambling machines spread across the gaming floor. The natural electricity of the casino was abuzz with thumping vitality as the girls walked through; yells coming from scantily clad women bouncing at the victory music of from flashing screens. Mia felt like the very floor of the casino reverberated energy into her body.

"Mia, Ting!" Shelby called. She looked effortless in her draped backless dress and bronzed skin. "You guys look great." She nodded at Ting's red Nike high-tops that closely matched the bright color of her dress. A man in a Hawaiian shirt attempted to take her picture, when Shelby barked, "Who the hell are you?" to the balding tourist. Looking scared, he shuffled away after his companion in a black floppy hat. Following Shelby to the packed casino lobby, a crowd continued to snap pictures of the latest arriving guests. "I hate all the dramatics, but we have to go this way." Shelby pointed to a grand carpeted staircase that took them to the second level to get away from the yells and flashing lights of photographers who mistook the girls for actresses. Mia enjoyed the quieter scene at the top of the stairs, where she followed Shelby across the landing toward a bridge connecting the casino to the hotel. Set with tables and chairs, Mia assumed they were going to have dinner there, the only problem being, the bridge was made of glass.

"Is . . . this safe?" Ting watched Shelby stroll onto the glass structure.

"No, it's going to break the second we sit — totally." Shelby placed herself at a crystal and silver set table as a waiter assisted her with her chair. "Just don't eat too much, and we'll be fine." Shelby winked.

Mia hesitantly sat while a waiter attempted to place a napkin on her lap. She grabbed it from him, and he awkwardly tugged it back, Shelby waving him away to get their drinks.

"Welcome to my house," she said as she leaned back in her chair.

"How long have you lived here?" Mia wondered how a place like this felt like home.

Sipping the mint-berry-infused water, Shelby shrugged, "Since I was a baby."

"But it looks so new!" Ting took a bite of the parmesan-encrusted bread that had just arrived, closing her eyes as it melted in her mouth. "Mud be 'mazing to grow up 'ere." She wiped her buttery fingers on a soft blue napkin.

"If you don't mind the crazies and the noise — yeah, I guess. But I'm planning on a hut by the beach someday." She took a bite of the soft bread, flicking her eyes to the two empty seats.

"I can't imagine living in one place for so long." Mia thought out loud. "We've only ever lasted somewhere about four years." She remembered a time before her father's letter. Her mother had promised her she could stay at her last high school all four years. So much for that promise.

"That sounds so adventurous," Shelby said as the waiters returned with salads and a steaming creamy lobster bisque. "Jared, what is this?" Shelby asked as he placed the warm dish in front of Mia.

"This is your birthday dinner, Miss Romeno, what you and Chef Ardeno planned . . ."

"No. I mean, why are you serving us the first course without my father?"

"Oh . . ." The waiter hesitated as another server shuffled over. "Miss Romeno, I am so sorry — your father let us know to go ahead and serve you and your guests. He is taking a bit longer with the press meeting but should be up shortly and extends his sincerest apologies."

Listening stonily, Shelby nodded as the waiter hurried away. "Okay, go ahead and eat; he won't be coming."

"Okay," Ting said, while Mia put down her spoon.

"I'm happy to wait," she said. "The waiter said he's just running late . . . ."

But before she could go on, Shelby retorted, "Ha, *late*, no that's code for he's not coming. It's fine. You guys like steak?" She took a taste of her soup.

Ting smiled eagerly. "Oh yes, I love all meats."

"But what if he's on his way?" Mia questioned. "I'm perfectly happy to wait."

Pausing before taking a bite of her salad, Shelby shrugged. "Unfortunately, there's one thing that drives most people in this town and always wins, Mia. Money. If there's money to be made, Dad won't miss the chance. It's fine, I'm used to it. Besides, he was going to bring his new girlfriend, so it's way better this way." She seemed at ease again.

"Hey, why don't we give Shelby her present?" Ting asked, while Mia felt the slightest tightness in her chest at seeing Shelby sit next to the empty chairs.

"Yeah," Mia agreed, while Ting reached down to grab a small box from her purse.

"Oh, shoot." She pulled out the semi-smooshed package and gave Mia an apologetic glance. "It's nothing breakable but — I'm sorry, I should have listened to Mia and not put it in there."

"What's this?" Shelby asked gruffly as Ting passed the package to her from across the table.

"This is a birthday gift," Mia said. "Most people say, 'thank you,'" she added, watching Shelby inspect the balloon-printed wrapping paper.

"Sorry," Shelby said coolly. "I don't really like presents."

"What? Everyone likes presents," Mia exclaimed, encouraging her to open it. As she tore off the wrapping, the girls watched as she uncovered a semi-flattened package that read *Bubble Tea, Make-at-Home Kit*.

Shelby stared at the small box while Ting explained, "I've used this before. I mean not this particular one — that would be gross — but I've tried this kit, and it makes pretty good tea. As long as you boil the boba right. It even comes with a metal straw, you know, for the environmentally conscious." Mia wondered if that was something a girl raised in a casino had cause to think about.

Shelby looked up, her eyes softening. "Thank you . . . This is . . . really cool." She placed the disfigured box tenderly on the table.

The rest of the meal passed pleasantly with a few good laughs as the girls shared the ironies of growing up in such nontraditional families; their differences somehow seemed to provide them a commonality they found endearing. At the end of the meal, after Shelby had excused herself to the bathroom, Mia leaned over to Ting to try to see what was happening below; a crowd had gathered over some late-arriving guests.

"Don't lean too much!" Ting nagged. "I don't want to put too much pressure on one spot, I ate a lot."

Jared, the waiter, was clearing Mia's plate when he explained the main poker tournament was about to begin in the west wing ballroom. "You should try to see it; part of it is being televised."

Shelby returned just as Mia decided she needed a bathroom visit herself. "I'll take you upstairs to my house," Shelby said. "We're heading to the elevators anyway," and within a few minutes, the girls were inside Shelby's grand penthouse by way of a direct elevator that shot straight to the top floor.

Walking inside the two-story residence, Mia was met with a city view through a wall of ceiling-to-floor windows.

"Bathroom through there." Shelby pointed to a set of double doors and asked Ting if she wanted to check out the balcony view of the city.

Mia followed her instructions and walked into a closet that more closely resembled an expensive boutique, lined with golden rods holding an endless array of color-coordinated clothes, shoes, and purses. It was one of the prettiest rooms she'd ever seen. Hurrying through, she came to the white-stone-floored bathroom that was accented everywhere with flecks of gold. The smell of lemon met her as she located the isolated private toilet, after mistaking it twice for linen closets. Washing her hands a few minutes later, Mia carefully placed the monogrammed towel back on its hook while reading different names of perfume bottles that lined Shelby's tidy bathroom counter. Most were full, except one fragrance that Mia picked up and smelled, catching the familiar scent of rose. Placing it back, she froze as her stomach flipped. Something electric, like a hit of adrenaline, rushed through her body. The smell, something about *that* perfume, set her senses afire and made her feel . . . cautious.

Running her clammy hands under the golden swan tap again, she looked at herself in the mirror. Regardless of having had a mild stomachache all day, she knew this feeling was somehow an unwanted warning. She'd had it before — the day of the bombing.

Returning to the family room, Mia found the girls yelling at the enormous screen while jamming buttons on a game controller. Sitting on the white half-circle sofa to still her shaky legs, Mia watched Shelby finish off Ting's virtual character by trapping her in the jungle with flying ninjas.

Why did she feel like this? Was there something not to be trusted about Shelby?

Shelby gave a victory cheer while Ting demanded a rematch, both girls offering for Mia to play next.

"No, I'm okay — never played." Mia took a popular women's magazine off the mirrored table and skimmed through the pages of makeup tips. When no one made any noise, she glanced up to see Ting and Shelby staring at her, bewildered. "What?"

"Storm girl, you amaze me," Shelby said. "You're just so . . . *not* LA."

"What does that mean?"

"It's hard to explain but easy to see."

Ting must have noticed Mia's irritation, adding, "Even if you're not — you know, super-rich or famous — you kinda try and act like you are. It's just what people do here to get attention or feel important. Actually, it's embarrassing when you say it out loud, really." She shook her head.

"That sounds awful." Mia's feeling of edginess grew. "I wouldn't waste my time with people like that."

"Yeah —" Shelby shrugged. "I mean, if you're not from here, I guess it seems odd, but it's how it is. If you can't keep up, like I told you, people will walk all over you. Besides, everyone changes when the world is watching. Everyone except . . . maybe you."

Mia studied Shelby. "What about you? Who do you try to be?"

"Me?" Shelby looked surprised. "What you see is what you get." Mia stared hard, trying to discern if that was true. "What? Don't think so?"

Ting stopped browsing a magazine to watch the two girls shoot looks at each other. "Ah, hey, should we check out the poker —"

"I wonder if you hide a lot," Mia said before Ting could finish.

"Oh, *really*?" Shelby straightened herself on the couch. "Go ahead, don't hold back, Stormie."

Mia scoffed. "I don't, and I'm not the one trying to be friends with someone I hardly know."

Ting's phone buzzed and both girls looked at her while she grabbed it. Feeling the need to pretend she wasn't listening, she started texting while Shelby answered Mia.

"Are you for real?" Shelby asked. "Have you never had friends before or something?"

"Nope, never had a friend before in my life. Is this how it works?" Mia felt her anger peaking. Something in her wanted to push Shelby, to test what she would do when she wasn't in control.

"Hey, guys . . ." Ting said.

"What?" Shelby asked gruffly. "Do you think it's weird that I would want to be friends?"

"Me . . . ? Wait, what?"

"Shelby, look," Mia started, unable to stop herself. "You don't need us, you don't *seem* to need anyone . . . being that you're rich and popular, apparently able to fit into the LA crowd, which I *clearly* don't. So, why invite me here and act like we're going to be friends at school come Monday?"

Shelby, who'd been standing, stared hard at Mia, like an animal cornered by its prey. She looked ready to pounce, and Mia prepared herself for a fight, when Shelby plopped down on the couch and sat staring at her hands. It felt like a good five minutes before she spoke, and when she did, her voice was soft and unsteady.

"Yeah, you're right. It's weird me inviting you here." She looked at Mia and Ting. "I have friends, a lot of friends that could have come but — I didn't want them to. I don't want to spend time with any of them anymore because, well, things have just changed. I've changed.

My tolerance, it wasn't high to begin with . . ." Mia could almost see inside Shelby, the struggle of what to hold and what to release.

"After the bombing, my mother called. She lives in Arizona, and I've not heard from her in years. Out of the blue she wanted to see me — see if I was okay." Shelby picked a tiny piece of lint off the immaculate pearl-white couch. "My dad got her here, put her up for a night, and she — like she always does — turned up drunk and wondering why I didn't want to stay and have breakfast together. She doesn't even remember I spent my fourth birthday cleaning urine off my new kitchen set because of her. My sixth, dragging her into bed and — there's too many stories. Dad doesn't know much, and he shouldn't. I guess she's my dark secret 'cause I hate her. Seeing her after the accident, I just, I don't know, but it did something to me."

Time seemed to pause as Mia and Ting listened to Shelby. Mia was quiet, her reluctance to believe Shelby melting away.

"After seeing my mom — my maid found this box of old stuff and wanted to know if she should throw it out, but when I opened it, I found this little candle my grandma gave me before she died. 'Use it, Shelby, when you need your guardian angel,'" Shelby said, mimicking her grandmother's voice. "Then, it was the weirdest thing. I was in the bath, lit the candle, and all of the sudden, Ting, you texted me asking how I was and explaining about Mia in the hospital. I guess it felt like a sign — you girls popping up when I was . . . when I felt so low." Shelby looked at the floor.

Mia couldn't help but think this moment was sacred, holy ground or something. Shelby wasn't trying to deceive them; she was trying to be vulnerable.

Mia stayed quiet for a while. When Ting cleared her throat, Mia spoke. "Shelby, I'm not by *any* means some guardian angel, but I'd like to be your friend," she said, watching Shelby's tiny teardrop land on the white silk pillow she was holding, the slightest mark of mas-cara and sadness.

"Yeah, me too," Ting said, her voice catching. "And I'm so sorry, Shelby."

"Sorry?" She looked confused. "Sorry for what?"

Ting blushed. "For judging you as an elitist mammet . . . You're nothing like that."

"Even though I have no idea what that means," Shelby shrugged, "I'm sure I've been called worse."

And somehow, in that moment the girls all knew they had just experienced an undeniable pull toward honest friendship, a close-ness they'd all been longing for that left them freer than they'd felt in a while. "Okay, now that I just bared my soul, the least you could do, Mia, is try a video game."

And with that, Mia made her first failed attempt at playing Flying Elves.

The girls grabbed water, hit the bathroom, and headed back downstairs where Shelby led them to the west ballroom. Handing each ten tickets, she explained her father had bought them to be used at the raffle, and if they didn't use them, they'd go to waste. Fully distracted by the six-foot chocolate fountain, Mia left Ting in the hallway and entered the ballroom where servers floated by with silver trays of biddable luxuries.

After walking the room twice and deciding against bidding on the adorable but barky Pomeranian, Mia dumped all her tickets in a box to win a pen that promised to never run out of ink, checked with Ting and Shelby, and headed back to the hallway to wait next to a group of guests attempting to toe dip in the chocolate, despite the watchful security guards.

". . . and if you win," Shelby was explaining to Ting as they met back up with Mia while she waited near a striking man in a fitted tuxedo shirt, "I'll be contacted. But don't get your hopes up. I've been playing since before I could count and never won a thing."

Heading down a back stairway to avoid the crowds, the girls followed Shelby outside alongside a diamond-shaped swimming pool; breathing in the cool night air, Mia tried not to laugh at the couple floating along on flamingo rafts, fully dressed and singing to the crowd of women walking by. The walk led them over a small bridge, alive with ginger-colored koi fish, to a hidden cave marked for employees only. Nodding to the men guarding the door, the girls traipsed through a kitchen steaming with smells of garlic and cooked strawberries and into a lounge set with giant screens, filling all four walls, that displayed the live poker tournament.

"There he is," Shelby said as they passed the screens and entered the poker room, her sights set on a gray suited man laughing as he lost another few thousand dollars. Shelby headed straight to her father while an officiant stopped Mia and Ting, explaining only players were allowed to proceed.

"And it will be televised so you can see all the action from the lounge," the man explained, as Mr. Romeno greeted his daughter, both sharing the same tanned skin and full lips.

"Princess!" He jumped up to hug Shelby while halting the card dealing. Mr. Romeno introduced his table to Shelby, kissing her cheek and beaming over her. Pulling her back at arm's length, Shelby chided him while he commented on how much older she looked now that she was sixteen.

"And legal to drive," he said while Shelby pointed to her friends. "Wonderful, let's meet them." Mr. Romeno said while Shelby waved them over.

It was then that a yell happened, followed by the ringing of a loud bell and an officiant yelling, "We have a winner!" The entire room cheered; some groaned as the winner took his chips to a large counter set at the bar and dropped the blue tokens into a machine that flashed the running total of his donations. Cheers and a collective applause grew louder when the counter totaled in gleaming blue letters, $1.4 million. The room brightened and festive music began; Mia clapped along with the celebratory moment, while Mr. Romeno thanked the man for his generosity.

Observing the winner, even from the side, Mia felt something magnetic. The man looked her mother's age, brilliant blue eyes and a rugged beauty that explained the constant crowd of women surrounding him. Ting pinched her arm and whispered something but to Mia, it was inaudible. Nothing could draw Mia from studying the stranger with such intensity. She almost believed it was her gaze that pulled him toward her with a bewitching stare she couldn't stop. He would later describe the moment as a force of the universe acting to bring them together, for when their eyes locked, it was then that Mia realized she was staring into the face of the man she knew to be her father.

The man, caught in a congratulatory crowd, was trying to move through the cluster of people toward Mia. The room, alive with laughter to everyone else, became a narrow tunnel of focus allowing Mia to only see one person, the creature who now stood before her.

With an empty chair between them, time suspended as Mia laid her eyes on Charles Marazza. It was strange to witness where her dark features had come from, his lean build and his straight-edged nose all resembling her own. She'd never had that before, someone to look like. His eyes, blinding blue like the sea, twinkled and smiled even as he stared back at her with the soberest expression.

"This is not how I wanted us to first meet, Mia," he said loudly enough for only her to hear.

Looking at him, she agreed, "Better than not at all."

Pausing to take her in, he smiled. "You're so grown. Such a beauty like your mother."

He had a rugged look to him that strong and brave fathers were supposed to possess, at least in Mia's imagination. Over the years, Mia noted most of her friends' fathers had potbellies and bald spots, but the man before her resembled nothing like those fathers. From his unbuttoned white linen shirt to his monogrammed shoes, he looked ever like the hero, someone who could rescue her from danger while showing her the world's adventure.

"Mia," he began, moving toward her, but the moment was gone. Waiters singing "Happy Birthday" filed out of the kitchen supporting a five-layer cake piled with strawberries and shooting sparklers for the boss's birthday girl.

The room joined Mr. Romeno in a second round of "Happy Birthday," while a red-haired woman appeared at Charles' side, eyeing Mia and trying to entice him to another drink. As he talked quietly to the woman, Mia watched him buy a few minutes alone. Turning back to his daughter, he smiled. "Mia, I have waited a long time for this." Noting her hesitation, he sighed. "I know. There's a lot to explain."

A group of admirers beckoned him over. Mia wanted to say something, but all she could think of was, "Guess there's time now," while Charles stopped a young man from approaching them.

Shelby appeared, cake in hand. "Chocolate with buttercream frosting, my fave, tell me you're not dieting . . . Mia?" She stared at the man staring at Mia.

"What's up?" Shelby asked Charles.

"Please forgive me, Mia, I have to go," he said, chivalrously kissing her hand. "The heavens opened up for us tonight." Mia watched him turn and walk away to his beckoning crowd, who embraced him like the captain of a ship.

"What the hell was that?" Shelby asked as soon as he was out of earshot.

Silent, Mia froze in thought.

"Mia? Ting, what's wrong with your eyes?" Shelby asked, biting into one of the chocolate-coated strawberries.

Mia watched Ting attempt to explain the situation through a series of nonverbal gestures, and let herself be brought out of the fog. She watched Charles disappear from the room, out of her sight, and, breathing a sigh of relief, looked at her friends. "Sorry, I wasn't expecting that."

"Oh, old men hit on me all the time —" Shelby took a bite of her birthday cake and offered some to Mia.

"No thanks, and that man, he's my father."

"What????" Shelby yelled, and as she did, she began choking on a chocolate curl. Instead of explaining more, Mia found herself standing at the bar, asking for something to drink for Shelby's coughing fit.

"Sorry, Miss, I'm not allowed to serve . . ."

"I just need water for my friend," Mia said, while Ting was trying to explain why Shelby should put her head between her legs.

"Sure, that I can do. Anything for you?" He was noticeably friendlier.

"How about . . . a lemonade?" She added a quick "Please."

"All right, I'll have to hit the kitchen; just ran out, but I'll only be a second." He jogged over to the kitchen while Mia stared at the various colors of bottles lining the mirrored wall and wondered if what she felt earlier was a premonition that she was going to meet her father. All day, she thought the feeling was about Shelby, but now, she realized, she knew why. "Sorry about the wait," the bartender said, carrying back a glass of lemonade decorated with a yellow umbrella, maraschino cherry, and a slice of what looked like pink grapefruit flowers. "Didn't realize you were important friends of the boss." He passed her a bottle of water with a shy grin.

"She's okay," Ting reassured Mia when she returned.

Shelby looked embarrassed and tried to downplay it while fighting the urge to cough.

"Honey, is it your stomach again? The cake is gluten-free," Mr. Romeno said rather sweetly while Shelby rolled her eyes.

"I'm fine!" She tried to shoo away her father and grabbed Mia's hand. "Let's go somewhere to talk." Shelby grabbed the lemonade from Mia and downed half the glass. "Ahh, just what I needed," she said with a small burp.

"Oh, I had this for you . . ." Mia's voice trailed off, and she set the water bottle on the table.

"Hey, Mia —" Ting checked her watch "— just letting you know, we have to leave in like forty-five if we want to get home by eleven. My grandma won't mind if I'm late, she encourages rule-breaking, but I know your mom might not —"

And with that, a few things happened. Shelby grabbed her stomach and keeled over, so suddenly, that she smacked her face on the nearest table, causing blood to spurt from her nose as her eyes rolled to the back of her head. Someone from behind grabbed Mia's arm, attempting to yank her away, while Ting started screaming for help.

It seemed everyone in the room descended on Shelby, some yelling, others covering their mouths, a few dropping their pieces of cake in fear of having the same reaction.

Mia yanked herself forward to break free of whatever was gripping her. Rushing ahead, she was just in time to spot Shelby lying on the floor, twitching and foaming at the mouth.

CHAPTER 6

Bad Lemonade

Mia knew she had to get to Shelby. Something inside her screamed go help the motionless girl, but too many swarms of onlookers blocked her way. Mr. Romeno sat cradling Shelby's lifeless body, yelling for help from anyone with medical expertise.

Only able to see the metal stud of Shelby's heel, Mia pleaded with the crowd to move. "Please!" she begged. "That's my friend!"

A waitress stood nearby sobbing, while onlookers whispered, and some even snapped pictures. A reassuring voice promised the paramedics were minutes away, while the man who had served Mia at the bar slammed his way through the crowd. "I'm a training EMT! I can help."

Mia managed to push past a heavyset male in time to see a woman appearing beside Shelby's father, clasping his hand and speaking calmly to him; she seemed as concerned about Shelby as he was, allowing Mr. Romeno to back off from the bartender, who was now thrusting Shelby's chest with compressions. A line of hotel staff bordered the inside of the circle, attempting to prevent anyone from breaking through or taking videos of the desperate scene. Mia, blocked by a stern-faced woman who did not understand her while she hysterically pointed to Shelby, noticed Ting had managed to get inside the circle. She shouted for her, and Ting rushed over just as the crowd broke into cries of relief that the paramedics had arrived.

"Mia!" Ting gasped.

"I need to get to Shelby; can you help?"

Ting opened her mouth to reply and let out a loud yell. Pointing to a spot just beside Mia, she screamed, "SNAKE!"

The crowd responded by jumping, some backing away, giving Mia just enough room to dive through an opening; Shelby, worsening by the minute with her bluish lips and ghostly pale complexion, remained perfectly still.

The paramedics arrived as Mia knelt beside her friend. Someone advised her to move back, but she shook her head; she had to stay, to do something for Shelby although she knew every second things were worsening. As Mia brushed her fingers against Shelby's leg, she felt an electric current of heat pulse between their skin. The spark was all she needed. Mia wrapped both hands around Shelby's leg, blocking out everything else around her. Something inside Mia drew energy from her own body, pouring it into Shelby's as she held on tight enough to bruise. Knowing she couldn't let go, Mia felt her hands burn under the constant heat pouring out of her. Squeezing her eyes shut to the sounds of yelling onlookers, Mia kept her hold, refusing to remove her grip, even against the blistering heat that flowed through her palms and into Shelby's frail body. Mia felt herself weaken; the channeling of energy was draining her; someone was hissing at her, another imploring her to let go.

The pretty brunette next to Mr. Romeno held him back from yelling at Mia, while Ting bent down, begging her to let them take Shelby to the ambulance, but Mia, using everything she had, held on.

Grabbed again from behind, Mia felt someone wrap their arms around her torso. Certain she couldn't fight off the vigorous hold this time, her grasp weakened, and she was yanked backward. Shelby's leg slipped through her hands; Mia kept her eyes pinched shut, afraid to open them and see what she was leaving behind.

"Mia!" She could hear Ting's yell as she was carried away from the crowd. Unable to respond, she felt herself slipping away from the present. A car system beeped, and Mia was lowered onto a seat that smelled of dirt and cloves. A door slammed shut, while someone pounded on the window.

Frozen inside her body, Mia could hear everything around her. *Maybe this was what it felt like to head toward death.*

A few minutes went by and the car beeped again. Doors opened and someone slid in next to her, a familiar voice mumbling in Chinese.

"Mia, please! You have to wake up," Ting whispered. "We've been kidnapped!" she said to the laughter of someone from the front seat. "Mia! If you don't wake up I'm — I'm going to lose it! I mean, really lose it!" Ting cried as the car roared to life and headed away from the casino.

"She'll be fine."

"Listen, you . . . you KIDNAPPER! . . . My parents know people!"

"And how is it you're kidnapped if you *asked* to get in my car?"

"I couldn't let you take her! What do you want with Mia?" Ting demanded, panic giving way to anger.

The driver tossed a tiny bottle into the back seat. "Put this under her nose; it will help."

"And WHY would I trust you?"

But the driver was already answering the radio beep. "Dregs here."

A muffled radio voice identified himself as Hunter 300 and asked if the target was secure.

"She's fine. I'm going to drop off, and then I'll go to the hospital." The driver merged onto the highway. "But I have a stray I need to get rid of."

"Mia, Mia!" Ting whispered, "please be okay."

"I TOLD you, she's fine. It can take a while," the person called Dregs said, when Ting screamed, "Oh MY GOD, DID YOU POISON HER TOO?"

The driver swerved and swore, while the receiver beeped again. Through gritted teeth, they barked, "DON'T scream in my car, and she's NOT poisoned!"

"But what's wrong with her? She was fine before you grabbed her."

The receiver beeped again.

The respondent on the other line instructed Dregs not to come to the hospital. "I need you to trail — meet after the Target is secure."

"Fine." Dregs hung up.

"Is Mia the target? Who are you going to trail?" Mia's stirring distracted Ting from questioning them, instead turning her attention to her friend's struggle to wake up. "Mia, MIA — I'm right here." Ting spent the rest of the car ride trying to help Mia sit up, all the while refusing to use the bottle the driver had given her.

"Out!" they barked once they stopped. "Quickly!"

But Ting shook her head. "I'm not leaving her with YOU! Why have you taken me here!"

They had already opened the door and grabbed Ting's arm. "I'm NOT a babysitter, and you need to go home."

And it was their insidious smile that made Ting move quickly out of the car and run toward her house.

Wishing she could yell to Ting that she was okay, Mia stayed in her trance until the car was stopped and she was parked outside her own apartment complex thirty minutes later.

"Come on," Dregs said, blotting something smelling strongly of jasmine and more cloves, under Mia's nose. "I'd prefer not to carry you again."

And like waking too early from a deep sleep, Mia felt her body awaken. Opening her eyes, she pushed herself up to a sitting position, the squeaky leather seats warm from where she had just lain.

"Let's speed things up. I need to be somewhere," they carped as Mia sat herself up, wincing at the painful blisters on her hands.

She slid herself along the back seat and out of the car while they grabbed her under her arms, hoisting her up as she stumbled out onto the gravel.

Feeling her strength return the more she moved her body and breathed in the fresh air, Mia stood on her own by the time they had reached the top of the stairs. She much preferred not having to lean on the jittery stranger for support. As she reached for the doorknob, raindrops patted the top of her head, the sky darkened, and the person named Dregs moaned, "Not the leather — come on, man, inside now."

Mia unlocked and opened her front door to a silent house. Apart from a panting Chip, all was quiet while she held out her hand to reassure her dog she was okay.

"Right," they said, grabbing Mia's phone. "I'm giving you my number. Do me a favor — don't go trying to save anyone again . . ." They handed back her phone and turned to leave.

"Wait, what do you mean . . . ?" Mia blurted. "Why were you watching me tonight?" she asked, as they descended the stairs.

Turning around so Mia had a good look, they seemed amused that Mia had pieced together their face from earlier at the casino. Flicking their hair to the side to prevent their fringe from slicking down and covering their eyes, they explained, "Let's put it this way, someone's decided your corpse is highly valuable. You *need* to be careful."

Mia stared at them in disbelief. The soft light of a few buzzing lampposts making it hard to read their expression. "But . . . why?"

she demanded as they turned back and bounded down the stairs. Despite Mia's calling, they jumped into their car and peeled out of the parking lot, leaving dust and upturned gravel in their wake.

Muttering "Thanks," Mia closed and locked the door. Gently opening her mother's bedroom door, she checked the time. 11:05. Pretty good considering her friend was probably getting her stomach pumped at the hospital right about now. Peeking at her mother's bed, Mia found Divana asleep next to a bowl of popcorn.

"Yay your home," her mother mumbled, reaching out her arms for a hug. Mia leaned in, cuddling her mom. "So sleepy," her mom whispered while Mia laughed and told her to go back to sleep. Pulling herself up, her mother's worn book on plants fell off the bed. No wonder she was tired, *how can she read this?* Covering her mother with a homemade knitted throw, she grabbed the book, when a folded printout of a newspaper article slid out. Unfolding the yellowed paper, she skimmed the short article that relayed the story of a young woman dying in childbirth some twenty years ago. Turning it over to the advertisement for a dentist on the back, Mia slipped the clipping back into the book and onto her mother's side table. Turning off the light, she exited the room and closed the bedroom door.

After dressing for bed, Mia stared at the ceiling that was now covered with tiny fairy lights. Her phone pinged just as she closed her eyes, and after sending off a good-night text to Ting, who was still ranting about their encounter with the person named Dregs, Mia went back to staring at the lights. With no word from Shelby after repeatedly texting her phone, Mia decided to go to bed. She felt it in her gut, Shelby would be okay.

Snuggling against Chip, who flipped over to his back and pawed at something in his dream, Mia drifted off to sleep in a haze of concern. The night's events cemented Mia's growing realization that unseen forces had somehow been set in motion against her, and she didn't know why.

Tomorrow she was going to meet her father *again*. Tomorrow, she wanted answers.

Half a day later, Mia walked up an absurdly long driveway as the afternoon California sun beat down on her back. She and Mom were going to meet her father.

"That was a beast." Mia caught her breath as her mother wiped her brow.

"Yeah, let's get a ride back down," Divana said. "Oh, hello!" her mother called to the four workmen positioned at the front door. Noticing Divana, as men always did, they nodded and smiled as she and Mia headed around to the back while her mother paused her at the side of the house. "One quick thing, honey," her mom said, turning to Mia. "I know you have a lot on your mind with meeting your father, but let's not ask all the tough questions today. I would love for you to just enjoy getting to know him. This is all new for him, me too . . . Let's go easy on each other, okay?" Her mother looked hopeful.

Suddenly the wind picked up, blowing Mia's hair in her face, obscuring her annoyance. Pushing her hair back and agreeing to try to be as respectful as she was able, Mia heard a man's voice calling.

"Divana! . . . Mia!" said Charles as they rounded the corner to see her father walking toward them, his arms open wide. "I cannot believe this is happening." Charles embraced Divana while Mia watched her parents hug for the first time. "All this time —" He stared in the face of her mother, whose beauty seemed to glow under his gaze, "together again," and he looked as if he could kiss her. Turning to Mia, he smiled. "Please forgive my emotion . . ." He wiped his teary eyes with a scarf wrapped loosely around his neck. "I'm just so absurdly happy to see you, Mia." And he took her hand and squeezed it while staring into her questioning eyes. "Come inside, please!" Flecks of gray salted his hair at his temples, the blowing wind revealing a small tattoo behind his ear.

"Such a view, Charlie," Divana said of the mountaintop scenery.

His house, set upon a hill, looked to be the most elevated property within miles.

"I know, it's the highest I could go without losing certain conveniences." He laughed while opening the mahogany-planked door and welcoming them into his personal study; warm oak furniture and walls of bookcases lined the room, decorated with artifacts and pictures of Charles throughout the years.

Mia felt claustrophobic.

"Welcome, welcome to my home." He gestured for Mia to sit near the fireplace. "I'm sorry for the secretive back entrance, but I almost had a break-in last night." He perched on the thick side of an armchair. "Yes, such a deep violation of my personal safety. I was gone most of the day and had given Nimmy the night off, so someone took advantage, and although nothing was stolen, I knew with, well, you gems coming, I had to upgrade."

Someone knocked on the door with three succinct raps.

A narrow woman in her sixties entered, her small frame taut and bony like someone who'd worked too hard for too many years. For all Mia could tell, she could have been eighty.

"Nimmy, you mind reader!" Charles exclaimed to the full tray of drinks and food.

Setting the tray down on the lacquered table, the woman began pouring drinks from a pitcher. "Divana." Charles took Nimmy's hand from the pitcher and pulled her over. "You must remember Nimmy — she worked for my father years ago and saved my life ever since." He squeezed the woman's shoulders while she smiled at his compliment.

Divana extended her hand to Nimmy, whose lingering smile stiffened. "You are *just* as stunning today as you were then," she said while turning to Mia, "and you look quite like your father." As she spoke, the light rain from last night returned as droplets began to slide down the windows, darkening the sky.

"Fool's luck — this weather . . ." Charles frowned at the windows. "I was hoping we could go for a walk, but let's toast instead." He passed the ladies drinks.

"Charles —" Divana smelled hers and glanced at Mia "— I can't have alcohol —"

"Shoot, Dee, forgive me, I forgot — Nimmy, would you mind," he started, as the woman nodded and hurried out of the room, while Mia put her glass down in support of her mother (and because she was not yet twenty-one). Hoping the moment didn't take her mother down the road of the past, Mia gave Divana a reassuring smile, who sheepishly returned one, reminding Mia that even though she'd made a career out of helping people heal from their addictions, her own demons might never fully leave.

Charles took a seat on the silky couch and began serving himself food while inviting them to join. "I have been a nervous wreck all day. Now that you're here, I'm famished. Please, come sit." He indicated for Mia to take the seat opposite him in a wingback chair smelling faintly of cigars. "So, Mia," her father said, noticing her quietly studying the room, her eyes flinching at the various framed pictures. "I'm sure you have so many questions . . . questions about the past, choices we had to make." He looked at Divana for a nod of reassurance. "I'm hoping that you feel the freedom to ask what you need to know." He settled back into the couch like they were about to discuss their favorite movies. With perfect timing, Nimmy returned with a tray of lemonade.

Staring at her father as he stretched himself across the couch, Mia felt yesterday's magnetism had been replaced with more of a raw curiosity; he seemed more human today. Who was this person so charming one minute and so dependent on his housekeeper the next?

"Honey," her mom said, "I think your dad is just wondering if there's anything worrying you or —"

"Yeah," Mia started. "Where's our picture?"

Looking surprised, Divana was about to speak up when Charles chuckled.

"You know, Mia, you remind me of your mother when we first met." He touched Divana's hand. "You're right. Your mother sent me pictures and I haven't displayed them. I wasn't able to. But I can now, and I will."

"But why, what's so dangerous about you being in our lives?" Mia ignored her mother's dagger eyes.

"Mia, I think . . ." her mother began as her father took a big sip of his fruity wine.

"It's fine, Dee, let's get it all out in the open." And Charles cleared his throat to indicate to Nimmy that he wanted to speak in private with his guests. "Thanks, Nim, you're the best," he said as she exited the room. "This whole father thing, ahh, it's nerve-wracking. People are always trying to get my attention, and yet, for the past month, all I've been able to think about is how to impress my daughter and my Dee . . ." Running his hands through his wavy hair, he looked forlorn. "Mia, I had a brother, a twin. He and I were close; he always had such a . . . an influence in my life. The only person who ever had more of a sway, I can honestly say, was your mother."

Mia's stomach knotted at the sight of her mother blushing, she never blushed. Apparently, Mia was witnessing small pieces of the connection her parents had once shared. It felt wrong.

"Maybe it's a twin thing." He took another gulp of the wine. "There's a saying, a twin's spouse is always second to their real other half. He and I, we were too connected, too close. My father wanted certain paths for my brother and — childhood was a set of rules, 'Be this person, Charles,' contrary to who I wanted to be or felt I was . . . deep inside." He gazed past the sea of pictures surrounding him with restitution. "Sensitivity . . ." he said to no one in particular, "it's always been my downfall. Too sensitive to what others wanted, expected to keep secrets." Looking like he had stepped back in the present, Charles sighed. "My brother lived my father's path, but it never suited me . . . It cost too much."

Mia glared at her father. "So, let me see what I understand — you were scared of your father and brother . . . and now they're gone and it seems you can suddenly be in my life with maybe even the possibility of getting back together with my mom and all the while acting like we're a family and you're my dad and nothing was lost except the fact that I had no father for my entire life!" Mia stood.

Her mother spoke first. "Mia! It's not just your father who had to keep his distance. I left; I had to get away from the danger I felt here. I'm responsible too. I'm responsible for taking you away." Clear sadness was etched on her face.

"But how *could* you stay if someone was going to kill us?" Mia scoffed. "We're not anyone important; there's no reason someone should be trying to hurt us. It's your fault! You're the — the someone, the one with the connections . . . I'm nobody. Why are *we* the ones who had to live like that . . . and you got to live like this . . . and then suddenly you get to say what goes!" A sweat broke out on her brow. Her heart pumped with an anger that had unlocked the day the note had arrived. An ugly three-headed statue stared at Mia from atop her father's mantel. Who had such a hideous decoration but not a picture of his own daughter? Mia felt the floor vibrate from the buzz of her phone. Fumbling to open her backpack, she pulled out her phone, ignoring her mother's suggestion to silence it, and saw a running list of missed calls from Shelby.

"Sheby! — Mom, it's Shelby."

"Excuse me — so?"

"Sorry, it's just, can I have a moment . . . to call Shelby? She was sick, and I was worried."

"Mia, this is not the time to talk to friends. I'm shocked you —"

But Charles jumped in before Divana could finish.

Unaccustomed to seeing her mother back down, as no one had ever needed to question her parenting before, Mia managed a small but brief smile. "Thanks," she mumbled as Charles closed the door, leaving her in the adjourning room, but not before Mia could hear her mother apologize for her outburst.

"Mia!" Shelby answered, followed by an exasperated, "EXCUSE ME . . . I said ALONE . . . oh my God, Mia, this is the first time I've been alone ALL day, I'm dying . . . well, not anymore." She laughed while Mia relaxed at hearing her friend's voice.

"Shelby, last night, I'm so sorry . . . ." Mia felt a knot in her throat that she couldn't swallow.

"Sorry? For what? YOU didn't try to kill me! But that's why I'm calling; we need to talk, in person. I don't trust anyone, well apart from you, and Ting . . . and my dad, of course, and Louie . . . and then there's that bartender who tried to save my life, but he's been arrested, so I'm not sure what to think there because maybe he was after you, so can you come over? Louie can come get you."

"Wait, now?"

"Yeah, I just got home from the hospital, and I'm already going nuts here."

"I mean, I want to but . . . Mom and I are at my father's, and there's no way I could leave now." Mia brought her voice down to a whisper even though she could hear them laughing through the walls.

"Wait — you have a dad?"

"Yeah, long story . . ." Mia assumed Shelby had missed some vital pieces of information from the night before.

"Seriously, A MINUTE PLEASE!" Shelby yelled to someone on the other end. "All right, how about after your dad's? I'll send Louie after your mom goes to bed?"

Never in her life had Mia ever had even the inkling of a thought of sneaking out of her house in the middle of the night. With her mind planning, she answered Shelby before all reason told her differently. Pausing to make sure her mother and Charles were still chatting, she whispered, "You know . . . I think I will . . . I'll see you tonight!"

CHAPTER 7

Puppies and Movies

Mia shifted in her seat, half awake, while Mr. Fallabee reminded everyone about final drafts. English was always one of her better subjects, but she was hardly scraping a *B*. Ready to be done and dying to get to lunch, she shoved her red-marked draft into her bag and stood from her table when Will Turlington walked over.

"Hey, Mia, how are you?" He smiled, his dimples peeking out from behind his stubbly, unshaven cheek.

Biting her lip to keep from frowning, Mia sighed. "Perfect."

"Ah, that's good, it was a rough start this year, but I'm hoping things will settle down for all of us. Fallabee's class is killing me, though." Will waved his paper, which was also marked in red. "I thought I was pretty good at this literature stuff —" his chuckle flattened at Mia's soured expression "— but apparently not, so, ah, you heard anything from Shelby?"

"Why are you asking me?" Mia crossed her arms, hoping to put some distance between her and his obnoxious dimples.

"Well, it was her sixteenth, but no one's heard from her. A few of us were going to get together, maybe a cake and some video games but — well, she's not here, and I saw you two hanging out at the memorial lunch, so I just wondered —"

"Well, I'm not her babysitter, so just call her yourself." When Mia swung her bag over her arm, it thumped across her back, still tender, still healing.

"I'm sorry, I didn't mean to upset you by asking." Will tried to read Mia's expression.

Wishing she couldn't see the concern cross his eyes, she sighed.

"It's fine. I'm just tired."

"Oh, I understand." Will smiled. "I was trying to get all the cruise info on the website late last night, but I passed out, have to finish during lunch," he said, and Mia began walking toward the door, hoping he got the hint.

Following Mia, Will continued, "You think you'll come? The whole school goes, and we go all out with the theme; it's really a good time." His friends passed, slapping him on the back and calling him to join them outside.

"Not quite my scene." Mia had been to only one dance and her night ended early when her friend's homemade sequined dress fell apart.

"As the individual personally responsible for organizing this affair, I am going to make it my prerogative to convince you it most definitely will be your scene." He grinned. "What do you love about winter?"

"Winter? Snow but . . ."

"Exactly. Last year we had real snow shipped in to go sledding on after the dance. It was amazing."

Mia said nothing, refusing to admit to him that it sounded . . . tempting.

"See, I promise this year not to disappoint."

Mia wondered why Will was looking at her. Wondering if she had that crusty eye goop from being so tired, she rubbed her eyes while a tall friend of his reached into the doorway and pulled him outside just as the bell rang. Their teacher, Mr. Fallabee, was already immersed in coffee and paper grading.

"Say yes!" Will called while she checked the time. Six minutes to get to the administration building, which meant no time for lunch.

Shaking out her hands in an attempt to get Will off her mind, Mia hurried to the far corner of the school grounds.

"I'm here for a school counselor appointment," she said, stepping into a Spanish-style cottage that from the outside, looked to have survived many centuries.

"Certainly, fifth door on the left, name on the door — *Mrs. TAYLOR*, can't miss it."

"Right —" Mia said, to the man pointing her down the hall, his pumps perfectly matching the neon sign, *MISS B-RAY* on the wall behind his desk.

"Can't understand the last one, getting lost with a simple walk down the hallway — ends up in the ladies room," the man frowned. "Scaring our new librarian half to death and far be it from me to complain that kids now a days can't follow simple directions with phones shoved in their noses and blocks for brains . . ."

Finding Mrs. Taylor's room, Mia was about to knock, when the door opened and a tepid woman with small glasses and a narrow nose greeted her. "*Jane Taylor.*" She extended her hand. "Come on in." She gestured for Mia to sit in front of her paper-ridden desk. Surrounded by old coffee mugs, sticky notes, and brochures from every college within the western hemisphere, Mia watched Mrs. Taylor study the computer and flip through a file, back and forth, back and forth, without uttering another word. Bored with staring at the woman's limp hair, Mia envied the small corner table set with tomato soup and what looked to be a grilled cheese, both wafting the scent of garlic and fresh-baked bread into Mia's nostrils.

"So," Mrs. Taylor began, looking at Mia and putting down the file. "What do you want out of your time here at North Elite Preparatory?"

Mia stared back. "Well, I'm, I'm not yet sure," she stammered.

"I see. Do you have any colleges in sight to build your résumé for?"

"Oh, I didn't think that I needed to think about colleges just yet . . ." Mia wondered if other sophomores were already preparing.

"I see." She glimpsed at Mia through the top of her blue-checkered glasses. "What brought you to this school then, Miss Storm?" Mrs. Taylor folded her hands.

"Um, oh, I just, well, I believe it was my father who found the school and wanted me to go here, I guess because it has such a good reputation." She forced a smile.

"I see. I think, Miss Storm, I must be blunt. You are a bit of an oddity here. No outstanding grades . . . achievements, no college preparatory work or aspirations. But since you're already here — let's just do what can be done. Now, you've not signed up for the necessary extracurriculars, and our students are expected to do at least one every school term."

"Oh."

"Right, so then, what do you want to sign up for?" Mrs. Taylor stared at Mia over the rim of her glasses while she clicked something on the computer.

"Sorry, I'm not remembering what the school offers." Mia was annoyed she'd never read the school handbook despite her mother's warnings that it may come in handy.

"Sure, just pull out your handbook. Everything is outlined. Disregard the summer and fall choices, some winter, too, since you would have already missed the deadlines . . . ."

"I . . ." Mia decided she was going to stand tall in her pit of shame. "I left it at home."

Mrs. Taylor turned from Mia to her computer. "I'll look on the portal to check what's still available. All right, we have Fencing, Polo; no, wait, scratch Team Polo — you need two years of dressage, so you'd not qualify. There's Runway Design, Pre-Olympia," pausing, Mrs. Turner turned her head to look at Mia, sizing her up from under her quirky glasses. Shaking her head, she continued, "Artificial Intelligence, and oh yes, the favorite among the males, Strategy & Survival," she said, leaning back in the desk chair as if it were all clear for Mia to decide.

"So — I just choose one I think sounds interesting?"

"Correct."

"Right, okay, um, would you mind refreshing my mind on Strategy & Survival?" Mia ruled out anything with a sword, or anything that involved wearing a leotard.

"Well, I always say it's one of those team-building pursuits like — what do they call it — capture the flag? Personally, I don't think any women have tried it."

On impulse and out of sheer defiance, Mia answered her, "that sounds perfect Mrs. Taylor, I'll do it," she declared to a look of resolute judgment.

After seeing to a few additional details, like making sure Mia was keeping up the dress code and where to log her community service hours, Mrs. Taylor was about to go over Mia's potential college options when there was a knock on her door. Popping her head in, Principal Florence stepped into the office. "Jane, so sorry to interrupt — but I need to take Miss Storm from you for the last few minutes of your time. I'm sorry to cut things short. I see you're resourcing colleges — wonderful place to pick up next time." The principal signaled to Mia to come with her.

Worried, Mia grabbed her bag, stood, and followed Principal Florence as the school counselor closed Mia's folder without a second thought. Principal Florence breezed past the vacant receptionist desk, speaking so quickly, Mia had to work hard to concentrate.

"I just knew this was the opportune moment." Principal Florence led her outside. "Of course, we didn't get our little chat in about the accident, but you seem to be doing well, which brings me to this moment, Miss Storm." Principal Florence stopped short and turned to face Mia. "I need a favor." Looking keenly at Mia, the principal continued. "You see, Mia — can I call you Mia? Our school has the potential of an incredible opportunity." The principal paused as if waiting for Mia to respond. When she didn't, she continued, "To be the location for an upcoming film — can you believe it?" She paused again.

Wondering why she was being told this, Mia tried to muster some enthusiasm. "Well, that's cool."

Principal Florence looked ecstatic. "Mia — this opportunity would mean international recognition, immediate proceeds, and of course, unprecedented exposure for our students to the entertainment industry, not to mention, I think, a good morale boost after the devastating accident, but — the small hitch of the matter is that we are only *still* being considered for the location — we've not yet been chosen." Principal Florence led Mia down the stairs and onto the path that veered back to the main building. From afar, Mia could see a small crowd gathered outside in the courtyard and hear the distant sounds of laughter. Trying to walk in step with the principal, Mia stumbled on the stone path. "We know the other schools in the running, and let me tell you, they are fierce competition. But the board and I feel so strongly that this project should go to North Elite. We may not have all the bells and whistles of an European castle estate or be on the

French Riviera, but we do have the most *natural* connection to the film . . . ."

Caught by the scene ahead, Mia stopped. Someone she recognized stood among a crowd of Mia's peers holding three golden puppies desperately trying to lick-bite his face.

"What's *he* doing here?"

Stopping to explain to Mia, who was ten steps behind her, the principal hurried back. "You see, Mia, and this has to be kept *very* quiet until the deciding time, your father is one of the producers of the film!"

Mia's eyes widened and her stomach dropped.

"I know! Incredible considering his only daughter attends our very school, of course undercover, I just felt fate calling when this all came to fruition."

As Mia listened, she felt the audacious question before it was asked; what could she do to make sure their school was chosen?

"Now, of course," the principal carried on, "your father explained the decision is not his, which would have made this so much easier, but nevertheless, the person who really is the deciding factor is the film's director. Good news, he's here for a bonus tour. We were hoping he could meet you and get a feel for how special this place is —" she hinted, while Charle's hurried over, two puppies in tow.

"Mia . . . what a surprise!" Charles held out a puppy for her to grab as its tiny legs kicked. Placing the second down on the grass, he leaned in to give Mia a kiss on her cheek. "How are you, darling? Yah, not there!" Charles jumped back from the puppy trying to relieve itself on his buckled, striped loafers. A short man followed Charles, his tart expression only drawing Mia's attention to his disheveled hair and vest of overstuffed pockets. "I want you to meet Maple Novak." Charles beamed and placed his arm on the man's shoulder.

Nodding to Mia, Maple spit out something brown.

"Oye! Careful, Nov, aim away from the ladies."

"You look very like your father," Maple said to Mia, a strong accent coloring his speech. "But not as good lookin'."

"Mia, I'm so glad we could surprise you," Charles said through a winsome smile. "Please don't hold it against me; I only found out this morning that Maple could make the trip. Delilah has been terrific about the whole thing, especially since the production company has not yet made a location decision." Charles let his voice trail in the air.

"I know, I get it, you want this school. But I cannot choose yet, too much to consider and I will not be pressured."

Patting Maple on the back, Charles interrupted. "No pressure, Nov, you just take your time."

"I wait for the inspiration and the feels."

"Well, then," Principal Florence interjected, "let's give you the full experience of our school," she said with determination. "Mr. Marazza, could . . ."

"God, call me *Charles*. I'll never consider myself the parental type, would much prefer to be friends," Charles said, and Mia rolled her eyes.

"Of course, Charles —" she stammered. "S-shall we put the puppies somewhere while we see the grounds?"

"Um . . ." Mia started, "I have class soon, but it's good to see you." Mia bent down to put the puppy on the grass with its sibling.

"Oh, I was hoping you could join us for the tour," Charles said, and Mia stared at her father as if he'd lost his mind.

"But I have class and tests and things." And the last thing Mia wanted to do was to be stuck with these three for the next few hours.

"So responsible, so studious—" Charles beamed at Mia. "I understand — work hard for what you want, right? Well then, we'll be off after you choose one," Charles said, looking down at the whimpering puppy at his foot.

"Choose what?"

"Oh, my girl, so unassuming. A dog!"

Principal Florence and Maple Novak were discussing the construction of a helicopter landing pad, while her father looked at Mia as if she was meant to pick a puppy and call it a day.

"But I already have a dog."

"You do, I wasn't aware. How 'bout another?" Charles shook his leg free of the puppies' nibbles while the bell chimed telling Mia she had zero minutes to get to class.

"I can't." He didn't know she had Chip? This is what fathers *should* know, things like having pets and not showing up to school unannounced. Normal things for normal girls from normal fathers that weren't Charles.

"Perhaps you'll change your mind. I wanted to do something special for you."

Mia bent down to pet the whimpering pup, and the creature began nibbling on her hand. She knew she couldn't take the dog, but the feeling that she was disappointing him or that she had even the smallest influence over his emotion made Mia feel bothered.

"Charles —" Principal Florence interrupted with Maple and his cigar. "I'm noticing the time, and I just want to make sure Mr. Novak has a fair view of the property, and we still need to make the drive down to the beach —"

"Yes, of course." Her father picked up and held out the puppy again for Mia.

"Listen, I appreciate your — the thought of it all but I can't."

Charles waved his hand. "Mia, I understand. You are your mother's daughter, unable to be selfish. It's okay you cannot keep the little guy, or girl, I'm not sure which one is which — do me a favor, though, watch them till we're done? Won't be longer than an hour or so." He passed the puppy to Mia and headed to the parking lot, before Mia could even think of a firmer response.

Why did he do that? Why did he make her doubt herself, act like she had to second guess a normal thought of something so basic like receiving a gift.

Jade, her least favorite classmate, called from behind. Her cropped uniform top showing scratches where the puppy she held had tried to claw her stomach.

"It's Maya, right?"

"No."

"Oh, well we can help you with these darlings next period," Jade said, and it took Mia a second to see the fourth dog nestled in her friend Vivian's purse.

"Yeah, I'm not sure I'm going to class now."

"Sure we are. Dr. Fern's a softie — He'll deal." She smiled at Vivian and the two headed towards the building. Mia's puppy barked for her to follow.

Sweaty from holding two squirming dogs, Mia apologized for walking in late. "Principal Florence had a meeting and — the puppies only need to be watched for an hour or so —"

Dr. Fern smiled. "Well, as a good poet once said, interruptions are life's surprise parties. Although we spend much time learning and diving into the technological world, we must practice attuning to life happening right before our eyes."

Dr. Fern promised to give the class (and puppies) time outside after their lesson on sequencing and profiling online scammers to as he put it, "ensure the carpets remain unsoiled," while Mia hurried to her seat, where Ting shot her a questioning look.

The rest of class continued with hilarious interruptions, including Jackson jumping up mid-lesson as one of the puppies slid down his pant leg. Happy to not fight the strong current of distraction as the end of class neared, Dr. Fern asked for one last bit of attention from the students so he could announce the midterm winners.

"Contrary to my previous expectations, I'm pleased to declare there are two winners for this midterm project. Both groups did an exceptional job on their projects and earned a visit to VanBoi Biotech Industries." Pointing to Mia's group, Dr. Fern announced that she, Ting, and Terry were the first project winners alongside Jade, Vivian, Shelby, and Jackson, who seemed most surprised at the unexpected accolade.

"Ting," Mia said, throwing her bag over her shoulder, thankful Ting was willing to hold one of the puppies, while the other nuzzled in Mia's arm. "It's awesome about the project, but you deserve all the credit."

"What, no." Ting asked, distractedly following the class outside.

"I didn't do much to help," Mia continued. "Maybe I can talk to Dr. Fern, explain that I was recovering from, well, you know — *Ouch!* — I'm sure he will let me redo some, at least make it fair."

"Okay — Ting said, as if stepping out of a deep thought. "Wait, no — Mia, you can't leave me alone with Terry on the tour. Don't even think about talking to Fern, I always do most of the group work, honestly, your just the only one who ever cared." Ting grabbed the puppy from sinking it's needle sized teeth into Mia's arm, and plopped it onto the grass. Flopping on its belly, someone screamed at Jackson to stop playing ball.

"Mia I think someone wants to talk to you." Ting said, turning her attention to Jade, a puppy peaking it's head out of her blue Togo bag.

"So Maya, I want this dog. How about I just pay you for him now." And she reached into the bag and grabbed a matching wallet, pulling out hundred-dollar bills, "shoot, all I have is five — JACKSON!"

"I wouldn't even know how much they cost." Mia said, shrugging at Ting for help.

"Everything has a price," Jade said, waving Jackson over and demanding he give her his spare cash.

"Two-fifty, that enough?" He held out a small card. "And a voucher for go-karting."

Taking his money and adding it to hers while discarding the coupon, Jade brandished it to Mia, while the puppy tried to paw its way out of the bag. "This should be enough."

"I'm not entirely sure I can just give you the dog." Mia tried to remember what her dad had said about where the puppies came from.

"Why? I heard you could keep one — are you keeping one?"

"Well, no."

Jade looked at Mia, softening her sour glare into something that resembled a smile.

"Look, my mom's a bit of a control freak, and this is the way I can get a dog. Just bring it home and surprise her, you know, pity story of how no one wanted him. I thought since I heard you say you didn't want one —"

Jackson had been standing a few feet away, eating a protein bar. "Who gave them to you, anyway?"

"Ah, boring story — okay, sure, I'll take your five hundred . . . That should be enough." Pulling out the money Jackson added and picking up his coupon off the grass, Mia passed it back, while Jade left with the dog.

"Uh, your welcome!" Ting muttered.

Jackson launched a football, "Cool, gotta go get that," he said running away.

Ting frowned, "I'm so sorry I'd skip my next class if I didn't have a test, but it's political science and my parents are pretty insistent that I get an A—"

Mia insisted Ting hurry off while she opted to skip world history, certain her teacher would not tolerate the three yelping add-ons. Left alone to juggle the puppies over to the familiar steps of the administration building, she spotted Maple Novak climbing into the back of a black sedan.

"I was just talking about you!" Principal Florence exclaimed seeing Mia, the receptionist from earlier standing with her. "Charles had to rush off, but we really think Novak is on the verge of choosing our school — meeting you seemed to seal the deal."

Mia plopped the puppies down, relieved to be done babysitting. She highly doubted she had any influence over the directors decision though she was scared to think about what this could now mean. "Great."

"I know, and B-Ray will take the dogs. So, Mia —" The principal leaned in, "A little friendly reminder not to tell anyone until things are decided. I know it's hard to keep secrets from your friends, but we wouldn't want rumors to spread or to distract the students. My students are my first priority." She patted Mia's shoulder and appeared satisfied with their chat.

Mia watched Miss B-Ray throw off his heels to chase the barking puppies and wondered how her school had become her father's new stomping ground.

CHAPTER 8

Maria and Mateo

Mia arrived home fantasizing about the mixing bowl she was going to fill with frosted puffs for dinner. Greeting a curious Chip, she spotted a note from her mom set on the stained kitchen table. *Mia, reminder to take out the garbage TONIGHT, love, Mom.* Last time she had ignored the instruction, the apartment stank for days and they had a bug infestation. Grabbing the bags, she leashed Chip and headed right back outside to the dumpster downstairs, knowing she'd forget to do it later. In the two months she'd lived there, she'd never walked around the apartment building (other than to visit the dumpster). Tossing the bags, she took the back way where her mom had mentioned there was a small community room and notice board that posted occasional jobs and events.

She heard a couple arguing over finances and veered herself towards an opposite hallway. Most apartment doors resembled her own, artificial floral wreaths and welcome signs to cover the chipped paint, apart from one that had a yellow eviction notice. Mia heard the lively sounds of the Spanish channel playing from an open door.

"*Hola!*"

Mia turned around to a boy standing in his doorway. Trying not to salivate over the incredible smells wafting out of the apartment, Mia pulled her dog back.

"Chip, down! Sorry, he's usually good with new people, I guess he's hungry —"

"Hola! *Mi nombre Mateo.*"

Mia didn't have a chance to respond, the boy seemed caught up in the new song playing, dancing himself into the hallway just in time for a few similar aged boys to round the counter and snigger shamelessly as they pushed past him.

"Hey, watch yourself." Mia barked at the one who bumped Mateo into the wall. Chip growled, scaring them away, while Mia continued to stand there, watching him dance. There was something sweet about him.

"*Mijo.*" a squat woman appeared, wiping her hands on a red-checkered apron. Smiling at Mia, she said something to Mateo, who smiled back and pointed to Mia. "Oew, Chip!" The woman said to the jumping dog, bending down to scratch his head and finally calming him.

"And you must be *amado* Mia!" She checked that her hands were fully dry and took hold of Mia's. "You resemble your mother, I can tell." She kept staring into Mia's face with her big brown eyes and full cheeks.

At once Mia realized this was the son-and-mother duo her mother had been telling her about. "So, he's not being naughty, he knows you!" Mia said laughing, a look from Chip telling her he was glad she caught up.

"I am Maria and this is my handsome son Mateo." Maria linked arms with the boy, stopping him from spinning again as a new song began. "We feel like we already know you and your Chip, as he has come here for many meals."

"Yes!" Mia said. "My mom has told me all about you and I'm so happy to finally meet you! Thank you so much for your kindness to us while I was in the hospital." Mia laughed at the bunny ears Mateo put behind Maria's head.

"Oh, don't you start," Maria chided. The television music had switched to the news and Maria asked her son to go inside and turn it off. Shaking his head, he said something back to his mother in Spanish, to which she replied, "I will ask, if you promise to practice your English." Turning to Mia, Maria asked, "Mateo and I want to know if you and your mom are free to join us for dinner. I'm making simple enchiladas; it's Mateo's favorite."

"That's so kind of you," Mia said, disappointed. "But my mom works tonight — she's not home. She'll be so happy I met you, though."

Mateo snapped his fingers at his mom, who held up her hand. "Mateo and I still wonder, could just you come? We would love to know you."

Mateo added, while bouncing on his toes, "Chip too, Chip too," in perfect English.

"That's my boy," praised Maria. "He knows quite a bit of English but sometimes needs the motivation."

"That is kind of you —" Mia said to Mateo's thunderous clapping.

"Please, then come in, and I'll finish up dinner so we can eat."

Mia quickly added, "Can I join you in a few minutes, just so I can pop home and change?"

"Of course, and feel free to leave *el perro* here with us." Maria headed inside while the timer rang on her oven. Smiling at the boy who held out his hand to take Chip's leash, Mia hurried back to her apartment for a quick change. Adding detergent to the washer where her dog-peed uniform was, she turned it on and grabbed a clean T-shirt and pants from her dresser. Stopping at the pantry, she picked her favorite chocolate bar that her mom stocked when money wasn't too tight, and headed back down to Maria and Mateo's apartment. Moments later, Maria popped out from the kitchen with a red plastic cup and handed Mia an iced tea.

"Thank you." Mia hoped they weren't making an extra fuss over her. "Oh, here, this is for you." She gave Maria the chocolate and took a sip of the sweetened tea as her stomach gurgled.

"What's this? Chocolate! How did you know my boy loves chocolate? This is so kind of you, Mia!" Maria held up the bar for Mateo to see. "Please, come sit now!" Maria went and returned from the kitchen with a bubbling dish. Placing the enchiladas at the table's center, Mia sat herself down to a rainbow sarape tablecloth and rose-patterned dishes in vibrant yellow and blues. Chip followed after Maria and sniffed the bowl of food and water already set for him near the humming refrigerator. Mateo parked himself across from Mia after washing his hands and smiled at her.

"Mia *bonita*."

Maria offered her hands. "Mateo, English please. Mia, would you mind if we say grace?" Mateo reached for Mia's hand. "God, thank you for the food you always provide. We have never gone without. Thank you for your help today with our car. Thank you for our guest tonight and that she is healing from the terrible accident. Please continue to keep her safe and protect her from harm; bless our time and this food." Maria crossed her heart and touched her forehead in a way that seemed significant. "Now, Mateo, what were you saying?" Maria passed out the plates and silverware.

"Mia *prretty*. Happy to have Mia."

"Yes, I agree with Mateo. We have been praying for you, Mia. You must excuse our informality, but we feel as if we already know you." Maria dished out the first steaming hot enchilada and placed it in front of Mia while Mia kept silent. It felt foreign to be so welcomed somewhere.

As Mia took a bite and was instantly transported somewhere else. "This is incredible!" she exclaimed, doing everything she could to chew properly and not shovel the food into her mouth.

"Why, thank you. I'm so glad you could join us on our enchilada night, much better than rice and beans." Maria handed out a smaller portion to Mateo. "Honey, eat your vegetables, and I'll give you seconds, remember." He took a well-appreciated bite of his tortilla.

With the food and company quickly warming her, Mia wondered out loud, "How long have you lived here?" She asked while helping herself to chips and Maria's homemade salsa. The colorful apartment was littered with old picture frames, statues of saints, and crosses along the walls. Some of the paintings seemed religious, others beautiful scenes of what Mia imagined to be Maria's home country.

"We've been here fourteen years now. Moved in when these apartments were first built and Mateo was just a little guy — in fact, we celebrated his second birthday in this very room, before we even had a dining table. He would throw everything on the floor anyway, so we just ate there on a blanket for a few years. How I would hate that now, getting up off the floor, not with these knees." Maria laughed while adding a spoonful of guacamole to Mia's plate. Mateo motioned for his mother again. "Mia, please excuse me, I am going to speak to my son in Spanish, as he's forgotten his manners." Turning to her son, Maria spoke quickly while Mateo scowled.

Mia ate her food wondering exactly how old Mateo was, while her hunger ebbed away for the first time all day. Glancing at Chip, she noticed he hadn't touched his food.

Mateo looked sad as he addressed Mia. "I sorry, Mia. I feed Chip too much."

Surprised, Mia let out a loud laugh. "Oh my gosh that's fine, he loves scraps," but Maria was clearing her throat when Mia realized she had just impeded her reprimand. "Gee, you know, Mateo . . ." she said, "one time I fed Chip some fish I didn't want, and that night he woke me up in the middle of the night and vomited all over my bed. Which, as I'm telling you this, I realize is bad dinner conversation . . . ."

Maria laughed and Mateo exclaimed, "She said *vomits!*"

Over the rest of dinner, Mia learned that the whole week Chip had stayed with the family, he'd stolen five pairs of socks and hidden two wooden statues under the dirty laundry. When dinner was over and Mia was full, she promised Mateo that he could walk her home with Chip. In the meantime, Mia sat on the couch while Maria served them chocolate pudding topped with whipped cream, sugared bananas, and broken bits of the chocolate bar from Mia.

"Is this a special family recipe?"

Maria laughed loudly. "Sadly, no. It's from a box. I usually use the genius of others to feed my boy his treats which is fine for me because I don't like many desserts. Poor boy, doctor says I need to put him on a diet, but that's hard for us. There are just some things in life that we need, and good food is one. I love my big cuts of steak smothered in hot sauce, the spicier the better." She kissed her fingers to her lips.

"Ha-ha, Mom is vampire." Mateo laughed while finishing his chocolate pudding.

"One vampire movie, and the boy is obsessed. You know," Maria continued, "I actually considered writing to one of those magazines about the funny things kids say and do, my son wanting his mom to be a vampire. Only, I have a feeling they won't appreciate his humor when they see his age."

"Vampire, vampire. Mia, you're a pretty vampire."

Mia laughed, thanking Mateo while eating her pudding, wondering about the lovely boy beside her who was so different from the kids she went to school with. What would it be like for him, out in a world full of people who didn't know what to do with different.

"You know, Mateo," Mia said, "if I'm ever feeling down, I'm going to come over here and talk to you."

His eyes lit up at the thought.

"You're so dear, just like your mom, although I never like comparing kids to their parents. Not good for them to have the pressure, you know? I had all this pressure growing up. Didn't live up to any of it." Her voice touched with indifference.

"My mom is the sweet one." Mia thought of how her mother had not only all the beauty but kindness too from the genetic pool, and Mia got, well, she was still trying to figure that out. "I'm . . . a bit more blunt, I think. I wish I could be more like her in some ways. You two both share the talent of cooking. She makes amazing meals when she has time. I am terrible in the kitchen." Just last week Mia burnt an entire plate of her mom's homemade cookies by microwaving them too long and turning them into a pile of dust.

"Well, I tell Mateo here, we are all great at something. It may just not be the thing we want. Maybe mine is cooking . . . Mateo, here, he's great at reading people. I tell you he can spot a fool from a mile away. He knows when someone is genuine or full of — excuse my language — *mierda*."

"That's impressive, Mateo." Mia wondered if she passed his test.

"Yes, like Mr. Daniels on the other side of the building. He's been roaming around down here, and Mateo is very stoic to him. Thinks he's up to something, so when he is around, we just shut and lock the door. No disrespect to him, but I trust my son."

"Wish I could take him with me to school to feel out the kids in my classes."

"Ah, that's right, new school for you."

Today was a mixed bag of emotions, and as Mia sat on Maria's couch, she realized she was having all sorts of conflicting feelings about her new life, especially about her father. After all, she'd just observed the man three days in a row after not seeing him for fifteen years.

"Yeah, it's not bad; I've met a few friends. Just different than I'm used to. This move, it's so different from the others. I'm not sure if my mom told you about my father, but . . . he's in our life now." Mia hoped Maria could read between the lines.

"Yes, your mother mentioned him. I must admit I heard he's very — what's the word . . . *heart-throbbish*? To have a father after all these years —" Maria looked at Mia as if thinking through her eyes. "Course, every momma dreams of a loving papa to heal their child's pains, brighten the future. I had a wonderful papa, the most loving man I've ever known. Right, Mateo, remember Pepe?" Mateo nodded and pointed to a few pictures mounted on the wall above the couch. Maria gazed at the picture of a white-haired man holding a baby boy. "He raised me and helped with Mateo. See, he was such a good papa, I had no idea a man could be anything but. When I met Mateo's father, I was sure he'd be like my papa ... but he was not. He left when Mateo was only a babe, after we got the diagnosis." Maria sat, looking at her son with tenderness. "Sometimes people surprise us in hard ways, and some surprise us in good ways. I think the trick, Mia is to never let the bad ways, turn us into someone who can't see the good ways."

Mateo clapped his hands. "Yes, the good vampire ways."

Lying in bed that night after a quick catchup with her mom, Mia kept thinking about Maria, Mateo, and of course, her father. She felt like something in her was holding her back from giving him a chance. After hearing Mateo's story, Mia realized they both had been abandoned by their fathers, and yet, here Charles was, trying to be a part of her life, offering puppies and time. So, why did she resist? It pained her to admit it, but Mia wondered if her father was the type of man who wouldn't have wanted to know her if she was . . . well, like Mateo. Her father had been steeped so long in the world of notoriety and wealth, Mia realized she didn't know if he liked her for who she was or who he wanted her to be.

Sitting with Maria and Mateo tonight made Mia realize she didn't have to worry about their intentions; she trusted them immediately. But with her father and his world, she felt out of place and unsure if she was able to measure up. One thing was certain, Mia went to bed thinking it may have been a whole lot easier if, like Mateo said, she really was a vampire.

November followed October with a cold front, bringing out Mia's love of warm cups of hot chocolate in the morning and oversized sweaters on the weekends. Mia loved and hated the fall for two reasons. She loved the cooler months and nostalgia of all that came with it; long runs outside, colored leaves, and the one time of year she tried anything pumpkin flavored. But ever since she was little, Mia hated her birthday, and the fall meant the challenge of celebrating turning another year older. She liked growing, but she hated the disastrous something that *always* seemed to happen on or around November 11. Thought she'd been optimistic in the past, she was certain that this year's birthday would be no exception considering someone had recently tried to blow her up.

"Let's just do dinner at home then?" her mom pleaded with Mia as she tried to discuss plans for the upcoming Saturday.

"Mom, he is not going to be comfortable here in our tiny little house."

"What? Mia, he doesn't care about the size of our house or the things we have or, I guess in our case, don't have. When we were young, we used to camp out in tents and go to the bathroom in the woods." Divana laughed at Mia's cringing face.

"One, that's too much information." Divana always seemed determined to portray Charles in the best light possible, but it usually backfired. "And two, you don't think he's different from us in *that* way?" Over the past few weeks, her father had sent flowers to her mom, presents to Mia, and asked them to come to upcoming events with him. Maybe that's what rich people did, but it irked her. "I don't think you can be in that world for so long and not have it change you." Mia thought of the kids she went to school with.

But one thing Divana was oblivious to was her own beauty and the advances of men, so in the case of her dad, Divana thought Charles was just making up for the lost time with his generous gestures.

"Okay, what do you feel comfortable with then, birthday girl? How do you want to spend your sweet sixteen?" her mom asked as they sat down to a regular weekend dinner of spaghetti and meatballs.

"How about sleeping in, a trip to the beach with Chip, and my favorite ice cream?"

Her mom looked disappointed. "Mia, that doesn't involve celebrating with anyone else."

"But you love the ocean, and ice cream."

"Are you for real?" Divana put down her fork. "And what would we tell your dad, hey Mia hates her birthday so even though this is the first time you can ever celebrate together, you can't do anything with us? What about your friends you mention all the time, Yu-Ting. . . Shelby? You went to Shelby's for her birthday."

But someone knocked and saved Mia from having to respond. Thankful for the interruption, Mia jumped up to answer the door.

"What, Chip, no crazy barking?" she asked as he popped up his head from where he was resting and cocked it sideways. Unlocking the bolt, she opened the door to see the detective from the hospital standing on her porch. "Hi," Mia said as he turned from looking at the parking lot to face her.

"Miss Storm, may I come in?"

Mia nodded, wondering if detectives normally made house calls. Closing the door and turning around, Mia was relieved she had not spent the day in her pajamas, which she usually did on Sundays. She made a mental note to give Chip an extra treat for getting her out of the house for their afternoon run.

"Honey, who's there?" Divana popped her head in the family room, holding a fork. "Oh, Detective —" Divana's tone was tense.

Thinking back to her time in the hospital, Mia wondered what it was about the detective that bothered her mother. Staring at him now, she thought he seemed professional and cordial. The most she could say about him, really, was that he was hard to read.

"I'm sorry to drop in on you both unexpectedly," he started, "but I can't put this off any longer."

"Put what off?" Mia asked.

The detective pointed to her desk chair to sit. "Sure." Mia grabbed her sweaty running shorts, balled them up, and stuffed them in a laundry basket. Sitting on the couch opposite the detective, she hoped he didn't see her teal sports bra lying behind him on her desk. Taking out a white envelope from the side pocket of his hooded leather jacket, Detective Batair opened the envelope and pulled out a stack of pictures.

"Would you mind looking at these and letting me know who you recognize?"

Divana sat beside Mia and gently pulled them from Mia's grasp. Mia watched as her mother sifted through the images. "Detective Batair, I've never seen any of these women, and I'm sure Mia hasn't . . ." She paused on the next picture. Looking over, Mia saw the picture was of a woman she had only recently met. Nimmy.

"Mom! That's . . . Nimmy — Charles's housekeeper . . . or family friend . . . or assistant person . . . ." she explained, studying the picture of the older woman dressed in a black trench coat and standing in line at a store.

"Can you tell me where you saw her?"

"We saw her at Charles's house. Charles — he's my dad but — long story . . . ."

"What was your interaction with this woman?"

Mia looked to her mom, who had remained tight-lipped, staring at the picture with a disdainful expression. "But, Mom, you were there." But her mother remained quiet. Too quiet. "What's going on?"

Divana pulled her stare from the pictures to Mia, and her eyes softened. "Like Mia said, this woman is Nimmy Smith. She works for Charles; she's been with the family for years. I almost didn't recognize her when we saw her at Charles's house — she served us lemonade."

Trying to remember more about that day, Mia thought back, frustrated with herself that she was so distracted about Shelby that she hadn't listened to her gut telling her something was off about the woman. Was she connected to the bombing? Why else would her picture be compiled in a lineup for Mia to identify? But she worked for Charles — he trusted her . . . Divana finally passed Mia the pictures. After Nimmy, there were a few photographs of women's headshots from a modeling agency. Neither of them recognizable, along with a picture of a middle-aged woman on a boat out at sea. The last picture, however, jogged Mia's memory. She had seen this woman with her father, the redhead who'd been hanging on her father all evening at the casino.

"This woman, the redhead." Mia handed the picture to Detective Batair, "She was with Charles at Mr. Romeno's fundraiser."

"And did she speak to you at all, come near you; was she ever standing close to your friend Shelby?" Detective Batair asked as Mia's stomach dropped. She was. Did this mean she had been the one who'd poisoned Shelby? She could have; she was close enough to them when she met her father, and she was certainly around before Shelby got poisoned. Before she left with her father, before everything went south.

"Yes!" Mia said animatedly, and Chip shot his head up in concern. Turning to her mother, Mia took a breath. "Mom — I didn't tell you before, but . . . when I was with Shelby . . . for her birthday . . . someone poisoned her. I wanted to tell you, but . . . Detective Dregs took me home and —"

"Dregs? Who's Dregs?" Divana snapped. Mia waited for her mother to channel her anger toward her but she kept at the detective. "Tommy, you know I only want you on the case, no one else, and —"

Mia sat dumbstruck.

"Mom?"

Detective Batair sat back in Mia's swivel chair. "I had to bring in another hand. There's been some developments, and I need more eyes on the situation. Dreg's is an original. I trust her."

Mia looked at Detective Batair and wondered what she was missing.

"Mia —" Divana said. "I know about the poisoning."

"What? But — how? Why didn't you tell me you knew?" Mia felt the wall of distance widen between her and the woman she sat only a few feet from.

"I could ask you the same thing."

Mia paused. "I — I just didn't want you to worry I — after everything you told me about your, our past . . . I seem to bring trouble —"

"No Honey, you don't — it's just . . . your father and I have our pasts, and together we —" Looking at the detective, Divana stopped speaking.

Focused on Mia, Detective Batair asked, "Mia, did you hear the woman say anything or see her with anyone besides your father?"

"I should have paid more attention. I just didn't think I needed to scan the room for murderers, but I'll remember that as a rule of habit now." Mia gave an unexpected laugh. "What do these women have to do with me? If they are trying to kill me, I need to know and WHY!"

"Tommy, I know Charles. He loves Mia. He would never hurt her. You're not saying he's involved somehow?"

"Who the hell is Tommy?" Mia demanded knowing full well it was Batair. Why were they acting like they'd known each other longer than a few months? Looking to the detective and her mother, Mia settled on the scratched front door. She felt like screaming or running, something to disrupt the miserable silence. Chip hopped up on the couch, nuzzling himself onto Mia's lap while Detective Batair rubbed the back of his neck. The feel of Chip's warm little body calmed her, while his little cold nose nuzzled against her leg.

"I'm not implicating Charles. I believe it's possible he may not know about Nimmy or the other woman. I'm talking about his father."

"His father?" Mia asked. "Whose father?"

"Dominic Broderick," said Detective Batair.

"Dominic who?" Mia looked at her mom pleadingly. "I thought his father died?" she said with the same rising anxiety that had first consumed her when she discovered her father was alive. It had taken weeks for Mia to be able to even look her mother in the eyes. Was it all about to be fractured again?

Divana paled. "I — I thought he was dead; I mean that is what Charles told me . . . that he died when you were a young girl." Divana sounded desperate.

"Despite what you were led to believe, Dominic Broderick is very much alive."

Divana gasped and covered her mouth. "You . . . you have to be mistaken," her mom cried.

"How do you know he's alive?" Mia demanded, somehow grasping to the belief that the detective was wrong. He had to be wrong; only, looking at Batair, Mia knew he wasn't.

"I believe he's using some of these women to track you at various opportunities —" Detective Batair pointed to the remaining pictures Mia had forgotten were in her hand.

Looking down at the face of the red-haired woman, Mia finished Batair's sentence. "— to try and kill me."

The next thing Mia did was the only thing that made sense, sense to her survival. She ran. She ran out of the apartment, down the stairs, and into the fading evening light that took her as far away as she could possibly get. Mia ran until she couldn't run anymore.

CHAPTER 9

Flight

The plan was to run indefinitely. It felt like she'd been running for hours when her legs cramped. Frustrated with her body, Mia slowed to a walk, quickly realizing how exhausted she was; succumbing to fatigue, she slumped herself against a mossy tree and closed her eyes. At the soft nudging of the detective, she awoke and took in a sharp breath.

"How did you find me?"

"It's what I do." Detective Batair offered his hand and pulled Mia up to stand, unsteadily, on her battered feet.

She'd forgotten she was barefoot.

"What do you do, sniff the ground for a scent?" Mia's cold hand buzzed in the detective's warm grasp, joined with the pinch of her right leg having fallen asleep.

"I just try and think like the person I'm hunting."

"Oh, well then, I guess I'm predictable," Mia said with a wicked laugh. "I'll try not to be — next time, but since I'm on a permanent hit list, there probably won't be a next time . . . ." A nagging pinching filled Mia's chest; she studied the ground while they walked toward an abandoned gas station.

"It took me a while to locate you."

"What time is it, anyway?" Mia felt pleased she'd inconvenienced him. When she rubbed the side of her rib cage, her skin was tender from where she'd tripped on a tree root.

"Just past midnight." Detective Batair walked slowly along the out-of-order gasoline pumps that were littered with old trash and cigarettes.

"I was hoping it was later. I don't want to hash it out."

"Then don't." Batair approached a motorcycle. Grabbing a helmet, he held it out for Mia.

"Right, I'll just avoid the topic for a while." Bitterness rose in her throat.

"Sometimes we hear best in silence." Batair waited for Mia to take the helmet.

The detective slid off his leather jacket and handed it to Mia, who had begun shivering. She slipped the helmet on but shook her head. "I'm okay, I don't need it." But her lips were bluing.

"I'll take it back from you once we get to your house; better use it while you can." Batair placed it on the back seat and mounted the bike. Mia felt embarrassed as she put her arms through the jacket, but it was so warm. With a pause, she swung her leg over the back of the bike and sat a few inches behind him. She'd never been on a motorcycle before. "You'll have to hold on."

"Right." She put her arms on the side of his waist; beneath his thin, holed T-shirt, she could feel a taut stomach.

Detective Batair kicked up the bike with his steel-toed boots and started the motorcycle, revving it to life. Mia held on to his sides as he took off, down back streets, along a winding unfamiliar path that led them to her apartment complex. She arrived in less than fifteen minutes, took off the helmet and jacket, and thanked him for the ride. Standing still, she paused. She wanted to say more, but nothing would come. Kicking an acorn, Mia turned toward the stairs when he spoke.

"It's okay to be scared, Mia."

As he said this, she turned back to face him. She didn't like the idea of him thinking she was afraid. Like she was some little girl afraid of the dark.

"Everyone is scared of something," he said. "Some, like you, have more to be scared of than others."

"What are you scared of then?"

A small smile drew on his full lips. "Losing things."

"Like your keys? Do motorcycles even use keys?"

He started the bike. "Get some rest." He put his jacket back on and slowly drove the bike out of the parking lot.

Mia walked up the stairs and opened the door of her apartment to see her mom, face down on her bed in what looked like one of her yoga poses.

"Mom?"

Divana jumped a good four feet. "MIA!"

"Hey," she said, closing the door while her mother jumped off her bed to hug her.

"Honey, listen, I know there's a lot to say," her mom began, pulling back from Mia when she put up her hands to pause her.

"I'm sorry I ran out, but I'm really tired, and with school tomorrow . . . ."

"Okay, yes. I hear you . . ." Divana paused as if trying to remember something. "I want to honor your request. I hear you saying you do not want to talk tonight, and that makes sense; we've had quite a shock."

"Yeah." Mia sat on her bed and pulled her foot up to assess the damage. Besides being covered in dirt and a few bits of leaf, she had only scratches and soreness from her trek across town. She needed a shower, but she was so tired.

"Honey! Your feet! Let me clean them." Divana ran to the bathroom to grab a towel and some soap.

"Mom, I'm fine." Mia lay down and closed her eyes. She was so tired now that she was home. Little Chip's wet nose pressed against her arm, and she forgot about changing into pajamas while her mother washed the grime off her feet, bandaging a few stinging toes. Pulling up the covers, Chip relocated next to Mia's leg, speeding the warming process as she sunk into her soft bed. Mia couldn't fight the inevitable pull toward sleep any longer. "Thanks, Mom," she said, peeking one eye open. "And hey, it's fine for you to plan my birthday. Why not? You only live once." Mia closed her eyes and thought of how her one life could possibly be a lot shorter than she'd once thought.

"Really, oh, honey!" Divana kissed Mia's forehead as her tired body began to relax into that glorious place of dreamless sleep.

Mia awoke to a darkened room. Grabbing her phone, she sat upright, surprised to see the clock read noon. The apartment was quiet, apart from the distant sound of a leaf blower.

"Mom?"

Unlocking her buzzing phone, Mia opened a slew of texts from Ting and Shelby.

Ting: Mia! Where are you, everything okay?

Shelby: Mia — are you skipping?

Ting: Worried 'bout U … I had a bad dump last night.

Ting: OMG autocorrect, meant dumpling, had bad dumplings, and I'm sitting in the nurse's office!

Shelby: What the — your dad is here!!! U skipping cause of that? The school is freaking.

Ting:	Hello???
Shelby:	TEXT me BACK!
Ting:	OMG did you hear about your dad!
Ting:	Call me!
Ting:	Your mom said you got lost on a run . . . U do know your phone has GPS?
Shelby:	Ting said your mom said you got lost running, UM. You're not that dumb! TEXT ME BACK!
Ting:	Dr. Fern wants me to remind you about the field trip tomorrow, please say you're coming?!!!
Shelby:	Tell me you're coming tomorrow!

Just as Mia finished catching up on her texts, the front door opened, and in walked her mom, carrying two full grocery bags and a look of relief to see Mia awake and grinning. "Honey, you were in such a deep sleep, I didn't want to wake you. How are you feeling about everything?" Divana closed the door with her hip and held the bags to survey Mia's condition.

"Good, better." Mia felt surprisingly well rested with only a lingering soreness on her side.

"I got a few things to make you lunch — well, breakfast, brunch — and then I thought we could do something relaxing like watch a movie!" Divana headed to the kitchen and put the bags on the table, quickly returning to Mia. Chip was nestled between her pillows.

"What about meeting Charles?" Mia scratched Chip. "I thought we were doing dinner or something later? And there's school."

"Yes, I tried to reach your father, but . . . he's busy today." Divana looked tired. "This is not the day I would want to share such news with you, but . . ." Divana took a deep inhale "Your father is actually at your school right now. I can't believe it, but, your school has been chosen for the site of his next movie." Divana reported the news mechanically, unable to hide an expression of budding anger.

"I called him this morning to talk and see when we would meet him, but he didn't put it in his schedule, something or other. He's busy with the movie. I mean, what the hell was he thinking? Mia, if I'd known, I would have tried my hardest to discourage him from it. He said he wanted it to be a surprise. Damn him and his surprises."

"It's okay, Mom," Mia said, determined not to go back to that place she'd lived in last night when she'd run through the woods. Somehow in the darkness, the despair she felt was deeper and scarier than ever before.

"No, Mia, this is *your* school. How on earth could something so absurd happen? Your father seems to keep making foolish choices and . . . ." Anger flashed gold in Divana's emerald eyes.

"I know about the movie; my friends texted me." She wasn't about to share that her father had possibly used her to land the location. No, it was better to keep that to herself. "I know this sounds crazy, but can we just not worry about this today?" Mia held her side as she wiggled her way out of bed, trying not to disturb a snoring Chip.

"But honey . . ."

Mia grabbed her bathrobe and headed to shower. "It's not going to change anything, talking about it . . . at least not in the way I want things to change. Can we just pretend to be normal people today, normal people who do normal things like eating." Mia paused at the bathroom door.

"Yes, food — let me get started on lunch." She eyed Mia, who seemed a little on the thinner side these days. Divana looked relieved as she headed to the kitchen and spent the following hour making a feast of poached eggs, roasted potatoes with peppers, glazed cinnamon rolls, and chai tea lattes.

The rest of the day Mia stayed indoors reading, texting her friends to reassure them she wasn't dead, eating, and organizing her desk. She wasn't much of an organizer, but things were getting desperate as she sifted through old books, papers, and new school documents that probably needed filing but for now would just be shoved in a drawer at the bottom of her desk, which, surprisingly, had an incredible amount of storage space. Under a pile of soliciting magazines that seemed to follow Mia through every move, she found a few cards addressed to her. The first was from school, and as she opened the blue card, a miniature paper model of a cruise ship rose from inside the card. Just as it fully came to life, something popped, and a tiny burst of glitter puffed from the ship's funnel. Along the back of the card were important details of the cruise weekend and directions to the website for final pricing. Below the typed wording was a handwritten note.

Really hope you come! — Will

"That's unexpected." Mia thought of Will stuffing and addressing every student's invitation. Feeling an odd shift of sentiment, she displayed the paper ship on her shelf despite her determination to not RSVP. The second envelope was more like a small package, which Mia unwrapped to see stationary from Sapphire Hotel and Casino. Inside the padded envelope was a thin box wrapped in purple ribbon. Untying the ribbon, she opened the box to see the pen she had bid on for the raffle. "I guess this means I won." Taking the pen out of its sleek velvet case, Mia held it in her hand and wondered why expensive pens had to be heavy. A sudden sweat broke out on her forehead as her memory flooded with a flashback of the lip gloss rolling down the bus aisle. Placing the pen back on her desk, Mia shook her head. How long would she feel damaged?

Grabbing the last envelope to distract herself before she fell into the darker space of time and thought, she ripped the thick envelope open and suddenly remembered what it was: the results of the DNA test kit she'd sent out weeks ago. Ironic. She'd been checking the mail for days waiting for the results, and now, here it was, weeks later and a day too late. Opening the document, Mia skimmed the letters that seemed to use a lot of scientific words and explanations to state what she already knew. She had a father and uncle, both sharing fraternal twin DNA and both the offspring of Dominic Broderick and a woman named Olivia Brown. Mia had never heard of her and added it to the list of things she had to confront her dad about.

The letter detailed the accuracy of the test results and statistical data involved in how to interpret the DNA findings. Alongside the test results for her maternal side, Mia only read her mother's name and in small lettering, the word *UNKNOWN* next to *parentage*. She'd always known her mother had no extended family since her grandparents had died young, but it felt lonesome to see it on paper. Putting the papers back into the bottom desk drawer, Mia took a drink of her chai latte and let the sugar rush to her brain. Just as she was putting the mug down on the desk, Chip jumped up and knocked her hand, sending the mug on its side, spilling spiced milk against the backboard of her desk.

"CHIP! What the heck!" Standing, Mia ran to the kitchen to grab tea towels and napkins

and wiped the desktop as best she could before sugary tea ran into every crack and crevice. "See, this is why I don't like fancy stuff," Mia complained, wiping the sweet clove-smelling drink with a frayed towel, focusing on the backboard of the hutch where most of it had splashed. Carved with intricate flowers and swirls of leaf petals, the ornate design of the woodwork meant Mia had to wipe the detailed wood tediously. Some of the middles of the flowers had tiny stones that reflected the light but needed something small to clean them; grabbing the new pen sitting on her desk, she put the paper towel up to the hole and used the pen to press the stone, soaking up the small dots of tea in each flower center.

Finished cleaning and annoyed at Chip for giving her a twenty-minute job, Mia grabbed some laundry and folded the towels and clothes on her bed as her mom came from her room to see if she wanted to watch a movie; Divana had just finished wrapping up client notes from the week. Throwing the laundry back into the basket, Mia jumped on her bed and spent the rest of the day laughing at romantic comedies that allowed them to get lost in the drama of other women's lives.

CHAPTER 10

Fight

School came too early the next morning as Mia dressed in a white shirt, black slacks, and her black loafers. Today, she tried to take extra care to comb and smooth her hair; Dr. Fern had instructed the students to dress in business casual in hopes of helping them appear mature and professional as they spent the day touring VanBoi Biotech Industries. Looking in the mirror after a good attempt, she put on a small amount of her mom's blush and lip gloss, readjusted her locket, and headed out the door. Waving goodbye to her mother, Mia headed into the tan pillared building an hour later to the confronting shouts of two high-pitched voices.

"I don't owe you anything!"

"Shut your mouth, no one wants to hear you!"

From across the lobby, Mia could see Shelby glaring at Jade in a standoff. Both girls were perched to attack, scowling at each other while Jade's sidekick Vivian cowered behind.

"You know," Jade retorted, "I feel bad for you; you're just as trashy as your mom."

And before she could finish, Shelby lunged forward while Vivian screamed and ran for cover behind Jackson, who was easily capable of breaking up the fight but instead, watched in amusement.

"Mia!" Ting yelled, spotting her springing toward Shelby. Grabbing Shelby by the waist, Mia pulled her away from Jade while Ting tried to convince the security guards the girls were only joking.

"She's done!" Shelby said while Mia wrestled her into a seat.

"What —" Mia kept her hand on Shelby's shoulder, blocking her view of Jade "— was *that* all about?"

"Thinks she can say whatever she wants," Shelby spat.

Ting appeared. "Um, guys, our liaison is on the way, which means we have to *try* and behave."

"Fine. Don't worry about me. I gotta pee." Shelby tried standing against Mia's hold.

"You're sure you're okay?" Mia asked, the sound of Jade laughing ringing in the background.

"Cool as a cucumber." Shelby grabbed her bag and disappeared into the lobby restroom.

Mia turned to Ting. "Am I going to get an explanation?"

"Oh, things have been brewing. Mia, I'm so glad you're here!" Ting lunged at Mia and pulled her into a hug, almost knocking her over.

"Thanks! I missed you too!" Mia righted herself and looked around. "But where's Terry?"

Ting smiled. "Oh, he got his wisdom teeth out last week, and thank God his head is still swollen."

"Well, it's too bad he's missing today. But really, why was Shelby so upset?"

Ting looked around the room as if wanting to make sure no one could hear them. Shifting

uncomfortably in her lime-green high-tops, she scratched her neck while pursing her lips.

"Ting —"

"Yeaah?"

"Ting, what is it?"

"Ah Mia, I really don't think —"

"Ting!"

"Fine. It's because Jade started speculating about how your dad knew your mom."

"What? Oh my God, how does she know about him?" Mia was so distracted with the news of her grandfather, that she just hadn't given any thought to things leaking about Charles.

"Oh NO, she doesn't know about *that*; it's more your *hypothetical* father." Now watching Jade from across the room smugly put on purple matte lipstick, Ting frowned. "See, your mom's so pretty, and she was kind of . . . see, in Hollywood sometimes . . ."

"TING, what are you getting at!"

"Oh, Mia, it's too vile to even repeat."

"I'll repeat it —" Shelby appeared from the bathroom. "She said your mom was probably a prostitute." Shelby looped her arm with Mia's and smiled. "Now, Mia, we don't want to resort to violence, do we? Trust me, she deserves it, but it's not you — stay classy, leave the violence to me."

"Why would she even say that? She doesn't know my mother!" Mia barked.

Shelby sighed. "She used to be likable, at least when we were kids. But she changed. Can you believe she requested I be removed from the project? Said I didn't pull my weight, which is very true, but she didn't need to tell Cheeks about it.

"Mia?" Ting watched her friend's deflated demeanor. "For the record, I am 99.95 percent convinced she cheated on the project and their group shouldn't even be here."

Shelby bit her thumbnail, which had chipped in the earlier scuffle, and shrugged. "I fully agree with that — she did all the extra work because she changed the concept and added way too much effort, but

I thought, *Hey, you do you; what do I care?* Until she called me lazy." Shelby spat out the nail in the near direction of Jade. "I'm a lot of things, but I'm not lazy."

"It's like my gram says, some people just have weak chi."

"North Elite Preparatory High School?" said a young woman reading out of her monogrammed notebook.

"Oh, us!" Ting answered excitedly while Jade, Vivian, and Jackson made their way over. Positioning herself near Shelby, Mia listened to the woman welcome the group while Jackson jumped to the front to collect his visitor's tag.

"Here —" Mia gave Shelby her tag as she stood and followed the woman named Harper to the security checkpoint. "Ting! What's in this bag?"

"Thanks, oh, I brought a few laptops just in case, you know, for the presentation. I've done a little more work and thought the upgraded version would be cool to explain, and — what?"

"You're amazing," Mia said, stopping Ting, who was walking forward with the group. "Wait, I didn't prepare for a presentation, Ting!"

"Yeah," Shelby leaned in, ". . . if I have to present, I'm outta here like right now." She nodded toward the doors.

"No, no, relax. Dr. Fern only asked one person from each group to present, you know, limit the possibility of —"

"Looking like dumbasses." Shelby glanced at Mia in relief.

The group followed the guide up a long flight of stairs, past various laboratories, where white-coat workers dropped brightly colored liquids into rows of coded trays.

Pausing at the glass windows, Jackson peered in. "What are they doing, Harper?"

"Oh, it's *Ms. Winton.*"

"Sorry, Miss Winton, what are they doing there?"

"*MS. Winton,* and this is our in-house testing center, where we look into genetic modifications. You know, mixing genes, splicing and dicing. It's restricted access, so you'll have to wait for the journal reports to come out for the findings!"

The group followed Ms. Winton past a coffee cart when everyone stopped to grab a cup, hastily dousing their coffees with packets of raw sugar and additive-free creamers. The next half hour was spent walking around hallways and watching employees work at their desks. Ting seemed enthralled with all the details of the place even though the rest of the group were bored out of their minds.

"So, as you will see inside," Ms. Winton began, referring to the bolted steel door that stood behind her, "we are in our second phase of testing in ocular forensics diagnostics." She checked her watch. "Just a word of caution before we enter, some of the scenes could be slightly disconcerting to those who are of the vegetarian nature. Of course. all the animals are protected under our Creature Care Act in honor of John Richards, who sadly lost his family pet in routine test-ing. So, with that being said —" Ms. Winton opened her zipper folder and pulled out paper face masks "— please put these on, and we have protective glasses just inside."

Taking her mask, Mia heard Vivian groan and asked if there wasn't something else they could wear considering the thick unbreathable paper was sure to give her *mask-ne.*

"Don't worry, it will improve your face immensely," Shelby said as Jackson tittered.

"Okay, right this way." And inputting a code into the door keypad, Ms. Winton waited for the heavy steel door to unbolt. As she pulled it open, the students walked inside, Jackson first, as they stepped into an oval-shaped room that, to Mia, looked just as a sterile laboratory should, with huge clawlike machines that resembled robotic hands operating from the center ceiling, while a long table set underneath held something covered by a sheet. The rest of the room was stark white with state-of-the-art equipment, computers, rows of plants, and a random jukebox in the corner playing soft ballads of songs from forty years ago.

"Oh, goodie, we're just in time," Ms. Winton explained to Mia, who watched two men in white coveralls uncover a sedated tortoise. "We've been testing the ocular response of the animal to familiar stimuli, trying to determine if we could shift and reprogram their intake data and set it to their long-term memory. Our theory is that with the right information input, we can change what it is we see, or want people to see, in this case, the tortoise. All our results thus far have proved promising."

At the very moment Shelby whispered, "I hope it's dead," Vivian started to scream. An overhead mechanical claw had inserted its tiny needle-like fingers into the animal's eye while the group watched in gruesome awe.

"Miss, I assure you this is routine. We've done this many times," she explained as a staff member nodded and continued to oversee the operation of the mechanical hand.

"But why a turtle?" Shelby asked, turning her head but unable to look away.

"This is actually a pond tortoise, not a turtle," Ting piped in. "This type of tortoise happens to have exceptional forward-facing eye movement ability, very unusual for a sideways-facing animal."

"She's right, and what's more —" But Ms. Winton was unable to finish. Somehow, the experiment had gone sideways, the claw snagging on the tortoise's eye, ripping it out and propelling it across the room, where it hit Vivian square in the forehead, which she tolerated by falling backward and onto the floor. Unsure if Vivian had fainted, Mia ran to help her as she screamed on the floor, thrashing about while the rest of the group watched Ting and Ms. Winton retrieve the rolling eyeball.

"I think we should go. Please follow me, and drop your goggles on the way out," Ms. Winton said, steering the group toward the emergency exit door located behind the scene of the crime.

Shelby was grinning as if it was Christmas morning.

"What?" Mia asked as they watched Jackson assist Vivian up the stairs while Ms. Winton led them to the third floor and toward a conference room, promising a debrief.

"Look . . ." Shelby pointed to Jade's shoes. The tan suede ankle bootie had sprinkles of red blood and green goo on the toe. "Don't you dare tell her."

"I'll leave that to you," Mia promised.

"Um, can you walk now?"

"No, I'm too weak." Vivian hung on tighter while Jackson pulled her up the stairs.

"I promise you —" Ms. Winton turned around "— I've been here three years, and this has never happened before, never. I can assure you, our human resources department will be launching a full investigation into the drone."

"These things happen." Shelby nodded.

Mia could tell Ms. Winton was feeling a little lost with the redirection of the tour. "If you could all come in here, the other groups won't be along for a little while, just make yourselves comfortable, and I'll be back," she said, leading them into a broad conference room and shuffling off while closing the door behind them.

"OH MY GOD! JADE — YOUR SHOES!" Vivian yelled, seeing the congealed goo up close once they sat on the couch.

Gasping, Jade jumped and ran out the door after Ms. Winton, while Shelby took her spot on the couch.

"What a great day this has been so far." Shelby closed her eyes in bliss.

"Mia?" Ting had settled herself in a seat at the conference table. "Would you mind switching the slides for me during the presentation? You just click here when I nod like this."

"Sure, but maybe you could just give me a look. I mean if you don't want to do so much of the head moving," Mia suggested, when the conference door opened. Expecting to see Ms. Winton or Jade, Mia was met with the faces of a group of professional executives, ushering themselves into the room and surprised to see anyone, especially a sprawl of teenagers laying about.

Standing and bumping Mia, Ting explained to a stone-faced man, "We're here with Ms. Winton, on the student tour."

"Oh, Mr. Boiton!" Ms. Winton said, rushing to Ting's aid. "Our group had to finish the tour a little early."

Holding up his hand up to stop her, the man picked up the wall phone, entirely relaxed, and said, "Kate, I'm in the conference room early . . . thanks." Hanging up the phone, he addressed the adults: "It seems some of our student protegees have joined us early," and indicated for them to take a seat while Mia helped Ting scramble to pick up her things.

"Okay," Ms. Winton said, after gathering the students together, "who can give the first presentation?"

"Huh?" Vivian asked. "Jade's supposed to, but she's not back —" Vivian looked faintly at Jackson.

"Don't look at me," he fired back, while Shelby added, "Not a chance."

"Well, someone has to go," Ms. Winton said rather desperately. "These people are investors and . . ."

"I can go —" Ting said at the nudge of Mia.

"Thank you, you dear girl, thank you."

Ms. Winton grabbed Ting and pulled her up to the front of the room, next to the screen.

"Right —" Ting said, flustered. "Um, Mia, computer?"

Grabbing Ting's bag and pulling out the laptop, Mia set it up as quickly as she could manage, while everyone stared at Ting pinking under the silence. Once Ting's presentation began, Mia leaned against the wall, relieved the day was almost over. She had a weird feeling after the eyeball incident, like she'd rode a roller coaster too soon after eating. Taking a moment to study the room, Mia noticed a sharp-looking young man staring at her.

She'd seen him before both with her father and on his wall of pictures. He knew her father, and here he was showing up again. Right across the room from Mia, smiling at her as if he knew who *she* was.

CHAPTER 11

Only a Girl

Running toward the soccer field, Mia slowed to a jog while Coach Drake yelled to take a cooldown lap. At once, a few of the boys stopped to catch their breath.

"Good! Y'all made it on time." Coach Drake nodded at Mia, who had stayed toward the front for the three-mile run. "Now, men . . . and a Miss," the burly coach proceeded in his thick Southern drawl, "we're picking teams today, and I don't want any switching, no complaining, and no having your mommy call me, all right?" Most of the boys nodded. "Captains, stand here." The bull-necked man pointed to opposite sides of the wide net. Stretching her leg, Mia watched a boy in soccer shorts step forward, muscular, resolute, and unsmiling, as he took his stance at the left side of the net.

The only person she knew from the whole group, and not even personally, was the tall gangly boy Phillip Henness, whose grandfather Carl, was forever seared in her mind.

The second captain, dark-skinned with thick curly eyelashes and a lean build, stood to the right and thought intently about his picks while the coach explained the team-choosing process. "In my games we coin toss, it's fair — pick a side and whoever wins gets his pick first. Might I remind ya, captains were chosen last year based on exceptional survival skills testing marks, so they are qualified, and I expect full respect for their leadership, right? Henry, heads or tails?" Coach asked the sandy-haired boy.

"Tails."

"Justice, you're heads." Coach Drake flipped the coin while the group waited.

"Tails it is; Henry you're up first."

The stone-faced Henry didn't miss a beat, pointed to his friend and immediately declared, "I'll take Simon."

"Yes, you will." Simon saluted his friend and ran up to join him while Justice glanced over Mia and called Chet's name.

Henry and Justice went back and forth, choosing friends and teammates while Coach Drake looked on, writing down which player went where and chewing on the end of his pen when someone took longer than a few seconds to decide. Phillip was chosen for Henry's team, which he seemed happy about. Walking by Mia, he joined the team while the captains continued to add to their roster until it seemed certain Mia was going to be the last not-man standing.

"All right, Henry, come on, one more choice; this ain't rocket science," Coach Drake said.

"Coach, team meeting first?" Henry examined the boy next to Mia, who looked years away from puberty.

Coach Drake was aghast. "Team meeting? No, you ain't a team yet, you knuckle brain, till your last pick!"

"It's just," Henry began, "I want to consult . . ." and with that Coach threw his hands up and yelled, "Rork, you're over there, and Storm, you're with Justice — taking forever to choose a dang player, come on man, and eh woman."

Mia walked over to the group of nine boys staring at their first female teammate.

"Hi." Justice extended his hand to Mia while a few guys groaned at having Mia over Rork the Dork. "I'm Justice," he said, a slight

English accent accompanying his broad smile. Shaking his hand, Mia introduced herself while a few of the guys grunted a "Hey."

"Right, now, sir?" Henry asked while the coach waved him back.

"Hold off a second, I gotta explain the rules to the new guys — *and* girl," Coach said, calling everyone to sit on the grass and running his hand through his short hair. "Okay, welcome to the official season of Strategy & Survival. We have some newbies here and, of course, all the veterans —"

The rest of Mia's group high-fived at having come back for another round.

"Couldn't keep you guys away if I wanted to," he said with a laugh. "Let's get to some of the rules, regulations, and safety procedures that have changed since last year — the rest I expect you to familiarize yourself with before next week."

Coach Drake handed out a bulky packet to each player, reminding them to shut up and listen. "Yes, fires are still allowed, Chet," Coach explained to the boy smelling dirt he'd pinched between his fingers, "but we need to have a better course of action as to how we can, eh?" Coach stared at him. "Contain and extinguish them in a timely fashion, so you, in particular, can familiarize yourself with section ten. For the rest of you, as you can see, we have a first this year, and that is our official female player, Mia Storm!" Coach Drake nodded at Mia. "We had to write a few additional expectations in our manual considering the lack of, um, diversity in the past, so do note the specifics required for overnights, tenting needs, and bathroom, *ehm*, situations." Coach cleared his throat as the boys laughed off the awkwardness. "I'll be enlisting my Mrs. on the weekend overnights as a touch-point person so that Storm has a female she can dialogue with should it be necessary for any — you know, female things."

Great, another way to stick out around here.

Coach Drake, in his blue windbreaker, spent the rest of his talk highlighting what he called the "absolutely do-nots because if I catch you — you'll be screaming for mercy," which mostly entailed threats against potential cheating, team bribery, and the inevitable stupid actions that lead to unnecessary injuries. Once again, Mia was berating herself for not reading her school manual. Bouncing around in a leotard was starting to sound a lot better to her than camping overnight in the woods with a team of boys who wanted nothing more than to exert as much male dominance over one another as possible.

"So, let's get you into your teams," Coach said to Henry's muttering, "Finally."

Henry jumped up and led his team to the opposite side of the field.

Mia sat where she was as her team members looked to Justice to instruct them further.

"You know," Coach yelled, "I wasn't entirely finished, but go on ahead and get started. We've only got a good twenty minutes left on the field before the prancing fairies arrive."

"Thanks, Coach. Guys, gather up in a tight circle," Justice called to his team, Coach having cleared his throat and nodded toward Mia. "Sorry, Coach, guys *and* lady person, gather up!"

Mia scooted toward the boys and placed herself next to the boy named Chet. His quad muscles were the same width as her waist, making her wonder how a high schooler looked thirty-five. The two players next to him were identical twins, both having the same almond-shaped eyes, dark spiky hair, and lean muscular build that complemented their hyper energy. Next to them was Justice, and beyond him Mia didn't know the remaining boys' names, but knew the three seated next to Justice were close friends because she'd seen them arrive at school together. The last boy hadn't spoken a word to anyone, like Mia, since the start of the meeting. He didn't seem unfriendly, and Mia wondered if she would gravitate toward him, seeing as the rest of the crew had claimed their friendship territories already.

"Right-O," Justice began. "Welcome to the winning team, blokes — shoot — and lady." Justice began, as one of the group of three quipped, "Good start, Cap." Ignoring them, Justice continued, "This year we are going to flippin' WIN! Against peers, against wanker schools and win that championship! We *all* know only real badasses play this game. We play, we win, we command the friggin' respect of the school!" Mia felt the guys go quiet. "Look, mates, you all know I was dealt a bad hand — born so early doctors told me mum I wouldn't make it. But who's here today to show them off? We've all got something to prove —" he motioned to them.

"*This* is our time, mates, OUR time to show everyone we can! We're not some posh prissies at a wanker school; we are REAL men, with guts and grit, and we have what it takes to kick —" By now the guys were rattling up and someone yelled "RULE!" as they jumped up, yelling and chest-bumping one another.

Mia, still seated, felt both the pull of joining in and rallying to the thought of winning and sitting in stupefaction at how comical this all was.

Standing only because one of the twins had almost stepped on her, the crew quieted down while Justice told the group they needed to choose a strength and conditioning partner. "Ideally, I want you training three times a week minimum, but Coach Drake said I can't require a specific number so, if you could just meet every other day, that would be the best." Mia looked in the direction of the silent kid only to see he'd already partnered with Chet. The last teammate left was one of the group of three friends who was already asking Justice if they could train as a trio. "No trio. Partner up with Mia. Mia!" he called as he dragged one over to her. "This here is Andy. Andy, meet Mia Storm. She's your new training partner."

"Hi." Mia extended her hand as Justice walked away.

Andy stared back. "Look, Justice is too much of a sheet to say this, but you don't belong here. This competition isn't for chicks. You better not mess with our chances of winning, and you better not rat on anyone for not kissing your ass." He glared at her.

Mia dropped her hand. She turned her back on him, walking to another spot. Fuming, she stood near one of the twins, waiting for Justice to rally the group again while Chet put the other grinning twin into a headlock. For the remainder of the training time, the captains assessed different skill sets within the group. Most of the guys spoke effortlessly to their strengths, Justice taking copious notes as to who could do what and how.

"I'm not sure." Mia said when it came her turn. She imagined there was hunting, chasing, some hiding — basic defensive positions, but she had little knowledge of what strengths she was meant to contribute to help the team.

"Well, you can run," Justice said.

"And that's probably it!" A boy named Oliver laughed, nudging Andy, who enjoyed the jab.

"Certainly not!" Justice said. "What else can you do, Mia?" Justice asked. "Would you say you're more of an offense or defense player?"

"Um . . . maybe defense?"

"Okay, great, and —"

"Right like she could defend the flag with Henry running thirty miles per hour at her," Andy chimed in.

"You nub, no one can run that fast," Oliver teased.

"You know what I mean. Justice, this is a joke. Let's just tie her to a tree and hope she can distract some of the players with her mediocre good looks," Andy said as the group went silent.

"What did you say?" Justice asked slowly.

"I said, she's mediocre at best, and I don't know what Coach Drake is doing putting an obvious loser on our team."

The boys had all eyes on Justice.

Dropping his clipboard, Justice looked livid. "Andy, I'm going to make this PERFECTLY clear. If I EVER hear you say anything along those lines again about ANY teammate, I am personally going to cut you from this program. Lucky for me, it's in the bylaws that as captain I'm eligible to submit a petition signed by Coach and another teacher to have you removed from the games due to unsportsman-like conduct. On top of that, I give Mia full permission, after I'm done with you, to kick your little ass if you ever speak like that about her again." Justice had stepped so close to Andy's face that Mia could see tiny droplets of spit fly from his mouth to Andy, who kept his face still as stone.

"Guys, come on —" Chet piped up. "Let's chill . . . it's the first day. Everyone's just wanting a good chance of winning, and we have an awesome chance. I should know since I was on the winning team last year."

But Justice was unmoved, standing so very still, Mia wondered if he was holding his breath. Everyone in the group sat watching, waiting to see who would break first.

"Guys?" Chet said again, lightly punching Andy in the arm while Coach came running toward the team. Andy broke his gaze, mumbling something while wiping his face just as Coach arrived.

"Hey, guys and girl!" Coach yelled. "Time to wrap it up! You can all do your texting later on 'cause it looks like the weather's about to turn."

Just then a gang of football players headed onto the field for a wet practice.

Andy caught Mia's eye as Justice turned back to his pernicious self to remind the team against shortening their workouts, and shot Mia a look that promised this wasn't over. A drizzle began as the sky darkened, indicating it was time to head home.

Patting a few of the players on the back, Coach held his clipboard over his head and quipped to Mia, "Welcome to the team, Storm! Hope you didn't bring the bad weather with you." Coach headed to his pickup.

Wondering what she'd gotten herself into, Mia made her way to the girls' locker room. Passing by Jackson stretching his hamstrings with a few teammates in practice pads and cleats, she threw him a slight wave, but instead of waving back, Jackson and the other football players burst out laughing. Mia put her hand down, wiped her face from the pelting rain, and headed toward school while the rain intensified. Her mother had gone on about the California weather, gloating it hardly dropped below the seventies or stormed, but that did not seem to be the case as Mia found her right foot steeped in a fresh mud puddle. Feeling her foot sink into the softened ground, she pulled it up, shoeless, and hobbled on one leg, trying to unsuction the other sneaker from the mud. Phillip and a few players swept by as the rain continued to downpour, ignoring Mia and heading inside.

Something told her this was going to be a long season.

CHAPTER 12

A Happy Birthday

Between Justice's strength and conditioning schedule, weekly practices with the team, and the added chaos at school of production beginning for her father's film, Mia's mind had been far from thinking about her upcoming birthday celebration. Only a day away, Mia had happily left any plans to her mother, who seemed very low-key about her sweet sixteen. Maybe it was the troubling news of her grandfather that had lowered her mother's excitement, but whatever it was, Mia was relieved the day would come and go with little fuss and hopefully no bad karma.

"So, dinner tomorrow with your dad still okay?" her mom asked for the third time while Mia reread the ending of her chapter.

Putting down the novel she was trying to finish before dinner, Mia yawned. "Yeah, it's fine." She wondered how many times she needed to assure her mom she wouldn't confront him until after her birthday.

"I know, I just want to double-check, seeing as we have some things to talk to him about."

All week she'd been trying to get Charles to stop by the house to discuss the revelation from Detective Batair, but the movie had kept him busy, and unavailable and Divana exasperated.

"Mom, I promise." Mia closed the book for the evening, giving up on finishing her English Lit homework till tomorrow. The story was confusing, and she was tired from having to look up so many French words.

"I want nothing to ruin your birthday, but I was thinking since you're well — if you felt you needed to get some answers, if it was eating you up inside, I wouldn't stop you."

"Mom, I'm fine. Please. If Charles is hiding something, he will still be hiding it next week, so . . ." But she couldn't finish her sentence because right then, Mateo's face appeared in the window.

"*Mia novia!*" Mateo pounded on the window, while Chip barked.

Laughing, while her mother opened the door, Mia tossed the book into her backpack and stood to greet Mateo. "Hey, buddy," she said, while he handed her a white box tied with a plastic yellow ribbon and bowed his head in a strange formal gesture. "Mateo?" Mia smirked, admiring his crooked toothy grin while she received the box.

"You are birthday queen. I bow to queen."

Her mother cleared her throat. "This is sweet, Mateo," Divana said, as Chip sniffed him expectantly. "But her birthday isn't till tomorrow."

"Me know, but Mom said it's okay," he said triumphantly, while Mia gave her mom a *don't be rude* look.

"Okay, well . . ." Divana started, while Mia asked, "Should I open it now?"

There was no denying Mia had to open it or Mateo would probably explode from excitement with his nods and claps. Untying the ribbon, Mia unlidded the small box to see bite-sized iced cookies covered in nonpareils neatly wrapped in parchment paper while the scent of vanilla wafted toward her. "Mateo, thank you! This is just what I needed!" She took one out as her mom eyed her. "Oh, sorry, here," she said, holding up the box to offer them some. As they shook their heads, Mia shrugged. "Good, more for me." She grabbed another and savored the buttery goodness as it melted in her mouth.

"Mia, wait till after dinner?" her mom said, while poor Mateo stared at Mia's lips as she licked the crumbs; he was almost drooling. Looking from Mateo to her mom, Mia thought it strange he turned down a sweet, and now that she thought of it, a little odd that her mother had mentioned dinner when she'd not been in the kitchen all day.

"What are you two up to?" she asked, as her mom and Mateo looked to each other in

exaggerated surprise.

"Mia, don't be silly. Mateo, do you think Mia could come and collect a bit of Chip's food from your house? I'm all out and don't feel like going to the store," Divana asked a distracted Mateo, unable to tear his eyes away from the box.

"Come on, buddy." Mia grabbed Mateo's arm and headed outside.

Mateo kept a slow pace down the stairs. It was his one fear, falling down stairs and off ledges and anything really that had something to do with heights. Maria wasn't even allowed a ladder or step stool in her house. Taking each step carefully, he asked, "Who that man, Mia?"

"What, the mailman?" Mia looked to the postman delivering letters and packages to the community boxes.

"No, the man who visit you." His eyes never left his feet.

No one, including her dad, had visited Mia at her house, except Detective Batair. Mia explained it was a detective.

"You in trouble?" he asked, holding the rail and pausing for a breath.

"Well, I don't really know, Mateo — I guess it depends on how you look at it."

"So, no trouble?" He reached the bottom and sighed. The entire time, Chip was stepping down the stairs with Mateo ever so cautiously as Mia joined them at the bottom.

"Let's just say, I seem to attract trouble despite my best attempts to avoid it."

Looking concerned, Mateo frowned. "No, Mia, you bring good," Mateo said while Chip pulled him toward the apartment, "but bad has to kill good."

Mia watched Mateo knock on his apartment and turn to smile at her. When no one answered the door, he covered his mouth with his hand to hide his sudden giggles. The neighbor down the hall, a hairy man who never seemed to get out of his bathrobe, opened the door and scowled at Mateo, who was thoroughly enjoying knowing something Mia didn't.

Mateo's grabbed Mia's hand, opened the unlocked door, and ushered them all inside when someone whispered, "Crap! She's here!"

Ting, Shelby, and Divana jumped in front of Mia, while Maria ran from the kitchen and everyone together yelled, "SUURPRIIIIISE!"

"What is this?" Mia asked, stunned to see her friends sporting sparkly blue party hats. Ting and Shelby took turns hugging Mia and wishing her a happy birthday while her mom kissed her on the cheek and decorated her wavy hair with a white party hat.

"I know you don't want a big fuss, but I couldn't help planning a little dinner with some friends." Divana searched Mia's face for a register of approval.

"Thanks, Mom, this is really nice." She felt a small lump in her throat. She'd had a few birthday parties as a kid — the typical school friends and cake, presents, and funny games — but never a surprise party. Mia felt sweetness inside as she settled herself at the table while Maria served them a four-course meal that began with beef-tipped tacos dripping in caramelized onions and spicy peppers. Maria's homemade queso dip with buckets of tortilla chips and tamales made the second course, and sugared churros with caramel and chocolate dipping sauces were piled onto their plates as a pre-dessert tasting that finished out the dining with a candlelit caramelized flan and a round of happy birthday to Mia.

"This is ecstasy!" Ting sang as she ate the flan. "I can't believe I've lived all these years and never tried flan!"

After the meal, Mateo played DJ with the downloaded music list he'd chosen in honor of the birthday girl; most of the songs were in Spanish, which he sang too, making Mia love the music even more. Ting surprised everyone with her K-pop moves, and Shelby demonstrated how flexible she was from years of ballet training. Divana pulled out a piñata, and Mia and her friends screamed in glee.

"I know you're mature teenagers, but I couldn't help myself." Divana laughed as she hung the piñata from an old hook in the ceiling, and Shelby rubbed her hands together.

Jumping to the floor, it was Mateo whose hit split the cardboard in two. Mia, Ting, and Shelby laughed and scurried after the treats, pushing and grabbing for various bagged candies, lollies, and lip glosses Mia's mom had stuffed inside.

A man appeared in Maria's doorway, holding an envelope and watching everyone scramble on the floor for trinkets. "Mia, forgive me," he said as she looked to see her father announcing his presence. "I'm late."

Mateo sat confused at who had arrived and what to do with a lip gloss.

Getting to her feet, Mia brushed off the shredded piñata papers from her jeans and walked to greet her father. "Hey," she said, startled to see Charles stepping into the humble home; Maria, quick with her welcoming spirit, swooped over and introduced herself and her son.

Hugging Mia, Charles kissed Divana on the cheek while Mia introduced him to her friends. "Oh, you're the Romeno girl; I've known your father for a few years now," Charles said and took a seat at the edge of Maria's old brown recliner while Maria served him an iced tea.

"Yeah," Shelby said, "my dad gets around." She opened a bag of sour candies and poured all the contents into her mouth while poor Mateo looked on in envy; his mother had capped him for the night.

"And this is my friend Ting Chen."

"Chen, you don't happen to be related to big boss Yoo Mon Chen, the foreign film director?"

Ting shook her head. "No, he's Japanese," she explained sweetly. "Although my grandma does love his films."

A weird noise started coming from behind the couch, distracting Mia while she seated herself on the couch ready to open presents. Taking her dad's envelope from the top, Mia and the rest of the crew turned to watch Mateo snarl aggressively at Charles.

"Mateo!" Maria said, chastising her son while Divana congratulated Charles for arriving just in time for presents.

"You okay?" Mia asked, but Mateo would not take his gaze off of Charles until Maria began saying something in Spanish that seemed to dissuade him.

"I'm so sorry, Mr. Marazza — Mateo is not always so warm to men," Maria explained.

"Oh, no worries, it's fine — " Charles laughed it off. "— kids are kids, right? In my business you see so many different kinds of people, I understand."

Mia stiffened.

Someone suggested opening presents, and Maria agreed, smiling broadly. Not sure what else to do, Mia added an "okay" and began with the envelope her father had handed her.

"Wow . . ." Mia pulled out a single ticket to the North Elite Preparatory High cruise weekend.

Her father explained, "I was so surprised to not see your name on the list for the cruise weekend, thinking it must be a money thing, so I got you a ticket and booked you in the best room money can buy. Well, the biggest one on the cruise at least."

Shelby muttered, "Oh great, now I have to go too."

"Well, I'm going." Ting added quietly.

"And —" Charles added, "I'll be making a little appearance!"

The three girls looked at him as if he had just told them sour news.

"Really —" Mia asked. "Why?"

"Well, there's going to be some movie people there, producers — board members, just a little schmoozing with the kids — a little PR and I need to publicize my documentary," Charles added to Mia's blank stare.

"Documentary? On what?" Divana asked.

"I'm up for a lifetime achievement award, such an honor, but of course we don't need to talk about this here. It's just a little film to show my life, my family, and highlight my upcoming projects," Charles tried to steer Mia back to opening her gifts. For someone who loved attention, he looked uncomfortable for the first time with all eyes on him.

"Charles, Mia cannot be in a documentary." Divana's voice was steady and thick with measured instruction.

Shelby began fiddling with Chip's ear while Ting watched Mateo.

"Well, of course she has to be; she's my daughter, Dee. I understand it's daunting to be on film, but the world is going to know sooner or later who you are, and . . ." Charles said as Divana stood up and Mateo lunged for Charles. Flying backward in the recliner, his feet went belly up while the chair crashed into the wall, knocking off the nearest picture frames. Charles jumped up faster than Mateo could get to him, dusted himself off, and tried to rehang the pictures.

Maria came to the rescue, blocking Mateo and taking the picture frame. "Do not worry, they need dusting," she said, setting down the cracked frame of her late father.

The ruckus had somehow calmed everyone, and despite her frustration, Divana had taken a step back, looked at Mia with her intense green-golden eyes, and determined she would be calm.

"I think I should be going; I only intended to drop in and give you my gift." Charles checked his black-and-gold watch. "I want you to have the best year here in LA, Mia, and I'll do whatever it takes to make that happen." He came to Mia and held her hands in his. Looking off to Divana, he added, "We'll talk about the documentary later, but if you don't want Mia to be in it, then that's just how it will be," Charles promised a tight-lipped, arms-crossed Divana. "We'll just have to be a bit more secretive about things. "He looked around the room at Mia's friends, who all nodded. "Right, Maria, thank you for the hospitality. I am so appreciative of your kindness to my family. Divana, please forgive my oversight. I'll call you after my dinner meeting tonight. Shelby, Ting, Mateo, lovely to meet you officially."

Shelby was still holding out her arm in what looked like an attempt to block Mateo.

Heading to the door, Charles turned to Mia. "For so many years, all I longed for was to see you on your birthday, lovely girl. Mia, you are perfect, but I'm not surprised because so is the woman who raised you." He left as everyone fell silent.

"Well," Maria broke the quiet, "he may not know how yet to be a father, but he does have a way of melting hearts." She stared at the vacant door where Charles had only just stood.

The rest of the evening passed smoothly, and Mia found herself enjoying opening the rest of her presents, beginning with a hand-knitted ivory-and-plum scarf from Maria, who insisted the colors would complement Mia's fair skin for the fall season. Mateo reminded Mia that his gift was the cookies and the self-control he had shown at not eating half of them before giving them to her. Ting's gift, a small flat box, was a running watch with a dusty-pink band, equipped with both GPS and a tracker that linked to Ting's phone and computer.

"You know, in case you get lost."

Thanking Ting and wondering when she could tell her friends the revelation about her grandfather, she opened Shelby's present next to see a jeweled framed picture of Mia, Ting, and Shelby taken the night of the fundraiser. Below was a small, elegant engraving that read, *Thanks for saving me.* The three girls knew the picture represented the weight of something unexplainable that had happened that night.

"This is really lovely, Shelby."

"It's nothing, not like a fancy watch." Shelby poked Ting, who was caught yawning.

"Sorry, I'm so sorry. I'm not bored. I ate too much, dang it."

"Don't forget mine!" Divana pulled out an unwrapped weighty book with a few ribbons popping out from inside the thick pages.

Her mother's gift was a homemade photo album. It was stocked full of gorgeous photos of Mia from birth to their arrival in LA, programs of things she'd done in school and ticket stubs from the past fifteen years. "Mom, when did you do all this?" Mia rifled through pages of glued pictures, birthday cards, and memorabilia from her different schools. Every page was jammed with memories of their life together.

"Oh, here and there, I've been working on it since the summer." Divana got up to start helping clean as the party was drawing to a close. Mia and the girls poured over the old pictures of uneven hair-cuts and years of missing teeth, laughing at Mia's adorable toddler years when she'd mostly run around in a diaper.

"Mia, you're so cute! I like how this shows all the different places you've lived, makes me feel like I know you better." Ting flipped through the pictures from her years in different states. Flashes of old rooms visited her mind. Drawing her attention to the picture of her on the little red playground, she remembered discovering the monkey bars that year. "Is that your mom with you?" Ting asked while Maria got up to clean after Divana refused to leave the mess to the host.

"Yeah." Mia remembered her elementary graduation where the fuzzy picture was taken.

"You know . . ." Ting dropped her voice. "That's the first picture your mom's been in."

Shelby plopped on the couch after her trip to the bathroom, the two girls bouncing up, flipping the book shut.

"What? No." Mia opened the book back to the picture of her as a little girl in her yellow-flowered graduation gown. Her mom was there, holding a small bouquet of daisies and standing behind Mia with a radiant smile. "Here she is." Mia flipped to an earlier page where she was a baby. Her mother was holding her; that much Mia could tell from her lean frame and long golden hair, but her face was out of frame. "Wait, not that one." Mia scanned through the rest of the book.

"Does she not like having her picture taken?" Ting asked.

"I would if I looked like her." Shelby put her feet on the coffee table and leaned in to see the graduation photo Mia had turned back to. "You know, Mia, you're really lucky. Your mom loves you."

"Yeah, she does. I am." She'd have to ask her mom about the pic-ture thing later. Looking at Shelby, Mia thought she saw something cross her eyes. "Are you okay?"

Shelby smiled. "I'm dandy. Happy for you, of course. Sure, it's sometimes annoying that the one thing mom's are meant to do, mine doesn't. Personally, to me, she's just the carrier. I guess, in a way it's encouraging to see you and your mom, that not everyone is screwed from attachment."

"You think?" Mia asked.

"Oh yeah. I mean, don't get me wrong, I used to hate girls like you." Shelby leaned into Mia "But that's the thing, being friends with you doesn't make me hate you or even want to strangle you, especially considering you get yourself into the worst predicaments. No, seriously, it's good — like an idea of what life could be like someday. If I'm ever a mom."

"I'm not sure I want kids," Ting added.

"What? You goof?" Shelby turned to Ting. "You're the one I would peg for having, like, five baby geniuses."

"Me?" Ting asked, shocked. "No way! I like my personal space, for one, and I'll probably never date till I'm forty, and by then my eggs will be too old to fertilize, so . . ."

"Ting!" Mia interjected. "Why can't you date until you're forty?"

"It's not that I can't; it's that I probably won't. No one ever wants to date the computer nerd. Did you know the higher a woman's IQ, the smaller the pool of men she has to draw from; men are attracted to someone they are equal with or slightly higher in intelligence, and then, of course, add the fact that I'm not a size small." Ting stopped when Divana and Maria entered from the kitchen.

"What?" Maria exclaimed. "No, no, you cannot speak that way about yourself, you beautiful girl. You should be proud of having enough food to eat and books to study." Maria patted her round belly. Turning beet red, Ting mumbled something about feeling bad for the less fortunate while Maria carried on. "Girls, you must remember, if you want to change, that is okay, but you change for you, or else who you become, you will not love." Mateo belted out his favorite television theme song. It was as if he was calling the room to see him as he was, someone who was different from and limited in the world's eyes but so alive and at peace within himself. Someone who liked himself. Mia hoped as she officially turned sixteen tomorrow, she could keep striving to be more like the Mateos of the world.

Chasing a Redhead

Rows of camera tracks lined the once pristine courtyard of North Elite Preparatory. Overnight the school was infiltrated by a small legion of Hollywood junkies, all scrambling to get the campus ready for filming, which began tomorrow, the day before Thanksgiving.

Mia spent the better part of the day running to classes and trying to avoid any interaction near the courtyard, which was manageable since the gym now doubled as a dine-in study hall with the school's cafe and courtyard overtaken by set designers.

"How are you standing all this?" Shelby drank from her eco-friendly water bottle and rolled her eyes at a cluster of passing junior girls. Three girls in the group were in matching pop art jean jackets, plastered with Charles's face on the back. Shrugging, Mia didn't answer. It had been two weeks since her birthday, and she *still* had not been able to speak to her father about the news from Detective Batair; that her grandfather was most likely alive, a homicidal maniac and gunning for her death. "I guess it could be worse," Shelby admitted while Mia and her friends watched one of the jacketed girls throw her banana peel at the garbage, giving Mia a full view of her father's smiling face. "He could be naked."

"There you are!" Ting bounded in through the open gymnasium doors. "I was looking for you guys outside." She waved a piece of paper and sat at their table. "Guess what this is," she started and, without pausing, said, "a scholarship letter to intern at VanBoi Biotech!" Ting wiggled when Shelby grabbed it and read the formal admission letter that invited Ting to join the prestigious internship program as VanBoi's new junior-level specialist in the applied sciences program.

"Ting! Wow and congrats! That's amazing!" Mia beamed.

"I had no idea I was even being considered, but Dr. Fern said they evaluated all the project finalists for the internship, so I guess they liked our presentation."

"*Your* presentation," Mia said, "but I can take credit for something. I finally got my learner's permit!"

"That turd!" Ting grabbed something inside her bag and scowled. "Sorry, Mia, that's so exciting about your permit! I can't wait to ride with you — he must have slipped it in this morning." She pulled out a small black plastic box. Ting threw it on the table while Mia and Shelby looked at the blinking device. "It's Terry's tracker, and *apparently*, it's been in my bag all day."

"A tracker?" Shelby pressed the flashing button. "What does he — OUCH!"

"Yeah, don't press that button." Ting logged into her device. "I can just hear Auntie . . . *Yu-Ting, your cousin is your responsibility; he needs you to graduate Yu-Ting, we expect more from you, don't stress-eat Yu-Ting . . . .*"

Mia didn't understand the pressure of extended family, but it still seemed unfair that Ting so often had to be responsible for her older cousin.

"I thought they were watching his phone." Shelby asked.

Grabbing her highlighter, Mia went back to circling paragraphs in her economics book, *How the Rich Rule Society and You,* while Ting explained that her cousin had lost his phone along with most other privileges for the time being. The little black box winking back at them, was his parents temporary solution to Ting's refusal to be Terry's babysitter.

"Such a troubled soul. Oh, what about this?" Shelby asked nudging Mia to look at her screen and clicking on the picture of a white mid-length dress with silver beaded fringe. "I'll take that as a maybe."

"I hate filling things out by hand." Ting searched her bag for a pen, pencil, or something to write with. "I can hardly read my own writing. Mia, can I borrow your pen?"

"Sure."

Shelby cleared her throat. "Aah, Mia . . . didn't you say Charles wasn't on campus?"

"Yeah."

"What? How is this possible?" Ting slammed her hands on the table, along with Mia's winning pen from the fundraiser and repeatedly pressed the power button. "My computer won't turn back on. Ohh nooo, not today! Why today!"

Mia caught the faint scent of singed hair.

"It's just, I think I saw Charles," Shelby pointed to a large line of people filing past the doorway, two men at the rear laden with bulky cameras.

"Crap, that looks problematic." Mia bit her lower lip.

"Guys, I *have* to go and get my backup laptop." Ting stood and shoved the broken device into her bag.

"Doesn't she need this?" Shelby picked up the beeper with her two fingers, but Ting was already scooting out of the gymnasium door, hurrying away apologetically from the red-haired woman she'd bumped into.

Red hair.

Grabbing her bag, Mia pulled crinkled papers out of several pockets until she found the crimped photographs from her time with Batair. Pointing to the water-stained photo of the red-haired woman she'd seen with her father; she knew it was the same woman she'd just seen.

"I don't know, Mia. I didn't really see her face, but the fiery red hair looks about right."

"It's her, I know it."

"Well then, let's go find out what she's up to next." Shelby stashed her tablet in her purse and stood.

"What?" But Shelby was up and already walking. Mia stuffed her things into her bag and hurried after her.

Trying to keep a quick pace, the girls breezed down the hall-way waving to Coach Drake who sat in his office enjoying a mochi doughnut.

Once outside, they were hit with fresh sunlight and a clear view of the woman crossing the west athletic field. Mia swung her bag in front of her and tried digging down to the bottom, from where she pulled out Maria's knitted scarf. Shelby watched her wrap the kit-ted muffler around her mouth, making sure to keep her hair tucked inside.

"Disguise," she muttered.

Shelby's eyes narrowed.

Taking something from the inside pocket of her school blazer, Shelby pulled a rhinestone beanie onto Mia's head, unwrapped Mia's scarf, and arranged it to fall over her shoulders, adding a pair of sun-glasses and stepping back. "Much better."

"Doesn't really matter."

The girls made it to the courtyard. Scanning the crowd, Mia saw the red-haired woman pause at a food truck, order, and speak with the barista, casually throwing back her mane of glory and laughing with the man behind the counter. She took a coffee and headed toward a black trailer.

"Shelby!" someone called, startling Mia.

"Will." Shelby nudged Mia to take off her glasses.

"Mia?" He squinted as he strolled up. "What are you girls up to?" He glanced at Mia, whose eyes drifted over to the woman, now showing identification to the security guards and pointing to the trailer.

"Oh, you know, just checking out the movie stuff. You?" Shelby asked.

"Yeah, it's wild around here. I feel guilty, I'm hardly doing any schoolwork these days, but hopefully it doesn't bite me in the end. I got a small role in the film though." Will watched Mia.

"Really?" Mia turned her attention to Will.

"Yeah, I was just instructing some of the freshmen on student council stuff, and one of the producers said he liked my aura, wanted me to come audition in his trailer, and then, next thing I know, Principal Florence is telling me I'm in some scenes. No lines, but hey, I'm pleased."

"Well, it can't hurt that you're gorgeous," Shelby said, causing Will to smile.

"Ah, Shelbs, you should audition too, both of you. They are still looking for small roles, I heard, probably want students so they can pay less, but money is money, right?"

"Yeah, thanks, but no." Shelby kept her eye on the woman.

Mia glanced over. Someone was waving the woman towards the trailer.

"Hey, Will," Mia said, "we gotta go, but congratulations."

Will sidestepped her. "Mia . . . I've been wondering . . . could you help me with some of the cruise decorations this weekend?"

Having caught Shelby in a rare expression of surprise, Mia stammered while trying to explain to Will why she would be a terrible choice to help with any type of party decorating. Her room still had bare bookshelves, apart from a few mementos, including the pop-up cruise ship he'd sent.

Unfazed by her resistance, he explained, "I really want a fresh perspective, someone with diverse life experience." He stared hard at Mia and stood close. "I think you have so much to offer, and I'd really love your help . . . ."

Mia had started to feel a little sweaty in the itchy beanie. "I don't think having lived in Texas qualifies me as diverse."

Shelby grabbed her arm to indicate that the woman was disappearing into the trailer.

"I'll make sure she's there Monday night!" Shelby pulled Mia into the crowd. They made their way along the edge of the grass, where students laid out in warmer weather, stopping at the campus café. The glass doors were closed, but Mia could see the inside clustered with movie set personnel.

"Thanks a lot, Shelb." Mia watched the trailer from across the courtyard. By now the woman had gone inside.

"I'll go with you, okay?" Shelby said, watching someone bounce toward them, her shoulder-length hair dyed many shades of caramel. "Oh, not her," Shelby muttered while Mia popped her sunglasses back on.

"Shelby girl! I've not seen you forever."

Shelby failed to dodge her side hug. "Gretchen."

"So perfect finding you because I'm working on gathering funds for our winter extravaganza. I know your dad's always a big donor and —"

Shelby held up her hand to stop her. "I get it, I'll tell him."

"Oh, you're the best, really, who's your friend?"

Mia laughed under her breath.

"Well, this is —"

"Oxana," Mia said, masking her voice with a made-up accent.

"Oh, hey, checking out our school? I'm sure you'll like it, just make sure you have other options, they don't let just anyone in."

Shelby looked dumbstruck.

"So, you'll talk to your father?"

"Ah, yeh . . . Oxana will come with me to ask, won't ya?" Shelby nudged Mia hard. "So, you Will's assistant now?"

"What?" Gretchen giggled. "I'm only helping; you know he does so much for the school. I'm just trying to offer my skills, helping lick away the details he's not crazy about."

"I bet your good with the licking and all, well Gretch, gotta go, lots to show Oxana," and she grabbed Mia's arm to pull her away and toward Pinky's Donut food truck.

Mia watched people walk away with blueberry glazed crumb cakes, and right when she decided she'd like one, Shelby let out an expletive. Turning to see what Shelby was gawking at, Mia saw that her father had emerged from the trailer, following the red-haired woman.

A small cluster of students inched their way closer to Charles the minute he stepped on the grass, begging the security guards to let them ask for autographs. Something about the way people idolized him, the way they were infatuated with him, the image of the woman on his arm, brought a bitter taste up in the back of Mia's throat.

"What is he doing with her?" Mia watched as the woman clung to her father's arm while he wrote something on a piece of paper and slipped it into her purse. "What's that he's giving her?" But Shelby wasn't standing with Mia anymore. Shelby wasn't anywhere Mia could see, and after waiting a good five minutes, her father disappeared back into his trailer. Mia's phone was silent, and Shelby was still nowhere to be seen.

With no answered text from Shelby, Mia didn't know what else to do but head back to school, this time taking the long way to avoid any Charles fans. She wove between tents and around staircases protruding from generator-fueled trailers, the largest tent full of seamstresses who beaded and buttoned yards of silk on dress forms. As Mia recovered from bumping a woman in a headset who seemed not to have noticed their collision, the woman kept pace with the stocky man beside her.

"Then FIND someone else," he spat.

"Sir, it's just, with the holiday, I'm not able to hire anyone until Friday and —"

"WHAT?" he blurted. "This is . . . I never heard that, no I refuse that. See, here, you! Come!" He summoned Mia over to him.

Hoping she'd misunderstood Michael Novak's instruction, Mia kept walking while he called to her again.

"You! Come here!"

He shuffled toward Mia in his coffee-stained vest, grease clogging his hairline.

"Me?" she asked while he scoffed at her.

"Yes, you! I'm offering you a part in my movie."

"Sorry, I'm not an actress."

But he was already instructing the assistant to get Mia's picture and information.

"If you could only smile slightly," the woman said and snapped a Polaroid of Mia. "Here, hold this while I take your information. Don't touch this part while it develops."

"Listen, I'm a student and —"

"Oh, that's not a problem. Michael wants you for the death scene tomorrow. It would only be half a day —"

"Mia!" Shelby called, barreling her way through a dress fitting while a model yelled that the seamstress had drawn blood. "I — what's this?"

"Excuse me, I am collecting her information." The woman frowned.

"Excuse me, who are *you*?" Shelby demanded while Mia tried to explain.

"They want me to play dead. Look, lady, I'm sorry but I can't."

"Yeah." Shelby pulled Mia away. "She's not dying today. Mia, I think the woman is . . . I think she's gone to your dad's house." Shelby pulled out her phone.

"Charles's house? But he's here."

"Yeah but she's literally pulling in to his residence." Shelby said, eying a map on her phone.

"And how would you know that?"

"I dropped it in her purse."

"You did? Why!"

"Not *why* but *what*. Mia, we need to go to his house and see *what* she's doing there," Shelby said with narrowed eyes and a look that told Mia her mind was already far, far ahead.

"But school and . . ." Only Mia didn't care about school right now. What she needed, what she'd been wanting for weeks now was information and answers, and if Shelby was willing to help, she'd take it.

CHAPTER 14

Dubious

"Jump on my back."

"No, you jump on my back."

"No, really, jump on my back . . . I do these at practice."

"I'm sure you do Mia, don't take this the wrong way but, you're a little scrawny."

"And you're not?"

"Well, I'm no Tia-Clair, but I did practice ballet for ten years and —"

"Okay, fine. You boost me." Mia hoped her compliance would speed things up.

Shelby leaned against the concrete fence, squatting and interlacing her fingers so Mia could step on her hands. Holding Mia's foot, Shelby hoisted her up, while Mia used her thrust to reach up onto the fence ledge and grab a handful of spiral evergreens that lined the wall. She could feel the plants rip from of the soil as she pulled and Shelby started to buckle under her weight. Down the girls went, Mia's arms flailing while she landed right on top of Shelby.

"I thought you had it!" Shelby moaned, rubbing her dirt stained arm where Mia left a footprint.

"I told you, I should boost you," Mia said, feeling the pressure to hurry and wondering what to do with the small tree she'd ripped out of its resting place. Throwing the bush aside, she positioned her leg deciding she'd hold Shelby this time. The sooner they got to the top of the hill and assessed what was going on, the better.

"Fine, you can lift me up," Shelby said, "but don't push too soon — and don't freak out if I get heavy and drop me if someone comes along —"

"Shelby, just do it!"

In the next few minutes, Shelby was successfully standing in a bed of wet dirt that rested atop the wide stucco wall guarding Mia's father's home from prying eyes. Leaning down, she offered her hand but Mia found it easier to jump up, grabbing the ledge and swinging her legs over until she was laying horizontally on the edge of the wall.

"That was different," Shelby said, not readily admitting she was impressed by Mia's agility. All the training for upcoming Strategy & Survival game was paying off as Mia's body, still small and lean, was retaining an unusual amount of strength. Even her teammates, Justice and Chet mostly, commented on how much she'd improved and how impressed they were that a girl could keep up so well.

Squatting down on the fence and peering up at the mountain of landscaping they had to hike through, Shelby fumed, "Why the hell is your dad's house up so high?"

"I guess he likes the view. Ready?" On the count of three, both girls jumped down, landing in soft mulch and wild wall germander. They began hiking up the hill, scaling boulders and pulling on shrubs and tree branches to compete with the steep incline and slippery soil. Sweating by the top, they came to a shorter, less threatening iron fence and easily climbed over it. Landing on the other side, they hid behind a row of blooming Japanese maple trees.

"Dang, your dad's house is probably one of the worst to do this with." Shelby wiped her eyes, and a salty bead of sweat rolled down her face. "AND makeup is smearing."

"So, I only know of three entrances, the study, office door, and back door, of which the last two are all glass . . . I'm thinking we go around back, to the study first." Mia said, reading a car license plate: *SEXY LIPS*.

"Look at you, going all sleuthy on me." Shelby patted Mia's sweat-soaked back and fixed her scarf, which had fallen down around her neck. "Now!"

The girls made a run for it, just as Mia's phone buzzed in her back pocket. When they made it to the side of the house, Mia threw herself against the stone chimney, holding her heart to calm her breath. She pulled down her scarf while Shelby crept to the corner, drew back, and muffed her own scream. Waving her hand in front of her face. "Just a creepy statue . . . But now that I think about it, does your dad have a guard dog? I'm having visions of a big black pit bull making taffy with my thigh."

Mia peered around the corner to peek at the stone muse playing a harp and shook her head. "Wait, I think I hear someone . . . ." She held up her hand and stood as still as the goddess statue.

"I think," Shelby whispered, "that's my stomach."

"Oh, then let's go."

The girls ducked, creeping along to the study door. Shelby grabbed the door handle, and to their surprise, it unlocked.

Peeking her head inside, Mia slid into the empty study. The tidy den was just as she remembered. Nothing had changed apart from a few fall decorations hung up over the fireplace and a single picture of Mia, in her favorite red rain jacket, sitting in a silver frame on Charles's desk.

"Do you hear that? Sounds like someone's on a treadmill."

"Right, that's the gym." Mia explained, pulling her attention away from the picture and remembering when she used the equipment filled room to talk to Shelby about the casino fiasco.

"So, what now? There's probably no way to get in there without being seen . . . ." But she paused at hearing a new noise coming from the opposite wall.

"What's over there?" Shelby probed.

"The kitchen and living room, which all connect to the dining room and main hall. It makes a big circle with the staircase in the middle." Mia remembered it well. *It's not every day a girl visits her father's house for the first time.* "It could be my dad's assistant, Nimmy."

Both girls' eyes widened when they heard the pounding stop. Someone was walking toward the door, and in seconds, Mia and Shelby dashed behind the executive desk and hid underneath just as the door opened. Mia could have kicked herself for not pulling the desk chair into the remaining space to conceal their hiding spot. If someone came around to sit at the desk, they were goners. The red-haired lady, she assumed, walked across the study, carrying a scent that smelled strongly of gardenia and sweat. Mia held her knees tight to her chest and shut her mouth in a thin line exchanging looks with Shelby.

Tempering her breathing like she'd seen her mother do for yoga, Mia waited, distracted by Shelby's heartbeat thudding against her chest. Shelby poked Mia in the thigh and asked, through the bulge of her eyes, the same thing Mia was thinking — what was the woman doing in here? She wasn't, thankfully, using the desk or sitting on the couch. But she wasn't leaving.

Mia heard beeping. She leaned forward. She had to see what was happening. Just as it sounded like something spun and clicked, Mia caught sight of a painting, swung open on a hinge from the wall, and beside it, a safe. Pulling herself back into the security of the underneath desk space, she smacked her head and silently screamed into her knees while the woman closed the safe, clicked the lock button to secure whatever was hidden inside.

So — Mia thought, as the pain in the back of her head subsided, *SEXY LIPS is taking something, possibly money, from my father's hidden wall safe. Interesting.*

Shelby nudged her, but Mia shook her head. Carefully listening to the woman shift across the room, Mia was hoping she was setting out to leave. Shelby twisted her flexible body somehow low enough to the ground. Mia could feel the woman walking toward them, and she silently swore at the approaching pink-and-black sneakers. Shelby was stuck, contorted with her face against the carpet. Mia began planning her confession. She'd tell them she'd thought her father was home. She'd say she got scared when she heard a woman's voice. Mia could smell rubber from the new sneakers. *Here it comes.* The woman stood by the desk, placed something down, and began walking away, back toward the door. Holding their breath, the girls waited in the silent room. Mia and Shelby looked at each other and exhaled in relief.

Unwinding herself out from under the desk space, Shelby rubbed her legs while Mia stretched hers, tingling with loss of feeling from being still so long. Pulling open the black-framed painting, Mia showed Shelby the safe.

"So, that's what she was doing?" Shelby whispered.

Did her father know?

The girls heard talking. They lunged toward the wooden door and plastered their ears to the wood.

"We'll take my car. Please excuse the mess. I've been doing a lot of traveling recently, so it's a bit of an office for me."

"Yes, of course."

"Do you have the chain and sedatives? I don't want to have to use it, but if she is not cooperative, we just need to be prepared."

"Yes, I have both ready. I must explain, I will be bringing protection with me. I don't know what kind of situation we will encounter, one moment please, Crystal."

Mia and Shelby stared wide-eyed at one another again. Protection . . . a sedative . . . a chain? What the hell were these women thinking of doing?

It dawned on Mia that the women were preparing to leave the house, and if left behind, Mia and Shelby would be stuck in her father's house with the security turned on. "Shelby, I think we need to go, like, right now," Mia whispered.

Shelby was still listening by the time Mia made it to the back door, motioning for her to follow. Just as the girls opened the door to the outside, the woman they now knew to be named Crystal, opened the door to the office, catching a glimpse of the outside door closing and clicking shut.

Confused, she hurried to look, examining the yard to see if someone or something was out there. Perhaps figuring it was her imagination, she closed the door, only the wind holding traces of their escape.

Plastered once again against the cool chimney of rare black stones, the girls paused to wait for the women to leave the house.

Mia and Shelby ran back down the steep hill, first over the iron fence and through the brush and dirt, in no time finding themselves scaling the stucco wall. They seemed to be making an easy getaway until a siren started that registered intruders had breached the premises. Shelby lost her balance, fell off the wall, and grabbed Mia's arm, taking her down.

"Run." Shelby jumped up, her knee scraped and bleeding; Mia's wrist was bleeding and already bruising from breaking their fall.

"What a rush!" Shelby yelled once inside her white sports car, peeling away from the parking spot and hitting the curb as she pulled onto the main road.

Mia agreed. For the first time in a long while, she was not so afraid of what was going to happen. A small part of her felt like this was fighting back. Her mom's timely text telling Mia she'd be home late and not to wait up was confirmation. Following the tracker via Ting's texts, the girls followed the dark Tesla into a mall parking lot.

"Won't it look weird wearing these inside?" Mia checked her reflection in the car mirror as Shelby added a beanie to her own head.

"I mean, maybe, but I can make it look like you just got a nose job." Shelby examined Mia's face closely, pulling makeup from her bag. "I mean, most people get one by twenty-five; just a little shadow and everyone would assume you're as vain as the rest of us."

Mia opened the car door. "Wait, have you?"

"Nah, that's the one good thing the carrier passed on."

The mall was buzzing with LED Christmas trees, and classical Christmas ballads, as the girls followed after Crystal past kiosks and around happy shoppers. It was easy to keep an eye from afar on her flowing locks of flaming ginger and easier that they only had to follow one person because Nimmy had stayed in the car.

"Are you sure we shouldn't have split up?" Mia asked, watching Crystal head into a jewelry store, look —" Mia stopped behind a pop-up stall of calendars and Japanese toys.

"What's she getting?" She watched a salesman pull out a small item from behind a glass counter.

"Miss, do you need any help?" A man in a checkered blazer eyed Mia curiously.

"What?" Mia realized she was standing in front of the bikini calendars. "Ooh, no, we're looking for the puppies." But Shelby wasn't standing with her anymore. Instead, she was positioning her-self a few spaces away from Crystal and talking to another jewelry salesperson.

Mumbling about telling Shelby to stop disappearing, Mia shifted over to a pretzel stand waiting till Shelby returned, smiling and swinging a little package around her finger. "Well?" she demanded once inside Shelby's car, the mats soiled brown from their run in the dirt. "What did she buy?"

"A ring. Gold band with a few diamonds."

"WHAT?" *Why would she buy herself a ring? Was it meant to be from her father?*

"People buy dumb things with stolen money —"

But Mia wasn't reassured.

The girls followed the women's car, out of the shopping district and away from the city toward a neighboring town. Ting kept a live stream off the beeper straight to Mia's and Shelby's phones so they could see in real time where the women were going.

"I think my mom's work is around here," Mia said, passing rows of tiny houses. "It's usually in a church. You know — friendlier to addicts."

Watching the tracker lead them to a corner street, Mia tried to remember the name of the church, certain it was just a few blocks away. *Was it St. Paul's of Hope . . . St. Peter's, St. Peter and Paul's?*

"How about, St. Peter! Of the Anglican Church?" Shelby blurted out. "Because that's it." And slowing the car, Shelby pulled it into a short strip mall that sat on the edge of the church lot.

Mia's heart dropped. Her mother worked at this church. Her mind spun, thinking of the conversation the woman had had at her father's house, and unstable thoughts clouded her mind. Were they targeting Divana? Mia tried to explain to Shelby what she was piecing together. "My mom works at *that* church, in there, Shelby

— remember Nimmy? She talked about sedatives and . . . and a weapon!" Mia could feel her anxiety rise with every word.

"Oh boy, oh boy," Shelby muttered.

Mia grabbed her phone and asked, "Who do I call?"

"Mia, are you sure this is where your mom works?"

"I'm sure!" She scrolled through her phone: *a chain, a tranquilizer, and A GUN!* "What if I call my mom and tell her to run?"

"Detective Batair!"

"But, I only have his partner's —" Mia fumbled with her phone, looking for the detective in her contact list. She waited for Dregs to pick up, wincing at the clock as time ticked away. They'd been in the parking lot only minutes, but Mia knew it took seconds for things to turn. "Come on . . . what kind of police person doesn't answer the PHONE!"

"Are you *really* calling to yell in my ear?"

"Detective Dregs, this is Mia Storm. I'm at the Anglican church in High Hills. My mom — she's about to be attacked. It's St. Paul Anglican church . . . St. Peter Paul's of the Anglican . . . It's on Flores STREET!"

Shelby dialed the police station and spoke to a lieutenant.

"Okay." Dregs said and hung up.

"No, I am not eighteen nor with an adult but — leave a note on his desk? What kind of public servant are you?" Shelby cut the phone call.

"The detective is on her way; we gotta go." Mia fumbled to unbuckle herself.

"Their way, okay but Mia — we can't go in there without — we need weapons."

"A weapon? I don't have a weapon! Dreg's, she'll have a gun!"

"I know, all I have is some jumper cables in the back — we can use those to swing around and grab some sticks. I can jam my earring on the end." Shelby showed Mia her pointed silver stud that stuck out like a sharp spike. "That should do, at least to draw some blood and, Dreg's ain't a she, you say they —"

"SHELBY! Not the time!"

The girls clamored out of the car, Shelby rushing to the trunk for jumper cables and Mia running to a nearby tree, jumping up and grabbing a branch, swinging all of her weight to try to break it off. When Shelby ran over, Mia was still thrusting her weight by kicking off the tree with her legs to break the branch.

"Why don't you use a stick? Here!"

"I wasn't looking there! Come on!"

"We should go in the back." Shelby veered to the rear side. "We need to sneak up on them, not give them any warning!" Shelby found the back door down a flight of stairs that smelled like cigarettes and skunk.

It was strange; Mia didn't feel any of the warnings she usually felt even though her mind flashed with the image of her mother lying on the floor looking just as Shelby had weeks ago.

The girls creaked open the door and entered an empty kitchen. Holding tight to their weapons, they were careful not to bump into any of the overpacked shelves filled with pans and baking equip-ment. Shelby reached her hand out to grab a cookie from a plate when Mia slapped it.

"I'm hungry," she pleaded, snatching the cookie and shoving it into her mouth.

"I know my mom's here," Mia said, the smell of peppermint oil and incense growing stronger as they made it to a stairway. The church was old but clean with posters on notice boards supporting holiday therapy groups and an upcoming cookie exchange run by a woman named Edna. Taking the stairs, Mia and Shelby peeked their heads into the empty hallway once on the second floor.

"Shhhh," Shelby said to the buzzing of Mia's phone.

The smell of incense was growing. The same smell her mom brought home from work.

"I hear talking."

"Really?"

"Yeah, oh my God," Mia said. "Can you smell that . . . It's bleach!"

Shelby sniffed and shook her head. "I can't smell what you're smelling!"

"It's this way." Mia turned down another hall. She was now able to see the opening to a large room. Her senses on hyperalert, her body strong and ready for impact — she believed that whatever faced her at the end, she could handle, even conquer if it came down to her and the two women. The girls inched their way to the end of the hallway as the talking grew louder.

"Ah," Shelby whispered. "I smell hay," she said, a note of self-satisfaction that she'd discovered something first. True to what Shelby smelled, a large stack of hay bales sat a few feet from the door, piled high with cornstalks and pumpkins. Mia could overhear conversations about the stress of the upcoming holidays. Creeping down along the threadbare carpet, Mia searched between the spaces between the hay for an open spot where she could see what was on the other side. She could only see a few people's feet and none that looked like her mother's — along with a circle of chairs and a table that supported refreshments. With the constant smell of coffee now filling their noses, a voice, like a woman in pain, cried out from somewhere beyond the group. Mia and Shelby froze. What if her mother was being tortured? The group quieted down, and someone mentioned Divana's name and something about handling a situation.

That was it. That was all Mia needed. She looked at Shelby and the two knew they needed to make a run for it. Shelby silently counted down with her fingers, *three, two, one*, and they both charged forward, jumping over the hay pile, through the shocked bystanders yelling over spilling their coffee, and ran toward the door, where another scream pierced their ears. Shelby yelled at the top of her lungs in Italian, while Mia burst through the office door, positioned with their weapons and ready to fight.

It took some time to register what they saw. Mia's mom *was* inside the room, only she was not screaming out in pain. Nimmy was there too, along with the red-haired woman, Crystal, but the only person who looked to be in distress was a puffy-eyed ill-kempt woman whimpering over a dog laying deathly still in the middle of the floor.

"MIA!" Divana exclaimed. "SHELBY! Girls, what are you doing here? And WHAT are you holding?"

Another body burst through the door from behind, shoving Mia to the side. Detective Dregs had arrived, holding a gun out and yelling for everyone to put their hands up.

"Oh MY GOD!" Crystal cried, running to the dog and putting her body over him, careful not to touch the stained blanket he lay upon.

"Storm, what's going on? Everyone else, quiet — NOW," Dregs yelled.

A few men had run to the doorway offering Divana their help.

"We . . ." Mia began, clearing her voice. "Something shady is going on here," Mia said accusingly to Crystal.

"Excuse me, I don't even know who you are." Crystal sneered.

"You don't know her, huh?" Shelby demanded, lowering her hands that still held the jumper cables. "Not working to try and get her killed!"

"Of course NOT!"

"Mom," Mia added, "we HEARD them planning something at Charles's house —something with drugs and a chain and —" "Mia pointed to Nimmy "— SHE has a GUN!"

Divana and the woman she was consoling looked aghast. Detective Dregs focused her gun on Nimmy, and Shelby swung her weapon for good measure. The woman looked like she'd swallowed a few of Shelby's explosive sour gummies as she stood against the wall and cowered. "Yes, I — this is so," she said, Mia and Shelby taken aback that she admitted it. "I had an incident years ago with a canine and . . . since then, I've been quite terrified of them." She watched the unmoving, soiled dog. "I have my permit thought if you need to see it." She nodded to her purse draped across her body while keeping her hands in the air.

"Why does that dog look dead?" Detective Dregs asked, triggering the woman to begin sobbing again.

Divana spoke up first. "This dog is *not* dead; he's sedated. I'm sorry, Detective, but there's been a BIG mistake. Mia, there is nothing here that needs police attention or your concern."

Dregs lowered their gun, clipping it to its holder and stared at Mia. "You called me for a sedated dog?"

"No!" Shelby retorted. "We saw her take money from Charles's safe. You took money; don't deny it!" Shelby pointed at Crystal, but the effect was not what Mia expected.

"Yes, I did, so?"

"So, you deny — wait, what?" Shelby began, but Divana spoke up.

"Mia, Shelby, I don't know what you are referring to, what this woman does on her own time with whomever is her business, but my dealings with her have been pleasant and professional. She is here to adopt this dog from Janet. Janet acquired this dog through me from Charles and, since then, has decided to rehome him due to personal reasons. Janet has been extremely upset during the whole process, and this is not making it any easier. Detective, I'm sorry to trouble you." Divana eyed Mia. "But would it be possible to request your help in getting Janet home so that she may get some rest and attend to her family waiting for her." Divana flashed her green-and-gold-flecked eyes to the detective.

"Yes." Dregs ushered the woman to collect her things. "Ladies, do me a favor and don't call me." They left the room and broke up the small crowd who'd gathered to see the excitement.

"Nimmy, would you get the blanket I brought?" Crystal picked up the sleeping dog in her arms and headed to the door while cradling the puppy.

"Certainly." Nimmy followed after with a small bag, leaving the stained towel for Mia to stare at.

Turning back, Crystal paused. "You are lucky I'm not going to press charges against your daughter and her reckless friend." She left the room.

"Really, Mia?" Divana watched her daughter. "What the hell are you two girls doing — skipping school and following two grown women . . . not to mention how you came to conclude they were doing something devious!"

"Mom, you have to believe me! It sounded so bad when we heard — Aren't you even concerned that she was taking money from Charles's safe! In his house!"

"No, I'm not. She has some loan agreement with your dad; she is short on cash, and he's helping her. Not the wisest thing, but he can do whatever he wants with his money. *But* how did you even get to the point of discovering that, if your father wanted to, he could press charges. As for the dog, my client Janet had a relapse. The poor dog got lost when one of her kids left the back door open. Not only did she lose her job, but she had to find a new home for the dog her children had grown terribly attached to. That is why, once her family found the lost puppy, we decided to rehome him quickly so Janet and the little guy could both get better and find the care and support they need."

Shelby was strangely quiet as Mia seemed to only be able to continue saying a muffled, "Oh."

"Look, we can talk about this more at home. Can I trust you two to get home and allow me to finish out this workday without any more unpleasant surprises?"

"Of course, Ms. D," Shelby said.

"Then, Mia, I will see you at home in an hour. Shelby, please wish your father and that wonderful family friend Louie a very Happy Thanksgiving from Mia and me."

"Yes, I will do that as soon as he's back from vacation," Shelby said. "And . . . I'm really sorry about tonight. It was my idea to follow the woman. We saw her at school, visiting Mr. Marazza's trailer and . . . I honestly thought it was a good idea to see what she was up to, considering Mia has her picture in her backpack and she was at our school — strolling around like she owned the place. It was dumb. I feel bad about begging Mia to skip her last two classes, even though today they were just study halls in preparation for Thanksgiving break . . . ."

Mia marveled at how Shelby could have kept going, talking her way out of this mess to her mom, but Divana stopped her and asked about Shelby's father.

"Oh yeah, he's in Singapore checking out a new casino."

"Well then —" Divana decided "— you'll join us tomorrow for our first real home-cooked turkey. If you attempt to say no, I'll remind you that you owe me some housework to make up for barging in at my place of work and partnering with my daughter to cause such a scene."

"Oh, what? Sure, I mean I can do that. Yes, ma'am." Shelby grinned.

Rolling down her window ten minutes later to collect her bag of tacos, Shelby shoved a salty chip into her mouth. "So, you think the dog is going to be okay?"

"I mean, he did look a bit banged up, not to mention the blood, but I don't think my mom would have been okay if she didn't think he'd be in good hands. That was so strange —" Mia accepted the taco Shelby had gotten for her after she'd insisted she wasn't hungry. She was actually starving, but all the misunderstandings, mostly upsetting her mom, had given her a stomach ache. Taking a bite after unwrapping the stuffed tortilla, her eyes widened in pleasure, realizing what she'd been missing.

"I know, heaven in a taco. Good thing I ordered extra." And the girls chowed down, relieved everything had mostly turned out in their favor.

Of course, Mia hadn't spoken to her mother yet, but with the Thanksgiving holiday tomorrow, she felt optimistic her punishment wouldn't be too bad considering Shelby was now coming over to join them.

It would have never occurred to Mia that after the day's events, she had somehow threatened Detective Dregs's safety. She had no idea as she sat in Shelby's car eating tacos that the detective was being taken to the hospital, alive but with three bullets in their back.

CHAPTER 15

Heat

Mia watched turkey grease drip drop into a saucepan while the room filled with the smell of boiled innards. "Are you sure that's safe?"

"Yes." Divana laughed. "It gives the gravy a deeper flavor. Now leave me alone to follow these instructions." Divana read from a cookbook and shooed Mia out of the kitchen, Chip hiding behind, hoping for scraps.

The doorbell rang and in no time, Mia, Shelby, Divana, and the Gallardos were all closely seated around their four-person kitchen table, bumping elbows as they passed plates piled high with whipped potatoes, onion-topped beans, spicy sausage stuffing, and turkey slices smothered in peppered gravy. Cloth napkins borrowed from the church, a crystal floral centerpiece from Shelby, and Maria's famous caramel-dipped churros completed the holiday feast, leaving Mia stuffed and sleepy as she stretched out on her bed while Shelby fiddled with her computer, still trying to find Mia a dress for the cruise.

"So, your mom is all good with everything?" Shelby closed the computer and scratched a sleepy Chip nuzzled on the bed.

"Yeah," Mia yawned. "I think so."

"And she believes them? Nimmy? Sexy Lips?"

"Yeah, she does, but there's something about that Nimmy woman."

"I agree. Who brings a gun to church?" Shelby sipped her mint tea and let out a loud burp. "You know, I don't usually say this about people, but that Dregs is intimidating."

Mia was about to comment on how she was debating sending an apology text to the detective when her mother opened the front door. "YOU turkeys! Why do I *still* see piles of dishes on the table?" The girls moved faster than when Chip had snatched Mateo's turkey leg and spent the next hour scrubbing stacks of dirty dishes clean from their Thanksgiving celebration.

The week back at school flew by, and by the time Friday rolled around, Mia found herself battling nerves for her very first Strategy & Survival weekend. She knew her team was ready to compete, but there was no denying her anxiety about the coming competition against Henry's team.

Justice had taken to sending daily texts, reminding the team what to eat and when to sleep and cautioning them against walking solo down school halls. Most of her teammates couldn't help but notice Mia's vast improvement. Her body had blossomed under the extra exertion at a far faster rate than her male peers; her tolerance for pain, endurance, and speed had reached beyond anyone's expectations, including her own. When the last practice before the big weekend arrived, Mia got to the field early to stretch, as per Justice's instruction. Watching the football team huddle at the finish of their practice, Mia saw Jackson bump heads with a player, notice Mia, and wave.

Oh, so we're friendly now.

He jogged towards her, the smell of grassy sweat wafting forward with every step. "Hey, Mia. You got a minute?"

Jackson fiddled with his helmet while Mia eyed him. Something about his posture, his earnest expression made her wonder if for some absurd reason, he wanted to ask her to the dance. It was happening all over the school much to Mia's annoyance. Having worked hard to avoid most conversations about that very topic (which wasn't difficult with Ting's obsession with her new internship and Shelby's determination *not* to date a high schooler). Mia secretly worried, while he scratched his sweat drenched head nervously, if he was going to do just that.

"So, ahh . . . eh . . . um," Jackson stalled. "Do you remember . . . back when you first started practicing with the team?" he asked, rubbing his temple as though it hurt. "I kind of laughed at you while you were leaving the field?"

Mia remembered.

Pulling a paper from his pocket, he unfolded it and began reading. *Oh God, here he goes.*

"Well, I am very sorry that I dissed you and did not give you the due respect you deserve . . . deserve as a chick, entitled to the support and appreciation from her peers, which is me, for something brave like being the first girl to join Strategy & Survival at our school, North Elite Prep." He stopped to look at her.

"Ah, oh, thanks?"

"Do you want me to read it again?"

"No, that's okay," Mia grinned, "I got it — and thank you."

"Yeah, well," Jackson said with immense relief. "My therapist said I need to break the cycle of male body supremacy in my family, so I made a list of people I needed to apologize to. To be honest, thanks for making that easy. Jade thought I was asking her to the dance."

"Oh, haaa-haaa, that's funny."

"So, have a good practice! Can't wait for the highlight reels!" He grabbed his helmet and smacked her on the back.

"Hey, guys," Mia said, joining her team, who'd circled up a few yards down the field. The twins threw Mia their smirks while the rest of the gang focused their attention to a stressed Justice.

"Coach Drake will not relent on his ban for the meeting on Thursday, so I'm sorry to say this is our last practice before the weekend. Of course, I thought that would be the case, so rest assured we are prepared — that I'm sure of — but, if there's anything we need to go over, fix, then you guys have to speak up, as it *has* to happen TODAY!"

The team spent the better part of the practice reviewing the weaknesses of their opponents and supply lists for the weekend. Mia had been practicing wearing the camping bag she'd borrowed from Ting loaded down with Maria's Spanish encyclopedias to build stamina. She was to bring spare clothes, toiletries, a single-person tent, a sleeping bag, and extra running shoes and socks. Apparently, socks were an inexhaustible resource in the woods, doubling as bandages, hand warmers, and earmuffs in the night chill. She'd been placed in charge of the team resources of toilet paper, waterproof matches, one liter of water, and the team's food source of protein bars (Justice had promised vitamin patches to compensate for the three steady meals of only protein bars).

"Now, and I can't stress this enough, do NOT do anything dumb from now until Friday. I mean it — don't even think about it! Chet, I'm so serious. Any last questions?"

The group was unusually quiet.

Mia surprised the group by raising her hand, which she quickly put down, remembering she wasn't in class.

"So, I was just wondering, what everyone means about watching the game online?"

"Mia? How did we not go over this?" Justice asked. "It's a way to keep the game regulated for fairness — it's filmed."

Oliver added, "With a student camera crew, kind of like a referee."

"Where everyone from school watches," Chet added.

"Yeah, so no one better make us look like morons," Andy glowered at Mia.

"It does sometimes add a little extra pressure, but I like to think of it as a safety measure, to make sure the other team isn't cheating," Justice said, but Mia had stopped listening.

Everyone was going to watch this?

Justice ended the meeting by reminding the team to go to bed early, catching up to Mia as she headed across the field toward the girls' locker room.

"Mia, I, well, um — I tell the guys this all the time — you know . . . so um . . . no dates before Friday. The weekend is mentally and physically taxing, and it's best for you to come into it as prepared as possible — ya know, limit the major distractions for a few days before —"

"Sure, Justice." Mia tried to hide her grin as they parted ways, knowing that was one issue, he didn't have to worry about.

Coach's voice boomed from the end of the athletic hallway. "Storm. TELL me you have your waiver or else I'm going to be driving you right now to your house and coercing your mother to sign it over a plate of whatever grub she's serving you for dinner. Stop that!"

One of the twins' dirty gym socks came dangerously close to the coach's head.

"Yes, Coach, I have it in my bag."

"Well, go get it! I'm ready to go home. If one of those hits any part of my body, you're cleaning the urinals!"

Mia hurried into the girls' locker room, a pleasant change from the rotten banana smell of the sports hallway. Heading to her locker, she stopped short. Someone had taken heavy-duty plastic zip ties and threaded them through the locker handle, sealing it shut. Who on earth would have done this? Peering around the corner, Mia half-expected to see the culprit sitting there, laughing at the prank, but no one was there. The room was silent.

Pulling at the handle, Mia could not get any leverage to budge the metal. The lockers down here were old and didn't run on keypads. She had scissors, but of course, they were in her backpack, and that was stuffed in the locker. Coach probably had a pair, but before she could think any further, the smell of sulfur, like a match being lit, wafted through the air.

Then smoke. First no more than a puff. Then a wave, like the opening of a steam room, and then — a constant stream of billowing black smoke that began to fill the room.

Mia slammed her hand on the locker, coughing, and took off running. She made it to the hallway, Coach at one end, waiting for her to deliver her waiver. Running toward him, Mia ran right past him and into his office, desperate to get something to cut the lock. "Storm, what the hell is going on?"

"Call the fire department!" Mia seized a generous-sized pair of toenail clippers from his drawer and ran past him. He tried to grab her arm, but she jerked it away. "CALL!" she yelled over his shouting to stay put. Mia covered her mouth with the crook of her arm and ran back inside, unsure why she was being so reckless. It was almost like once her body was in motion, it was functioning apart from all sense of logic. Finding her locker amid the thickening smoke, she began trying to cut the plastic. The strips were jammed so tightly, they were bound together like one, and while Mia snapped away, she found she was hardly able to make any progress. Keeping one arm to cover her mouth, Mia was forced to use only one hand to chip away at the plastic. Vaguely aware of Coach yelling from behind, Mia felt her eyes burn from the sweat dripping down her forehead, waves of smoke surrounding her while the fire's heat kept Coach back.

"Storm! FORGET YOUR THINGS AND GET OUTTA THERE!"

Mia gagged and dropped the clippers, clutching her chest. Falling to the floor, she began to dry heave, trying to cough out the thickened mucus that tasted like tar. Puttering around on the floor, she searched to find the clippers, but the smoke was making her head throb. She could hear Coach coughing as he inched toward the fire with the extinguisher. Shaking her head as if it would clear from the scene, Mia pulled off her shirt and tied the breathable fabric around her nose.

Coach Drake blasted the extinguisher, while Mia kept clipping away at tight plastic ties, promising herself to gift him a new pair for Christmas . . . if she got out of here okay. A blast of something cool hit Mia's leg, and she looked to see that Coach had dropped to the floor. The fire extinguisher blew wildly while Coach spewed profanities through bouts of retching.

Mia rushed over; he was convulsing on his side and turning blue. She dove under his arms, yanked him upward, dragging him out the door while he whimpered something about asthma. "Get him OUTSIDE!" she yelled to the twins, one of them catching Coach from Mia's arms before she ran back inside the smoking locker room.

Heat hit her face and Mia dove to the floor crouching down on all fours, manically sliding her hands along the warming tiles in search of the clippers she dropped. She touched something and found them hiding under the wooden bench. Squatting at her locker, she stayed as low as she could while working at the plastic; piece by piece she snapped and pulled until only two remained. Mia pulled at the handle while her body prickled from the encroaching fire. Jerking the handle up and down, up and down, the plastic was pulled into a thin line. She dropped the clippers again, but she was so close. She grabbed the last two plastics with two fingers and pulled, until they snapped.

Hands shaking, Mia fumbled open the locker door, grabbed everything inside, and ran into the hallway, down the long corridor, and to the exit. Reaching the door, she turned for a split second to see the fire reach the hallway, engulfing the extinguisher Coach had left behind, a loud bang assuring Mia something had just exploded where she'd last stood. Bursting through the exit doors, Mia doubled over toward the stone wall, gasping for breath.

"MOVE!" a firewoman yelled, suited in her sixty-pound gear.

The fire rescue team proceeded into the building, yelling back at the EMT to attend to Mia.

Shivering, she sat on the grass, while someone covered her with a blanket and tried to offer her crackers to go with the lime-flavored sports drink that the EMT promised would help with the nausea. Mia hugged her bag and put her head down to rest, when, minutes later, Coach Drake was at her side.

"Storm," he growled, cough-yelling at the EMT to get away from him, "what were you thinking? It was hotter than hell in there!" Coach pulled at her arm to see how it wasn't burned. "You really scared me, kid, really scared me." Coach gave her arm back with a gentleness he hadn't had when he'd taken it.

Mia coughed, unable to use her voice. With sore, throbbing fingers, she opened her bag, took out her locket, and put it around her neck, shaking as she tried to clip the clasp.

The locket, a faded golden pendant etched with intricate markings and glass stones, was the only thing she had from when she was little, and she wasn't going to let it burn away in the fire.

Mia held the pendant while dialing Shelby's number to see if she could come pick her up. Somehow, she just couldn't stomach taking the city bus home today.

"But anyone could have done it."

"I know." Mia scratched out her drawing and put her pencil down. She'd become accustomed to doing so many things on her device in school, it sometimes felt foreign using a proper pencil and paper to draw, something she had little talent for anyway.

"I don't think so," Ting said.

Shelby and Mia stopped their attempts at cartooning and waited for Ting to explain.

"There —" she said, satisfied with her drawing of a pineapple sitting at a computer. "I was just thinking, based on what you told us, it definitely seems, to me at least, it was a student. What did you have in your bag that someone would have wanted to burn up?"

"Nothing. Just my books, device, wallet, which I guess still had a few hundred dollars in it from selling the dog to Jade, my phone." Nothing was of great value, apart from her necklace, but who would want that?

"So," Shelby said, "you don't think it was someone from the list of pictures Mia carries around to remind her of people who want her dead?"

Ting continued. "I don't think anyone but a student could have gone so undetected in our school. First of all, we have security cameras in most of the high-traffic areas. Then, there's the use of the plastic ties. I've seen them all over campus, securing cable cords and such. I think anyone could have swiped some, and whoever did was fairly impulsive about the whole thing, which speaks of inexperience. It couldn't have been a professional job, at least not from what I can see."

"But then . . . how would the fire have started?

"Could be as simple as getting kerosene from one of the grills the crew uses to prepare meals." Ting looked up at hearing her cousin laugh at one of Jackson's jokes.

From what Mia could tell, the current status of Ting and Terry's relationship had deteriorated since Thanksgiving, when Ting was blamed for the loss of Terry's beeper.

"Yeah," Mia chimed in. "The firewoman suspected someone poured kerosene on the shower curtains, and then all it had to do was reach the lockers and *bam*." Mia noticed a lingering nervousness whenever anything smelled remotely like smoke, including Ting's pork-stuffed dumpling for lunch yesterday that set Mia off in a full-body sweat. "I just feel so frustrated I didn't look around the bathroom more. It was quiet and I swear no one was inside but me."

"So, here's my thoughts," Shelby proposed. "Why don't we rig Mia with body cameras." Ting stopped drawing. "What? That's what dad does at the casino. Sometimes when there's someone we know is cheating, we have to send out a scout and *WHAM*, we got 'em."

"Speaking of your dad." Mia hid her amusement. "How are things with his girlfriend?"

"She'll be gone by New Year's — I bet it was Jade." Shelby drew her thoughts to the laughing girl across the room. With Dr. Fern's permission, Terry and Shelby switched groups, which seemed to bring Terry into his own, surrounded now by the attention of Jade, Vivian, and Jackson. Apparently, a boy with his talent fit nicely into their little posse. It served Mia and Ting fine since it afforded them an extra hour of the school day with Shelby.

"That's really good." Mia watched Shelby sketch another scene.

"Nah, lacks dimension . . ."

"It's meant to be two-dimensional," Ting explained.

"You guys are funny." Shelby scratched out her drawing.

"Whoever it is," Ting said, "I think that it's not related to the person who shot Detective Dregs."

Shelby shook her head. "I still can't believe that happened right after we saw them. I don't know how, but it has to be connected to the dog thing. I mean, not that I'm claiming that. Hell no, they brought that upon themself, telling you to never call again."

Mia had wondered the same thing. What if by bringing them there that night, Mia caused Dregs to be in danger? Only, Mia knew they were long gone from the church when the shooting happened, Ting discovering the news in the paper the day after Thanksgiving.

"Ladies, how are your cartoons coming?" Dr. Fern approached their table and looked over Ting's and Shelby's comics with interest. "I hear a lot of quality brainstorming."

Mia glanced at her two stick figures. "Dr. Fern, I'm not really much of an artist."

"Naturally, Miss Storm, one cannot be good at everything or even many things. One can only be good at a few of the important things or even one thing at a time . . . ."

"Yeah." Mia hoped that meant he was okay with her sticking to line drawings.

"Do you have everything ready for tonight?" Ting asked as Dr. Fern left.

"Mia, just do me a favor," Shelby started. "Whatever you do this weekend, keep clear of sleeping near Chet."

"Okay . . . why?" But Mia never got her answer. Dr. Fern interrupted the group time to draw the class's attention to Terry's artwork, caricatures of some of the kids from class, including Dr. Fern, which closely resembled an old, blind chipmunk.

CHAPTER 16

The Games

Dropping her pack onto the floor alongside her teammates, Mia waited for Coach to finish the emergency reminders. "Like I said, ONLY for emergencies." Coach Drake passed both captains bagged phones. "Does anyone need further clarification on what constitutes an emergency to call for help like say, a fire, Storm?" Coach glared at Mia, relieved he had allowed her to continue in the game after only a mild protest.

"Coach!" Dillian lifted his hand.

"What the hell are you raising your hand for? We're about to start the game!"

"Coach, I just need to use the bathroom before —"

"DILLIAN!" Get down and give me twenty right now! The rest of you, we're going to start the ode."

Clearing his throat, Coach Drake began, a little sharply, the chant. The others apart from Dillian, joining in and hitting their arms like a drumbeat.

> *Forge A path*
> *Lasso the sun,*
> *Never stopping till the game is won.*

Shape the stone,
Rule the night,
We won't wilt, we're born to fight.

The soul holds two,
It's honor we choose,
Sly the evil, take the heat, don't lose.

Shape the stone,
Scale the tree,
Unearth the beast, set the wild free!

Beast, Beast, unearth the beast,
Set the wild free!

To finish, the boys stuck out their tongues and growled, casting deadly looks at their opponents. Mia picked up her backpack, secured it to her back, and readied herself for the hike deep into the woods. Coach Drake signaled for four students to come forward from across the lawn and introduced them as the selected filming crew from Berkins Academy.

"All right, on my horn and not a moment before," Coach said, alongside Coach Bender and Junior Coach Ray, who were point persons for the game with the addition of his wife, who he reminded Mia was available in the event of any "female necessities."

As the horn blasted, the students took off sprinting. Mia pushed herself forward and started running, falling in step with the twins, who were busy ramming into one another to see how adequately their packs weighed them down. Henry's team headed north, Dillian holding his bottom and disappearing with his team into the beginning tree line. Once inside their side of the forest, Justice increased the team's pace to a rigorous sprint. Avoiding tree stumps, Mia kept her eyes trained on the ground, only snagging her pack once against a low branch. Coming to a clearing, Chet followed behind Justice, slowing to a jog.

"Cap?" he yelled when Justice didn't seem to lessen his pace.

"We're not staying here, come on," he yelled, taking the team an extra half mile until coming to a smaller clearing, bordered by sparse pine trees and a few small mounds of dirt hills.

"Justice." Chet threw down his pack and panted, while taking a swig from his water jug. "This isn't where we agreed to camp!" He rubbed the spot where he balanced the metal heat lamp and generator across his shoulders.

"I changed it." Justice tossed down his pack, chugging water and beginning to mark everyone's spot.

"That's kind of a jerk move, man," Chet rigged the generator up near a tree.

"Why?" Justice said. "What's the problem?"

"No problem, Cap." Chet mumbled something about how Justice could carry the heavy stuff himself next time.

Mia set up her sleeping bag and things at her allocated spot, saving the tent for if the weather changed. Set on the opposite side of camp from Chet, she smiled at Shelby's warning, but the distance meant she was farthest from the heat lamp. Thankfully, Ting had lent her a down-filled sleeping bag, which promised to retain warmth in below-freezing temperatures, along with heat packs and a plastic mat for the cold, wet ground.

"Everyone," Justice called, "we need to start the rotations. Remember, it's subjective to what happens when attacked, so prepare to use your intellectual flexibility. Let's do a roll call, so I know that everyone is in check with their first rotation. Andy, Kai?"

"Scouting!" The boys grabbed their camouflage water canteens, saluted the team, and headed out into the forest, where their first job was to identify and spy out the other team's camp and supplies.

"Stag, Chet?"

"Building camp defenses." Chet said and cracked his neck.

"Tai, Andy, Pierce?"

"Checking traps, surveying the land, disposing of human waste."

"TAI!"

"Sorry, Cap-ee–ton . . . We are off to locate the box."

"Mia, Oliver?"

"Camp watch," Mia called in tandem with Oliver, a job that involved a few specifics to comply with game rules. First, the flag needed to be visible at all times and at least six feet off the ground but no more than twelve feet in the air. The flag had to float unobstructed within a ten-foot radius of anything. Only the captain could string the flag, and it had to be done within the first hour of the game. Mia and Oliver's job, before patrolling the perimeter, was to keep watch over the captain while he fitted the flag from a high tree branch.

"Where's the camera kids?" Justice checked his watch. He had less than five minutes to get it on film that the flag was airborne.

"We're here," said one of the kids, emerging from the woods, a squishy sound accompanying his footsteps. "Stepped in something disgusting."

Mia kept guard while Justice secured the flag, the boys from Berkins recording it. Hanging it between two trees with enough distance that someone couldn't easily reach it from the branches,

Justice checked the measurements to show they were in compliance with the game rules. The camera crew did a quick interview, asking Justice for his predictions on eliminations (to which he refused to dignify such a question with an answer) and Mia took off around camp, keeping up a steady pace of walking the circumference for any encroaching opponents. Feeling hungry from the excitement and running, she watched through the dense trees, a darkening sky as the sun set low and the first chill of the evening breezed in. It was beautiful here in the woods, surrounded by nothing but earth.

Approaching Oliver, Mia suggested possibly patrolling the area a bit farther out.

"So, I guess I'll head west, make sure the traps are coming along. Oh, and if you can, lay some extra twigs and leaves for noise," Mia suggested, remembering some of the tips from the manual. Overall, the way to win the game wasn't very complicated. Be the first team to steal the flag and get it successfully to the winner's box. The locked metal box was hidden somewhere in the woods and could only be opened with the team's code and the opponent's flag insignia. Mia's team, named after their likable captain, *Justice's team* (and because no one could think of anything better), had the school insignia on its flag, a woman holding a gauntlet standing in waves and pointing to a sun. All of it was embroidered in gold thread and rather ugly in Mia's opinion.

"Cool, see you in a bit," Oliver said as Mia tossed him a protein bar she'd stored in her jacket pocket, figuring if she was hungry, so was he. Walking around and eating the nutty mush, she came upon Chet and Stag, who were covered in dirt and digging a wide hole.

"Urghhh, TAI!" Mia yelled, when he jumped out from the net-covered ditch. Getting the message from Justice to keep it down, Stag and Chet went back to finishing their traps while Mia continued to patrol, wondering what was happening elsewhere. The team was not allowed what was called any first- or second-level technology, which included things like phones, computers, drones, or anything that could advantage one team over another. They could use clocks and compasses, maps, and things to heat food, heat lamps, and generators to power lights. The team's main source of communication was walkie-talkies that buzzed when announcing updates from teammates about what they were scouting, evidence of the other team's advances, and who was currently digging their own bathroom hole.

"Chet, how's your neck?" Mia asked, when he came to collect his protein bar. He was severely disappointed by its size.

"Ah, just tight, but I'm good." He threw the whole bar in his mouth at once and looked to snag another. "Ugh, this is disgusting," he said after she passed him three more; a kid his size needed sustenance. The night carried on uneventfully. Most of the communication from the walkie-talkies was explaining how the other team seemed to be doing a lot of arguing about who should do what and conflict on how to divide their food supplies. Upon hearing the reports, Justice couldn't wipe the glee off his face.

"I knew it!" Justice smudged black dirt all over his face and hands as he covered his pants and top with army gear and strapped on a headlight. "Guys, Mia, I think we could win this game by dawn, but stay sharp!" Justice tallied the extra points their team would earn from an early capture.

Mia had roamed camp, hung out in a tree for two hours to watch the flag, gone to pee in the woods twice, and was now settling into her sleeping bag to catch a few hours of sleep before her rotation as a lookout. Setting her alarm, she snuggled, breaking her heat pack and instantly feeling her sleeping bag fill with glorious warmth. Resting her head on her rolled sweatshirt, she closed her eyes and threw the blanket over her head to keep the warmth in and occasional bugs out. Drifting off for a few hours, she was awoken to the sound of her watch alarm, ringing that it was 2:00 a.m.

"Oh, hey, Mia, sorry, just getting a bar."

"What did I miss?" Mia sat up and scratched her head.

"Well, we lost Oliver," Justice said, unable to hide his shaken confidence.

"What, how?"

"Well, we had them. No one knew what was happening while we charged their flag. I was the diversion, straight shot to grab it and then ran about half of 'em away. Oliver was supposed to climb the tree, get the flag, and pass it off to Andy, but he wasn't wearing his glasses strap. Dropped the things and accidentally passed the flag to Bronx from the other team . . . then ran himself into a tree."

"Ugh." Mia rubbed her eyes. "How did you get back?"

"Ran like hell. Andy gave me some help, but I felt bad leaving Oliver," Justice explained as the two camera guys arrived, asking if they wanted to see the footage of Oliver knocking himself out. "Might as well," Justice conceded.

Mia dressed in the extra layer of pants and jacket Shelby had lent her, stuffing her pockets with a small water bottle, flashlight, walkie-talkie, and protein bar. Scheduled to partner with Pierce, she looked around the campsite, not able to see him. Assuming he went to his spot early, she checked the locational coordinates, making sure she knew exactly where she was headed, and set off on the ten-minute hike into the dense, dark woods. Approaching the spot quietly, Mia recalled the first thing Justice had ever taught the team was never to whisper each other's names during the game when on site, which was anywhere off base camp. So, while Mia looked for Pierce, she hit two sticks together, listening to the echo filter upward, absorbed into the trees. A stick hitting a tree sounded, and Mia paused to try to gather where Pierce's reply had come from.

Hitting her sticks again, she headed toward the sound when a light flashed, leading Mia towards a thick oak tree. Approaching ever so cautiously, Mia was only just able to spot him in his camo jacket and dirt-rubbed face. Sitting against a tree trunk with his eyes closed, he somehow faded into the wide tree trunk like a large protruding root.

"Great camouflage." She crouched.

Holding night binoculars, he nodded and pointed around the tree where he'd been watching, offering them to Mia.

"Sure," she said, peering around the corner and having a look. Surprised by how much detail she could see, she almost regretted not having a pair as she looked at the crisp outline of the tree leaves and an intricate spiderweb set in the bush next to Pierce. "Thanks," she whispered, passing them back to Pierce, knowing she couldn't justify the steep price for a school game.

Settling herself on the other side of the tree, Mia sat alert, spying the rich night darkness with her naked eyes, and focused on any movement or sound around her. After a good twenty minutes and spotting a squirrel running up a tree, Mia shifted herself into a different position, stretching her back and tightening her jacket's hood. Pierce hadn't made a sound. Mia found it strange sitting in the dark with someone. Another half hour passed while Mia, thankful for her wool socks and insulated coat, shifted to lying on her stomach in a pile of wet, wilted leaves to stretch her back. She'd never realized how strenuous it was to stay still in one position for so long. She took a noisy sip of her water bottle.

"*Shhh*," Pierce snapped.

"Sorry." The plastic *was* a little loud for the silence of the night. A canteen was another item on her list she hadn't bought. "So . . ." Mia murmured, her back to Pierce, "how many years have you played?" she asked, recently learning he was in the senior class with Justice and Chet. Pierce didn't seem as obsessed with the competition as the other two, and he didn't try to exert his seniority over the other teammates.

"Four."

"How does this year compare to the last three?"

"Fine."

"Oh yeah?" Mia asked. "Justice thinks we have a good chance of winning."

". . . maybe," Pierce mumbled.

About to ask something else, anything to kill the dullness, Mia was interrupted by Pierce's walkie-talkie. Someone was yelling, "Attempt on camp, attempt on camp!" followed by a string of static, scuffling, and the news that the other team was down two men, Rork and Carey both having fallen into the booby trap and one of the two with a twisted ankle.

"Nearly dawn." Pierce covered his watch.

"You know," Mia started, "I think I'm going to watch from the tree. It's getting lighter now, and I'm freezing." She stood and looked for a good climbing tree, not that she was terribly comfortable ten feet above ground, but it beat lying on the wet ground and seemed logical to have the height advantage as she waited out the last thirty minutes of her post.

"We're almost finished here, though."

"Well, I could use thirty minutes off the wet ground." She pulled herself up into the low branches of a pine tree and climbed up. It was the instant she was concealed in the thickness of the needles that she heard something from a hundred feet away. Loud, thumping footsteps, like someone running toward them, drawing near at a very fast pace. Mia held on to the tree with one hand and tried to snap her fingers with the other in hopes of alerting Pierce. It seemed impossible for him not to hear the intruder, the incomer unconcerned

with concealing his approach, thumping on snapping twigs and rus-
tling fallen decomposing leaves.

What the hell is he doing? "Hey," Mia whispered. "Climb up!"

Mia recognized Henry by his agility as he ran at full speed toward
Pierce, who was standing wide open. Swinging herself down the
branches, Mia reached the lowest limb and positioned herself in the
crook.

The idea came to her in slow motion, and she knew she had
just enough time to execute it. Mia jumped at the precise moment
Henry crossed the ground underneath her, seconds before he would
have collided with Pierce. Her feet met his thick, tough shoulders.
Thrusting her weight onto his back, she took Henry down to the
ground and flat on his face.

CHAPTER 17

"Man" Down

Mia grabbed Henry's arms and pulled them together behind his back, her body exploding with instinct from training. Using pressure where she didn't have the mass or weight, she forced him to the ground while he thrashed and kicked up his feet into her back with his heavy-soled boots. Wincing from the blows, she pulled his arms tighter and jammed her knee into his hamstring while digging her thumbs into the pressure points Chet had taught her, forcing his fight to slacken.

"Ahhhh!" Henry yelled.

Mia dared not to speak. If she could appear stronger and larger than she was, she could buy some time until she got him tied up. Wondering what could possibly be taking Pierce so long to come and help with the rope, Mia heard someone crashing through the trees, and a second later, Chet burst through the woods and slammed into Pierce. Pausing only to steady himself, he yelled, "DOUBLE DOWN!" and took off in a full sprint past the trio.

Just as Chet ran off, giving Mia a congratulatory grin, Phillip appeared. His long legs carried him quickly after Chet, followed by two members of the camera crew in hot pursuit. In the confusion, the crew debated staying with the chase or filming the current predicament, deciding to follow Phillip and Chet. Pierce appeared with the rope and tied it around Henry's arms, then legs, while Mia held Henry down, her legs cramping from the strain. Once Pierce had secured the rope, he helped Mia shove Henry over. The feeling of pure pride and a rush of elation coursed through her at taking down the other team's captain.

Upon seeing Mia's face, Henry laughed. First a little chuckle of surprise, then a full-on belly laugh, while Mia grabbed her mini-spray can from her jacket pocket, ready to mark Henry out of the game. Pierce held out his hand to stop her, pulling out his spray can, the sound of Henry's laughter echoing against the trees. Parting clouds revealed the warming sky, a glow highlighting Henry's amused face. As if on cue with Henry's quieting laughter, Pierce took Henry's spray bottle and struck Mia's chest with a bright yellow line. Pierce grabbed Mia's arms with determined force and finished a second line, completing an X across her front.

Staring in shock at the wet paint staining her front, Pierce began to untie Henry.

"WHA- WHAT are you DOING?" Mia yelled at Pierce, but the deed was done; he'd untied Henry and was now backing away to let the meaty boy rise.

Dusting himself off, Henry let out one last chuckle. "You should really check out your teammates, little girl." He grabbed his spray can back from Pierce and ran off into the darkness. "We're even now, Petterson!"

Pierce stared hard at Mia. His face of defiance was betrayed by his fumbling hands. He grabbed his walkie-talkie. "Guys, it's Petterson, the girl's out. Tagged by Henry. I'm coming back." And he turned and left Mia standing alone and eliminated from the game.

It took Mia some time to hike across the forest, back to the starting line, where she was to call the coach on duty for pickup. With her compass to guide her, Mia reached the clearing at the same time dawn appeared. The first rays of morning hit the open field while Mia made her way to the pop-up tent and seated herself in a foldable chair. Opening a bar of chocolate, Mia grabbed herself a Coke and chugged the carbonated sweetness while racking her brain as to what could have happened for Pierce to go rogue. He'd always been cordial to Mia, but by *cordial*, she realized he was rather quiet, sometimes seeming indifferent toward her. Pierce didn't strike her as mean or as someone trying to cheat his teammates. Mia tried to think back to anything that might have happened that caused him to be untrustworthy. While stewing in her anger, a tall, dirty figure emerged from the woods and headed toward Mia.

"How'd you get here? Last time I saw you, Henry was a goner." Phillip limped toward a foldable chair.

"Let's just say things soured."

Coach pulled up to the grassy clearing in his two-door pickup truck, while Mia finished her chocolate and helped Phillip to the truck. It seemed his ankle was only bruised, a possible sprain. "But really, this happens . . . us Hennesses have skinny ankles."

"Two more down." Coach sipped his extra-tall steaming latte.

Mia climbed in the back, letting Phillip take the front seat of the midnight-blue pickup. A soft twang of country music played over the radio while the coach waited for them to buckle up. In less than a few minutes, they were back at the school parking lot.

"I'm so relieved we don't have the circus here today. After the fire, I tell ya, I need a holiday bad."

"Not coming to the cruise, Coach?" Phillip opened his door and moved the seat for Mia to climb out.

"Not a chance. The Mrs. wants a vacation somewhere *ethnic*, so that's what she's getting. Trying to get it all planned this weekend." He walked with them toward the school building. "So that means, I'll be in the music wing if you need me."

"Thanks," Mia said while Phillip held the door open. He shared the same kind eyes as his grandfather. "Where are we meant to go since they are fixing the gym?" Mia asked, but Coach was already out of earshot.

Phillip let Mia to the student lounge (that she never knew existed until now) and it did not disappoint. "It's nice too, but reserved for seniors which is why underclassmen never get to see it." Complete with retro vintage arcade games, massage chairs, and a walk-in refrigerator, Mia parked herself on the extra-wide couch next to Rork, asleep and drooling onto a pillow.

"The only thing I hate about these weekends is the lack of food." Phillip sat down to a tub of cookie dough and frozen chicken nuggets. "I can't stomach any more tuna."

Mia's stomach bubbled from the chocolate soda while watching Phillip scoop bites of raw dough with the chicken.

"So, how did it happen?"

"Oh, I ah, the rope I used to tie Henry came loose." That seemed a logical explanation.

"Ah, man, that stinks. Probably would have ended differently if Pierce hadn't been acting like a deer in headlights. Thought he was doing much better." Phillip washed his meal down with a carton of orange juice.

"Doing better?" She straightened herself up on the green uphol-stered cushion.

"Oh, I was just meaning, I thought Pierce was doing better since the accident." Phillip looked at Mia very cautiously.

"What do you mean?" Her mind spun. The chocolate and fizz churned in her stomach as she became alert to something. Somehow, Mia was remembering. Something she'd never been told, a face that she could now see shared a striking familiarity with another. The girl who'd died on the bus — Sarah Petterson — Pierce's sister. How had she not seen it before? He had arrived at practice blotchy-faced and solemn. Justice handled his aloofness with tentativeness, not pushing him as hard as the others. Pierce, never using Mia's name directly, always referred to her as "the girl." Somehow, Pierce must have known Mia's secret, that the bomb that claimed his sister's life had been meant for her. Mia stared at Phillip eating his cookie dough and excused herself.

Standing from the couch, she scooted herself around the leather ottoman and hurried to the girls' bathroom, where, once inside, she leaned against the cold wooden door. She tried to calm the sick feeling rising in the pit of her stomach. Pierce's sister had died. Phillip's grandfather had died. She was meant to die. Phillip had no idea the real reason his grandfather was gone. She'd lived and his sister hadn't, and because of that, Pierce hated her. It all pointed to her, the cause and reason for so much hatred, hatred she hardly understood herself. Swallowing something sour, she knew it was too late to stop, and she ran to the toilet to throw up.

Mia thought she was dreaming when a gang of exuberant voices, shouting and grunting, woke her up. She very well could have been dreaming because she felt her pleasant mood drop when she opened her eyes to see her team pouring into the student lounge, where she had slept for who knows how long. Phillip and Rork were gone.

"What time is it?" Mia watched the guys raid the kitchen for anything they could stuff into their mouths.

"Mia!" Justice tossed her phone over. "We won!"

"We did?" Mia asked, checking the time and for messages, mostly from Mom. She'd slept all afternoon.

"Of course!" Justice poured cereal into a square baking dish. Sniffing the milk, he settled for a serving spoon and started digging away. "You doubt?" he asked through a grinning bite of oaty puffs.

Mia sat at the counter, afraid to eat anything with her stomach still feeling sour. "How?"

"Well, after we lost you, Chet and I decided we needed to change up the plan, so we did an unexpected ambush, and it worked! We'll catch you up Monday night." He shoved the cereal in faster than he could swallow.

"Monday?" Mia retied her messy hair into a ponytail.

"Monday, our winner's celebration!" Justice shoveled in another bite, while Chet seated himself at the counter next to Mia.

"You've gotta come, Mia." Chet munched on a bag of carrots and inferno-flavored chips. "Last year Justice cried."

"You both cried." Oliver emerged from the pantry followed by Pierce, who beelined it to the couches where the rest of the team had settled themselves. Mia was startled to see Pierce, even if it was just the back of his head. Her stomach dropped, and her throat went dry.

"Listen eh', there's nothing wrong with showing a bit of emotion," Justice said, having moved on to making butter and ham sandwiches. "Ladies like sensitive blokes."

"Whatever. Mia?" Chet nudged her with his big muscly arm and caused her to wobble as she stood transfixed on the couch where Pierce sat, his back toward her.

"You can't ask her," Justice interjected.

"Why not? She's a girl."

"I mean, yeah, she's a girl — you're definitely a girl, Mia," Justice explained as if Mia needed reassurance, "but she's not in that category anymore."

"Ohh." Chet nodded.

"Sorry, boys." Mia yawned, too tired to work out what they were meaning. "I've got something Monday night."

"What?" Kai and Tai yelled from the couch. "You can't miss. It's part of the team code."

Chet looked affronted.

"I just promised I'd help with something. Next time, okay? I'm expecting a winning streak." Mia tore her eyes away from the back of Pierce's head.

"You better," Justice threatened. He started cleaning his dishes in the sink, calling the rest of the guys to get their rides home sorted. "And put your dishes in the washer, if you think I'm cleaning up after you—"

Mia waited for her mom to text back, when Justice offered her a ride home.

"It's fine, I can swing by my dad's—" he said while Mia loaded the dishwasher and punched the blank screen, hoping something would light up and turn on. Most of the guys had left, leaving their mess, while Justice hurried to clean up after them, promising retribution come Tuesday's practice. Climbing onto the front seat of his silver Audi, Mia buckled herself and thanked him again for the ride.

"Of course, Mia, my teammates are my tribe."

"Yeah." Mia had actually begun to feel that way too. Until Pierce.

"So," Justice said after driving in silence out of the school grounds. "When are you going to share what really happened with Pierce and Henry?"

Mia snapped her head. "How did you . . . ?" He kept his eyes on the road and shook his head.

"Hell, Mia, it's the grief—my dad says it makes people do weird things. I'm just mad Pierce took it out on you." Mia laid her head against the headrest, hoping her unwashed hair didn't smudge the monogrammed initials woven into the tanned leather. She'd not expected to discuss this with anyone, at least no one on the team. Finding out about Pierce's sister cemented her decision to keep what happened between her, Pierce, and Henry — even if it meant letting them get away with cheating. She'd thought about it while she lay on the couch listening to Rork snore and Phillip chew. Somehow, she just knew she needed to swallow this one.

"Mia, you're going to tell Coach, right?"

"NO. But *how* did you know?"

"Well, I've been wondering about Pierce. How 'bout I tell Coach and —"

"NO."

"Mia, obviously we all feel bad for what happened to Pierce. It's horrific. But that doesn't mean he should get away with cheating and taking it out on you — besides, Henry tricked his entire team, and giving people passes doesn't help them in the long run."

"But we won," Mia said, while Justice turned into her apartment parking lot. Flickering Christmas lights now wrapped around porch railings, while Mia's door was decorated with her mom's homemade evergreen wreath.

"Yeah, but come on, I care more about what's right than whether we won."

But Mia shook her head.

"If Pierce needs to do this to feel — I don't know — a sense of control or resolve, then I'll let him have that."

"Mia, that's ludicrous; you don't owe him anything. You can't let this go unchecked; look, I know him fairly well, and he's not in the right headspace these days. I thought he was better, but —"

"Is that how you knew? How he was acting?"

"No. He said you cried."

"Oh."

"Yeah. We all expected Henry to try something shady, but I never saw it coming with Pierce."

"That's the thing, Justice, I don't know Pierce or Henry, and I didn't know his sister. I just know that she died, and — and no amount of cheating or — revenge is going to fix that. You can't say anything. Please! We won despite it; let it be."

Justice took in Mia's dour expression and put up his hand. "If that's what you wan —"

"Yes."

"Okay, I'll chill. But, Mia, if something were to happen again or there's even an inkling . . ."

"Yeah, sure, I get it." Mia unbuckled herself.

"Hey, before you go, look, *ehm* . . . about the dance coming up . . .."

"Uhh —" Mia tried to think of something to say to derail the question. Surely, he wasn't thinking of asking her, not after the "she's not in the girl category."

"I was just wondering if you, well — is your mate Shelby going with anyone?"

Mia felt so relieved, she giggled. "Ha, ohh, Shelby! Yes, I mean no, she's not going with anyone, but she already said no to a few people; she's planning to go solo."

"Really? That's too bad. Maybe I'll just go solo too and happen to bump into her."

"Well," Mia said, smacking his arm, "if you do, I'll fully help her *accidentally* bump into you."

"Ahh, thanks, mate." Mia got out of the car, thankful to be one of the guys again.

CHAPTER 18

Omission

Mia and her mother climbed the set of metal stairs and knocked on her father's trailer door, hugging her jacket around her. Skirts in winter was getting old, but she refused to sport colorful knee socks as a fashion accessory. "Are you sure he said to come here?" Mia asked as the smell of burnt plastic seeped out from the trailer.

"Coming —" Charles opened the trailer door in his bathrobe. "I'm sorry for the smell, I can't get this damn coffee maker to work."

The trailer felt more like a one-bedroom studio that clearly surpassed their apartment in square footage and beauty. The appliances, furniture, and light fixtures were new and shiny: an exercise bike, seventy-inch television, king bed, and built-in desk space where a kitchen table would go, showed Mia her father had a pretty nice place to "camp" out during his work day. Turning off his watch alarm and sitting on the suede couch, Charles stared at Divana.

"Dee — would you mind?" He stretched his legs out on the coffee table, his manicured toes pointing at Mia. "You'll have to excuse my fatigue; my trainer came yesterday, and we hit it hard. I knew I'd be stretched for time this week."

Charles looked happily at them with sleepy eyes, and Mia wondered if he had any clue that she'd been avoiding him. He seemed so secure within himself, like it never occurred to him that someone wouldn't go out of their way to be in his presence.

"I'll take mine black," he said to Divana, who was busying herself sniffing chocolate sauces and French branded creamers.

"Here, honey." Divana gave Mia a mug filled with what smelled like Christmas. Sipping the bittered sweetness, it slid down her throat while perking up her brain.

A script lay on the table. The bottom of the thick bound stack of pages read:

A Story of the Unfavored

By: Charles Marazza

"What's this?" Mia asked, interrupting her mother, who tried to explain how many coffee beans equaled a shot.

"My script." Charles gave a careful look to Divana.

"You wrote it?" Mia picked it up, Divana leaning over to see.

"Yes, it's been a dream of mine. Actually, this is as good a time as any to share. I owe it to you both; having you in my life has ignited the young man in me that I tried to hide away. It's been so liberating to walk into that place again, the place of hope and possibility . . . ."

Mia took another sip of her coffee and felt the heat warm her body. She'd been thinking about what to say to her father. Looking at her mom, she wondered why she was staring him down. Not in the *what-he-just-said-was-so-charming* way but the way Chet looked when he played dodgeball, like he wanted to annihilate whoever crossed his path.

"I never knew *you* were a writer."

"Well, I had some help, of course. Nimmy is incredible; the woman has her law degree and got it at night school when she was our age, if you can believe that."

At the mention of Nimmy, Mia felt her stomach pinch. Or maybe it was the coffee.

"Charles," Divana interjected, "Mia and I received unimaginable news. We need to speak to you, and I beg you to be honest."

Charles looked concerned and hugged his robe around him, drawing the cashmere wrap closed to shield his smooth chest. He picked up his coffee and held it to warm his hands.

"Anything for you — you know that, Dee."

Mia's mother spoke quickly. "We heard your father is alive. I need to know the truth; do you know this to be true?"

Mia watched her father put his coffee down on the table, staring at the blank space where the script used to be. He sat back and folded his hands. He seemed calm, apart from running his thumbs over each other in a small circle. "Yes, I know he's alive."

"CHARLES!" Divana's eyes flashing a brilliant gold, like a warning call. "You NEVER TOLD ME!"

"I know and I am regretful of that." He paused. "It wasn't my intention to hide it per se, just . . . to make sure that *he* didn't interfere with our being together or my meeting Mia."

Mia watched Charles and, against her own volition, believed him.

"It's terrible who he is and what he's capable of, but you have to believe me — I've not been in contact with him for years. He knows where I stand, and I am not part of his family. Not anymore."

"But Charles —" Divana lashed, "terrible things have happened. He could be behind it!"

"Yes . . . he very well could be. He's done his fair share of terrible. I've pondered so many times confronting him, but in the end . . . the best thing I can do is stay away."

"What the hell does that mean?" Mia joined the conversation.

"I mean, he's no good to me, and I, to him. I have no influence or power over that man, so to try would be ineffective. As long as I live, I *vow* to *not* be involved with him. Whatever he's doing, he's doing it apart from me. My hands are clean."

"But . . . BUT he's trying to kill me! And you're hanging out with women who are helping him!" Mia stood and spilled her coffee on the tan-carpeted floor. Good, she hoped it never washes out.

Charles glanced out the window where it was still dark. "I don't know what he's doing, Mia." He held up his hands as if to try to calm her. His robe unfolded to show his ugly silk shorts and tanned stomach. "He's an old, baleful man who I want *nothing* to do with. However, as far as the people I keep in my life, I trust them. Just like I trust you . . . even after you and your friend broke into my home." He sat back on the couch.

Mia looked at Charles. He or her mom had never said anything about him knowing she and Shelby had snuck into his house.

"Charles, the girls meant no harm; you know that."

"I know that. Of course. Yet I am showing Mia that there are things we don't always explain, but sometimes we have to give someone the benefit of the doubt."

If he wanted an apology, well, he wasn't getting one. She'd sneak in all over again if it meant finding out the truth. Pacing the small room, Mia couldn't comprehend Charles's reasoning.

"How can you SIT there and — and just ignore that *your* father wants to KILL ME!"

Divana stood to join Mia. "Charles, if your father wants to hurt Mia, don't you think you have some role in how to stop him, to HELP HER!"

"Help?" Charles stood. "What could I do? I don't know anything about him, not anymore —" And he walked over to the window to pull down the tan window shade. "Look." He turned to face the women, his look of frustration and despair mildly comforting to Mia. ". . . if, if you need help, financially or some extra level of protection, I can certainly offer that . . . ."

Mia felt on the verge of tears. She didn't want money; she wanted him to care. To fight for her, to protect her in a way every girl wants of her *own* father. Looking at her mom, she pleaded with her eyes, *do something, make him help*, but Divana's expression was hardened. Where she thought her mom would be riddled with shock and despondency, she showed something else. Something that looked a lot like pity.

"You're *still* afraid of him, Charlie, aren't you? After all these years."

"Well, aren't you?" Charles crossed his arms and pulled his robe tight.

Divana stood and looked at Mia. "I need air. Mia, you're welcome to come with me to the car or stay and ask your father anything else you need to get off your chest." And she walked to the trailer door, opened it, and left Mia standing by herself, staring at her father.

CHAPTER 19

Will's House

Mia didn't talk much longer with Charles after her mother left. When she got to their car, easy to spot with its dented bumper and rusted hood, she found her mom staring out the windshield window. "I'm hungry," was all her mother said, and the two drove until they found a cafe specializing in organic pastries. "Oh, who cares," her mom muttered when they saw the exorbitant breakfast prices listed on the menu.

Keeping to their own thoughts, Mia and her mom ate in silence. The rest of Monday passed like any other, except that Mia's day was clouded by a deep feeling of betrayal. How could the man she dreamed of as a child be such a coward, a disappointment, again?

What good is a father if he can't even protect you from his own?

Justice found Mia after lunch, asking one more time if she wanted to speak up about what had happened with Pierce and Henry to Coach Drake. Mia suspected his question had been brought on by the rumor spread around school that Justice's team had cheated, but Mia was adamant in her position. She finished the day in a stupor, not wanting to think about her dad or his dad. She couldn't bring herself to muse about the approaching dance that everyone was now fully obsessed with preparing for, including Shelby, who applied a self-tanning cream that had turned her skin orange.

"How was I supposed to know that my skin absorbs this stuff like a dry sponge?" Shelby took a tight turn into Will's neighborhood. Mia rang the doorbell of the Turlington home despite Shelby's insistence that they had a walk-in, open-door policy. A pigtailed child opened the painted front door, recognizing Shelby and smiling to show two missing bottom teeth.

"Hi, can we come in?" Shelby asked as Will appeared behind his littlest sister.

"Shelb! Mia, come in!"

Sailor latched onto Will's side, hugging him around the stomach and peeking at the newcomer. Pulling Will's arm to signal for him to bend down, Sailor whispered something.

"Hey, Sail, go tell Mom the rest of my friends are here, okay?" Will pushed her toward the kitchen, and she scampered off.

"Let us know if she needs any help!" Shelby called after the twiggy child.

"I wouldn't offer that if I were you," Will said. "Mom's a little controlling in the kitchen; it's like the one time we're all scared of her." Will led the girls toward the stairs. "Everyone's in my room."

Mia turned back to see the kitchen door swing shut, followed by something loud crashing to the floor and an adult grunting in exasperation. Will's home was everything Mia imagined: baby pictures lining the walls, signs wishing visitors welcome, and toys beyond anything Mia had ever had as a child, filling the rooms with clutter and life.

Trailing Will to his room, Mia walked in to see a handful of kids from school working on snowflake cutouts from flimsy pieces of Styrofoam.

"Everyone, Mia and Shelby are here."

Only a long-haired boy, Emery, cared enough to look up, his double-pierced eyebrow stuck with foam shavings.

"This isn't workin' man," he said, shredding a piece of foam into dust.

"Shoot, you're right . . ." Will scratched his head. "I just thought that we could save some money doing it ourselves . . . ah, forget it. I'll just tell Gretch to buy some of those hanging paper ones." He glanced toward his closet.

"Save money?" Emery asked as hundreds of floating bits of foam now swirled at their feet.

"Let's just throw this around, and we won't have to wait till after the holidays for the illusion of a white Christmas." Shelby tossed handfuls in the air, some flecks landing on Mia's shoulder.

Mia watched Gretchen emerge from Will's closet.

"Ah, Gretch?" Will asked, wondering why she was wearing his hoodie.

"I got cold; your floors aren't heated . . . Shelby!" Gretchen said. "You made it — I didn't believe Will when he said you were coming to do decorations. So, can you help me out? I really need your dad's annual dance donation. I know you were going to talk to him, but I've not heard from you —"

"Oh, right —"

"Great. If you guys are all good with stuff, Mia and I can get started on the trees," Will said and grabbed her hand to pull her from the room. "I don't know about you, but I hate being stuck inside all day," Will said once they made it to his fenced backyard. "Figured we could do this out here and get a little breather."

Mia was quickly distracted with the massive pile of artificial evergreens, all of it needing a paint makeover within the next few hours.

"So, how was your weekend?" he asked, kicking one of the dozen empty paint cans lying at their feet after they'd given a good half hour of work.

"Well — it was fine, different than I expected but eventful." It was weird standing here with Will, the fumes of the paint reminding her of Pierce's betrayal. Maybe it was being older or the type of kids North Elite attracted, but Mia had never before felt how confusing it could be making friends. Or at least confusing figuring out Will.

"I think it's great you're on the team — you looked good when they caught you on camera, which wasn't as much as I thought. Justice spoke highly of you, though." Will checked the fake pine needles to see if the white paint had dried.

"Really?" Mia did feel a kinship with Justice after Sunday, now that they were privy to each other's secrets.

"Yeah, he's cool." Will looked out into his yard. Mia followed his gaze to the playhouse, strung with pink fairy lights and a flower-twined swing.

"You two close?"

"I guess, compared to the rest of the team." Mia grabbed a new paint can, pulling back horrified at the magenta color shooting out the nozzle.

Will, who looked just as offended, went over to check the paint. Sure enough, half of the remaining cans were the near-blinding hibiscus color that he blamed Gretchen for choosing.

"But should we use them?"

"I mean, yes, sadly." Will looked up at his window and frowned. "I don't have time to change it."

Mia followed his gaze up, unfazed to see Gretchen's face pressed against the glass, waving for Will's reply.

"You know if Justice is taking anyone to the dance?" Will asked.

Mia looked at Will in surprise. "Yeah, actually, he's not."

"Oh really? I thought he liked someone and was sure he'd asked her by now —"

"Not unless things changed in the past day," Mia said.

"Good, I mean, he's cool, but I hate it when girls all go for the same guy."

"Don't you have that same problem?"

Will laughed hard. "No way, not the guy who everyone thinks is going to report them to the principal." Will smiled.

"I don't think that; besides, I think you have an admirer upstairs." And she looked up to see Gretchen watching them still, Shelby attempting to pull her away with a thumbs-up.

"Yeah, she's . . . something. I should explain, Mia, I did like her for a time, but then I didn't. Now, I just feel bad because I think I've confused her."

"That's fair, but you don't have to explain anything to me."

"I should tell her it's not going to happen. I struggle with hurting people's feelings, ya know?"

Mia tossed the now empty can in the pile. "Will, somehow I think she'll be okay."

"Yeah, but it's just, I have to tread carefully — it's hard to explain. Ah, nevermind it's weird." Will took the finished tree and moved it over to the done pile, wiping his hands on the grass. "Do you ever feel like you're just living for other people's desires?"

Mia had stopped painting her tree to watch him. He seemed burdened, although she wasn't sure she wanted to care.

"I guess, I mean yeah, I do. But I have to."

"Yeah." Will stretched his arms above his head so Mia could see his arms flex and his rising shirt expose his taut stomach. "Sure, we're at the mercy of our parents I know but, would it be better if we just figured it out our own way? I don't want to look back and see I got it wrong."

Mia thought about her dad. She wanted something from him that she was beginning to realize, he wasn't capable of giving. Maybe Will knew that feeling. Maybe she'd judged him too soon. It was clear something was bothering him.

Looking at the darkening sky, he asked, "Do you think much beyond high school?"

"Honestly, Will, I've been trying not to think past the week; I mean, so much can happen in a year's time."

"Wow, how do you do that? That's so refreshing. I obsess about the future. It's like my part-time job. You know, I've wondered, our school is pretty hard to get into for people who aren't — I mean, parents who don't —"

"You mean for poor people?"

"No, I just mean . . ."

But Mia waved her hand to stop him. "It's fine, although — I'm offended you didn't assume I got in on charm and pure talent."

Will laughed hard again, his face lighting up, easing the worry from his boyish eyes.

Realizing she was warming to him, she sighed. "So, up until recently, it's always just been me and Mom . . . but I found out I have this . . . uncle who wanted to help us — get to know us, and he sent me."

"Yeah, I assumed it was something like that. Good for you, Mia. Maybe something like that will happen to me with college."

The wind picked up a lock of Mia's hair and threw it across her face.

As if he'd done it many times before, Will took his hand and brushed her hair behind her ear, smiling just enough to showcase his beautiful dimples. "Stranger things can happen, right?"

Mia froze just as a woman called from the back door for them to come inside for dinner.

Between bouncing her youngest daughter on her lap and feeding the next youngest unwelcomed bites of chili, Mrs. Turlington attempted to get to know Mia with questions: "How do you like North Elite?" and "What's your favorite city you've lived in?" A California girl herself, she was curious about Mia's unusual upbringing and articulated it with *oohs* and "that's incredible" every time Mia explained something different from their Californian culture.

Amused by the attention Mia was getting, Shelby sipped on her iced tea, throwing a rather obvious eye roll when Gretchen chimed in asking Mia what her mother did.

Will dropped his spoon at the scream of Flora, his youngest sister, who'd wound a rubber-handled fork into her baby-fine hair. His parents excused themselves to help untangle Flora's mess, when Gretchen continued, "And how does she support you?"

"Gretch, what is this, twenty questions?" Will leaned back from the table and decided he was full.

"I'm just trying to get to know *her*."

Mia answered casually, "My mom's job is really admirable; she helps people deal with their addictions and find recovery."

"Whoa, that must be so hard being around junkies and alcoholics all the time."

"Sort of like your house," Shelby mumbled as Will stood, offering dessert.

"Omg, yes!" Gretchen said, jumping at the chance to follow him somewhere.

"I hate her," Shelby said, not quite whispering. Emery, the only one left at the table, smiled and got himself up to join the others in the kitchen for warm chocolate chip cookies.

"What was that about?" Mia wondered, but Flora was already bounding her way back into the room to show off her new bangs, freshly cut out and adorable on her chubby face. Mia spent the rest of the evening painting white glitter onto votives and stringing lights around the sprayed trees that, despite her reluctance to admit it, looked pretty good all piled together — a winter wonderland on steroids.

The second Mia and Shelby were in the car, Shelby blurted out, "Why didn't Will ask you to the dance?"

Mia shrugged. "He should ask Gretchen." She texted her mom that she was on her way home.

"Mia! I was sure if you came tonight he was going to ask you. Don't you like him?"

"Like him? I mean — I don't know," Mia said, relieved she didn't have to consider giving him a response.

"Wait, I thought you were into him." Someone honked at her for switching lanes too closely to their front bumper. "I mean he's kinda the best our school's got, so it's downhill from here. Don't laugh; it's true unless we get some foreign transfer students, but even then, it's so hard to understand them."

"Sounds like you have firsthand experience," Mia said, laughing. "I can't like someone I hardly know. He seems confused about life." Not that she wasn't.

"But I know he's into you, and I thought you kind of — oh, who knows? I can't even figure myself out; how am I supposed to help you?"

"Maybe I don't need help." Mia closed the car door and leaned in the window to thank her friend for the ride. "Make it home safe!" she yelled as Shelby drove away hitting the curb.

Surprised to see her mom and Maria having a cup of tea at the kitchen table, Mia greeted the women while her mother jumped up to hug her. "How was your time? Oh, you smell like . . . cumin?"

"We had chili." Mia wanted to tell her about the night but saw her mother's tear-stained face.

"Just finishing up." Maria brought her mug to the sink and gave Mia a hug on the way. "Gotta get home to the boy. He's so particular these days about being on time and schedules. Has me up in the morning every day at seven before school to walk and get our exercise, driving me nutso!" Maria headed out the door with a promise to see them tomorrow and an extra hug for Divana.

"Mom, is everything okay?" Mia asked while her mother washed the mugs and put the kitchen towel back on the oven handle.

"Yes, just processing our visit to see your dad." Divana smiled at her daughter and grabbed Chip's leash from the post.

"Oh, um, did you want to talk?"

"Oh, honey, I'm good. I feel better just getting the feelings out, ya know? Something about saying it, even though it doesn't change anything, I feel better. But I won't if I don't get this pup walked—he's been glaring at me all night. And please, your Christmas list? I need it, like, yesterday!"

After her mom left on a walk, Mia showered and settled into bed thinking of what her mom had said. It seemed pointless when she shared how she felt with her father—he didn't want to do anything out of his comfort zone to help Mia, and where did that leave her? And what would she gain if she shared how she really felt about Will? If she had to be honest with herself, she did feel some interest in him. How deep, she wasn't sure, but it dawned on her that she was becoming one of the few girls at school *not* to get asked to the stupid dance.

"Ugh." She turned on her side just in time for Chip's return snuggle.

"And so, what does my girl want for Christmas?" Divana lay down at Mia's feet and rubbed Chip's side as he sprawled out, ready for sleep.

"A sweatshirt," Mia said now that hers was permanently blotted from the day of painting.

"You want a sweatshirt for Christmas?"

Mia nodded. She didn't really care. If Mia asked for something small, she worried her mom would feel insulted that Mia thought she couldn't afford a nicer gift. If she asked for too much, Mia faced not getting what she'd asked for, like the time she'd asked for the doll every girl in her school seemed to want. It was a life lesson she'd been practicing for years, culminating today in seeing her father cower away from helping his own daughter. *Don't ask for what you can't get.* She never got the doll.

"How about a cute jumpsuit? I saw a few young girls wearing one the other day and thought they looked so smart."

"Mom, please, I don't like things that make it harder to go to the bathroom."

"Yeah, I did think of that. You know, I never understand why people spend all this money on fancy lip cosmetics that make your lips all swollen when this stuff is just perfect." Her Mom took a swab of Mia's bedside Vaseline and moistened her lips.

"I think because they can, and not everyone looks like you." Mia poked her with her foot.

"Ouch, well whatever people have or do with their face I don't care — as long as they are generous. I hate selfishness."

"So, then what made you fall for Charles?"

"Still calling him that? Well, I can't blame you, not after this morning. But that's not your *father's* failing. Let's see, when I met him, I was actually beginning school to be a nurse." Popping up on her elbow and startling Chip, who rolled over, Divana smiled. "I know, sometimes I wish I'd given it a go. I think I would have been pretty good at it too, apart from the needles, but I've heard you just get used to it. But that's where I met him, found him sitting outside the hospital one day on my way in. I sat right next to him on the bench, and we talked. I joked he was waiting for me. I guess we both fell quickly."

"What drew you to him?"

"Well, full disclosure, I'd actually seen him in the hospital ward . . . so, I can't say I didn't have a heads-up. He had a softness to him — delightful, generous . . . all the nurses fought over who could treat him, and when they left his room, they were beaming from his attention. I was just shadowing for the week, but he was all the entertainment. Some people like to take up all the space in the room, and Charles certainly can, but I always felt he had the ability to make others feel seen too. I liked that about him. I liked how he saw me, and I saw him for who he really was." Divana smiled at Mia. "You're certainly asking curious questions after visiting this Will's house."

"Mom, it was a student council meeting."

"But do you like this boy?"

"No! I mean, probably not —"

"Probably — that's practically a maybe." Divana looked so hopeful, Mia sat up.

"I like Will, but not like that. I don't know what you felt for Charles when you met him, obviously, but I imagine it was something pretty strong . . . like some force of nature that can't keep you apart like . . . of all the people in the world — this is the person you need to be with, and nothing about their weaknesses or opposing destinies can keep you from running back to them, even when it seems completely impossible."

Divana stared at her. "Mia, is there someone you're not telling me? You can tell me . . . ."

"What? No. What are you talking about?"

"But how do you know that?"

"I don't; it's just a guess. I mean, I figure if love isn't earth moving — like, I'll die and give everything up for you right now, then, at least for me, I wouldn't really want to bother with it."

Divana sat grinning at Mia while her phone buzzed.

"What?"

"Nothing, you're just special, that's all. Time for bed, missy, no late-night texting, okay?"

Mia murmured good night and turned off her phone without even checking to see who'd texted. She'd had enough of the world for one day. Too many unknowns, including the vault inside. Forcing herself to think of frivolous things, she went to bed imagining fresh-cut Christmas trees and love stories with happy endings.

CHAPTER 20

The Cruise

A winter warm front swept through Los Angeles. The mild December temperatures shot up to the eighties, just in time to pique the students' excitement for the weekend cruise. Festive in her navy sailor dress and hair wreath of mistletoe, Mia's choir teacher, Madame Cherry, welcomed everyone onto the *Isla Florbol,* their floating home for the next few days.

"You know we're only on this thing for three days?" Shelby stopped one of Ting's six suitcases from rolling off the ramp. She herself had two black hard cases, easily maneuverable in her navy romper and matching cord mules.

"Don't be scared. These things are built like tanks —" Terry offered, alertly on the lookout for someone else to meet up with. "You don't need so many supplies; all I have is my suit, a shirt, and some deodorant."

But Ting looked too nervous to listen. "I have a panic list — and floating somethings are at the top."

Mia helped Ting secure her bags while she checked in, wishing she'd thought to bring a hat as the sun beat down on their backs.

"Mia, hello, dear; don't forget tomorrow's choir practice —" Madame Cherry ran her finger down the rooming list. "Hummm . . ."

"I'm rooming with Shelby Romeno."

Shelby saluted the teacher at the mention of her name.

"Yes, but, dear, I don't see you on the list, you *did* register?"

"Yes, of course I —"

"We would be booked in a suite." Shelby explained.

"A suite?" Madame Cherry checked a different list. Finding Mia with the weekend VIPs, she explained, "Oh, it looks as if you're in the king's quarters."

The girls made their way onto the ship, promising to see Ting after she and Terry had settled into their cabin. A slow elevator ride to the suites led them to a gold-stamped landing with walls of mirrors and gaudy railings. Shelby keyed her card onto their suite door, entered the room, and stopped short at the sight of a man waiting to greet them, dressed only in an Egyptian tunic, offering drinks and promising to be of service for the weekend.

"Well, thank you." Shelby ran past him and landed herself on one of the king beds.

The bare-chested manservant excused himself and left the girls to unpack their things. Mia set her backpack in the smaller closet while Shelby checked out the bathroom, yelling in excitement that the shower had an ocean view. Lying on her own bed of silky linens, Mia checked the schedule to see they had three full hours before the dance began at 8:00 p.m.

"Want to go explore the ship?" she asked while Shelby opened her bags.

"Mia! That won't be enough time." She pulled out neatly folded garment bags and hung them in the larger closet. "We have to set your hair, choose dresses — at least get our nails done, if not toes . . . then there's makeup, accessories — you shaved, right?"

"Nope, going free and natural."

"Whatever, I say we order room service, my treat." Shelby headed to the shower with her periwinkle bathrobe and tote of hair products.

An hour later, after the girls had eaten their fill of steak sandwiches with sweet potato fries (chocolate milkshakes, thick), Mia sat in a rattan gold-twined chair while Shelby fiddled with her hair, trying to roll Mia's long tresses around a hot curling wand.

"Isn't this bad for your hair?"

"Mia seriously — ouch— not if you put in the right product; by the way, I love how you don't know a thing about cosmetics." Shelby yanked Mia's hair and snapped her head sideways. "Sorry," she said, a clip falling to the floor. "I think your hair is just too thick and long for this."

Someone banged on the door, and before Shelby could open it, Mia heard Ting yelling outside.

"He locked me out! Put my suitcases in that tiny hallway, took my key, and LOCKED ME OUT OF MY ROOM!"

"Well, of course you can stay with us!"

"Thanks, Mia, really, this is great." Ting heaved all her suitcases inside.

"My GOD, woman!" Shelby yelled, taking in the mess Ting had created once she opened her bags and spilled everything from several pairs of multicolored high-tops, life jackets, and boxes of ramen noodles to rolls of extra toilet paper, now strewn all over the floor.

"Mia, your hair is so voluminous." Ting tilted her head.

"I'm not wearing it like this; Shelby just lost hope."

"Oh good," Ting said, relieved.

"I am only taking a creativity break," Shelby called from the bathroom, steam escaping from the crack in the door.

Ting studied her friend's hair and decided to give it a try, tugging and braiding while Mia grimaced. "You know —" she wiped her brow "— it's really a matter of knowing what type and texture your hair is. If you apply the right pressure, products, and perseverance — it *should* do and look as you want." Shaking the braids free, Ting tried pinning Mia's hair into a messy beehive, but she quickly took it down. Complaining of sore arms, Ting tried one last attempt at straightening Mia's hair but gave up when they refused to unkink in the back.

Finished steaming dresses in the bathroom, Shelby came out sweaty and excited for Mia to try on all the options she brought.

"You mean you bought these?" Mia asked in shock at the $900 price tag.

"Don't forget, this is your Christmas gift, and I didn't pay for them in advance; the store loans them to me, and I just pay for what we keep. Come on, try it on!" Shelby shooed Mia into the bathroom.

She emerged minutes later in a lacy black off-the-shoulder dress. When Mia dropped her arms, the dress slid right down to the floor, leaving Mia standing in her underwear.

"Built for someone with a few more curves?" Ting summarized while Mia backed up into the bathroom and closed the door. The next dress was a white silk cap-sleeve that fit her waist and shoulders like it was tailored just for her. "It would be perfect . . ."

"If you were about thirty and getting married," Shelby said. "NEXT!"

Mia went through two more dresses before she agreed to re-exit the bathroom to model a black-and-gray ombre paneled dress that, as Shelby promised looked, "so hot."

"I think it makes her look too mature," Ting said.

"Yeah, I agree, doesn't look like you. I mean maybe a sexy villainous version of the badass future Mia, but how about the other black one?"

"Too many straps," Mia said.

"Well —" Shelby jumped up "— that just leaves the blue one." And turning a reluctant Mia around to go back to the bathroom, she pushed her friend forward and let out a startled breath. "Mia!

Your back!" Shelby put her hand to Mia's back and touched the skin. "Does it hurt?"

"No —" Mia chastised herself for forgetting. "I know it's not something anyone wants to see," she said while they gawked at her back, but Shelby wouldn't let her turn.

"Wait, can we see the whole of it? It's just, I've never seen anything like this. . . ."

Mia hesitated. She'd never looked at her own back since the accident. Walking over to the full-length mirror, she wondered, how bad was it? Reaching behind to undo the zipper, the stretchy fabric easily separated while she pulled it down, leaving her back bare and in plain sight.

"The scars . . . the way they run on your back, it's almost like they make a pattern —"

"Wings," Ting answered. The small markings of damaged tissue ran the length of Mia's spine, stopping just above her hips, each side mirroring the other in its arched pattern of scars on the smooth white skin of Mia's back.

"How is this possible?" Shelby asked. They stared in silence.

"It's really lovely, Mia," Ting said, her eyes showing something of sadness and awe.

Mia grabbed her T-shirt, deciding she'd wear her mom's green dress when Shelby begged her to try on the last dress. "Pleaseeee look — I have something . . ." she said, hurrying to her suitcase and pulling out a silk bag. "The blue dress, this somehow in your hair, and we can figure out the shoes later."

Stepping outside the bathroom five minutes later, Mia was a vision in a periwinkle-blue lace tulle gown. Ethereal sleeves draped softly over her shoulders; the hand-sewn flowers over nude mesh, shielding Mia's back. She'd pulled her own hair off to the side, wet it to get back some of its natural wave, and secured it with the platinum black diamond clip of Shelby's that had been kept in the silky bag. Maybe it was the ornate detail of the flower dress or the way it pulled to a V in the front of Mia's chest and showcased her fair skin, but somehow, she looked like a winter goddess. Her brown eyes, now brushed with mascara, her lips, coated with pink stain, looked like the kiss of two flower petals touched with dew.

"I can't believe it!" Shelby said, high-fiving Ting. "We did it!"

"Too bad that won't happen when I get ready." Ting sighed, taking her black sequined dress to the bathroom.

The girls walked under a canopy of twinkling birch trees one hour later, and Mia beamed. Will and the other student council officers had outdone themselves. Spinning to the master DJ's music, students danced atop a color-changing floor while snow dropped from the ceiling, cooling the sweaty dancers and sprinkling the trapeze artists that hung from the ceiling.

The night passed in a blur, and Mia danced longer and harder than she could ever remember. Jackson ripped his pants break-dancing and was forced to go change by B-Ray, stating bare buns were a violation of the school handbook. Will did his best to find Mia throughout the night, having to duck and run for cover when Gretchen appeared at the slow songs. Mia tried to find her way over to Justice, spotting him at the food station and portrait corner, but just when Mia had gotten Shelby and Justice near enough to each other, Principal Florence floated down from the ceiling in a sleigh, enjoying a glass of celebratory wine and announcing prizes and awards for the semester student achievements. Mia clapped hard when a stunned Ting went to receive her award for exceptional service to the school and community through her project with VanBoi Biotech Industries. Dr. Fern emerged from the pizza station with his wife to shake hands, and afterward Ting explained, or rather yelled over the cheering of classmates, that her project had been adapted by Dr. Pika Waters and was to begin testing this summer. Mia was so proud of her friend, she almost missed her name being called.

Suddenly all eyes were on her. "Mia, Mia Storm?"

Shelby and Ting tried to push her forward. "Mia, that's you."

"But I haven't done anything . . . ." Mia shuffled slowly toward the sleigh.

"This award . . . oh, there she is, come on over! Let's see, yes, this is our good steward award — going to Mia Storm in recognition of the first woman to compete on the Strategy & Survival team! I must say, had I had the luxury of going to this school, I might have given you a run for the title." Principal Florence laughed. "And secondly, we recognize Mia for her fearless action in saving our Coach Drake from the terrible and accidental fire that happened in our athletic department. Thank you, Mia." Principal Florence clapped while B-Ray (standing in for Coach Drake) presented Mia the pointy award and shook her hand with his clawlike nails and matching red fur cape.

Most of Mia's teammates cheered for her as she found her spot back in the crowd, some classmates patting her back in a congratulatory gesture. "Thanks," Mia said, recognizing the sophomore Natasia, next to a frowning Gretchen.

"I knew someday someone would see your attraction to danger and death as a noble attribute," Shelby exclaimed, while Ting hugged her.

Principal Florence finished the award ceremony with a surprise dedication to the students lost in the bombing. Immediately, girls broke down in tears, a few even running off the dance floor to collapse at their tables. And just like that, Mia felt like she had whiplash. Her jovial high plummeted at the reminder of Pierce and his sister. Mia hadn't seen her teammate at the dance and had the nagging feeling that it was because of her.

"You guys want to go outside?" Mia asked, but Shelby was talking to Ting about how to get revenge against Terry. Trying to strengthen her shifty voice over the thumping music, she yelled "I'm hot, WANT TO GO OUTSIDE?" The entire dance floor vibrated as Mia pointed to the exit and yelled, "ME — FRESH AIR!" Taking off her heels, she made her way to the hallway where a mauve staircase ushered students to and from the ship's top deck. She could feel the cool air soothe her burning cheek, sighing in relief at the cold deck floor on her throbbing feet.

It was an endless sea and sky out on the open water, and something about looking out into the unknown calmed her. She couldn't change what had happened with the bombing, or that people had died . . . but how long would she feel punished for living? She wanted to do something to rectify things, to erase the danger so clouding her future . . . but how? What could she do to make sure her grandfather and his payoffs stopped? Mia leaned against the railing and watched a few students trickle out onto the deck, some trying to air out their shirts, others grabbing their date to flirt, away from prying eyes. Mia, noticing a couple cozying up behind her, decided it was time to go back to the dance. Walking along a narrow hallway, she held the glass plaque in one hand, her pointy silver shoes in the other, with her thoughts fixed on visiting the pizza station.

"How did you know about the contract?" Will Turlington stood at the top of the stairs looking at Jade in her sleek fitted dress, the exact style of Shelby's, only all in black. On impulse and before she could be seen, Mia ducked into a hallway where a maintenance door stood and waited.

"Kirk's been trying to snag my mom for years, now that her divorce is final, and she's not getting any younger; they're official and I'm privy to his boring business dealings at occasional dinners,"

Jade explained coyly. "Will, he wouldn't have moved your father to the top of the list had I not mentioned what a good family you all are."

"Jade, that's incredible. I mean, I don't know what to say."

"Then say you'll help me with the information I want about the Storm girl."

Mia nearly dropped the heavy award on the floor. Sliding down to a squatting position, her spirits dropped.

"But I already told you, there's nothing to find out. I told you what I know, and —"

"Oh, Will, we *all* know Florence keeps dirty files in her office. You can't run a school like *this* and not have receipts."

"But Principal Florence has cameras in her office."

"But *you* know how to turn off the cameras, and you're the *only* person who could do it and *not* get caught. Come on, Willy, it's you — the guy everyone trusts."

Will seemed to pause. Mia pleaded in her head for him not to do it — *stay strong, Will, don't let her pressure you* — but it was too late. He was agreeing to do what Jade wanted *with* the condition that she made sure his father got the deal. Mia listened as the two made their way down the stairs and emerged from the hallway, not caring about the giggling girls passing by. So, that's how it was. All that talk while painting the trees, and he was going to do what Jade wanted to get his father a business deal. Was everyone around here a sell out?

Shelby came running from the ballroom just as Ting exited the bathroom and Mia reached the bottom of the stairs. "There you both are!" Shelby called. "You have to come and see this. B-Ray is having a dance-off with a very competitive Madame Cherry and Jackson, who, for the sake of team spirit, has been granted permission to continue dancing in his underwear, considering all his other clothing ripped off . . . by himself." Shelby tried to get Mia to follow her back to the ballroom. "Mia?"

"You know, I'm tired. I think I'll head back to the room."

"NO, Mia, you can't leave. That teammate of yours keeps turning up whenever I'm by myself. If you leave, I'm going with you!"

"Oh." Mia said, feeling sorry for Justice, who, at that moment, poked his head out of the side doors.

He called Mia to come join the fun as their team was now going to enter the limbo contest and though she wanted to go back to the room and sulk, she knew Shelby wouldn't let her. Following her friends back onto the dance floor, she ended the night with so much cheering and laughter that her sides hurt. Grabbing a final cupcake and feeling the small sparks of popping candy and gooey caramel gush into her mouth, she headed with her roommates to the elevator.

"Wait up!" someone called, and Mia's stomach dropped at seeing Will run after them.

"Mia! Shelby, hey, you guys coming to the after-party?" Will jumped in the elevator with the girls and nodded to a very sweaty Ting, who struggled with trying to keep on her right eyelash.

"Nope," Mia said, while Shelby looked intrigued.

"What is this after-party you speak of?"

Ting announced she needed a nice long shower as soon as possible.

"We're all planning on gathering at the pools in an hour and staying up till sunrise. We are scheduled to dock in Mexico at five, so we'll go ashore for food, hit the beach, and then be back by the afternoon."

"When are you going to sleep?" Ting asked seriously. "We have the banquet tomorrow."

"We'll get a few hours here and there." Will grinned. "Mia?"

"No thanks." Mia stuffed the rest of the cupcake in her mouth and watched the numbers climb.

Following the girls to their floor, Will stepped out onto the landing.

"I guess we're good." Shelby shrugged, watching Mia's eyes. "Besides, I'm beat. Even though I wake up looking like this, I still need *some* beauty sleep, so we'll see you tomorrow." Ting opened the room with her key and waved goodbye to Will.

Once they were safely all inside, Shelby turned to Mia. "What's that about?"

Mia placed her award on top of the baby grand piano and shrugged. Her mind drifted to a hot shower, getting into her pajamas, and thinking about anything besides the new problem she had.

"Did Will say something dodgy? Did he do something weird, Mia?"

Mia took off her borrowed shoes and checked for any scuff marks on the red-soled heels.

"It's nothing. I just don't want to give him the impression I like him." Mia rubbed the shoes with a tissue to remove the dirt marks, tenderly putting them back in Shelby's closet.

"Mia, you do know I can tell you're hiding something, right?"

"I promise, it's nothing. It's just something about Will; something about him bothers me."

"Ah . . . okay, in that case I'm going to shower and get these eyelashes off," Ting said. "I've been practicing for weeks with these things, and they still feel like I'm wearing spider legs."

"By the way you were acting, I thought it had something to do with that Justin kid," Shelby said, relieved it didn't.

After taking turns using the shower, Mia and her friends settled into their beds, scrubbed clean and comfortable once again in their pajamas, which for Mia was an old T-shirt and sports shorts. Ting rested on the semi-cleared chaise lounge and talked about the activities happening for the rest of the weekend. Tomorrow the cruise was docking in Mexico for the first part of the day, then turning around and heading half-way towards LA, where they were picking up guests for the evening banquet. Mia wasn't actually able to do any of the afternoon activities because she had choir practice for what Madame Cherry had called the greatest performance of their lives.

The next morning Mia awoke to rays of sunshine peeking through the black-striped curtains above her bed. Opening her eyes, Mia saw Ting's face at the edge of her pillow and yelled.

"Morning, Mia." Ting stretched and turned on her back. "I kept falling off the chaise and Shelby middle sleeps."

"Oh, that's fine, sorry for yelling at you."

Yawning, Ting replied, "'s fine, Gigi sticks her head in my face all the time to wake me up. It's terribly shocking, although you'd think I'd be used to it."

"Ladies, less talk, more sleep!" Shelby grumbled, smooshing a pillow over her face.

"But we've got to go and explore Mexico while we can! We only have six hours." Mia got up and used the bathroom first.

The hotel suite looked like someone had ransacked the place, except it was Ting's things strewn all over every available crevice. Mia got dressed for the day in a pair of jeans, flats, and a light blue T-shirt, which matched her dress last night, and a tan cardigan sweater. She busied herself with heating water for some tea and asked the girls if they wanted anything hot to drink.

"I need fruit, bacon, and a matcha latte, pronto!" Shelby picked up the room phone.

"But I think they offer breakfast in the dining hall." Mia looked for where she'd left her phone to check the online schedule. "Yep, here it is." She located it under Ting's life jacket. "Meals in Dining Hall 2 or self-service stations in the cafe area."

But Shelby shook her head. "Have you ever seen that show, the one where they have butlers, and they always bring their breakfast in bed so they don't have to be seen in their pajamas? Well, that's my way. Hello, I'd like to order . . . ."

"I'm happy to go with you and find something," Ting offered, and they agreed to meet back at the room in an hour.

Mia and Ting found their way to the crowded café full of hungry students all trying to hurry breakfast so they could get off the boat and tour the pastel-hued fishing village. Mia bumped into Jade with her tray while trying to get some cream cheese for her bagel and didn't apologize. She glared hard through Jades sun glasses. Even if there was dirt to dig, Mia imagined herself a fierce tiger and that she had B-Ray-length nails, forcing Jade to walk around her.

"Some people have no manners." Jade said to Vivan as they walked away. "I guess that's why you can't breed class." She laughed while Mia dropped her tray down on the table where Ting sat, rather loudly.

"Oh, she's just rude, ignore her." Ting said, dipping into her chia pudding. "My cousin said she's super nosey. I know that's a lot coming from him, but he said she just asks questions all the time about how much money his parents make and who he knows and this and that. It's actually annoying him, which pleases me greatly. His mom and dad are accountants, so around here, that's about as dull as you can get. Doesn't win him a lot of brownie points when he tells people."

"And what about Jade, what does her mom do?" Mia asked Ting.

"Oh, she's a scouter."

"What's that?"

"She scouts for rich men and marries them. And, she's a talent agent. One of those jobs where everyone kisses your butt because you have connections. I think that's where Jade gets her charming personality from."

Mia laughed and the two sat down at a table to eat their eggs, sausage, and boat-shaped waffles. Just as Mia was about to start on her fruit, Will sat at the table with them. He looked exhausted but wired.

"HEY! I just had my second cup of coffee; how'd you ladies sleep?" Will smiled broadly in his tank top and swim shorts. "Mia, it's not so cold once you get outside." He noted her sweater and jeans. It looked like everyone was dressed for the beach: bathing suits, sundresses, and shorts that showed long tan legs. Mia didn't say anything to Will's comment; instead, she drank her juice and picked at her fruit. Ting covered Mia's silence by asking Will about details of the evening's banquet dinner. "I'm so glad you brought that up. I have three spots at my table, and I need dates. Was wondering if you two and Shelby could sit with me and help me entertain some of the sponsors as upstanding students who can convey just how important and necessary our school is."

Mia waited to deliver a big fat *no* when interrupted by Ting. "Wow, yes, we'd love to join you!"

"Um, no I don't think so. I have a singing performance for chorale," Mia said, but Will was too fast for her.

"You perform before dinner, so you can still join me! I'll see you tonight!" he said while being pulled, once again by a determined Gretchen and a gang of peers, toward the main lobby, where they were all going to disembark the ship.

"Ting! Now, we have to sit with him."

"But I thought you were cool with him?"

"What? No! I — he's . . . I can't explain, but just for future reference, let's have some sort of yes-or-no code."

"Oh, I like it, a code. Terrance X-Code style. I saw in this movie once this girl pinched her nose like this every time she was trying to signal to her boyfriend who the killers were. So, we could do something like that?" Ting pulled at the under-part of her nose.

"Okay, that could work. So, does that mean no or yes?"

"Okay, if we go like this it means no. This means yes."

"Sure, then tonight if I'm doing this —" Mia rubbed her nose in all different directions "— it means 'get me outta here.'"

The girls headed back to their room, pulling at their noses and testing the signal with each other to make sure they knew what to do. The day flew by with the visit to the Mexican village, where Mia got her mom a little beaded coin purse and gave some of her money to the girls selling packets of gum. After a long practice of unembellished Christmas songs following lunch, Mia found herself back in her suite with her friends and getting ready for the evening's banquet. Grabbing her mom's green dress, she put it on before anyone could convince her otherwise and settled with her nude flats. At least her feet had stopped throbbing. Shelby managed to figure out the strappy black dress, and Ting donned her red dress again that she'd worn to the fundraiser. When she came out of the bathroom, she exclaimed, "Mia, we're dressed like Christmas again!"

Although the choir was performing at the beginning of the banquet, Madame Cherry wanted the singers to arrive an hour early and serenade guests as they arrived. A few people were milling around the hall, doing last-minute setups while Mia met up with her selected chorale group. Poor Madame Cherry had not used enough sunscreen, and in her rosy-red Christmas dress, she looked to have transformed into a giant cherry from head to foot. Mark kept staring at her and losing track of what she was saying as the round teacher fanned herself through a hot flash and covered her chills with a sweater on repeat. Grouped with Mark and two quiet girls from class, Mia was stationed at the door between the auction room and the banquet hall. Most people passing their singing quartet appeared annoyed they were in the pathway of their table seat. The room began to fill, and with that, so did the noise and excitement of the evening. Patrons, former teachers, alumni, and some students' parents were arriving, all excited to see one another and to have a night of schmoozing. After someone stepped on his shoe, Mark shook his head and stopped singing.

"This is bogus; no one can hear us, and I'm thirsty. I say we peace out until the performance." He walked over to the bar and ordered a soda.

Mia looked at the two shy girls who didn't know how to disobey instructions and admitted, "I think he's right. We should take a break."

And the girls agreed, the three dispersing to grab seats. Mia headed toward the front of the room, looking for her friends, reluctant to sit at Will's table without them. She decided, for the evening, she would be cordial but tight-lipped. Hopefully, he'd take the hint to leave her alone. Ting waived at Mia, and she headed over to the table where Shelby stood talking to Will. They all turned to greet Mia, Will commenting again on how lovely she looked, while she forced a smile and pretended she was pleased with the compliment.

"So, this is our table," Will said nervously, ushering the ladies to sit down. "I hope it's okay; we are sitting with Principal Florence and a few big-time donors, so when they come, if you guys could just greet them and act interested; let them know about the school, that kind of stuff."

"Wonderful, I'm a fantastic schmoozer." Shelby took a seat and put her purse on the table.

Mia sat next to Shelby with Ting on her other side, while Will sat across from them, the remaining seats reserved for the principal and whoever else was designated to sit with them. Waiters came around offering the girls drinks and hors d'oeuvres, but Mia passed on anything but water. All day, she'd been managing a queasy stomach made worse when it was time to get up in front of the filling tables and sing Christmas carols and one song about a dreidel. The performance went as well as it could have, but Mia was relieved to be done, happy they'd managed to stay on key and even project some harmonies.

Mia headed to her table while people clapped, and Ting jumped out in front before she could reach her seat, rubbing her nose in all sorts of ways.

"Ting, I don't —" But she saw why her friend was trying to warn her. Sitting at the table, next to the principal, was her father Charles.

CHAPTER 21

Unlucky Again

It was times like this that Mia was beginning to believe she was one of the unluckiest people in the world. Here she was, having dinner with her father, although she couldn't or wouldn't admit it. Ting sat quietly watching her. Shelby was scrutinizing everything that came out of Charles's mouth, and then there was Will, unashamed of showing his infatuation for the actor as Charles shared his long history of Hollywood breakouts that had led him to become one of the most in-demand actors of his generation. On and on he went as the wine kept flowing.

"And just what do you aspire to do in the future, Miss —?" the broad man seated next to Mia asked.

"Storm," she replied. Charles winking from across the table while he enjoyed glasses of both red and white French wine. "I've not given it too much thought." She prepared herself for the adult-ish dump of dull advice meant to give direction to her sixteen-year-old life.

"Well, you have time, don't you?" he said with a kind smile. "No hurry, you have all the time in the world. Such a short season to be free of the weight of the world right? The years coming for toil and labor, well, the math isn't great when it's all said and done." He took a drink of his sparkling water.

"Thank you, what is it you do, sir?"

The man signed. "Yes, I wonder that myself."

Maple Novak arrived at their table, his mouth holding a smoky cigar, wanting a word with Charles.

"Novak, old pal," Charles said. "I believe there's no smoking in here. You know, young lungs."

But Maple wanted to know how much longer this dull procession was going to take.

"We're barely started," huffed a curvy woman.

"Hey, you, I let you in my movie." Novak pointed to Shelby.

"Not him again," Shelby muttered.

"Let's talk when the formalities are over," Charles insisted.

"Sir, I believe there's a designated smoking lounge I can show you." Will jumped up to help, Mia secretly hoping his pants would fall down and he'd trip on the way.

"Charles," the woman purred, sliding into Will's chair, her fitted leather top squeaking and squeezing as she leaned in. "You're such an example to these young people; it's a wonder you never had children of your own to carry on your legacy."

Ting coughed and shot out chewed tomatoes all over the centerpiece of winter flowers. With her face turning a deep shade of purple, she flicked the tomato pieces off the white roses, and shrunk in her seat.

"You know, Sasha, life has a funny way of working out." Charles winked indiscreetly at Mia or Ting, Mia couldn't be sure. "You live your life, make the necessary choices, and yet, things have a way of coming back to you, full circle."

Shelby took a drink from her water bottle but tried to convey something through her eyes. Mia was tapped from behind to see Madame Cherry standing at the table, her burn starting to blister.

"Mia, this is for you." She handed Mia a small box tied with ribbon. "Nothing fancy, not on a teacher's salary — oh hello, Sasha,

Mayor Brinehart, Mr. Marazza! Cherry-covered chocolate — chocolate-covered cherries for my students. Merry Christmas!" She leaned in and gave Mia a small hug with arms that felt like hot wax.

Wonderful. Mia had been talking to the mayor of Los Angeles about having no aspirations in life, and now it seemed her teacher was heating up over her father.

"Why, I just love all your performances, Mr. Marazza. It's such an honor to have you filming at our school. I was so proud when I heard you helped write the script, one artist to another." Madame Cherry said, a slight squeal escaping her blistering lips as she shuffled off to her own table while Principal Florence began the banquet formalities.

"Really, Florence," Sasha said, minutes later when everyone was seated for dinner. "It's time to hire someone more competent than that lobster. I mean, we don't prioritize our music; it's just not logical with Sound Wings and the LA Performing Music school in our district, but we can do so much better than her."

"Oh, Sasha." Principal Florence laughed uncomfortably. "I love your competitive spirit. We can discuss it at the school's next budget meeting."

"You know, I loved the performance." Charles now spoke to Mia. His voice stopped Principal Florence and Sasha from their side conversation. "You were marvelous, and the other students, so raw and unfiltered." His compliment won the table's approval.

"A real gentleman," Sasha praised. "All the stories about you are proving to be true: a gentleman in the streets and a tiger in the —"

This time it was Shelby who spat something out, across the table, and onto the forehead of Will, who'd returned smelling of cigars. The black olive pit bounced off his forehead, onto the table, and settled under the edge of a plate.

"Sorry, I was aiming for the open chair," Shelby said while Will wiped his forehead.

Charles leaned across the table to Mia and asked, "Is this a kid thing, something fun to do at dinner nowadays, shoot the food?"

The banquet formalities paused for a dinner of escarole salad with shaved fennel and short ribs, asparagus seafood soup, and a family-style platter of sashimi.

"Ooh," Ting said, excited by the array of raw fish, while Mia passed, her stomach turning.

"Excuse me." Mia stood and put her napkin on her chair. Walking towards the bathroom, Shelby ran after her as she made her way to the bathroom. "You okay?" she asked. "It's a lot, sitting there with him — let's ditch them. We can text Ting and tell her to meet us back at the room."

Mia looked at Shelby, and something in her chest lightened. Most of her peers would be dying to sit at the table with her father, and here Shelby was, happy to walk away.

"Yeah, not gunna lie, it's weird. I'm sitting there going, *wait, is he really my father?* Sometimes I don't think it's possible we're related and then, sometimes I even like the guy. But I really do just have to go to the bathroom."

"Okay, well, use our room. Last I went, it stank of skunk. Do you need a key?"

Mia nodded, heading to the elevator. Following the golden carpet, she got quickly to their suite and saw the door was ajar. Wondering if Ting or Shelby could have been so careless as to leave it open, she looked inside, assuming the cleaning service was tidying up, and reminded herself to tip them.

In life, sometimes, people who are very brave, can, in fact, act very foolish given the right amount of bravado in uncertain circumstances. This was precisely what happened when Mia decided to proceed through the open door of her suite.

Fully inside, Mia surveyed the room. With curtains blowing in the wind and some of Ting's papers strewn around the carpeted floor, the room looked empty and quiet. No sign of someone cleaning.

She made her way toward the bathroom, when something or someone struck her hard from behind. A normal girl of sixteen would have succumbed to the blow, but Mia, armed with months of training, was prepared.

Grabbing a wrist, Mia wrenched them forward, turning so she was facing the woman whose face had haunted her dreams for months. The woman who'd planted the bomb. A smile crossed her scarred lips as she wrenched her arm free from Mia's hold and kicked her shin, sending Mia to the floor. She slapped Mia's face so hard, her vision blurred; the woman kicked her in the gut and pulled a syringe from her jacket.

She's going to poison me. Mia gasped to catch her breath and regained her vision. Thrusting her knees upward, she kicked at the woman, hitting her chest and sending her backward. Turning to crawl away, Mia made it only a few feet when her legs were pulled from behind, the woman slamming her up against the wall. She was fast and let out a wisp of a laugh while smacking Mia's head against the golden wallpaper. A sticky red substance now filled part of Mia's matted ponytail, confusion clouding her mind. Her thoughts swam with images of her mother. Her kind, ageless face that rarely looked angry. She heard a whisper, someone telling her it was time. Time to go? Time to go where? Was it time to go somewhere else? *I can just give them what they want*, she heard herself telling the voices.

Uncapping the syringe with her teeth, Mia's attacker located a vein on her arm and stabbed. A burning pain flooded her arm. Mia watched the needle enter her arm like an interesting science experiment. First the jab, then the burning, and then it was as if her whole arm was on fire — shooting to her fingers as she prepared herself to feel her body disintegrate. *This is how I'm going to go.* Dying on a cruise ship . . . left for her friends to find . . . her father getting drunk a few floors down . . . .

The burning stopped. Instead of fire and poison spreading into her body, Mia felt a cold sensation of ice and water, chasing down the fire like a balm, down her arm and into her chest. *Something's wrong.*

The woman's face showed what Mia could feel. *It wasn't working.*

Her thoughts were clearing, and she needed to move. With every ounce of strength, she slammed her legs into the woman's stomach and began fighting like a wild animal, clawing and crawling her way away from the evil-eyed attacker.

The woman grabbed Mia's legs again, pulling her down, this time holding a pillow, ready to smother her, but Mia's strength was returning. Her will to survive grew. Maybe it was the awakening from the cooling fire that now filled her insides, but something gave Mia the determination to wrap her legs around the woman just as she'd done with Henry, then she pulled her to the side, and slammed her against a table, splitting the woman's lip and sending her through the glass table and back onto the floor. The woman's grip slackened as she fell, giving Mia the chance to slip away, her clearest path taking her out to the balcony.

"HELP, Please! SOMEONE HELP! ROOM 520!"

The woman lunged at her from behind, slamming Mia into the deck railing.

"WHY," Mia gasped, yanking herself around. "WHY ARE YOU DOING THIS?"

The woman glared, her black eyes devoid of emotion.

"Tell me!" Mia yelled. *Someone please be listening.*

The women pulled and grabbed at each other, the background behind them only the vast sea. It dawned on Mia that one of them could not survive this. Pushed against the banister, Mia felt her feet slipping. Gripping the railing, she intertwined her legs through the banister and let the woman shove her backward. Keeping her legs locked, she bent backward, and in one fluid movement, pulled the woman with her, sliding her over her own body and down toward the water.

It happened. The woman hit the water. The only sound drumming in Mia's ears as she lay still on the patio floor was the pounding of her heart.

Whatever the woman had given her hadn't worked. But it did make her head pound, or maybe that was everything else. The throbbing inside was hitting all corners of her brain, and she knew she was going to black out. She needed water or drugs or something to lessen the banging against her skull. Staggering to the bathroom, Mia turned on the tap with shaky hands and started drinking. She managed to open her toiletry bag and popped a few pills her mother had given her for migraines. The pills, mixed with her normal medications for aches and pains, were probably expired, but she choked them down anyway. Adding a few more, she swallowed them and stumbled to bed.

What felt like seconds later, Mia fluttered open her eyes to see Ting's, bulging inches from her face.

"Ahhhhhhh! SHELBY! MIA'S AWAKE!"

"Whoa, Ting," Mia whispered, "morning breath."

Shelby rolled over and sat straight up. "I'm up." An unusual cautiousness in her voice.

"Mia," Ting explained, "when you didn't come back to the table, we got worried, only with Principal Florence there, we couldn't leave until Mark's uncle performed and no one knew he was going to perform an entire set, and seriously most of the song sounded the same, so when we could, we came straight here, and —"

"Ting fainted," Shelby said.

"I was overwhelmed! I mean finding you like that Mia — we thought —" Shelby shot Ting a look. "Look — I warned everyone, I don't do well on things that float." Ting slid herself carefully off the bed, her eyes trained on Mia as if expecting her to go unconscious again.

Mia lay in bed, examining her injuries. Her arm was bruised and tender from where the woman had jabbed her with the needle. Her pinching headache surrounded the scabbed lump protruding from the back of her head. Her chest and stomach were both so sore from where she'd been kicked. Wincing at the flashback of the woman, she shivered. What had happened last night was unsurvivable, only she was still here.

The room service came quickly. Mia sipped the strong coffee along with taking her three remaining pills and let the pounding subside to a dull ticking. She began to share with the girls all that had happened, from finding the suite door open to passing out after she'd crawled into bed. The more she shared, the more she remembered, but how to explain what had happened at the end . . . to the woman. The thought of saying it out loud was . . . .

The girls nodded when she got there. Shelby filled in the pause by whispering, "We almost never saw you again."

Ting was staring out at the balcony with a look she sometimes carried while navigating her way through a class project. "You know, I think it's worth it to try and see the ship's surveillance cameras, get an idea of how she got on the boat. She obviously boarded in Mexico —"

Shelby stood, alert with energy from breakfast and coffee. "Ironic that I myself never had the meddling parent, so forgive me for being hypocritical and I'll only say this once, but, Mia! Next time you see a door open like that, please don't be such a dumbass!!!"

Ting and Shelby spent the better part of the morning trying to make sense of what had happened, while the ship sailed to a private beach. The students would spend the early afternoon challenging each other in water games, and, for those less inclined, parking themselves on the sand to improve their tans in time for Christmas. Exhausted and bruised, Mia wanted to stay in bed and sleep, but the thought of being alone in the room all day was less welcoming than people wondering why she looked like she'd been in a boxing match.

"Mia, you are not leaving our sight." Shelby pulled a few bathing suit cover-ups from her bag for Mia to try on — insisting jeans and a sweatshirt (Mia's preference) were going to draw too much attention.

The plan was for Ting to meet them out on the beach; she wanted to see how close she could get to the captain's control room to sync her cipher-tech to their online security log. Once home with her personal equipment, she could infiltrate the ship's system and begin running the footage to track the woman's activity on the ship.

"I promise, you'll fit right in," Shelby said to Mia, dressed head to toe in yachting wear.

As they stepped onto the beach, Mia could see Shelby was right; the entire female population, apart from those already in the water, seemed to be dressed alike in wide-brimmed and bucket hats hiding expensive dye jobs. Oversized sunglasses and flowy dress shirts covered bright-patterned bathing suits with matching totes. To hide her bruised and blotchy legs, Shelby put Mia in high knee socks and sandals after a failed attempt at using a combination of self-tanner and concealer. She promised that knee socks were a new trend. Unable to catnap on the beach with so much running through her mind, Mia enjoyed the distraction of students jumping off moving Jet Skis and piling onto blowup floats. Kai and Tai's favorite activity of the day was to jump between each other's tubes while riding behind a speedboat and then cannon bombing the girls on rafts as they swung by. In North Elite fashion, the kids were given full service on snacks and lunch by sweaty waiters bearing the unusual heat. "Hey, ladies, anything to drink or eat?" a young man asked, not much older than the girls themselves.

"If you happen to have any bottled water, I'd love some," Mia said.

"Something carbonated for me." Shelby closed her eyes to soak in the sun in her black one-shouldered two-piece.

"Can't serve you alcohol. What do you want?"

"Anything clear and bubbly."

"Miss, I'm not a mind reader. Either you tell me exactly what you want, or you can go and get it yourself."

Shelby sat up looking shocked. After she stammered about a *Spritee*, the server wrote it down and promised to be back in a few minutes.

"I think he's about our age," Mia said quietly.

"Yeah, well . . . I wasn't trying to be rude." Shelby said.

When the waiter returned, drinks in hand, Shelby scribbled something on the bill tab and hid under her hat and glasses. If Will hadn't come over to speak to the girls, the afternoon would have been reasonably restful. The sunshine, and company of her two friends was just the thing she needed to not drop into a complete tailspin of despair over what had happened last night. Mia even tolerated Will's interest when he expressed concern over her disappearing from the table.

"Something Mia ate didn't agree with her, if you know what we mean," Shelby answered for Mia.

"Sorry — feeling better now?" He observed her through her round, mirrored glasses.

"Yes, a little better. Just hoping it's that and not something contagious." Mia played with the brim of her hat.

They watched as Will left to go join some familiar faces, Gretchen, Jade, and Mark all getting in a game of beach volleyball before they had to head back.

After a relaxing and hot afternoon, the girls made their way off the cruise ship to head home. Mia had planned to ride with Shelby until she stepped off the ramp, onto the dry stable land. Standing in a crowd of waiting parents was Detective Dregs and Detective Batair.

Mia knew they were here for her.

CHAPTER 22

Bloodlines

Mia limped after the leather-clad detectives to an unmarked police car. Once inside, Detective Batair turned from the front passenger seat. "What happened, Mia, and are you okay?"

"Yes, I'm fine," she said quietly.

"Take off the glasses and hat, and we'll see how fine you are," Detective Dregs grunted while making their signature peel out of the marina parking lot.

Mia turned to see the golden glow of the afternoon sun paint the harbor line. With Dregs's fast driving, the scene disappeared, and along with it, her feelings of hopefulness.

"Looks like you had a hell of a boxing match." Dregs glanced in the rearview mirror to assess Mia's face. Her right eye was swollen and cut, a yellowish crusty substance congealed across the eyelid. Her cheek had changed from a deep red to purple, outlined with yellow-lime bruising that crawled down to her chin. Shelby had tried her best to cover some of the damage with makeup, overlaying Mia's lips with scarlet-pink lipstick, but had given up after Mia complained the concealer was stinging her. Turning around in his seat, Batair looked at Mia's battered face and for a second, a pained look crossed his eyes.

"Am I going to jail?" Mia blurted.

Dreg snorted.

"Mia—" Detective Batair handed Mia a small plastic container "—the woman you fought, as I'm sure you've pieced together, was the woman who planted the bomb months ago. She found a way to get to you by boarding the ship in Mexico. The injection she used, Ostium Iris, was a lethal toxin designed to shut off your circulatory system within minutes."

"Why then was it not strong enough to kill me?" she asked, twisting off the lid of a grassy-smelling ointment. Dregs let out a whistle. "You're an odd one — put some of that on your wounds — bruises too."

"Mia, it should have killed you," Batair continued. "That was her intention, but your body rejected the poison." Batair pressed his lips into a thin line.

"But how?"

Batair turned to the front. "We're going to take you home. Your mother needs to know what happened," he said, dialing Mia's mother to explain that the three of them were on their way.

In a short while, Mia sat in the exact spot where she'd first heard that her grandfather was behind the attempts on her life. This go-around, she found herself doing most of the talking, mechanically running through the fight as if she were relaying a scene from a movie, certain she'd never be able to remove the memories from her mind.

"Mia, we need to know that the woman is dead," Detective Dregs said as Mia struggled to finish the story of what had occurred after she'd been held against the railing.

"Yes."

Divana had been holding Mia's hand. When Mia said yes to Detective Dregs, she grabbed Mia's hand with both of hers. The action calmed Mia in the way only her mother could.

"We understand you acted in self-defense," Batair said after observing the moment between mother and daughter. "But," and Batair focused on Divana "Mia is aware that the poison should have killed her."

"She needs to know why." Dregs interjected. "If this were to happen again —"

But Batair cut his partner off from finishing with the simple raise of his hand. "This won't happen again — they will soon know Mia survived, and using that knowledge, they won't make that mistake again."

"No," Divana said.

"No? No what." Mia asked, glaring at her mother. "Who is they?"

"Mia, I — I can only speculate." Divana explained. "Because of your father and his bloodline, you were able to fight the poison since you have his blood type in you."

Mia looked from her mom to Detective Batair. "Okay . . . he has some sort of unique blood that I inherited, and it makes me immune to poisons?

"Yes, in a way." Divana continued. "He's part of a history of certain people who carry the genetics that are . . . evolved more than the average person. It's part of why you've been gaining so much strength from your training. This — ability . . . is why Dominic is so convinced of his superiority and right to rule over others. He believes it makes him better than everyone else."

"But why kill me if I'm like him? Why not, why not let me be?" Mia looked from her mom to the detectives.

"That's what I once hoped for . . ." Divana said, her expression growing more despondent as she spoke. "I can only speculate it's because you are a threat."

"That's insane!" Mia shrieked. "Who would think I'm a threat unless — am I some sort of mutation?" Mia watched Dregs tap their foot. "So, the woman had to kill me because — because I share his bloodline but, not all of it?" Mia glanced at her mom. "I have your bloodline too. What does that mean? If I only had your blood, would I have died? Are you in danger too?"

Maybe Dominic suspected that Mia only had her mother's genetics. There was a moment when the woman looked so angry that the poison hadn't worked — wouldn't they have known that she'd have both her father's and mother's DNA in her? What kind of idiot who at least makes it through seventh grade science doesn't know kids get both of their parents' genetics?

Divana wasn't watching Mia. She focused on Detective Batair, her golden eyes flashing. "Mia, I think that it would be best if I finish out with the detectives. Before you arrived, Maria called and was very upset over having an issue with her employer. Would you be willing to go and check on her? Chip's there anyway." Divana said padding her back as Dregs mumbled something under her breath Mia couldn't discern but thought it involved the word blindness.

Mia hesitated. She wanted to know more, *needed* to know more. What was her mother not telling her? It felt strange that Mia stood and did what her mother asked her to do, excusing herself from the room and going down to see Maria. Almost as though she was compelled to mindlessly obey, she walked straight into Maria's apartment without even knocking. A tall and overly chubby Christmas tree sat by the front window behind the worn couch. Decorated midway with colorful glass ornaments, tinsel, and white lights, the tree permeated the rooms with the smell of cedar wood and berries, twinkling against the added Santas and winged angels scattered on tabletops and along the scratched bookshelf.

"Mia, what a lovely surprise. I was just — MIA!" Maria shrieked, running over, her own eyes puffy and red from crying.

"It's a long story, Maria, but I'm okay."

Mateo emerged from his bedroom with a dog brush in hand.

"Ah, there's my guy," Mia said to Chip, who slipped out from behind Mateo and sniffed Mia, whimpering and licking her wrist to avoid her scratched hand.

"Mia, *que paso?*" Mateo asked, coming close to Mia's face and touching her bruised eye.

"Mateo!" Maria scolded.

Chip growled in protection.

"Everyone, I'm fine." Mia backed away from Mateo's prodding finger but tried to reassure Maria she felt better than she looked. "Look, I can still dance." Mia jumped on her good leg and winced.

"Oh, Mia, I am going to get something to help you." Maria directed her to sit on the couch, where Chip had taken up a seat waiting, pleased to get away from Mateo's vigorous brushing.

"Maria," Mia called while she shuffled to the kitchen, "my mom wanted me to check on you. She said you're having trouble with work?" Mia craned her neck to try to see Maria while she rummaged for something to hold the mess of ice cubes that had fallen on the floor.

Maria looked flustered, tears welling in her eyes. "It's okay, just my employer, Mrs. Bayer. She says her daughter-in-law is right now driving here to take her ring back that she gave me. She believes I stole it!" Maria burst into tears.

Trying to help Mia with the icepack, Mia took it from her as Maria heaved heavy sobs.

"But, Maria —" Mia tried to lead the women to sit on the couch. "Mrs. Bayer gave it to you! For Christmas! Doesn't her daughter in-law understand that?"

Maria shook her head. "They tell Iris she forgets things and that she doesn't know what she is doing, and they treat her poorly. Her memory is fine. She's smart as a whip, but this is so much trouble.

I am going to put the ring on the doormat, and she can just have it. I don't want trouble. I can't believe this, someone telling me I am a thief and this all happening right before Christmas." Maria went to her room and got the ring she had lovingly put on her dresser to admire until Christmas Eve, when she was going to wear it for the first time.

"Wait." A thought came to her mind. "Maria, can you stay here and not open the door for five minutes until I get back? Don't put the ring out either —"

"But if she comes, I cannot have any trouble. It would upset Mateo, and —"

"I know, but if you can just wait, I'll be right back. Less than five minutes, I promise." Forcing her achy leg to hurry as she shuffled back up the apartment stairs, Mia got to the door just as Detective Dregs opened it to leave. "Please don't go yet!" Mia said while her mother, carrying a hardened expression, looked ready to argue. "It's Maria. There's a mix-up with her employer. Maria's being accused of stealing. Can you come down and help?"

Detective Dregs spoke up first: "Sorry, kid, don't work domestics." And they stepped out onto the landing and waited for Batair to follow.

"I know." Mia tried to catch her breath. "But it won't take more than a few minutes. I think your presence would help smooth out a misunderstanding. This woman is abusing her power over her mother-in-law and Maria is so kind and honest. Mateo, her son is my age and — I promise it won't take long." Mia now looked to Batair, who was still standing in the same spot, listening to Mia's plea.

"Tommy," Dregs said, but he narrowed his eyes at Mia.

"Go ahead, I'll catch up."

"Tommy."

"I'll catch up." Batair left the apartment, Mia trailing behind and taking the lead down the back staircase, while Dregs left without a backward glance.

Mia knocked on the door this time. "Maria it's me, Mia. I have a friend with me," she called, and the door slowly opened, Chip's nose the first thing to be seen. "Maria, Mateo, this is my friend, Detective Batair. He can help you speak with Mrs. Bayer's daughter-in-law to clear everything up," Mia explained, stepping inside with Detective Batair and closing the door quickly behind her. "Remember him, Mateo?"

Detective Batair nodded to Mateo, but the young man shook his head.

The doorbell rang and Maria gasped.

Detective Batair asked Maria to stand by the couch with Mateo while he opened the door and let himself out into the hallway to talk to the woman. Mia and Maria exchanged worried looks, hearing the hysterical woman demanding her mother-in-law's jewelry, yelling something about a ring in hostage. Mia winced hearing the woman speak about Maria so poorly, misnaming her *Marie*.

Mia couldn't make out what the detective was saying, but somehow, he was able to calm the woman, and soon they couldn't be heard in the hallway any longer. Opening the apartment door and slipping inside, Divana came and hugged Maria, explaining that the detective was walking the woman to her car (and was on the phone with Mrs. Bayer).

"But how did he do that so fast?" Maria teared up in relief. "Dee, I need a cup of tea to calm my nerves." Maria asked Mia if she wanted one.

"No, I'm okay, I think I'd like to go unpack." Mia hoped to catch the detective before he left, while her mom eyed her suspiciously, as if she knew what Mia wanted to do.

Mateo expressed his disappointment.

"Mia, stay, watch wrestling," he said, pointing to the dramatized match ensuing on the television screen and copying the bronzed, mustached wrestler, showing off his budding biceps.

"Oh, dear, he likes the workout now so much — go Mia, save yourself." Maria laughed from the kitchen and answered the ringing phone.

Mia heard the utterances of Maria promising Iris she wasn't quitting and accepting her apology for her meddlesome family member as she headed out the door. Mia's mom promised to be home after tea.

"Detective!" Mia called to Batair, who watched Mrs. Bayer's daughter-in law pull out of the parking lot. Evidently, she'd not changed out of her pajamas for the day from what Mia could see as she drove away in her light blue sedan. From afar, the detective didn't seem as intimidating standing in the parking lot, his back turned to Mia. Sundays for Mia and her mom were stay-at-home days, for catching up on housework or laundry, and usually, the parking lot was full of others doing the same. But today, the parking lot was mostly empty. The neighbors were out. *Must be doing last-minute Christmas shopping.*

Approaching the detective, Mia called to him. "Hey, thanks for your help." She tried to hide her limp as she passed a neighbor lingering around the mailboxes. Batair could easily pass for a college guy, except for the holster he wore under his jacket. "She didn't give you too much trouble?"

"No," he said. "She seemed to appreciate the law — that's always convenient."

Mia laughed, and for the second time ever, she saw the detective smile. How had she never noticed his facial hair before, his small, manicured goatee that outlined his taut jaw — his gray eyes glinting against his dark, smooth skin . . . his soft, kind lips . . . . Clearing her throat, Mia asked, "Detective, do you need a ride? Although I'm not sure you and my mom want to be in the same car together."

"No. Can I help you up upstairs?"

Mia shook her head. The last time she'd had physical contact with him, she forced herself to review quadratic formulas to avoid thinking about his warm body pulsing underneath his thin T-shirt.

"Please?" He held out his arm.

Mia leaned against him and groaned. Somehow, the physical contact made the whole of her body ache worse. Even wrapped in his leather jacket, she could feel his strength as she held onto his steady arm, catching the scent of peppermint and oranges.

"Mia." His solemn gaze settled on her puffy face as they reached her door. "What's on your mind?" Now that she was standing close to him, she had no choice but to observe him again. His guarded eyes, his well-proportioned nose (not small like the ones at school), and that mouth that kept far away from smiling.

"Mia?"

"Yes." She said snapping back into focus. Unlinking her arm from his, she pulled away, brushing his hand and feeling that instant stir within. The moment was gone but not before Mia could admit the spark of electricity she'd felt go through her. Stealing a glance, she looked up at him, wondering if he felt something too. His gaze was trained on her apartment door.

Quickly before she lost her nerve she blurted, "Have you ever — has anyone ever died in front of you?" And unable to stop herself, her eyes filled with tears.

"Yes. Part of the line of work I'm in."

"How do you handle the guilt?" She stared at the faded Christmas bow someone had tied to the rail post.

"I don't try to handle it. I accept it."

"Oh."

"Feelings are meant to tell us things Mia, to move us, keep us alive inside. Your guilt, from seeing someone die, it's necessary. It means you value life."

"But . . ." Tears rolled down her cheeks, stinging her cuts. Maybe she was more like her grandfather than she wanted to admit. Both killers, both trying to save themselves.

"I just wish there was some other . . . I keep wondering why she was so intent on killing me. If she could have just given up or backed off, maybe I . . . ."

"People choose their paths. What you need to understand is why the woman was so intent on giving you no choice but to fight her to the death. You hold the power to understand."

"I don't hold any power!" Mia regretted her outburst as Batair looked almost hurt at her retort. "I just mean, the last thing I have around here is the power to do anything except . . . die." Maybe, instead of jail, he would haul her away to a lonely island where she could never hurt anyone again and no one would try to hurt her.

"Mia, I hope you take more stock of your life than that." Batair pulled up her hand so he could give her the jar of ointment and that feeling hit again. His hand, so beautifully brown, hers . . . scratched and bruised. The charged exchange pulsed through her as he looked deep into her troubled brown eyes. "I know I do."

A familiar car pulled up below and scraped the sidewalk with its front bumper. Detective Dregs, in the driver's seat, nodded to Mia while they revved the engine. Batair was already down the stairs, Mia watching him jump in and close the passenger door, while Dregs whipped out of the lot and onto the road. They were gone, leaving Mia to think on what Batair could possibly have meant.

The fast-approaching holidays were the perfect distraction. Half-expecting her mother to threaten to chain her to the house, Mia found herself enjoying the feeling of teenage normalcy that included hanging out at Ting's house, shopping for Christmas presents, and the occasional drifting of her mind to think about Detective Batair's striking gray eyes.

This distraction had never happened to Mia before, although she'd had plenty of friends who had explained similar experiences of infatuations with their crushes. There was one time, in the sixth grade, when Robert Custa defended her by yelling at a classmate. Mia was being teased for not having a father to come to Parents' Day and instead of letting her hide in the bathroom because her mother had work, Robert made Mia join him and his father for ham-and-cheese sandwiches while they explained the basics of football, and how to make the foamiest root beer floats. Mia never forgot his kindness that day, and for the rest of the year, she felt something soft toward the boy who faithfully waved whenever he spotted her. When she found her mind wandering to the detective, Mia would shake her head and begin singing her favorite Christmas carol.

"I think you just kind of shove them into the tree," Divana said, attempting to string colored lights around their first real Christmas tree. The skinny balsam fir sat lopsided in front of the window in a pot of rocks and water. "Maybe you wrap them around the branches?" Divana looked at the blinking lights as if it was a complex puzzle and then startled Chip by yelling at him as he tried to relieve himself on the tree.

"I never understood till now why people got so excited for these things." Mia found herself enjoying sitting on the couch and watching her mom decorate.

"I know, and I could *never* justify cutting down a tree," explained Divana, an avid plant lover who'd gotten the tree from a client who'd decided to drive east for the holidays.

"Well, we could go artificial in the future." Next year they could save up to get a big tree and some ornaments; this one only topped out at about four and a half feet.

Divana looked at the tree and smiled. "Sure, a big tree. Hey, that reminds me, your dad, did he contact you yet?"

"No." He was busy with the movie and documentary, and it was better for Mia that he stayed away after his refusal to help with Dominic. The memory of Charles's cowardice pricked her every time she thought about that visit in his trailer. It almost suffocated her when she added the fight with the woman on the cruise ship, knowing he was downstairs, shmoozing, while she fought for her life. "I have a gift for him, though." Mia texted Ting her Christmas wish list, which consisted of a pair of running socks, a sweatshirt, and a reusable water bottle.

"You do?" Divana stood back from adjusting the tree.

"Mom, don't look so . . . He's still my father," Mia said, thinking there wasn't much to a personalized handkerchief, but how was she supposed to know what to get him?

"You know, Mia — I worry sometimes that all that's happened to you would dampen your spirit."

"Hey, I thought no serious talk."

"I know. I just want to let you know that I'm really proud of you. Despite this place and despite things with your dad, I'm proud of how you've kept your goodness in there." She poked Mia in the abs that she'd only recently developed. "There, that's all I wanted to say." Divana tossed her brassy blonde hair behind her while she pinched her lips shut and indicated she was headed to the kitchen to start on their Christmas Eve dinner for two.

CHAPTER 23

A Gift

Mia's mouth was wide open. Before her in the dusty gravel parking lot sat a brand-new, gleaming pearl-white Range Rover. It was almost midnight when Charles woke Mia with a few startling bangs on the apartment door. He paraded the pajama-dressed women outside and downstairs to give Mia her Christmas gift.

"Go ahead. Let's give it a drive." Charles was boyishly giddy as he showed Mia all the upgraded features of her new custom-built car — down to the hidden security cameras, bulletproof windows, and a glittered sheen added to the paint job. Not one to spend a lot of time wishing for material things, Mia recalled texting Ting earlier in the night that she had no hopes for presents this year, apart from her own car (something she'd said only in jest). An unsettled feeling had been growing ever since the cruise ship. It wasn't something she could put her finger on, but the thought of her own mode of escape gave some ease to the tension that had led Mia to daydream about getting a car. Now, here she was, hours later, as if someone had read her mind. But this time, it wasn't the nine-hundred-dollar clunker she'd pictured. The Range Rover smelled just as a new car should, every button and knob unused and for her fingers alone.

Charles buckled himself in the passenger seat, while Mia hesitated, not knowing how to turn on the keyless car. "We have to program it to your voice, but for now we can click this." Charles tapped a button on a remote that started the car as he clicked on his seat warmer. "It won't bite," he said, smiling at Mia's jump to the automated female voice welcoming the passengers.

"I just . . ." Mia listened to the quiet purr of the engine. "I feel like this is too much," she said, glancing back at her mom. Divana's car had begun whimpering whenever she drove it over the fifty-mile mark. "And I don't have my license, technically."

"Oh, well, that's fixable." Charles turned on the radio so Mia could hear the ten-speaker surround sound.

"How about limited distractions for the new driver?" Divana leaned forward and turned off the radio, the car reverberating from the sound waves.

"Sure, good point. Okay, Mia, are you ready? I'm thinking about a drive-thru for some fries — it's my cheat day," Charles pointed out two black buttons on Mia's doorframe, the same color as the sleek wooden panel. "The first allows you direct access to the police, and the second will put the car on autopilot and take you to the nearest hospital."

Mia rolled the car onto the main road while Charles took the reins of reteaching Mia the rules of the road. He was calm when she hit the curb at the drive-thru and encouraging when she did a near-perfect parallel park. It had to be close to 2:00 a.m. when they pulled back into the parking lot so Charles could head to the airport to catch his flight to Switzerland.

"Must follow the weather," he said, referring to his next scenes needing the backdrop of snowcapped mountains. "You know, you could both join me?" Charles waved to the black SUV.

"Charlie, we can't." Divana looked at Mia sadly. "Besides, we have an urgent license to get."

"Well, then, since I can't whisk you both away, here's your gift, Dee. Promise you won't open it without me." Charles kissed her cheek.

Mia waved to her father from the stairs, double-checking that the car was locked and secure, even though she'd heard it auto-lock the moment she was three feet away. Their neighborhood was not accustomed to seeing this style of vehicle in the parking lot, and Mia went to bed hoping no one would worry that she had acquired it illegally or try to take it for themselves.

"Don't you *want* to open it?" she asked her mom as Divana placed the silver-wrapped box under their tree.

"Well, yes, of course, but he asked me to wait." Divana gave a shake to what sounded like a piece of jewelry. Mia climbed back into bed, where Chip sat grumpily at being abandoned in the middle of the night, but she couldn't sleep. She tossed and turned, the growing feeling of excited hesitation bubbling her insides. She'd never felt the giddy joy of receiving something so extravagant, and although it felt good, it also bothered her that she liked it so much. She didn't care about the type of car, but she was bothered by the fact that it was the one thing she'd wanted, a vehicle of freedom, and it was Charles who'd given it to her. What if she was indebting herself to him? What if accepting this gift meant she was absolving him of his cowardice? She was still so hurt by everything.

So much had happened since Mia had met Charles that fateful day at the casino. Meeting him felt like finding a landing place finally, after looking for so many years. But since then, too many twists had taken the dream of a dad and pushed it into a different reality.

Besides, she couldn't even bring herself to call him Dad.

By the time New Year's came, Mia decided she was going to keep the car, get her license, and take the gift as a sign that she was heading toward a better year. The last one had been a doozy. The change in Mia's stance toward her father was not lost on Divana, who reasoned the car and the hope of a new year had brightened her daughter's spirits.

Mia couldn't wait for her friends to return from their winter vacations, a ritual everyone at school seemed to take. Ting and her family always traveled somewhere tropical, this year trying a remote resort in Jamaica, where her grandma learned cliff diving.

Shelby and her father were headed north to spend Christmas at their chalet in Aspen. She was almost giddy talking about hitting the slopes and drinking hot chocolate while breathing in the pure mountain air. The only thing was her father had an unexpected surprise, his new girlfriend joining the two for the tail end of their trip and imposing on Shelby's only father-daughter time.

Mia's hopes of seeing her friends before school began were shrinking. Both girls had to take later flights and would not be getting back until late Sunday night. Ting's grandma had ended up in the emergency room after sampling some fresh berries in the Jamaican rainforest. The berries were edible, but, as the hotel on-call doctor explained, it wasn't the berries that had caused the trip to the emergency room but, the *number* of berries that Gigi consumed, bloating her stomach with uncomfortable gas.

Shelby's flight was delayed due to a winter storm, and she was stuck flying back with her father's girlfriend, Maribelle.

"AND *she* kept asking me all these personal questions. *What's your favorite food? What movies do you like? What hobbies do you have?* Blah, blah — creep." Shelby doodled on her paper while Ting reread the next test question.

"Sounds like she's trying to get to know you." Mia sighed. The woman didn't stand a chance.

"Ladies, a little less talking and a little more group work, please," Dr. Fern instructed, walking by to see their progress. "I like to allow students the freedom to work in tandem, building talents together, but if you prefer to work individually —"

"Nooo. Sorry, Dr. Fern," Ting apologized, even though she was the only one who was filling out exam questions.

"Of course, Miss Chen. I was more so speaking to your teammates here. By the way, I had a jolly time completing the evaluation for your internship," Dr. Fern said, not that Mia doubted Ting was to get anything but a glowing review from her favorite teacher. Mia had to complete a peer review over winter break for Ting's internship, answering questions from what kind of team player she was to what scientific breakthroughs did she see in her future.

"When do you begin?" Mia asked as Dr. Fern directed his attention to Terry, Jackson, and Vivian's group, as they debated who had the correct answer for question two, with Jade absent.

"April 1st if everything goes through with the board's grant, which reminds me, would you both want to come to my house for Chinese New Year? It's February 22nd. My parents are throwing a little party to celebrate the New Year and starting my internship," Ting noted quietly, a sideways grin peeking out. Mia hadn't often heard of Ting's parents making too much of an effort over her accomplishments, nor had she met them yet.

"I'd love to, Ting —" Mia started but knew it was dependent on her Strategy & Survival weekend winnings. Her team was set to compete against three schools, two weekends in a row at the start of February. If they won them all, the team would advance to the semifinals and then the finals. The final game was scheduled for mid to late February, which just so happened to be around the time that Mia's father's documentary was set to debut.

"You mean he's having a premiere?" Ting asked Mia, who nodded reluctantly as the girls stood at Dr. Fern's instruction to go outside and begin filming voiceovers for their animated cartoon. Not only was Charles having a premiere for his life documentary, but he invited most of the school to attend. "Well, at least we know he won't be bringing Crystal," Ting said.

Much to the shock of everyone, Crystal's face had been blasted all over entertainment news after eloping over Christmas with a security guard who worked for Charles. The pair was still on their honeymoon in the Maldives, pictures of her with the ring Charles had paid for flaunted as her new wedding band.

"Was that why your dad was drinking so much on the cruise?" Shelby asked.

Mia shrugged. "I guess he was bothered that he'd lost a good security guard."

"I just hope someone responsible is watching that poor dog — come on, people, any day now," Shelby barked at the group ahead finishing up with the sound equipment.

Ting leaned over while the students scrambled to finish and whispered, "Did they hear anything about —?"

"No, her body was never found," Mia said quickly, swallowing the atrocious thought of the woman she fought, her body sinking to the ocean floor, rigid and lifeless, never to be seen again.

"I have been doing a little research, and ever since you told me about, you know —there's some really fascinating theories about different tribes in history with superhuman abilities."

"Aren't conspiracy theories political ambitions made up to redirect the public?" Shelby took her seat at the table the group had just left.

"Well, yes and no. Some theories have been validated, but most are what you call unresponsive logic, meaning if someone were to prove a conspiracy theory, people still wouldn't be responsive or accepting of it because it doesn't seem to be based in logic that suits their rational daily experience. Like people who have unnatural physical strength and such, in our world they are basketball players and gymnasts, but some conspiracy theorists believe they're aliens from another planet and —"

"And today, ladies, just got a lot more interesting." Shelby said, waving at the group down the hall.

Mia accidentally knocked the computer screen as she stood to greet the crew walking toward her: Detective Batair, Dregs, and Principal Florence all headed straight to her, along with a young man Mia had never seen. Thanks to Ting's quick hands to steady the screen, Mia picked up the headphones from the floor as Principal Florence approached, looking warily at the classroom door. Mia smiled, trying to mask her panic while guessing what could possibly bring them all here.

"Miss Romeno, would you mind taking Miss Chen inside the classroom and letting us speak to Miss Storm alone?"

Shelby looked aghast. "I mean, sure, but —" Shelby got up from the table, shadowed by Ting, and walked as slowly as possible into the classroom.

"Well, Miss Storm, what a year it's been, and it's not even February." Principal Florence sighed and nodded while Dr. Fern closed the door to the prying eyes of Shelby and Ting. "It has come to my attention that there seems to be a need for additional security for you for the remainder of the year."

"For me?" Mia tried to avoid Detective Batair's intense golden-gray eyes, which lingered on hers. Just his mere presence flustered something deep within and caused her to want to smooth out her frizzy hair. "But I'm fine; all good here," Mia said, her face flushing.

Detective Dregs crossed their arms.

"Mia," Detective Batair said, catching her with his tender voice, "Principal Florence has agreed to allow us to station a bodyguard here, at the school, for you." He nodded to the man now grinning. "Kryder will be posing as a student in hopes of preventing anymore situations that could place you in danger."

Mia felt her cheeks burn. She was being given a babysitter.

Wanting to object, she wondered if Detective Batair was as frustrated as Detective Dregs looked at being here and having to bring someone to help Mia get through the rest of her school year. How was she going to explain this to her friends or her mom? Or Charles?

"Good, Kryder, get the lay of the land, and report to me when you're done for the day," Detective Dregs said, snapping the young man's attention to them and looking to the window, where the movie commotion was in full production.

"Is this all necessary?" Mia asked quietly, only Detective Batair hearing her question.

Principal Florence was now explaining what was happening in the movie saga to Kryder as he looked out the window into the courtyard — lines of ropes, security, and movie crew members helping to prepare for the next take.

"Yes, Mia, we need to know you are safe." Detective Batair watched Mia as if trying to read her thoughts.

Looking like they might combust if they didn't get some air, Dregs asked Batair, "Are we done here?" with such a stony glare that Mia decided, right then and there, that Dregs officially hated her. "Good," Detective Dregs said at Batair's nod, and off they went in their black studded boots, clomping all the way down the hall.

"Oh, I was hoping to have a chat with them in my office," Principal Florence said, watching Batair follow his partner without a goodbye to anyone. "I guess they have some important business, which leaves me to figure out exactly how to integrate you." Principal Florence evaluated Kryder, who easily stood a good few inches above six feet. "Possibly the basketball team . . . ."

The classroom door flung open, and out came Shelby. She planted herself next to Mia with her arms crossed, daring Principal Florence to send her away again.

"Miss Romeno, so glad you're here — could you take our new student, Kryder, into the classroom and introduce him to Dr. Fern? I'm going to have a quick chat with Miss Storm." Principal Florence instructed a disappointed Shelby that Mia would be missing for the remainder of class. Leading Mia down the hallway, Kryder ignored the principal's request to join Shelby for introductions and began tailing Mia like a shadow.

"Sorry, ma'am, I have my orders," he said as the principal looked to be constraining herself.

"All right, come along, but you can wait outside." Mia had never been to the principal's office, but then, why would she? What could possibly be the reason for a simple teen like Mia to be singled out, particularly by the head of school for anything like a disruption or disturbance to school events or having a secret father, and that felt to Mia like only a piece of the larger pie that was beginning to color her arduous life.

She braced herself for a new round of awkwardness as she sat behind the principal's acrylic desk. The various trophies and awards lining the built-in bookcases distracted Mia from what Principal Florence was saying as she took off her shoes and massaged her sweaty feet.

"I thought today was going to be a low-key day, but then detectives showed up. So, Mia," the principal leaned underneath her desk and popped up with a can of chilled seltzer. Sticking a metal straw inside the lemon carbonated fizz, she continued, "Now that it's just us, we can speak frankly, can't we? I really wasn't able to glean much from the detectives, but I do feel a level of concern that you are afraid for your life while here at school. Can I ask, has anyone been bullying you? Have you been receiving threats? I mean, it's just us women —"

"No, Principal Florence, really, I'm okay," Mia said, wondering if there would ever be a day when she could speak to how things really were and how she really felt.

"You know, Mia, we have someone you can speak with, if all this fame and secrecy is too much for you to handle. Our therapist is not here on site, but I can make a call and bring him in, very highly regarded, excellent with adolescents . . . ."

"That's thoughtful but . . ." Mia said, her eyes widening at the thought "I'm fine. I promise."

Finishing her drink with a tiny slurp, Principal Florence seemed satisfied with Mia's answer. "Well, the offer remains open if you need it. I just, can I be frank? I secretly hoped, by now, I'd have a VIP pass to the upcoming premiere of your father's documentary," she confessed. "But so far it's only a select group, and, as the principal of the school he's filming at, well, what would you say to having a little chat with him about getting me on that list, oh, and B-Ray if possible too?"

"Huh?"

"Well, it does sound forward of me, doesn't it — but I've always had the mentality, 'you scratch my back, and I'll scratch yours.'"

It came to her quickly, the chance to scratch her own back, and she agreed before she could second-guess her plan. "Why, sure! I'd be happy to speak with Charles for you."

Thinking the conversation was over, the principal adjusted her seat to stand, when Mia took the lead. "Principal Florence, can I go ahead and call him now? The premiere is so close, only a month away; I'd hate to lose the last VIP spot because I couldn't reach him with both our busy schedules of school and filming."

The principal's eyes danced at the news.

"Well, of course! That makes perfect sense." She smacked her lips together.

"But my phone, it's back in my bag, and I don't have his number memorized. I *would* love to ask him right away . . . ."

"Absolutely, of course." Principal Florence opened her desk drawer and grabbed a set of bronze keys. "Say no more; I have access to his personal cell; he *is* your sponsor." And while Principal Florence unlocked the cabinet door behind her desk, Mia popped her head over to study which cabinet held her file.

"Oh, I didn't realize you kept paper copies of all the students' information; how tangible," Mia said, needing confirmation that it was the secret file she was looking at.

"Well, to tell you the truth, Mia, I keep my students' records on my computer, but this —" she opened Mia's file "— is not for public eyes. I have to keep a few details off the grid, mostly from my staff, as they don't need to know the nitty-gritty concerns of the families. We're not royals, but we have had dignitaries here, children of presidential candidates — oh, here it is. Okay, I'll go ahead and write it down for you."

"Thank you so much, I'll be quick." Mia stared at her file. The principal picked it up and put it back in the filing cabinet where Mia heard a click of the lock. "Oh, Principal Florence?" A giddy feeling of rebellion grew. "This is embarrassing to ask, but if there's any way our conversation could be recorded . . . well, my father is really private, and . . . " Mia said, thinking of the cameras that Jade had mentioned, "there was this one time my father was recorded, and, well, it was all innocent, but he immediately shut down the movie and found a new location, so I just —"

"Right! Of course, naturally, we'll take the necessary precautions. I keep the cameras running on busy days — helps with the memory, but they are not on today," she said, and Mia felt satisfied her plan could really work, as if fate was on her side. Principal Florence went over to a carved white armoire and opened the cabinet to show it lined with screens, recording devices, headphones, and logged tapes. "Honestly, I really only use this from time to time, parents saying I promised this and students lying about that. Emergency uses —"

Pretending to dial her father, Mia talked to the empty buzzing of the other line while the principal grabbed her jacket and left the room. Quietly grabbing the keys from inside the desk, Mia put down the phone and made her way to the filing drawer. Five keys later and she couldn't believe she found the one that opened the drawer to hundreds of student files, cataloged alphabetically beginning with Adele Asteroid. Grabbing her own file, labeled *STORM*, Mia opened it.

It was just as she expected. Pages of information about Mia's father and his acting career, details on the movie and his financial contributions. Not much about her mother or Mia's life before coming to North Elite, apart from a few school references, her interest in psychology, and her mother's salary, which was marked in big red letters *INCOMPATIBLE*. It wasn't a scandalous file, but to the outside world, it was leverage, and she was more than happy to erase this from the eyes of Jade, Will, and anyone else who wanted to use it against her. Taking most of the papers from the file and stuffing them down her shirt, Mia grabbed a few pages from a random file, checked to make sure they were boring and uneventful, and added them to hers. Whoever read this would think that Mia had had LASIK eye surgery at the age of ten and was the great distant cousin of a sultan heir. About to close the drawer, she spotted Will's name and paused. Opening the file marked *TURLINGTON*, Mia read a submission for financial aid attached to a lengthy letter from Will's father about bankruptcy and promises to catch up on his tuition. It seemed Will's family was hardly able to pay for his current schooling, let alone future colleges.

Mia grabbed the papers from Will's file. Shoving them down her shirt with her own, she locked the cabinet, put back the keys, and left the office bustier than when she'd entered.

Hurrying outside and across the courtyard, she made her way back to school, followed by Kryder. Turning to face her shadow, she demanded, "Look, I need to pee. You're not going to follow me in there, are you?" She pointed to the bathroom she'd been locked in during the first week of school, when someone thought it was funny to prank the new girl. As Kryder nodded and motioned for her to lead the way, Mia found out she now had a constant companion for the foreseeable future, even to the bathroom.

CHAPTER 24

A Hinge

The month of January ended with Mia deep in preparation for another Strategy & Survival Games. This round, her team was playing against Catan Academy, a military preparatory high school that Justice had heard often made their opponents cry.

Mia and her team were spending the second half of practice watching highlight reels of a brutish student slamming his frightened rival into a tree, the hollowed trunk cracking in half.

"I think it's their ability to out-mass," Oliver guessed, intimidated by the sheer size of the opposing team.

"Well, then, beef up, everyone," Chet said as he patted his stomach, which had grown from bingeing over the holidays. "I told you, Cap—we don't need more training, we need team burger outings!"

Justice ignored Chet, as he did to anyone in practice who tried to steer his focus from the task at hand, winning the upcoming games. The team had a hard loss last week, after Andy's suspension for having too many accumulated detentions. One player down wouldn't have cost them the game, except they'd lost the twins hours before the starting horn, both Kai and Tai coming down with the flu after visiting their auntie who ran a home daycare. They tried to convince Coach Drake that their game performances would not be impaired by fevers and urgent bathroom visits, reasoning they could manage their symptoms with high doses of vitamin C and caffeine. But Coach Drake made them stay home, and without Andy and the twins, the team lost the game early Saturday morning. Although Mia felt sorry for Justice and Chet (both wanting to take away the championship title for their senior year), she was pleased to have an unexpected Sunday to spend with her mom.

Mia was so close to feeling ready to take her driver's test that she scheduled it for the coming Monday. If all went well, she'd be able to drive to school for the rest of the year, all on her own.

"That doesn't make any sense, honey, it's a gift for you." Divana watched Mia pull into the tight parking spot and breathed a sigh of relief.

"But *you're* the parent, and *you* should have the nice car."

"Oh, I don't care about those things. Besides, if I showed up to work in such a thing, people would start to wonder — a lot of my clients have such deep struggles with finances — truly, I would feel uncomfortable throwing something so lavish in their face."

"What about asking Charles for something less extravagant?" Mia was getting in last-minute driving practice in her mother's old sedan, which added its two cents by spurting something from the exhaust. "See, this thing is on its last legs," Mia guessed, while her mother clicked her tongue and pretended to coddle the car.

"Don't you let her speak that way to you. Honey, gifts are meant to be enjoyed and appreciated. I think you need to understand something," Divana said while Mia waited for her mom to hop out and grab Mia some pre-license celebratory ice cream. Looking at Mia, Divana's eyes held that stunning golden halo as she became serious. "I believe this is your dad's way of helping protect you. I know it's not what we wanted, but it is incredibly thoughtful. A gesture of love. He spared no expense making sure your car is as safe as he could make it, and I know. I recently saw the insurance premium."

Mia patted the peeling steering wheel and watched an older gentleman scuffle into the store, a suited woman impatiently trying to cut in front of him.

"I agree, it's generous," Mia said, not wanting to credit her father too soon. She had noticed how much thought he'd put into designing the vehicle. Especially after Charles had sent a man from the insurance company to visit them and train Mia on how to use the "unique features" the car possessed, including a series of voice commands that somehow would — the man wouldn't say more — "derail outside danger."

"Charles's heart is good, Mia —" Divana said, and if it weren't for the bright sunshine hitting her mother's face as she stepped outside, Mia would have sworn her mother teared up.

Friday afternoon came speedily, and Mia couldn't help but notice that every player on the opposite team *was* double her size in weight as they made their way into the forest after the starting bell. This time, her team was on foreign territory, the base woods next to Catan Academy, a school that had similarities with an Eastern European fortress. Thankfully, Chet had been continuing to show Mia how to use her strength and speed against larger opponents, a skill she knew would be needed in the next few days.

After she unloaded her gear once Justice chose their camp spot, Mia's first post was to scout the forest with Tai; he'd been given a clean bill of health from Justice along with an extra allowance of protein bars to regain some weight. Making their way around the forest's edge to the backside of the woods, Mia hunted for the winner's box. Chet and Kai were already reporting no sign of the box on their side of the forest as the four teammates approached Catan's camp, Mia and Tai coming from the east, and Chet and Kai coming from the west.

As he looked through his night vision binoculars, Tai let out a low growl and passed them to Mia. Two large boulders sat on opposite sides of a tall row of thick tree trunks, currently being stacked and woven together with taut rope. To Mia, it looked like they were erecting a massive fence around their purple flag, barely visible as it dangled like a carrot from a lean tree branch in the middle of the fort. The remainder of the team was busy stacking stones around the base of the fence, securing any openings with mud and crushed leaves.

Backing away, Tai and Mia crawled some fifty feet north toward camp, where they found a low brush to hide in, frantic to radio the team and share what they'd discovered. Mia lay on the ground while Tai listened to Chet confirm, out of breath, that he, too, saw the predicament.

"And I lost Kai — I mean, we got separated, and I have bad news," Chet said.

"What about the winner's box?" Justice kept his voice tempered.

"That's the bad news! The winner's box is in their camp!"

"But it can't —" Justice retorted. "That's not the rules — I should have thought something was up when they said there was no camera crew!" Justice yelled, his voice carrying a level of manic over the muffled walkie-talkie. Mia signaled to Tai it was time to head back, Justice was calling for an emergency team meeting. "Look, we've been duped," he said while the team circled around the flag. "We could report them, but I don't want to be remembered as the captain that snitched, and personally, I want to beat these cheaters even more now."

Mia stole a glance at a focused Pierce, his gaze unwavering from Justice as if he knew Mia might be thinking of his own betrayal.

"Agreed—" Stag said, his forehead wrapped in a black bandanna. "If we call the game, and report them, they'd have enough time to replant the box, and it'll be our word against the barbarians."

"So Cap, what's our angle?" Andy asked, Oliver and Simon nodding.

"I say we ambush them, every man, woman and weapon," Chet began, "take as many out as we can, full demolition of their team, and hope one of us gets the flag." He said chewing on some bark.

Kai stumbled back into the clearing just as Chet lowered himself, ready to pounce on whoever approached. "Oh great! You're back," he said to the mud-splattered boy. He'd slipped in a ravine — or at least he hoped it was a ravine; the smell permeating from him was undeniably foul.

"I know we can do this." Justice pulled up his chest. "We have skills, we have brains, we have been training, and we have loyalty to one another. We can use all that and do something they wouldn't expect, something that would confront their weaknesses." His eyes moved to Mia.

"Ah, what?" she asked as a grin crossed his mouth.

"Mia, how much do you weigh?" Justice asked as the group of guys shifted uneasily.

"Well," Mia stammered, "I've gained some weight since we began training, so I don't really know." Mia trusted Justice but couldn't gauge where he was going with this.

"But can you guess, is 120 close?"

"I mean, I really don't weigh myself," she admitted, Kai having joined his brother in the circle, punching his twin's arm. "See, I was right; she *could* take you, little brother."

"Perfect. Mia, guys, this is what I'm thinking . . . ." And Justice huddled the team close.

In no time, Mia was harnessed to a climbing saddle and weaving her way up a young California redwood, while the twins and Chet watched from behind, each in their own tree.

"Come on, Storm," Chet said into the walkie-talkie. "You got this."

"I think you're distracting her," Kai said over the channel, while Tai informed everyone that he'd just found a bird's nest, to which Justice barked for them to "Update! Not commentate!"

"Hey, guys," Mia said, out of breath, "a little quieter," and she threw her weighted line to the next tree.

"Okay, Storm girl is flying through the trees, each move taking her closer to the military base — she reminds me of a squirrel I once shot with a BB gun; no sign of fear in this one, maybe a little bird poop on her helmet, and some sweat running down her cheek —"

Mia ignored the dialogue and leapt onto the next tree, using her line as a pulley to swing herself against the trunk. Grabbing branches, she slipped and fell a few feet.

"And that was a close one," Tai continued as Mia regained her composure, finally seeing the purple-white flag. Her stomach growled at the smell of grilled sausages wafting toward her from below. Whispering into her walkie-talkie, she reported what she saw: half the team eating dinner while four guards were stationed outside the fortress, two at the movable door and two patrolling.

"Probably fueling up before the attack," Andy guessed, back at camp with the rest of Mia's team.

"Then, we'll be ready —" Justice promised while Mia debated her next move.

The beefy blonde guarding the door, pulled out a shiv (another outlawed item) and began carving something into the wood.

"Frakus, what was that?" His partner asked, returning from the woods.

Looking around quickly, he shrugged. "There's nothing. The *skizzies* have no chance. Can we switch soon? I'm starving."

Mia had three trees between her and Catan's flag. Looking to Tai, she gave him the signal that she needed a distraction. Tai signaled back to Kai, and Kai motioned over to Chet. The two boys climbed down the tree to begin Phase Two of Justice's plan. Mia waited for the cue, Tai remaining close for the toss-off.

It happened so fast, Chet and Kai ambushing the enemy's camp, yelling like hyenas and causing all hell to break loose. Frakus cut his hand, the patrolling guards smashed into one another; the fort door jammed when all five boys inside tried to open it. When they did, Mia watched Chet and the twins draw Catan's players into the forest, leaving Mia unattended and able to swoop in.

It was as if a wild animal spirit had awoken in her body, her dexterity and weightlessness overpowering all other senses as she maneuvered herself to the flagged tree. Her mind shifted into a trance, her intuition taking over reasoning and thought. Mia used the memorized codes to open the winner's box, and she had the congratulatory praise of her teammates as she delivered the news, flag in hand, that they had won the game.

The elation of winning the Strategy Games, and becoming licensed to drive by the state of California, sent Mia into a sanguine bliss as she strolled through February. Even Chip, in his new collar, seemed to be walking with an extra bounce (Divana insisting it was Maria's homemade treats that appeared weekly on their doorstep). Mia's school workload was at a manageable pace, now that she knew how to better anticipate the teachers' expectations of each class (after spending half a year catching up). She earned her first *A*-minus in English, and after she was able to get Principal Florence

VIP access to the premiere, Mia heard the good news from her guidance counselor, Mrs. Taylor, that she now believed college was more likely in her future.

At her final checkup with Dr. Millard, Mia was given a clean bill of health and the stern warning to never return to his office again under such circumstances (which Mia worried was aided by her mother's rejection of his request for a second date). With such a collection of goodness, Mia felt like she could better see the colors of life, the darkness only occasionally sneaking into her late-night dreams.

Somehow, the deadly fight with the woman on the cruise allowed Mia to gain a deepened sense of confidence, knowing she'd faced death three times and come out alive. Like she had a shield of protection around her that she hadn't seen before. Like the super blood that ran through her veins had afforded her a safeguard against all that had come to attack her, and she felt, she could be okay. Her mother seemed to believe so too, as Mia twice found her spring cleaning everything from old photographs to her favorite artworks from a younger Mia.

Before bed one night, Mia found her mother organizing pictures, when she popped her head into her room to say good night. Divana looked up from her collection of crayon drawings and misspelled notes at Mia's question.

"Hate having my picture taken? Well, yes, I've never liked it, but why do you ask?" Divana grinned at a seven-year-old *Hap-e Bert-day* card.

"I just noticed in my scrapbook you're rarely in pictures. I guess I could believe that if you weren't so pretty, but you're the last person who should shy away from the camera."

"Sometimes the camera catches angles of us we want to keep unseen —" Divana found another picture of Mia on a particularly bad hair day in the sixth grade. The day before that picture was taken, Mia had decided to cut her own bangs.

"You know what I mean. Can you *now* tell me what you were talking about with the detectives when I went to see Maria? I think it's time — it's not fair that I don't know." Some days it bothered her deeply; others, she was able to push it from her mind. But whenever Detective Batair's face crept up, which was more than she cared to admit, she would remember.

"I'm practically an adult." She could drive, after all.

"Are you now?" Divana asked playfully, looking up at Mia from her memory box and feeling the growing seriousness of the conversation. "Well, I never thought of someone as an adult until they were able to take full responsibility for their own life and didn't have their mom wash their dirty underwear." Divana put the keepsakes back into the shoebox. She closed the shabby lid with a laugh, but Mia didn't smile. Divana crossed her legs on her bed and settled herself back on her pillows.

"Okay, talk here . . ." She patted the bed for Mia to join. "The detectives were worried about my safety because of my relatives. Like your dad, mine had . . . abilities too; that's all." Divana gave a pained smile.

"But you said you were safe."

"Yes, honey, I am. Nothing's going to happen, I wouldn't expect —"

"What does that mean? Maybe we should see what else we can do to protect you; have you considered a gun? And what kind of abilities are you talking about?"

"A gun? No, Mia, that's not for me."

"But what if it could save you from —"

"I'm sorry honey, but I'll never operate that way. So easily take one's life to save another. I know my limits, I know my weaknesses. I can live with them. And the healing, that's from me." Divana looked lost in a memory Mia couldn't see.

At the word *healer*, a spinning wheel of memories hit Mia's consciousness: falling off the playground, the bus bombing, Shelby almost dying from poison, and of course, the brutal attack from that woman.

"But *why* didn't you tell me this before?" Mia touched her temple as her voice grew in pitch. *Not* another *secret*.

"I planned to; I've just been waiting. There's much we've dealt with this year. I honestly wasn't ready . . . ."

"Mom. Why do you think it's okay to keep things from me, things I need to know?" Mia said. "It's not fair. I keep getting these little pieces of pertinent, life-changing information that you just throw around, like —"

"Excuse me?" Divana sat upright.

Mia was standing now, unable to stay still as she paced the room.

"It's not fair you're — you're treating me like a child, and I'm NOT A CHILD anymore. No one who had to endure what I did — you say adults are responsible but . . . where were you when I fought off that woman? I've had to deal with things NO ONE understands."

"Mia, do not think I am unaware of all you've had to deal with. I, too, have had to take an unexpected path that I wouldn't deem fair." Divana stood and clenched her fists.

Taken aback by her mom's posture, she knew she should back down. But she couldn't. "Why, because you got the bad end of the stick too, so I can't feel bad? Well, I do feel bad! I DO! You choose a coward of a man, and HE'S MY FATHER! I DIDN'T CHOOSE HIM!" Mia stomped her feet and threw her hands. She felt out of control, her body moving and taking over what had been locked inside.

"I . . . we . . . your father and I were destined for each other — there was nothing . . . I couldn't stop it . . . I knew the risk, but I never thought it would go — to be so hard, being here, dealing with everything. You have NO IDEA!"

"SO, then GIVE ME AN IDEA!"

Divana was shaking; Mia, seething; both in so much pain, but Mia needed more.

"Mom, is there anything — ANYTHING — you need to tell me that I don't know that would help me understand?"

Divana unclenched her fists and took a shallow breath. Leaning back on her window, her body parted the curtains, the sun warming her and lighting her silhouette. It was peculiar that in one of her most disappointing moments with her mother, she still seemed to feel the universe telling her there was something incredibly lovely about the woman, something even the heavens couldn't ignore.

Her mother shook her head. The answer was no. She was telling Mia there was nothing more to share. Mia knew she was lying.

With the whole of North Elite Prep invited to Charles's documentary, students could speak of nothing else. Scheduled for the last Sunday of the month of February, Mia was planning to spend the weekend celebrating the Chinese New Year with Ting and decided not to attend the premiere, despite her friends' insistence.

"But I can't go without you, Mia, that's perjury." Ting pinched shut a dumpling and placed it carefully onto wax paper. "Besides, Grams is so excited."

Somehow Mia's dumplings looked nothing like her friend's, the ratio of dough to meat grossly disproportionate. Relieved Gigi scooted them out of the kitchen, the girls stole away to Ting's room to discuss the surveillance tapes she'd taken from the cruise ship security.

"This doesn't show us much except that our school has a tremendous lack of security." Shelby viewed the tape that Ting had edited into a video timeline of the woman's whereabouts on the ship.

"You're right; it only shows where she boarded and how she was able to get to our suite," Ting explained. "However, it struck me as odd that she knew where to go. Somehow, she had prior knowledge of where Mia would be staying. But according to Madame Cherry, the rooms were only assigned the morning of the cruise. So, I looked into who had booked the rooms. Turns out, it was that woman Sasha, who we sat with."

"So, we need to find out from her who requested the King's room?" Shelby asked.

"Or I could just ask Charles." Mia wondered if her hunch was right.

"Yes, it would be convenient to ask him," Ting said, "or we could ask Sasha."

"She's not going to tell us unless she knows why we want to know," Shelby said.

"I was thinking — maybe Will could help us," Ting said hesitantly as she watched Mia's face. "I know it's not ideal, but —"

"No, not him."

Shelby narrowed her eyes. "And just when are you going to tell us why you are holding a grudge?"

"I'm not holding a grudge. I just don't trust him and —"

But Terry burst through the door to announce that Ting's parents were giving out red envelopes, and lunch was being served.

"That's it." Shelby wiggled her finger in her ear.

Ting had screamed in surprise at Terry's intrusion, and Shelby's eardrum bore the brunt of it. "We weren't able to get him on the cruise, but mark my words, by the end of the year, I'm going to get him."

Mia and Ting didn't dare doubt her.

CHAPTER 25

The Premiere

Combing her long hair back into a low ponytail, Mia studied her reflection in the mirror and decided she needed to use some of the hair spray Shelby had given her. Applying a thin layer of mascara and peach lip gloss, she brushed her teeth and walked out of the bathroom to put on her shoes.

"The most beautiful girl in the world." Divana held Mia's shoulders to stare at her daughter.

"Ah, it's the best I can do," Mia said, thankful she was in pants, a black jumpsuit on loan from Shelby with low-heeled mules that were infinitely more comfortable than any heels she'd borrowed.

"And she's even in a onesie." Divana smiled at Mia, who hadn't realized the outfit was a one-piece until an hour ago.

She was set to be picked up by Louie in less than thirty minutes, and the thought of trying to find something else to wear made her perspire.

"Have a wonderful time tonight," Divana said while Chip jumped up on Mia's leg and pawed her pants.

"Hey, bud, don't worry, I won't be gone long." Mia grabbed his paw and bent down to scratch his head. "I don't have any of Maria's treats, I'm sorry." She looked at her mom for help to prevent her from going to the premiere covered in dog hair.

"I think I'll be taking this one for a nice *long* walk, as his tummy is undeniably widening by the day," Divana said, telling Chip to get down before he scratched Mia's leg through the thin silky material.

Paying no attention, Chip continued to jump up and paw Mia. "Geesh, you'd think he didn't want me to go." Mia caught her mom's eye as they shared a tentative look, both not wanting to admit they felt apprehensive about the evening ahead. It took a bit of convincing for Mia to relent about going to the premiere, but in the end, a sleepover at Ting's with Shelby changed her mind. Kryder was going to accompany the girls at the theater, which put her mother's mind at ease, and Mia was sure her father would be so busy, he wouldn't notice her, which put her hesitation to rest.

"So," Divana said, "how about a pair of earrings?" And she returned a moment later from her closet with a pair of drop stone earrings, sparkling blue with hints of plum.

"I forgot about these." Mia took the heavy stones and remembered her mother wearing them only once. "Are you sure?" She examined the vintage set.

"Yes, you need a little something extra." Divana said. "It's pointless to keep them locked away in old socks forever."

"Well, thanks, Mom." And she took out her small gold studs to replace them with the antique-set stones. Mia dumped everything out of her backpack onto her bed, trying to decide what she could stuff into the tiny, beaded clutch. Ting promised pajamas and whatever else they needed for the evening, so apart from her phone, the premiere passes, mints, and some cash she had from the dog sale and her first Chinese New Year, she decided that was it.

"Can we take a picture of you all dressed up?" Divana grabbed her phone from underneath the pile of Mia's things. "Shoot, the battery is dead; that's inconvenient — I thought it was at 50 percent."

Taking her phone from the tiny box clutch, Mia snapped a selfie with her mom just in time to see Shelby's text that she was outside waiting.

"I've got four-inch satin heels on, so I'd rather not destroy them on the ghetto gravel," Shelby called from the window as Mia hugged her mom at the bottom of the stairs and apologized to a whimpering Chip.

Two bags of candy later, including a flaming hot gumball that made the car smell like smoke, Mia and Shelby arrived at the old historic theater and instructed Louie to take them around to the back entrance. "Let's get away from all the lights and cameras," Mia said, only the back entrance was closed, even though Louie demanded with the security team to let them through.

"It'll be fine," Shelby promised. "I've done a ton of these. Don't be intimidated, just follow me and don't smile too much." They waited their turn to walk the carpet. "Don't trip, don't fiddle, but don't not smile either," Shelby instructed, and while Mia tried to process all of that, she passed a gigantic billboard of her father Charles' face.

CHAPTER 26

It's Him

The arrival of the two teenagers barely drew a sideways glance from onlookers as Mia and Shelby appeared on the red carpet. Alongside hundreds of waiting fans, Mia and Shelby walked beside a handful of actors, while paparazzi snapped pictures and fans sought autographs.

Behind them, friends of Charles filtered in, each taking their moment in the spotlight. Red-headed Crystal and her new husband ogled each other as they claimed to be Charles's biggest fans. Principal Florence walked with Sasha, both dressed in sleek black blazers, accompanied by the mayor, who Mia thought looked tired. Everyone seemed to be biding their time until the man of the hour arrived.

"She wanted to wear matching outfits, but I drew the line," Ting explained, meeting the girls outside the historic theater, while Gigi visited the bathroom. Mia saw her father arrive in a black SUV, Michael Novak and a young actress from the movie accompanying him alongside the young man Mia had seen both on his wall of pictures, at the casino, and at VanBoi Biotech.

"Shelby —" she leaned in "— who is that?"

"The movie director, the guy who never showers."

"No, the younger guy," Mia said, while Gigi appeared, following in their line of vision, and added, "the sexy one."

"That's the former governor's son," Ting explained. "He's predicted to follow in his father's footsteps if his career keeps on track. Remember, we saw him at your father's casino, and he's on the board at VanBoi — also on the list for sexiest up and coming politician and . . ."

Something had crossed Ting's mind, causing her to frown.

"Don't do that, you get wrinkles." Gigi patted Ting's hand and stroked her cheek. "This only lasts so long."

"Ladies, I must insist you go inside," a short-haired pregnant woman gently pushed Mia forward.

"Yes, sorry!" Mia pulled the group along.

Once inside, Mia walked down memory lane and into the decorated years of Charles's career, from his first film, *Underdogs in Chains*, where he trained a fighter pit-bull, to his current movie, *The Unbound*. Year after year, her father's relatively unchanged face showed the projects he had dedicated his life to, Mia absent for it all. One film showed Charles holding a little girl, a father-daughter relationship that he proudly acted out while his own daughter had no idea of his existence.

The irony, the bitter irony.

Maybe she shouldn't have come.

"Mia." Shelby nudged her at the sighting of Jade. "Looks intense . . . Mia? You okay? Not drinking any lemonade, are you?"

Mia didn't laugh.

"I am just wondering where Kryder is."

He'd been expected to meet her here, and he was usually so prompt.

"Probably caught in traffic. Your — Charles, I mean — has quite a turnout." Shelby smiled at Gigi, who was listening.

"Yeah, I don't know, doesn't feel right." Mia thought she'd been so dismissive of her gut warnings in the past. Something was stirring, and she could feel it. Mia spent the next half hour scouting the theater, but nothing seemed amiss. She analyzed every person within sight, swearing to Shelby that she'd seen Detective Dregs in the crowd.

"Well, if you do, please make them arrest that man." Shelby complained of the bearded drunk who kept calling her *Jenny* and asking for her phone number.

The VIPs were shifted into the theater for the first viewing of the documentary, followed by a second showing reserved for most of the North Elite students. Mia waited for Shelby to return from the bathroom, and Ting left her to take a seat with Gigi, who was panicked she'd miss even a second of the beginning credits.

"It's okay, go ahead, we can just make the second showing." Mia reminded herself to ask Shelby about her frequent bathroom trips that always seemed to happen when they needed to be somewhere. Waiting by the wall, Will waved Mia over, when an usher asked her to please make her way inside the theater so he could close the doors. "I'm just waiting for my friend. It's okay, we'll get the next one." But Mia wished she was going inside now that Will was walking over.

"Not going in?"

"No. Waiting on Shelby." Mia saw the brunette materialize across the room. Waving to Shelby, Mia excused herself before Will could talk anymore and shuffled over to the usher. "Sir," Mia said as they both approached the usher. "Can we sneak inside? We don't mind missing the first few minutes." Shelby added a flirty, "Pretty pleeee-ase," even though he'd just closed the doors.

"Sure, I can let you in, but we'll have to go through the back."

He took them down a wallpapered hallway and up a flight of carpeted scarlet stairs to a landing. Passing the hallway of box seating, the girls followed the usher through the side door. As they looked around for any open seat, he walked them to the very last row, the lights darkened as the documentary had begun.

"It looks like you'll have to split up." The usher motioned for Shelby to follow him.

She found her seat in the fifth row from the front. Mia waited while another usher asked if he could help seat her.

"Ah, yes" she said, distracted by the film showing her father as a young boy playing in the sand at the beach with his brother — their father smoking a cigar and a young nanny attending to them.

"Right this way." The man led Mia to the back and explained he was taking her to a private box. *That's probably better.* She was relieved to hide from the gallery of people spending their evening adoring Charles. Following the usher up another staircase, this one much narrower . . . he opened a creaky door to a darkened room and escorted her inside.

"Is no one using this?" She stepped into the room, while he flicked a light switch to reveal a tiny hanging bulb and old broken furnitures that had years of dust. "Sir?" A deadly chill overcame her.

The man put something on the door, removed his usher's hat, and spoke in a silky voice. "How I've anticipated this moment, Mia."

Dominic Broderick stood before her. His silver hair pulled the blue from his eyes that once must have been striking. His skin was thin and lined, a dirty bandage wrapped around his neck under the ill-fitting usher's coat.

Late at night when Mia woke in a cold sweat from a dream, she had wondered about this moment. He'd always been a faceless monster haunting her . . . the man standing here. Her grandfather.

She stood transfixed. The image of him in person, his visual frailty, somehow beguiling. Sounds from the laughing crowd awoke

Mia from her trance, stirring the thought that she could scream for help, to which he replied, "No one will hear you if you yell, Mia. I've made sure. Soon —" he said, referring to the audience clapping again, some women gasping "— the world will discover my son has a nephew." His forced smile showed fake white teeth. At the sound of his words, Mia's stomach constricted. His words, his voice was so enticing, despite the deep horror she felt within from desiring to listen. "Curious, are you? I've noticed. Not necessarily as curious as I expected, but that's your mother's doing . . . always trying to stifle."

Dominic unfolded a ripped chair from where it was propped on the wall and sat. "Oh, the paradox of this entity, old and frail, and yet there is great strength left. Some things grow weak in age, some evolve to unmatched powers. The question is, what will become of yours, Mia?"

The sound of her name splintered her from the fugue state she was in. "Why won't you leave me alone?" The sound of her own voice sharpened her senses as she planned how to get out of there.

"Greatness needs to be tested. Without me, you would never have seen what you are capable of." He crossed his long thin legs in a way she'd seen her father do.

"Nothing you say I'll believe." Mia wondered if this was what the face of pure evil looked like.

Dominic eyed Mia. "But everything I have told you is true. I will tell you anything you want to know, secrets your mother has long hidden from you."

At the mention of Divana, Mia's anger flared.

"Don't you speak of her!" She wanted to destroy this man. To eliminate him from existence and yet could not help but wonder at the word *hidden*. "If you're talking about his nephew, I know who he is; I've seen him. If Charles wants to adopt him and forget me forever, so be it. But you . . . you will leave me and my mother — you will leave us alone and . . . *if* you don't —" Mia finished the sentence in her head.

"So, you would leave your father, just like that?" Dominic picked a piece of lint off his pants and dropped it to the floor. "I'm intrigued to hear that, for I thought you two had more affection for each other. He must know your contempt. You are more like us than you know."

"I'm nothing like you," she whispered, looking around the room for any way to escape, the feeling of water rising too high and threatening her mere ability to breathe.

"Yes, you are different, simpleminded and weak like the others and still magnificently different. There's few others like you Mia. Surely, you know that by now."

He was baiting her, baiting her to hear more.

Shaking her head, she shouted, "NO!"

"They will not hear you, Mia, but I *will* release you, on one condition. That you let me tell you what it is that everyone has been hiding from you." And with that, Dominic eased back in his chair and watched Mia decide, unsmiling and calm.

Like a foul game of trickery, Mia tried to anticipate what he imagined she would choose. If she agreed to hear him out, how could she believe he would let her go? But assessing his curved shoulders and his papery, veiny hands, she believed she had a fighting chance against him.

"The truth, and I'll let you go." A look of impatience crossed his face.

"Why . . . what are you wanting from me?"

"I want what any proud grandparent wants, to see what you become . . ."

"And if I don't?"

"Then I will kill you."

She scanned the room for weapons, but his smirk and the small rubber-looking ball that appeared in his hand stopped her.

"What . . . what is that?" She tried to make sure her voice was steady and measured. It wasn't.

"The bomb that should have killed you. Not powerful enough at the time but now laced with Arthenium Phivenstum. Very hard to come by, even harder to harvest, but will be effective."

"What—what are you going to do? All these people—" Mia's heart raced. Her friends were out there! Gigi, her father. Thank God her mother was at home, but how could she survive it twice?

"Oh, it's not active yet; only you can decide if I use it or not." He leaned forward and motioned for Mia to sit. Crossing her arms, she pushed her back against the wall, trying to press herself as far away from him as she could, wishing she could melt through to the other side.

"I first must explain the attack seventeen years ago for you to understand." He paused.

The memory of her mother telling her never to reason with hatred whirled across her thoughts.

"Many years ago, my people, of the highest position and power, found themselves . . . restricted. Unable to live freely, my people left their home to seek a land of new possibilities of freedom, although they were marked as traitors. We grew. New bodies, new abilities and gifts that extended to us an . . . unusual influence. We found our balance in this new way, our people, the *De Summa*. You can imagine my dismay when my young son, privy to this new world, cast away his heritage to be with someone from the old world."

Mia thought his eyes gained a darkness: cold, red, and drooping from age.

"But Charles has always been weak. In his weakness he tried to find partnership with someone who could never accept him for who he truly was — it is not your mother's fault where she came from, but what she wanted of him, impossible."

Mia's legs trembled. Why was he telling her this? How could she believe even a word, and yet, not wanting to show any sign of weakness, she slid herself down along a bare spot in the wall, unable to stop listening.

"The variable of a child that possessed the powers of the two lands was complicated. Do I let it live and discover what it would become or destroy it? The predicament I was faced with, a cumbersome choice. I had to test. See if the mere fetus within could survive, and you did."

Mia felt her breathing slow, almost as if her heart was freezing, everything inside of her turning so cold.

"You, Mia, the evidence that there no longer need be those trying to stop us, trying to take away our kingdom."

"I am not that person."

"Oh, but you could have been; you can be."

"No," Mia said. "I promise to you, to my father, I'll leave you all alone and go away with my mom if you just let us be. We're nothing to you."

He let out a small one-note laugh. "If only. If only you had stayed away . . . not let your weak father draw you here. But after tonight . . . things will change." He checked his watch. "Tell me, Mia, does it feel good to know you possess invincibility?"

"What do you mean?" She felt a hard, guttural scream of fear hit her stomach.

"You've faced death many times now, each time proving more exceptional. You must sense it, growing stronger by the day. We met once before. The little playground where you fell, protecting your weak little friend; you must have sensed it — both the power of the De Summa and the power of your mother's people inside you."

"My mother's a healer; she —"

But his eyes flashed with venom.

"That is a cover! Your identity is anything but, borne from one of the goddesses of light! A healer — insulting!" And he spat on the floor.

"What are you talking about?" Mia shook, inclined to laugh, and she closed her eyes and pretended this was a hallucination. Maybe she should start crying, but she opted for another laugh.

"Our time is up. What is your choice? Choose to live and I will train you to be what Charles could never be — along with it you'll get a life of power, prosperity, unlike most have known."

Mia shook her head. "POWER! I'd DIE right now to avoid one second on your side."

"Then, I see," he said as the crowd applauded, cheering on Charles, who promised a speech. With force unmatched by his feeble appearance, Dominic gripped Mia's wrist and slapped something on it that "clicked" and tightened against her skin.

"What the —" Mia looked down at the small blinking globe, but Dominic was already stepping back to the door.

He sighed. "*You* could have been something glorious. I saw the vision, you just needed an unleashing." And he pressed a button on his watch. "Eleven — the perfect number."

Mia watched Dominic unhook the door and grab the handle. Without a turn or word, he opened it and walked outside, and into the crowd.

CHAPTER 27

Death

Dropping to the floor, Mia screamed as hatred spilled out of every pore of her being. If Dregs hadn't shown up at that very moment, Mia was sure she would have died screaming.

"How long ago did he leave!" Dregs demanded before Mia could get to her feet.

"I — just moments ago," she stammered.

"Get downstairs; find Batair, and —" They spotted the cuff on Mia's wrist. "FIND BATAIR NOW!" And they were gone.

Mia scrambled out of the room and stumbled down the stairs, tripping over half of the people exiting and landing at the bottom. Jumping up, she scrambled through a mass of people migrating to the back terrace.

"Mia!" Kryder yelled from across the room. He ran over, and Mia saw Shelby materialize behind him.

Before they could speak, Mia demanded, "Where's Batair? I need to find Batair," only just noticing Kryder's swollen right eye. A roar of laughter came from the back patio, where Mia's father was beginning his speech, but Mia pleaded, "Batair . . . ."

"Follow me." Kryder grabbed her hand and pulled her toward the foyer.

Only then did Shelby notice the blinking bracelet on Mia's arm. "What the hell is that, Mia?"

But Mia shook her head. Barreling through a growing crowd of reporters, Kryder pulled Mia to the front door, where Batair waited alongside Ting, a look of fire in his eyes.

"Hunter!" Kryder called, but Batair's eyes were trained on Mia alone.

"Mia, when did he put that on you?" Batair asked with a warning in his voice.

"I . . . I don't, ah — two minutes ago."

Batair grabbed her hand. "How did he activate it?" he asked, and Mia saw in his eyes what she'd been denying, that she had a bomb strapped to her wrist.

"What the hell is happening!?" Shelby demanded, Ting grabbing Mia's arm for support; the small act warming her and dropping her stomach. She had a BOMB strapped to her arm and at any moment . . . .

"I have to get OUT OF HERE!"

Batair grabbed her arm and pulled her through the crowd of crazed fans and security guards, Batair paying no attention to anyone he forced out of his way. His motorcycle was parked one block from the theater. In an unspoken synchrony, they sprinted to his bike, the security system beeping at the click of his remote.

He handed Mia the helmet and she took it, but grabbed his hand. "Please . . . please tell me what's going on. I — I know Dominic told me. I know the secret," she said, piecing together that this was the final answer Batair had wanted Mia to know. "I don't want to die, Tommy," Mia said almost in a whimper. "I don't want to —"

"We have six minutes." Batair jumped on the bike, shoving the helmet at Mia. "Dregs has Dominic in sight; we need him to deactivate it."

"But can't we just cut it off?"

"If it's an upgrade from the last, it will detonate when it breaks contact with the skin."

Kicking the stand and ripping the bike down the side street, Batair commanded the machine to move. His phone beeped, a voiceover from Dregs reporting where to go. A car swerved out in front of them; Mia screamed and closed her eyes, anticipating the impact while he nearly leaned the bike fully on its side, skimming so close to the ground, Mia's shoulder could have tasted gravel. Upright again, she held on to his side, and the bracelet light switched to yellow.

Mia cursed. A gunshot rang, and they swerved onto the sidewalk. Another shot hit a lamppost, evening strollers screaming and diving out of the way.

Batair pulled out his gun and shot back, driving with one arm, the thrust of the motorcycle rumbling beneath her. She tightened her arms around his chest, his pounding heart syncing her thoughts to something besides terror. Mia spotted Dreg's car, the sedan edging just beside it, trying to run it off the road. They went on like this for a few miles, squinting her eyes closed with every gun shot, racing toward a back part of town. Darkened streets and abandoned shops gave way to one long road and as Mia opened her eyes, she knew the end was here one way or another; the road ending in a restricted pier, and then there was only ocean.

The sedan was at full speed when suddenly, it turned, swerved, and crashed into Dregs, spinning their car in circles until it landed on its roof.

Swearing again, Mia closed her eyes and leaned into the turn, while Batair shifted the bike sideways, skidding to a halt and slamming Mia's leg into the railing. Jumping off the bike, Batair held up his gun, yelling for Dominic to get out of the car. Mia slid off, unable to put much weight on her leg as she limped toward them,

Batair yelling at her to stay back. Dregs's bloody hands appeared, pulling themself out through the car window and stumbling toward the sedan. Flicking on a lighter, they threw it onto their car and ignited it.

"OUT OF THE CAR!" Batair yelled while Dregs shot at the open window, jerking open the driver's side.

Mia couldn't believe the size of the man Dregs pulled out. His arms were a mass of muscles and veins, and he looked ready to kill, with a gun in each hand. He yelled something in a language Mia didn't know, and it became apparent Dregs had killed his accomplice in the passenger seat. Mia worried for the rangy detective, as the man shot at them.

"HELP DREGS!" Mia yelled, but Batair kept his gaze on the blackened windows.

The gas tank exploded, and the back door swung open.

Dominic stumbled out of the car as Mia's cuff switched to red. A quiet beeping sound teased an explosion was only moments away.

"Kill him, I don't care." He coughed. "You're all dead anyways." But Dominic was stumbling. "Even if you survived the explosion, it's laced with Mia-tested gas." His laughter started a coughing fit.

"Deactivate it NOW and I'll let you live!" Batair barked, his gun trained on Dominic.

Dominic was bent over, heaving and coughing blood. "The omega has come," he sputtered, coughing out so much, Mia thought part of his organs were now on his shirt.

The beeping was increasing—a simple mathematical calculation—and she knew she was out of time.

She had to get away. She looked at Batair's bike; there was only enough time for him to take Dregs and make it a few blocks.

Dominic dropped to the floor as Dregs popped up. Somehow, they had disarmed the hulk and handcuffed his arms and feet together. With their gun now trained on Dominic and a stream of blood dripping from their head, they demanded he deactivate Mia's cuff. Shaking, he fell face-first into the dirty concrete, spilling more of his insides in far too large a pile for Mia to know that survival was not possible. Dregs ran up and kicked his leg. Dominic was motionless, frozen in his own decay. Dregs grabbed his wrist. As they tried to decode his watch, they dropped his hand, shaking their head.

"Go!" Mia shouted.

Batair strode toward her. A deeply frightened dread shaded his face.

"Mia." His eyes showed light and fire and that golden glow her mother had whenever she was upset.

"You NEED to go — GET OUT OF HERE. NOW!" Mia yelled, backing away. She was shaking . . . but Batair kept coming. "GET AWAY!" The cuff was beeping so fast, it had begun to blur into one note. There was no more time.

"Mia, look at me! LOOK AT ME!"

But she was shaking too hard.

Taking her face into his hands, Batair pleaded with her to look at him. "In the water —"

"BUT YOU'LL DIE!" Her whole body, her head, the ground she stood on, was shaking. Everything trembled and she was about to crumble with it.

As if he was calling her back to the living, Batair yelled her name. "MIA! You don't remember the explosion, but you saved your friends that day. We can survive this, but we need to get in the water NOW!" He jumped atop the railing, reaching down for Mia to do the same. She had no idea what he was talking about. No one could survive a bombing twice. Dominic had made sure of that. Even though she wanted Batair to run away as far as he could from her, even though she knew it was her most selfish act to try, she reached up for his hand. She climbed the rail, and when she slipped, he grabbed her waist to steady her. He looked at her and held up three fingers, two, then one.

Together they jumped into the sea. Plunging feet-first into the chilly water, Mia kicked to the surface, popping up to see him swimming to her. Grabbing Mia's arm, Batair covered the cuff with his hand.

"Hold on as long as you can," he whispered and pressed his lips against hers.

He was warm and alive and . . . the last thing she'd ever feel before he pushed them both down below the surface . . .

. . . just as the bomb exploded.

CHAPTER 28

Twisted Fate

Mia watched her body absorb the explosion, a mass of energy emanating from the explosion into her chest, down through her legs, and into the very marrow within. She was still connected to Batair, and the two seemed to create a force field the energy couldn't puncture.

Mia's arm was alight with fire, every appendage crying in agony. She whispered goodbye kisses to her beloved mother, as she was unable to make out Batair's face, blurred in the water or possibly melting from the heat. She didn't want to let go, but she had to. The recurring thrusts of pressure and her weakened body made it impossible to resist. Flying apart, Mia drifted deeper into the Pacific Sea, Batair hitting the concrete wall.

"Air," she gasped, trying to reach the surface. *Breathe . . . breathe . . . live.* It was all Mia could think as she kicked her legs, pushing to reach the surface, gasping for breath as she broke free from the suffocating water, then turned around to see where Batair was.

"Mia!" Batair yelled, barely audible beneath the sound of the wind and the thrashing of the water surrounding her. Mia started swimming over, her lead-filled arms too slow, as she fought a terrible fatigue, much like when she'd saved Shelby. Batair met her halfway, grabbing her just as she felt she couldn't take another stroke. He pulled her close to him, against his warm body. He swam her to the stairs, grabbed the railing, and clung, holding Mia for a moment . . . time pausing as they clung to each other in relief and desperation.

Dregs called from above, and Batair pulled Mia to the stairs, the two sloshing up the steps, Batair holding Mia's waist and blackened wrist. When they reached the top, Mia stood back as Batair went to Dregs. She found it hard to stand on her own but tried as she heard the hushed tones of the two speaking.

Dominic had called her mother a goddess of light. It must have been how she'd survived. Whatever she had, if Mia had even half of what her mother was . . . .

She could see Kryder body-bagging Dominic. The disgusting mess he'd left on the floor, the mess he'd made of her life. Maybe now Mia and her mom could have some peace. Now Mia could give her dad a real chance, and her mom, maybe she'd be able to have her happy ending with the only man she'd ever loved. Mia caught herself wondering about the future and a smile crossed her lips.

She'd survived. Batair had survived. She could have a future.

But when Batair turned around, he was stoic. "Mia — we have to go."

"Go where?" She shivered. If she could just lie down for a second, but Batair was on his bike.

"It's your mother," he said in a low, pained voice.

"My mother?" Stumbling toward him, she shook her head. Her mother was at home. Safe. The only one safe in all this mess. She slowly approached the bike.

Dregs appeared at Mia's side, holding her waist as she climbed on the murmuring machine. "What's going on?"

"Mia, you need to go. Please."

Turning the bike toward the street, Batair took off fast and without pause, on an unfamiliar road. Shaking from the cold of wet clothes and with a deep chill within her, Mia reminded herself her mother was the strength of what she had. There wasn't cause to worry. Mia had survived; her mother would be fine. When she began to recognize the familiar roads. She felt the vehicle slow and turn onto the strip mall down the street from her apartment. It was late, and the shops were closed, except for the twenty-four-hour convenient market Mia sometimes picked up milk from. Batair slammed the break, and the bike skidded across the parking lot, Batair jumping up on the curb, fishtailing it to a halt in front of the convenience store.

They both hopped off, Mia unsnapping the helmet, throwing it aside, following Batair into the mart. A panicked woman stood over the body of a woman with long white-golden hair.

"What happened?" Mia gasped, running to her mother, who lay still on the floor. But when she reached Divana's body, she choked. It looked as though someone had sucked her dry from the inside, her face sunken, her chest caved, and all vitality gone from the woman Mia knew to be so, so beautiful. If she hadn't noticed her hair first, or the favorite blanket sweater her mother loved to wear while home, she would never have believed this was her.

"NO!" She grabbed Divana's cold hand and closed her eyes. She'd done this once before, she'd saved someone. She could do this. She put her other hand under her mother's head, like a new baby and pleaded for her to be healed and to wake up. She began to whisper chants, call the forces that be, to bring her mother back to life. "This is possible." It had to be possible.

But instead of heat and life beating back into the sunken remnants of Divana, Mia could feel whatever was left of her very presence evaporate from the room. Tiny droplets of her mother's glorious essence, fading away, leaving Mia alone.

"Do SOMETHING! DO SOMETHING!" she screamed at Batair and to the kind shop owner who'd given Mia and her mother smiles and coupons all year.

But they did nothing. They stood watching Mia watch her mother's entire being disappear from the world, a shell of a mutilated woman left behind. Divana's limp hand turned so cold, it matched Mia's insides.

Mia rested her head on her mother's caved stomach, her first home, and sobbed. The sudden loneliness was unbearable. Her mother had been her entire life. She let the many soundless tears roll down her cheeks, some dropping onto her mother and soaking into her white shirt, soaking her lovely hair.

"Mia," Batair whispered, "we only have minutes."

He said something about other police officers coming, the store needing to be locked down — she faintly heard the shopkeeper crying, offering Mia something to drink, but it all sounded to her like quiet murmurings of a song with the melody of death. Mia sat up and undressed her mother's arms from the knitted gray sweater, pulling it from her body and onto her own. She hugged herself tightly with the soft yarn, wondering how she'd ever take it off.

As if on cue, two police cars hit the parking lot, Dregs flying out of the passenger side. Hurrying to Divana's body, Dregs called for the dressed officers to stay back, instructing them to seal off the area before anyone else arrived. Mia watched Dregs check that her mother was dead. With a look to their partner that confirmed it, their eyes flashed gold together, and they bowed over Divana's body.

"Go, I'll deal with them," Dregs said, referring to the police officers out in front of the shop who were almost done marking the area in yellow police tape. Batair grabbed Mia's hand again, took her outside and to the bike. The heat of his hand comforted her icy skin. She felt dazed watching the world pass by as the motorcycle traveled deep into the city of Los Angeles, away from Mia's home, her mother, her everything.

She wondered if she'd ever feel warm again.

They arrived at an alleyway deep into the east-central city side. Batair drove his bike into a dark parking lot, to a spot marked on the ground by a blue spray-painted *X*. Mia stared at the beaded bracelet on his wrist, small black beads and a blue one she'd never noticed . . . blue, the color of her earrings . . . the earrings her mother lent her . . . hours ago . . . before the premiere, before Dominic . . . before her mother died. Batair looked alert at Mia's sharp intake of breath, pausing from helping her remove her helmet.

"Dominic, he said — said things were going to change tonight!" Mia said, her eyes wide. "While — while he was talking to me . . . ." Mia let out a wild yell, an animalistic call that reverberated deep into the blackened parking lot. For the second time, she wondered if this was how she would die, yelling and calling out to the heavens, her heart stopping from grief.

But then a hand came and touched her own. His warmth stilling her, quieting her, containing the pain . . . somehow. Detective Batair led Mia out of the parking garage and into a narrow street set between two tall buildings. A rusted outside staircase climbed the building's side like ivy. He pulled down a ladder, while a woman warming her hands at a tin-can fire whistled.

Quietly telling Mia to climb up first, Batair nodded to the woman in rags. Batair swung himself around Mia, jumping onto the metal porch and offering his warm hand again to help her off the ladder. Opening the door with a key, he led Mia inside his apartment.

Switching on the kitchen light, the detective grabbed a teakettle and filled it with water. Mia stepped inside and watched him take three tins from his pantry and pull a flower off a plant on the grated kitchen window ledge. He added the collection of herbs to a mug, along with the flower, and poured in steaming water. Adding a few drops of honey, he handed the mug to Mia. "It will help you sleep."

Mia was glad she trusted him because she felt like she would do anything anyone told her to, just to escape the looming darkness. Batair took Mia down the hallway, stopping at his linen closet, and grabbed a towel and washcloth.

"You can stay here," he said to her as they stood outside the doorway of a bedroom. "I'll be on the couch."

Mia wanted to say something, but she couldn't even look into his gold-flecked gray eyes, too reminiscent of her mother's. Maybe he could read her mind, and in her mind, she thanked him.

Stepping into the plain room, she went to close the bedroom door and let out a gasp. She remembered Chip, her dog, her sweet loyal dog, waiting for someone to come home. He wouldn't know one of them would never return. Mia remembered the dog's earlier restlessness at her departure, his nagging her to pay him attention. He must have sensed something and was trying to tell her. How was it he knew? How had she missed it?

Mia opened the door and called to Batair, a hoarse gasp coming from her throat that he somehow understood.

"I am going to call your neighbor. Chip will be okay." He headed down the hallway.

Telling herself her dog would be okay, that Maria and Mateo would take good care of him, Mia realized she needed something to drink besides the herbal-smelling tea and went to the bathroom sink to drink from the tap. She washed her hands and face in the ensuite bathroom and looked into the mirror at her reflection, her skin, emitting a warm golden glow. Wondering if she was running a fever, she wiped her face with the washcloth and rinsed her mouth with water. No mother to take her temperature, to remind her to brush her teeth, to annoy her about her homework. No mother to ever mother her again. How was she meant to adjust to being so wholly alone?

Mia left the bathroom and went to the window, pulling back the curtains. Three-quarters of the moon shone through the paneled window, and somehow, she felt comforted by the light it cast onto the centered bed. Settling in the simple room, Mia drank her tea and covered herself with a heavy blanket, warming her body just enough to take the edge off. She tried closing her eyes, but every time she felt the soft pull of sleep, she snapped awake and remembered.

Taking the blanket with her, she crawled out of bed and walked down the hallway. Tiptoeing into the living room, Mia saw Detective Batair sleeping shirtless on a futon, his hands behind his head as he breathed in and out, the intricate tattoo markings across his chest moving with his breath, in and out, up and down.

Hoping he didn't wake, she climbed onto the futon and laid down on the edge, her back resting against his blanketed feet.

Her heart hurt, but her mind retained a strange blankness, her eyelids growing heavy now that she was lying down. Mia closed them and wrapped herself tighter in the blanket, everything feeling unfamiliar and different.

Nothing could *ever* feel the same without her mother.

Nothing.

CHAPTER 29

It's Okay

The funeral for Divana Storm was held at a small burial site near a vineyard, outside of town. Charles insisted on paying the steep prices to lay Divana's ashes in an Italian garden that grew grapes for wine claimed to have been touched by angels. Mia had no fight in her to dispute her father's choice. In some ways, it satisfied Mia because it kept away too many people wanting to attend, including Divana's clients. Only Mia and her father, Maria and Mateo, Ting, her grandma Gigi, Shelby and her driver Louie, Detective Batair, Dregs, and Chip found themselves surrounding the small plot of land where Divana's headstone rested on that glorious spring day.

Mia opted not to say anything, leaving the words to a kind minister who had worked with Divana at the church. Looking around at the group, Mia sighed. Her mother was one of the kindest people she'd ever known, so many people she had touched in her life, and yet, the group celebrating her life was barely a dozen. The world was carrying on as if she'd hardly been known at all.

All the times they'd moved, all the people in their past, Mia hadn't told any of them.

She was learning grief changes a person into someone who no longer cares what is right and wrong but only what will still the haunting voices that called them to stay down in the depths of sorrow.

Her friends were wonderful. Ting and Shelby took turns staying by her side, distracting her, making her drink a new flavor of bubble tea, and sometimes admitting only to one another that they were afraid to leave her alone. Mia stopped eating much, having just enough to get her through. Food seemed to lose its flavor, her stomach constantly aching, or maybe it was her heart. Somehow, her lean and strong body continued to retain its robustness. Her mother's lovely green dress still looked stunning on her at the funeral.

Detective Batair now carried a continual look of concern in his kind eyes but knew enough not to ask Mia anything beyond what required a yes or no.

It wasn't known who had killed Divana or how, although Mia knew Dominic was behind it. She reasoned it was poison, but trying to understand how she was spared while her mother . . . now that Dominic was gone, the *hows* were irrelevant. Mia told no one about what Dominic had revealed that night, apart from what she shared with Batair. After all this time, she knew the secret of her mother's life, and now she couldn't share it with her, and that made her not want to share it with anyone. What a joke life could be, the irony impossible to stomach.

Kids at school sent Mia notes, cards, and some, even flowers. She put each one in her mother's room, sometimes pretending she was on the bed admiring the expensive bouquets that rich kids were able to afford. Mia's team, having missed her for the last championship game, sent her a lemon tree. The card explained that without Mia on the team, they were a bunch of lemons, but her presence brought a sweetness to all of them that allowed them to become something more. They signed the card with a *P.S.: We lost the championship, but it feels right without you here.*

Shelby, when she wasn't with Mia, began going to church, a small chapel down the street from the casino. Most of the service was in Greek, which she found refreshing, just listening to the sweet, steady music and watching the robed priest wave incense. She would wear her sunglasses, cry, and beg for wisdom on how to help her hurting friend. After two weeks of settling her mother's affairs, Mia went back to school, mostly because she didn't know what else to do. Her grades dropped, her effort toward school minimal at best. But Will told Shelby that Principal Florence had gathered all of Mia's teachers into her office and threatened their jobs if anyone so much as attempted to give her below a *C*.

Grandma Gigi cooked for Mia, and Ting offered an open invitation for Mia to stay at their guesthouse. She assured Mia she and Chip were welcome for as long as they needed, her parents sending a sympathy basket to express the same invitation. But for now, Mia was splitting her time between her apartment and her father's house on the hill.

"It will be fun," Charles said one afternoon while Mia packed a few things in a box to keep at his house. "I mean, there's a pool . . . ."

Mia wanted to stay right here, close to her mother's things, close to Maria and Mateo, who had become her and Chip's second family. Not a day went by when Mateo didn't stop over to give Mia a hug and tell her he missed Divana. He would remind Mia of what his grandfather used to tell him, "'Mateo, the sun will shine tomorrow,' so Mia, I will tell you, the sun will shine again."

Spring released its goodness and beauty upon the land. Delicate prismatic flowers, newly hatched baby birds, and for the school, the excitement of summer plans all flourished. Although California kept much of its resplendence throughout the year, the spring here was a new level of beauty that Mia knew her mother would have loved to see.

"I think that's it for now," Mia said. "Oh, what about this?" She held up the small, wrapped Christmas box from Charles.

"My God, she never got to open . . . Mia, that's for you now." Charles smiled sadly. "Just don't tell Nimmy; I paid cash, so it's all yours — and it's off the books."

"Do you want me to open it?"

"You know, I think . . . hold on to it for now — you can open it a little later, when things settle." He teared up. Charles was doing that a lot lately, crying randomly and forcing smiles. At first, Mia assumed he was being dramatic, but six weeks from Divana's passing, he still seemed heartbroken.

"What can I make you for dinner, kiddo?" Charles asked, as they walked to Mia's car.

She hadn't felt like driving much so he took the keys, excited to show her more of the car's features.

"I'm okay with whatever." He was a terrible cook, so she suggested pizza.

"Well, sure . . . It's not my cheat day, but that sounds perfect."

The last week of school came and with it, final exams and end-of-year celebrations for departing seniors. Mia joined her friends in the auditorium for the senior send-off; three of Mia's teammates graduated, although she cared little about Pierce's departure. As Mia walked down the athletic hallway on the last day, the smell of fire still circulated in the air.

"I hope they install those toilets that clean you like Pinewood has," Shelby said of the beginning construction on the women's locker rooms. Mia headed outside, across the cleared courtyard, where production had been paused. Dressed in silver and black for Spirit Day, Mia saw a familiar face leaning against a tree on the edge of the school's garden.

"Do you want us to come?" Ting spotted Detective Batair.

Shelby and Ting traded worried looks.

"No, I'm okay. I'll fill you in."

"Okay, but if you need anything," Shelby said.

"Thanks." Mia headed over, stares from her classmates following as she neared the striking detective. His hair was back in tight braids, his facial hair neatly trimmed, his expression soft. Mia felt her stomach flutter at his smile. "Is this place softening you?" She noticed him offer her friends a grin as they watched them meet.

"Impossible," he said, while Shelby yelled, "Talk to him about Europe!"

"How are you, Mia?"

"I'm doing okay."

"You look healthy."

But the truth was, she was changing by the day. Something had happened when her mother died, something strange. It started gradually: glowing skin, her lips rosier; her hair began to grow out with highlights; her body was strong and lean despite her lack of care for it. Little scars and imperfections faded away, although her back scars remained unchanged, and her face was as radiant as it had been the night her mother died. It was as if the beauty of Divana had made its way into Mia.

"Thanks. It's probably the green tea," Mia joked, but it touched her every time Gigi sent over a gallon.

"What's this about Europe?"

"Oh, Shelby wants me to go with her to Italy this summer to visit her grandma and stuff, but I'm not planning to go."

"That's why I'm here, Mia. I wanted to inform you that I am going away."

Mia frowned. "You are? New assignment?" She felt her heart drop.

"Yes, for a few months, but Detective Dregs has made the official move to our LA precinct, and they will be in contact. Kryder too."

"Oh. Well, thanks for letting me know," she said, trying to read his stoic expression. She wondered about him a lot over the past few months, about the day they'd both survived . . . how they'd survived . . . about the moment before the bomb exploded. When she wasn't deep in grief over her mother, when her future didn't seem only gray, she let her mind wander to the moment he had kissed her. Playing it over in her mind, she sometimes questioned if it had happened. The feelings she felt, sparks of attraction, moments of connection . . . . Was it insanity that she thought he felt it too?

"Mia, your mother would want you to keep finding the goodness in life," Batair said, his serious eyes staring into hers.

"Find goodness . . . yeah, she did that well."

The sun beat down, highlighting her hair an even brighter golden brown.

Looking away from his gaze, Mia couldn't help feeling the compulsion to ask something that'd been nagging her for months.

"Do you think . . . you think if we had gotten to her sooner . . . ?" she started, watching Jade and Vivian point in her direction.

Detective Batair pulled a branch from a budding bush and twisted it in his fingers, watching the leaf spin around until it spun off the twig and floated to the ground, leaving the branch bare.

"I don't know, but I believe your mother was aware of the risk."

"I should have been there!" she blurted, immediately wishing she'd not raised her voice, for it drew stares.

This time, Will stepped right in front of Jade, standing in her way so she wasn't able to watch Mia. A small bubble of coldness inside Mia's heart popped; only a million more and she might feel normal again.

"To be finite is one of the hardest truths of this life," Batair said.

"Well — don't worry about me. I'll be fine." And she forced a smile.

"Now I'm convinced," he said with a chuckle, his laugh deep and songlike.

Why didn't he say more? *Hey, Mia, remember when I kissed you? How we thought we were going to die? Well, now that we didn't, I need to explain, I'd like to kiss you again . . . .*

Detective Batair straightened his jacket, signaling it was time for him to go.

"Have some fun this summer, Mia. Live with the living." And he took a few steps away, his badge strung around his neck, shining out from under his open jacket.

Mia watched him leave the school courtyard and sighed.

With her grandfather dead, maybe Batair felt he didn't owe her any answers. Maybe, in truth, he didn't want to be in her life any-more. She was young; he was — older, although she never quite got a handle on how old he was. Relieved that disappointment didn't hurt like grief, she headed back to her friends. Mia watched them join the underclassmen in a paint-balloon toss, Ting and Shelby covered in yellow goop from losing.

"This . . . is . . . disgusting," Mia said as she stood on the sidelines, opting out of the games.

No one questioned her resistance to joining things. Shelby came to stand with her, trying to wring the paint from her dripping hair.

"Do you really mean it — your dad is cool with me coming to Europe?"

Shelby stopped fussing with her ponytail and looked at Mia.

"Wait!!! What are you saying?"

"I don't know . . . something the detective said about . . . living with the living." Mia shrugged and second-guessed herself now that if she went, she might dampen Shelby's time.

"My dad was the one who *suggested* you come — Mia! I mean, don't give him the credit. I want the same thing, but I couldn't believe he brought it up first! MIA! Seriously, if you come, I'd . . . I'd — my nonna will love you, and there's sooo much to see. Please, please, pleeease, this is what I've been asking — hoping for! Say yes, Mia!"

Shelby's excitement was unmatched by Mia's tentative posture as she considered the grip of grief, always so near, threatening to press in. But holding her friend's elation broke the tiniest crack of joy into the sadness, and Mia said yes before the warmth evaporated.

Shelby screamed, the winners of the paint game cheered, and the sun hit Mia's face, planting a kiss of comfort on her forehead where her mother used to. Maybe this was her mother speaking. Maybe she was somewhere, now as an ethereal being, telling Mia to press on. Wooing Mia to live and, in time, hope again.

Mia was still here, whether she wanted to be or not. It had to mean something that she had survived. There had to be goodness waiting . . . There had to be living she was meant to do. Her mother's fate was set, but Mia's story was still unfinished.

Author's Note

Your voice matters. If you enjoyed *The Unfinished Storm*, I would be so grateful if you'd leave a review on Amazon or Goodreads. Reviews help authors like me reach readers like you — thank you for your support!

∽

COMING SOON

The Unseen Storm

∽

LET'S STAY CONNECTED!

I'd love to hear from you. Follow me on Instagram and TikTok:

@JACKIE_WRITES